ORIGINS: TRUTHS REVEALED

Wes Easton

ORIGINS: TRUTHS REVEALED
Copyright © 2020 by Wes Easton

For information contact:
Email:
Wes.Easton.Writes@gmail.com
Instagram:
Https://www.instagram.com/author.wes.easton

Edited by: Amanda McFarland

Book cover design by Germancreative from Fiverr.com.

ISBN: 978-0-692-05165-8

First Edition: June 2020

DEDICATION

To my wife, kids, and family for always believing in me, being my cheer team, and consistently pushing me to write, even when I was exhausted from the stressors of everyday life and work. Thank you! This book would not have been possible without you all.

TO THE READER:

Thank you for reading my book. Your continued support fuels my writings. Please leave an honest review and rating if you enjoy this story.

Please note, sexual assault is never something to take lightly. If you or someone you know is a victim of sexual assault, please seek immediate help from law enforcement, organizations such as the National Sexual Violence Resource Center, or someone you trust.

ORIGINS: TRUTHS REVEALED

CHAPTER 1

Family Ties

"Life is 10% what happens to us and 90% how we react to it."

— DENNIS P. KIMBRO

In the low light, only the faint glow of yellow and orange embers struggling against extinction permeates the night. Trees rustle against billowing winds. The girl sat wide-eyed, transfixed and focused on the darkness. It shocked Mae to find she was holding her breath; her pulse continuing to rise at a steady pace. "Did you hear that?" she whispered.

Her sister replied in the same non-committal tone she had the last half a dozen times Mae asked her, "Nope."

Mae felt as if time passed by pulling a ball and chain. She checked her watch: two minutes. That was it — the total amount of time that passed since she'd last checked. She hated these "bonding outings" (as her father likes to call them). Mr. and Mrs. Daniels were the epitome of what a loving marriage should be. Now, her father struggled to keep it together, always trying to present a strong face for his girls, the only ones who meant anything to him anymore.

Mom's death really hit Dad hard, Mae thought. *He's clung to our camping trips even more now than before. I wonder if he knows we'll still love him without these mandatory monthly bonding trips. He means well; I know that. But he hasn't realized we aren't his little girls anymore, that I'm heading off soon. And that's a problem, but then again, I think he needs us more than we need him. Who'll remind him where he left his wallet in the mornings or fix his tie before he leaves for work when I'm gone?*

Mae eyed her dad as he continued preparing their camp. *Daddy means well,* she thought, *but after Mom passed away, well … he's been a bit different, a shell of who he was. To top it off, he's become too protective of us — which is why I'm not telling him when I start dating. He'd kill the poor guy.* She chuckled at that prospect. She could only imagine … Ryland Daniels stature intimidated people before he ever spoke and they found out his true nature.

Mae looked up at the firefly lights her dad was setting up. The lights low luminance complimented the slivers of moonlight dancing across the water, casting gentle shadows across their lakeside campsite. She pulled her knees in close, encasing them in her orange-and-red plaid flannel shirt. Mae returned her attention to the tree line, surveying it with a hawk-like gaze. A feeling told her something — someone — was out there, watching them. It became a chore to try and shake it.

"You know you're out here tripping, right?" Keyera said, giggling, "Ain't nothing out there, and you know this. We've been coming to these same camping grounds for years, and it's the same old things … wolves howling, wind blowing, and a bunch of pure nothingness!" She motioned for her sister to come closer and whispered in her ear, "See Dad over there?"

Mae nodded.

"I bet I can scare him," Keyera said. "Besides, I'm his favorite, so he'll forgive me; he has no choice."

Chuckling, Mae gave her sister a playful punch on the shoulder. She knew different. Keyera might have been older, but Mae was the prettiest, smartest, and more level-headed of the two of them. She knew her daddy's heart and affection leaned in her favor, but to stave off sibling rivalry, she let her big sis believe what she wanted. Besides, she was a few weeks away from graduating high school and knew she couldn't take Keyera in a head-to-head fight — if it came to that. Keyera was quick to anger, so it wasn't always easy to predict her actions.

Mae studied her sister in the low camp light. Keyera was the captain of her softball team, had an awesome muscular definition, soft curves, and a mean right hook. People always mistook her beauty for weakness, until they found themselves gasping for air on the ground, cradled in the fetal position.

Mae stopped smiling as a cold chill crept up her back. She'd always had the ability to sense when something was off, and now was no different. Her gut told her something did not feel right. Mae's senses told her something or someone were in the trees. She felt cold eyes on her, making her skin prickle.

Camping in the fall always gives me the heebie-jeebies, Mae professed to herself.

Whatever was out there was staying just out of sight. She couldn't shake the possibility that maybe one of the neighboring campers thought it would be fun to be some sort of Peeping Tom.

It's probably nothing, Mae thought to herself. Being out here in the woods always gave her the creeps, and tonight her senses may just be getting the better of her.

This trip might be our last camping trip for a while, at least until spring break or maybe summer break from college. But either way, it'll have to be awhile after we get settled into our new college routine. I guess we'll come back and go camping with Dad again during our sophomore or junior years of college, Mae thought to herself.

Images of frat parties and boys raced through her mind. She imagined meeting someone who loved the outdoors as much as she did, someone who was an expert with the party scene since she had no expertise in this area.

Keyera often referred to Mae as a prude, in not so many words, and college would be her redemption, her saving grace. She'd go to a semi-prestigious college like the University of Maryland, College Park or something, and explore in ways she'd never allowed herself to do while living under her father's roof.

Breaking her concentration and snapping back into reality, Mae focused on her dad's words.

"Hand me that bit of tinder, will you, dear," Ryland said. "Yes, of course, Daddy," Keyera said before sticking her tongue out at Mae as she took some tinder to their dad for the campfire.

Ryland gestured with a nod towards Mae, "Sweetheart, go into the tree line and grab a bundle of fresh, not wet, branches and twigs for our fire, would you."

More of a statement and less of a question, but Mae got the hint. She rose from her warm mossy seat, acknowledged her father's orders, and strode off in search of their life's blood for the night.

Keyera stood before her physically imposing father. Even when he knelt down, his size and mass were impressive. With those soft brown eyes and stern features, Ryland looked up, asking, "What's the matter, honey?"

With a quizzical expression, Keyera asked, "Daddy, why are you so hung up on doing this the hard way? You know, there's no shame in using store-bought starter material and equipment for your fire. It won't make you less of a man, you know."

Ryland smirked, "What will you do when you are out here on your own, trying to survive after the fall of civilization?"

"Dad, you are the only one who believes civilization will fall one day. Have you seen the world lately? Our scientists are discovering new ways to solve world hunger, they're searching for ways to draw power out of nothing, and President Branson is actively trying to end hostilities with those few nations still trying to undermine the Coalition. Times are good, Dad.

Our civilization won't fall ... at least not during our lifetime."

They both chuckled; he at her naivety and her at how crazy she thought her dad to be at times.

CHAPTER 2

Conscription

Thourn stood erect with his eyes closed — or as erect as a man could stand who'd been around for millennia. He often enjoyed the serenity of his privacy amongst the plants in his garden. The air, crisp and cool, enveloped him, reminding him of the beauty of the world. Medium-high clouds hung overhead, lightly peppering the evening sky with billowing white wisps resembling hundreds of sparse pillows.

How long had it been since it rained? Thourn wondered. Rain, he found, was the great equalizer. It could operate as a benign catalyst for harvest or as a ruthless iconoclast washing away all traces of civilization from the historical timeline.

The sound of quick-paced footfalls carried with it enough urgency to release Thourn's mind from its meditative-like state. *No rest for the weary*, he thought.

"Sir! Sir!" the young boy called out. "Forgive me for the intrusion, although I must insist you loan me some of your time."

Thourn turned around, watching his slim-figured protégé approaching with haste. "Perleases, slow down!" he cautioned.

"But, sir ..." Perleases faltered on his words, trying to ex-

plain his reasoning for interrupting the venerable Watcher —
often referred to as the First One amongst their fellows.

"I know you are new to this life and our duties, but you
really must find your balance, young one."

Looking a tad bit embarrassed, Perleases paused, straight-
ening his tunic while preparing to deliver the only news that
was sure to make the First One distraught. Rubbing the back
of his head, he continued, "Sir, our Watchers in the field are
reporting an increase in rift detections. Some even had visual
sightings; the volume and frequency of rift openings are growing at an exponential rate. Not only that, but we have good
reason to suspect Oralee is in trouble!"

As the last sentence finished rolling off the tip of Perleases
tongue, Thourn actually stood fully erect, his pulse threatening his existence. "Why did you not lead with that last tidbit
of information first, Perleases!"

"Sir, I was reporting the facts in a congruous and succinct
order, as I received them," retorted Perleases.

"Young one, do you not know why we are here?" Thourn
barely registered his own words as his brain began racing,
assimilating all the facts. Extending his essence, in the blink
of an eye, Thourn passed over landmasses and several bodies of water as if he were the man of steel himself. *Of course,
that fictitious demi-god in blue tights never astral-projected his essence halfway around the world in a matter of seconds either*, he
thought.

With his astral-senses on full alert, absorbing everything as
he moved, Thourn pinpointed Oralee's location in a matter
of moments. He came to a resting position slightly above the
trees as he took in the situation. *There's some time. Good. I can
work with that,* he thought.

There was a time and a place for conferring with his fellow
First Ones, and there was a time for him to make a direct
decision. All decisions came with consequences, and based
on what Thourn had in mind, he hoped the resulting conse-

quences would be minimal.

Trees whirled past faster than Jax's eyes could keep up. Jerking the wheel, a bit to the left, the car swerved as he worked to steady it out. Jax's skills with manual driving only manifested within the past year once he had enough money to buy his own car. The vast majority of people didn't drive; no one needed to when all they had to do was send a thought to the network, and a car magically appeared to take you wherever you needed to go.

Once the government did away with you-drive cars and replaced them with self-driving cars, vehicular death rates dropped catastrophically. Old-style gas guzzlers were still on the roads in tiny numbers, but in a few years, even those would become a faded relic of a world and a society long since passed.

The lady in the car coming towards him was a classic beauty — olive skin, high cheekbones, and soft flowing hair that seemed to sway and bounce with a kind of angelic appeal to it. *Wow,* he thought. He couldn't see her eyes, although he imagined them to be a shade of a light hazel.

Jax redirected his attention back on the road, trying to reconcile what he was seeing: a man standing in the middle of the road like a lunatic. No sane person would do that. His gut told him something was off about the man, though he didn't have long to think about it. His speedometer told him he'd tear through the poor guy in less than a few seconds.

Continuing to stand there, the man looked as immovable as a force of nature.

Jax swerved hard to avoid the lunatic, sending the car hurtling towards the right. Struggling to regain control, he overcompensated as he jerked the wheel hard left, causing the car to veer into the opposite lane lightly smattered with oncoming traffic.

His front end slammed hard into the ass-end of a mid-sized pod, sending them careening off at an odd angle.

Jax's knuckles flushed as he gripped the steering wheel tight. He spun the wheel right and then left again to regain control. The front end of the vehicle spun to the left, and with the help of forwarding momentum caused by Newton's first law of motion — a body in motion stays in motion — the car continued on as two of its tires lifted off of the ground ... and then the road melted away and was replaced by light wisps of shimmering white clouds ... then to the gray asphalt smitten with road grime. For several iterations, the car tumbled over, side for side, tossing Jax around several times before sliding to a screeching halt.

Jax tried to think. He could tell he was badly banged up. His thoughts trickled in, slowly at first and then progressively faster. *What ... the ... hell ... just ... happened! Jesus Christ, that hurt!*

"Jax, it would appear you were in an accident. I've taken the liberty of informing local first responders. Please try not to move as you may have internal damage." Jinx, Jax's EMCD artificial intelligence personal assistant, said through the embedded fiber optic nanorelay system traversing his cranial cavity.

"I figured as much. Thanks, Jinx." Jax contemplated listening and staying put to wait to be rescued, but then again, he never was good at taking orders. Using an old Swiss Army knife he'd picked up from a 'going out of business ... everything half off' sale at an old Army surplus store, he cut his seatbelt and fell onto the roof.

The impact was slightly more jarring than he'd braced for. Rubbing his temple, trying to massage away the pain, Jax supposed the fall hurt more than normal because of the searing pain that moving caused. His head throbbed, pain searing his nervous system with each beat of his heart. Jax wasn't a medic by far although, the glaringly abnormal angle his shoulder bone stuck out of its socket told him more than he needed to know.

Jax used the roof for leverage as he slithered across, crawling through the window with one arm dragging behind him. A lifetime passed as Jax pushed and pulled himself out of the car, gaining his freedom from the ruined wreck of his 1969 Ford Mustang Boss 429. Vehicles like his were scarce these days. Luckily, he knew a guy who knew a guy willing to part with the salvaged vehicle for, "Oh, ah ... just a small fee of 60 thousand ..." he recalled the guy saying.

The air smelled of radiator fluid, burned tires, and an entire year's worth of savings down the drain. The sun, radiant and strong, stood at its highest point of the day. Cloud wisps were reminiscent of a mild ocean current.

Today is too nice a day to crash a car. I'll never hear the end of this from Mom, he thought. "Mom! Shit!" Jax struggled to breathe. Each breath came more labored than the last. A sense of urgency assailed his thoughts. *"Jinx, I need ... you to ... call ..."* his thoughts trailed off, *"What! No, that's not right!"* he thought, watching a man step through burning debris, walking purposefully towards him. *"That guy's the freakin' reason I crashed! What's he doing? Coming to ... finish the job?"*

Thourn surveyed the scene, taking in the destruction he'd wrought onto this young man. By the looks of it, he should add bodily harm to the list of rules he told himself he'd never break. This had not been his plan. He'd never — of his own volition — hurt another human unless it served the 'Exit Strategy.'

Looking back, Thourn saw the smoldering wreck of a midsize pod. A man and a woman lay inside, burning; two small children were beside them. Their bodies mangled and distorted, the smallest of the children, a four- or five-year-old boy, was listless and missing an arm. Smiling inwardly, Thourn allowed himself to consider those four lives and their essences. *Your rides are over, my friends. Until next time,* he thought.

Had it been any other time then now, Thourn would not have bothered with breaking the rules, even if they were his rules. What he would make would be a first. The Council of Elders — his senior Watchers — flirted with the concept, but their stagnation was replete.

This was Thourn's realm. He himself wielded the power to overrule the Council. *The demand is present — Oralee requires a protector! The time to act is now,* he thought. He would circumvent the Council's molasses-style of voting on change and implement the plan without their consent. He'd pick the recipient himself.

This man — no, that's not right — this boy was far too young when compared to Thourn, an entity whose seen civilizations rise and civilizations fall. A being who has watched continents shift, form, and reform.

To compound Thourn's concerns, he could see this boy was not only hurt but scared.

Jax kept crawling. Looking over his shoulder at his would-be attacker, he croaked out a few words, his voice labored and raspy, "Get ... away ... from ... me," he stammered.

"Jax, perhaps this man is here to help," Jinx said in Jax's head. *"It may be prudent to ..."*

Jax felt his temper flaring at his AI's naivety. *If he was here to help, why was he standing in the middle of the road like a madman?* he thought.

"Calm down, son," a disembodied voice from over Jax's shoulder said. "I am here to help."

"I don't want your help! I don't know you!" Jax's head thrummed beyond measure. His consciousness was holding on by sheer will as he tried to maintain focus beyond the insufferable pounding in his head. With every fleeting moment, Jax knew he needed to communicate with his mother. To let her know he loved her and probably wasn't going to make it home for dinner today or any other day. With that thought, he mentally sent an instant message to his mother:

"Mom, I'm sorry, but I won't be able to make it for dinner. I know you were really looking forward to my fried chicken and I'm glad, but let's take a rain check. I love you, and you'll always be my number one."

"You don't know what you want, nor what you need," the man said. "You will become more than the sum of today's events have allowed once I'm done." As he spoke, Thourn felt time constraining. His patience for pleasantries evaporated.

Reaching down, taking care not to grab the protruding shoulder bone, Thourn flipped Jax over onto his back. "You'll thank me for this later." He placed a hand on Jax's forehead.

Jax felt himself plunge into pure darkness with bits of light sporadically piercing the veil of nothingness. His body convulsed and contorted into ungodly positions. Bones cracked. His skin heated. He felt — electrified, as though he was standing in the middle of a field during a lightning storm with a metal rod taped to his body.

A few cars began to slow, stopping shy of the recent traffic accident. *I must deal with them later,* Thourn thought.

Light flooded Jax's vision. He blinked, breathing in a trunk full of air. He felt different, almost new. He'd dare to say born again, and more importantly, he felt healed. No longer did his shoulder threaten to rip a hole through his skin and spill on to his newly-bought Finn and Ricky shirt. *Those guys are hilarious,* he mused.

"What ... what did you do to me?" Jax said in amazement, "I can remember ... everything!" Beyond astonished, Jax bellowed, "I thought this wasn't possible?"

"It is possible, and now I need you to fulfill your duties."

"My duties? What duties!"

Rubbing his thumb in the palm of his hands, Thourn said, "You are now a Watcher. I've activated you for a very specific mission: Find and protect Oralee."

"Whoa, man. Who said I wanted this? I was minding my own business when you damn near killed me!" Jax knew he had this man to thank for patching him up, but he didn't care.

"Listen!" Thourn urged. "We do not have a lot of time. My strength isn't what it used to be, and as we speak, Oralee is being wronged. I need you, she needs you, everyone who will ever live needs you to find Oralee and save her! Can you do that? Time is a luxury! Tell me now if you'll accept this mission. If not, I'll put your mind back to sleep and awaken another one."

CHAPTER 3

Darkness

Walking through the dark, sullen trees, awash with the glow of the moon, somehow put Mae at ease. The elegance of the rays dancing through the canopy, gently tapping its way across trunk after trunk, painted a surreal scene.

The autumn leaves crunched beneath Mae's footfalls. Each step brought a waft of the light scent of the forest up to her nose and she smiled. "I will miss this. I will miss Daddy and his ability to make us feel warm during such a cold time in our lives. I'm going to miss Jordan and the way his butt fit into his jeans. God, I wish he knew how I felt about him."

A light snap of a twig from behind brought Mae out of her reverie.

The sound was faint, and Mae could barely hear it. *Is that ... footsteps!* she thought, not sure if her mind was playing tricks on her.

Her heart raced, her eyes widened, and her pulse quickened. Sweat now trickled down Mae's bronze forehead, matting stray hairs to her brow. Her flannel shirt began to cling to her as if it were electrostatically charged.

"Who's there?" Mae whispered, "Keyera, is that you?"

Nothing.

"Dad?"

Nothing.

A long pause passed before Mae steeled herself and called out again, "This isn't funny whoever you are!"

The man, obscured by the trees, stood idle from his vantage point, patiently waiting to claim his prize. *This bitch has blown me off for the last time!* He thought to himself, *I'm going to do it. I have to do it. I've come this far; it'll be a hell of a rush when I get away with it.*

With that final thought, he stepped out from behind a nearby tree, lightly bathed in moonlight.

He stopped and watched Mae for a moment as she fought to see who was there with her. She turned this way and that before spinning fully around, coming face to face with a strange masked man. She stood motionless. There was something familiar ...

Those eyes, she thought, *something about those eyes.*

Mae didn't have time to think about them for too long. In the seconds it took her to register the fact that she was face to face with a vaguely familiar stranger in a ski mask, she was already flying backward.

Mae slumped over, reeling and gasping for air, and collapsed from the force of his blow.

Her vision was distorted; everything was upside down. Mae tried to focus, but she couldn't. Her would-be attacker appeared to be walking on the wall. He grew closer and closer. As the distance between the two of them waned, her blood pressure increased, her eyes darted from side to side, and her breathing intensified.

Get up! Get up and run! Now! Run now! Mae's thoughts were as clear as day; if only her body would respond.

Coughing and wheezing, Mae held out a hand and begged the man to stop. He didn't. His delight was palpable. The man moved faster than she could track in her dazed state.

He stuffed a handkerchief into her mouth, gagging her, then planted a knee on her chest and bound her hands. Mae noticed the man was leaving her legs free. Something about that invoked a wild feral panic in her.

Jamison had pondered how he would do it — in what manner he would constrain the girl. In the end, he settled on leaving her legs untied. They posed no real threat, and besides, he had decided earlier that he wanted a bit of a struggle. The idea of a struggle excited him.

Jamison tore at Mae's clothes, ripping her blouse off with such ferocity and force that her bra threatened to slice through her body before ultimately giving way as the metal brackets bent, finally divorcing each other. His brutal eagerness began to show. He yanked his pants down, almost tripping as he fought to get them around his ankles. He kicked his pants away and they flew through the air, landing a couple of feet away in a mud puddle.

Mae's tears screamed in silent protest. She was alone — no witnesses, no help, save for the small animals foraging for food during the cold of the night. Tears streamed down her face. Had her mouth been unbound, she would have gasped as he flipped her over, cut away at her jeans and panties, and illicitly entered her.

The scent of blood permeated the night's air, bringing a smile to Jamison's face.

Jamison, a boy whom Mae previously regarded as an arrogant punk, stood and looked down at her, sprawled out, defenseless, and in shambles. His still-erect penis dripped a combination of seminal and vaginal fluid. In the darkness, his shaft looked like a menacing snake, erect and hungry for prey.

Sobs seeped through the gag in Mae's mouth as she mumbled, "Please leave ... just leave."

"You know, Mae," the man said, careful to disguise his voice,

"You had this coming. I want you to think about that. This all could have been prevented if you weren't such a bitch!" Mae recoiled as the last words seethed out of her attacker's mouth.

Taking a knee, Jamison wrapped a hand around Mae's throat and whispered in her ear.

"I'm going to put my sticky, wet cock in your mouth now. You are going to suck it like you mean it, and if you attempt to make a sound, I will kill your sister. But not after I have fun with her too. I like my fun. Do you understand me!"

Everything that happened next felt like something far worse than a nightmare — the immobilizing waking dream kind; the kind you try to wake up from but can't.

The taste in Mae's mouth was foul and repugnant. Between her sobs and her attacker's thrusts, she pictured her sister sprawled out over a fallen tree with this monster atop her. As her thoughts raged on, she sucked and licked, and gagged.

Jamison held one hand around Mae's head and the other around her throat, ready to crush her windpipe at a moment's notice. He knew he was close to cuming and had one more trick in store for his victim.

The pressure was light at first, but then the pounding intensified. He increased his thrust, forcing his way into her throat as he held her head tight. His pubic hair tickled her nose, and her tears moistened the inside of his thighs. Mae struggled to breathe, but the man held her head tighter and tighter.

In a fit of coughing, Mae tried desperately to separate her head from this sadistic, treacherous monster. At that moment, he came again, exploding into her mouth, choking her as it jetted down her throat, some making its way down her windpipe.

Mae's attacker pulled his flaccid member from her mouth. She coughed violently. In the low light, she watched a smile creep across his face before he returned the gag to her mouth. Mae continued to cough, now muffled, trying to recover from the large amount of bodily fluid her attacker just pumped down her throat. Writhing on the ground, half-naked and used, she wondered, *Why me?*

Mae watched the deviant stand and look around, then stroll off into the trees, the dark woods offering sanctuary for dark deeds. Her attacker walked ever deeper into the night until his figure was a not-so-distant memory.

CHAPTER 4

Safety Through Technology

The moonlight lit a swath of land imbued with the outline of a human body. Trees rustled slightly in the cool, crisp autumn wind. Jax's breath coalesced into a light fog in front of him. The cold dry weather forced the warm air from his lungs to condense into tiny droplets of ice, forming fog.

The scene was almost surreal for him. Not too long ago, he was simply another human, going about his daily affairs, trying to put his stamp on life and carve out a niche in history where he'd be remembered, even if those memories would be of him with his shirt off. Jax's mother never approved of his profession as a model. He knew that and planned to stop once he made his mark on the world and then found a higher paying job.

Now he was standing here, in the middle of the woods looking down at a battered, badly used girl whose only mistake was being alone in the woodlands with a well-concealed attacker.

Bending at the knees and hips, Jax reached down and cradled Mae's head in his hands. Some sort of fluid ran out of her mouth and onto his arm and shirt. The night's light made it hard to tell what it was, although the smell was repugnant.

He gazed up and down her body, taking in every inch of her. Goosebumps were ever-present and prevalent all across Mae's body. The night's air made her skin cold to the touch.

In the dark, Jax could make out Mae's torn shirt. Her pants had been ripped off and left dangling from one ankle. He put Mae down for a moment while he moved behind her to break the ropes binding her arms together. Picking her up again, Jax stood and began walking towards her camp.

Mae felt warm and safe. The kind of safe that comes after years of knowing someone and spending countless evenings in their arms. There was a sort of familiarity with the level of safety she currently felt. She opened her eyes a crack and saw only a jawline slightly obscured by the night.

Where am I? Mae thought. *Why am I being carried? Who ... who the hell is carrying me! Oh God, no! Not again!*

Screaming and flailing, Mae tried to wriggle herself free from Jax's strong, cradle-like embrace.

Stopping, Jax looked down and gently said, "Miss, you're hurt. You were attacked. I'm here to help. Please stop fighting me."

Mae cried out, kicking and screaming, "Help! Please! Someone! Help!" Her voice was raspy from the recent trauma to her trachea.

"Stop it! Please let me help you. He sent me to help you." Jax said, his frustration rising.

Mae focused her thoughts. *I don't know this guy, and for all I know, this is some sort of elaborate trap by my attacker. Maybe he wants to play mind games with me. Maybe not. One thing is for sure — I'm not sticking around this guy any longer than I can help it. I need help! Please, someone — help me!*

Mae hollered and screamed. Much to Jax's dismay, he had to hand it to her. She was a fighter. Voices came from up ahead. They sounded like they were quickly getting closer. Swatches of lights swung back and forth, not too far from where they were.

Jax had a choice to make. Stay, continue to try to help and probably get himself arrested in the process, or flee and check back with the girl when she was feeling a little less vocal and scared. She was half-naked, showed visual signs of abuse, and was distressed at his presence. Staying would only make matters worse.

With that final thought, Jax slowly and gently lowered Mae back down to the earth. Her frantic screams subsided some. Turning, Jax allowed himself to blend into the darkness. His previous position devoid of motion and life, as if he'd never been there.

◆ ◆ ◆

"Mae! Mae! Are you out here??? Baby, are you out here?" Ryland's heartbeat threatened to shatter his chest cavity.

Mae heard Keyera's voice a few paces away, in tune with Ryland's, frantically crying out for her sister.

"Here! I'm over here!" Mae yelled, shuddering. Her eyes hurt from the agony of the recent hour.

Relief washed over Mae as her dad approached, followed promptly by her sister. The grief she observed in their eyes mirrored only a portion of what she felt. The things that had happened in these woods moments before were abstract concepts to her family, but it was all too real for Mae. Her mind and body felt dirty; they'd betrayed her, by no fault of their own. The things he'd done to her — made her do — shook her to her very core. No one had the right to enter her sanctuary, to violate her inherent rights and destroy the constructs of societal norms, without her expressed permission. Yet her attacker had, and he'd done it with such ease. Throughout the entire nightmare, Mae's main concern was the safety of her family, and looking at them here, like this, allowed her a moment of reprieve.

Ryland took his oversized flannel shirt off of his body and placed it around his shaking daughter. He eyed her, his baby girl; at that moment, he knew he'd failed. Mae was in shambles. He'd failed to keep his baby girl safe, the sole responsibility of any dad who had daughters.

Nothing on this planet will stop me from finding the filth that did this to you. I promise you will have your justice! Ryland thought.

◆ ◆ ◆

Mae's hospital room was fairly decent, as far as hospital rooms went. The small fold-out couch on one side housed her sister while her father reclined in the chair opposite the couch, next to the bed she was lying on.

There were a few light raps on the door before it gently slid partly open. "Ms. Daniels, it's Nurse Taylor. May I come in?"

Nurse Taylor entered with a hovering cart in tow following Mae's nod of approval. "I've brought you more food. How are you holding up, dear?"

"I just want to leave," Mae said, not feeling too keen on talking. Following her attack, talking was low on her list of priorities. Earlier, she overheard her father whispering to her sister. *"It's as if her attacker stole more than her virginity,"* he'd said.

Mae began to believe her dad was right.

The nurse dimmed the lights. Mae's bio-signs sprang into her mind. Mentally she studied the readouts hovering over Mae while externally she remained impassive.

Mae knew she was safe; she knew her attacker was probably long gone, but how could she sleep, how could she relax knowing that he was still out there?

The detectives' EMCDs — supercomputers the size of a grain of rice embedded at the base of the cerebellum — had provided them with augmented vision, allowing them to pick up her attacker's genetic trail and track him through the woods down to a lake. But that's where the trail went cold. They said the perp used a DNA scrubber to mask his getaway. The police explained that they suspected the perp must have gotten away on a watercraft, but there was no telling for certain. Mae thought back on Mr. Stanly's tech class. "Scrubbers are relatively cheap to come by and are sold by most dealers of paraphernalia. Don't be the one to get caught with one," he'd said. "The police won't go easy on you, kid or not." *Yeah, if they ever catch you*, she thought.

Mae's mind wondered, *just about everyone has one of those EMCD things. They're supposed to make life easier — more fluid and stress-free, the ads said. They did nothing for the police. Like Daddy says, people over-rely on technology. Whatever happened to classic detective work? It seems that even the EMCDs have their limits. Of course, in my case they did nothing. Typical.*

"Please, just leave," Mae told her nurse.

"I'd love to leave, just as you would like, however, not before my job is done. There are more tests I need to run, Ms. Daniels."

The nurse turned and sent a mental message to Ryland.

"Mr. Daniels, your daughter is in a great deal of mental distress. It would be easier for me to treat her if she had an EMCD. The typical age to receive one is five. Might I inquire why she lacks one?"

"Nurse, my wife, Anise, and I thought the children might benefit more from life if they were allowed to actually live life instead of constantly being jacked into the social consciousness. Everyone else's thoughts floating around in your head ... It's just not natural."

"Sir," Nurse Kennedy said, *"the technology is so much more than instant communications. What people used to do with cell phones, we can now do with a thought. Televisions are a thing of the past ... well, for some ... now that we can immerse ourselves in our favorite shows anytime we want. This technology can afford your daughter ..."*

"Enough, Ms. Kennedy. I've heard this all before," Ryland shot back, wondering why he should continue to listen to this woman. He and his wife had decided this long ago, and he had

an obligation to continue to carry out his dead wife's wishes, didn't he? *"My children will be fine without that technology."*

"Mr. Daniels, how do you get from place to place when you do not know the lay of the land? When you need a new recipe, what do you do? When was the last time you have spoken to a friend or," Nurse Kennedy gave a hard look at Mr. Daniels, *"— called the police?"* Her eyes met his.

"Ms. Kennedy," Ryland said, resigned. He knew this lady had a point. Tears started to stream down his face, *"I do not ... no ... you are right. The EMCD has its usages, and without it, I doubt the police would have made it to our location and responded as quickly as they did. But I am still not completely sold on why Mae would need this device. Isn't it too late for her? Isn't she too old now?"*

"Mr. Daniels, if your daughter getting brutally attacked is not enough to sway you, perhaps this little fact might help you decide what is best for your daughter. At the moment, she is in a highly depressive state and may or may not pose a threat to herself once released from this facility. If she had an EMCD, we could track her mental progress and you could check-in on her whenever you wanted via the parental control function. And best of all, there are therapeutic programs which can be used, free of charge, which would allow her the opportunity to heal at an accelerated rate. Much faster than if you allow her to go without it."

Ryland walked over to the nurse, placed a hand on her shoulder, and mentally asked, *"Will it hurt her? To receive the implant this late in her development? I understand there's something about neural plasticity and such, but I don't fully understand all the technical jargon."*

Nurse Kennedy looked at Mae, studying the floating display of her vitals. *"Slightly,"* she replied. *"Your daughter will need to undergo a somewhat modified version of the procedure. By this age, the EMCD's microscopic nanofibers should have grown with each new neural pathway created, fully embedding itself within every part of the brain and throughout her nervous system. Because of her age, we'll have to force that process along at an accelerated rate. It won't be an easy process, but the benefits outweigh whatever she'll go through to get her EMCD."*

Ryland looked at his baby girl and knew he had failed her. *How could I have been so stupid! I should have been there for you. Never again, baby.* "I'm sorry! he whispered, "so, so sorry." He wiped away the last tear rolling down his cheek. Ryland gripped his daughter's hand and silently said, *"Do it."*

◆ ◆ ◆

Mae stared as the iridescent lights passed by at regular intervals. Two orderlies floated her into a cold and spartan-like room. She wasn't sure what was happening, but she knew it had to do with her somehow. The room scared her.

"Ms. Daniels, hello. I'm Dr. Craig. I assume you've been told why you are here?"

Mae looked incredulously at the man. "No!"

"Shame. Well, we're going to remove your restraints now; do remove your clothes," Craig said matter-of-factly.

"I don't want to." Mae trembled visibly, twisting and pulling against her bonds.

"But you must and you will. There is no other way to add the tactile interface, young lady. We have to graph the interface to the neurons throughout most of your body. Unfortunately, that isn't something we can do *through* your clothes. Had you received the EMCD implant when you were five like everyone else, this unpleasant experience would be unnecessary. The neural interface would have grown, spreading within you as you aged. Now, either you can remove your clothes or my assistants can. Your choice."

The bonds holding Mae in place fell away. She sat up, eyeing everyone in the room — the slender orderly with yellow-stained teeth, his short female companion with a buzz cut, an unassuming Dr. Craig, who looked impassive save for the growing bulge in his trousers, and several other nondescript help. She felt repulsed at where her life had taken her.

Mae closed her eyes as she slowly began to remove her articles of clothing. She thought she could feel the old doctor's eyes groping. She shifted from side to side in the sparsely furnished room. Her arms and hands covered her girl-bits. She couldn't have felt more uncomfortable.

From behind, two strong hands grabbed Mae's arms, pulling her towards something materializing out of the ground in the middle of the room. A black chaise lounge chair rose in stark contrast to the rest of the sterile white room. As Mae approached, the straps opened, waiting to embrace her body.

"This is for the benefit of society. Once you're successfully linked in, you'll become a more productive citizen. Not like those, those darn Upgraders!" Dr. Craig spouted, disdain dripping from his last words.

"Ouch!" Mae yelped as a needle penetrated the base of her skull. In one swift motion, hundreds of mechanical needles jetted from the chaise lounge chair, penetrating her skin and spreading their tendrils throughout her body like fast-moving slime, attaching themselves to their pre-targeted neurons. The numbing agent pumping into Mae's body afforded her relief from what would otherwise be excruciating pain.

Again, Mae found herself naked and duly afraid — unable to change her circumstances, unable to maintain a modicum of modesty. Again, she found herself at the mercy of another man — baring it all to someone she didn't know, except this time there were multiple men and women here who'd just robbed her of her remaining dignity.

Tears of anger, insecurity, distrust and panic streamed down Mae's face.

As the sedative began to take hold, the world started to fade away. Again, Mae contemplated embracing death.

CHAPTER 5

New Knowledge

The heavy D.C. traffic was an awful sight. Kurt Carter never cared for the view from his office window, which overlooked Vermont Avenue leading into Logan Circle. *When will these people ever learn to drive!* he thought while reflecting on his small hometown of Framlingham, Suffolk in the United Kingdom. *At least back home, no one's ever in a rush, and they don't run over you to get to where they're going. Getting rid of that darn law that still allows people to drive themselves is step one.* His mind trailed off, considering the ramifications of such a law.

"Margaret, dear, cancel my 5:00 meeting along with my 5:30 and 7 p.m. virtual meetings. I plan on taking the rest of today to myself."

"*Yes, sir,*" replied his aide mentally.

The Englishman released a deep, exasperated sigh. *This new generation is so reliant on the use of EMCD technology that I'd swear they'd forget how to speak and live in the physical world—if they could muster it,* he thought.

"Margaret, again, please refrain from replying to me via the EMCD. I'm old-fashioned, you know that. I like good old run-of-the-mill verbal communication."

Kurt's statement drew a look of satirical annoyance from Margaret. "Yes, sir, Mr. Presidential Science Advisor," she said, giving emphasis to his title as if he hadn't known who he was. Kurt found it quite funny that he was in charge of advising the President of the Coalition on all matters relating to science and technology, and he was repulsed at the idea of completely losing himself in such matters. To him, humanity was selling their soul to the devil for added conveniences; he wanted none of it.

Kurt stood deep in thought in front of the 20-foot-high windows adorning the wall behind his faux mahogany desk, with his hands in his pockets. "Sir, your avatar is receiving a ping. Would you like to take it?"

"Margaret, sweetheart, I really would like to be left alone for a bit. Just have the avatar conduct the meeting, and I'll download the meeting specifics when I'm free."

"Sir, I think you might want to take this. It's the Director of SETI himself, Dr. Bimala Aadrika. He says this can't wait and that he has to talk to you face to face."

Aadrika himself, huh? Kurt pondered, *I haven't spoken to Dr. Aadrika in quite some time. Not since I first took this office. The search for extraterrestrial life has proved fruitless for so long that SETI only maintains its funding to keep up pretenses with the civilian population. If he's contacting me and he says it's urgent, perhaps hearing him out wouldn't be such a bad idea.*

Kurt replied to Margaret then answered the virtual meeting space (VMS) request from Bimala Aadrika. Closing his eyes — although this wasn't necessary, it was comforting — Kurt allowed his consciousness to be drawn into a VMS of his own design. Bimala was already seated in the plush leather chair as Kurt materialized and spoke, "Bimala, what can I do for you? What was so urgent that the Director of the Search for Extraterrestrial Intelligence couldn't meet with my avatar?"

"About that — my apologies, sir. I'm sure you have more pressing matters, but I had to see you. You have the President's ear," Bimala said.

"Well, spit it out, son." Kurt was teetering on the edge of vague interest and professional tolerance of Bimala's presence. The man was Indian-born and American-raised and educated in various countries, including the U.S. and the UK. He held degrees from MIT, Harvard University, the University of Oxford, and ETH Zurich in Switzerland. He was bright, having been only 24 when selected to be the Director of SETI two years ago, although he lacked humility and interpersonal skills.

"Sir, we've, ah, discovered something, and to be frank, we are excited!"

Kurt perked up. *The SETI team discovered something? Of note? That's almost unheard of ...*

"We've had satellite dishes around the globe positioned towards various points in the sky, with many of those dishes set to overlap their scans." Bimala continued, "We discovered strange signals coming from one of our colony planets orbiting a star only 11 light-years from Earth back in 2017 by the Arecibo Observatory in Puerto Rico. We here at SETI have been running a background program designed to cross-coordinate various points of data as it pertains to random strange signals."

"Wait a minute," Kurt said. "So, you're telling me we've detected multiple unexplained signals from different star systems for the past 60 years, and no one's said anything?"

Bimala's eyes were alight with a brightness akin to the joy a toddler might feel at the sight of a new toy. Continuing, he said, "More than that, sir, we've detected a signal like no other. It's alien for sure, and it is strong, sir. Frankly, I'm surprised it took our computer systems and astronomy guys so long to detect it. The signal appears to be originating from — and this is the exciting part, sir — the Eskimo Nebula."

Kurt fell back into his virtual seat, pondering the implications of what Bimala had just told him. *There's life out there other than humans? We. Are. Not. Alone.*

"Bimala, refresh my memory. I'm not as fresh on my astrophysics as I should be. Where is the Eskimo Nebula, and what does this actually mean?"

Dr. Bimala Aadrika leaned in, a cool, confident smile splayed across his face, and said, "Sir, the Eskimo Nebula is located some 5,000 light-years from Earth. This signal discovery means that we are not only not alone, but that they are either trying to make contact with us, or ... we think, maybe themselves!"

Kurt reeled back with disbelief, "What? Son, are you mad! I'm no expert, but do you know how far 5,000 light-years from Earth is? Do you really think some alien species outside of our local group would be here on Earth? Not only on Earth, but trying to communicate with themselves at such a distance? The technology for that feat would be astronomical. I can't believe that."

Bimala spoke calmly and pointedly, "Sir, that form of communications is beyond our means, certainly. But can you really be so narrow-minded to think there wouldn't be a species among the stars that couldn't accomplish such a feat?"

Kurt disregarded the man's jab at his intelligence in light of the important information he'd just delivered to him.

Not waiting for his boss to say something, Bimala went on, "That's not all, sir. You know those string of disappearances that are always airing on those late-night crime solver shows?"

"No. What are you talking about? I don't watch that rubbish."

"Well, the discovery of these signals and the large volume of unexplained disappearances got me thinking ... what if there's a connection? So, I ran a correlation algorithm and, sir, they are connected! I don't know how, but the date and time stamps on the transmissions from the Eskimo Nebula directly correlate to thousands of disappearances around the globe!"

Kurt sat, beyond silent, his mouth draped momentarily open. "Ok, listen," he said, snapping into action. "Tell no one, and those who already know need to be informed of the same.

I'm classifying this information. The public can't be allowed to know about anything related to this discovery. Not until the President has been read in. Lastly, I want you to realign every radio dish we have towards the Eskimo Nebula. We need more data — ten years ago."

The pair stood and shook hands. "Understood, sir," Bimala said, assuring his boss he was on top of it before disconnecting the virtual meeting.

CHAPTER 6

Decisions

The menacing creature, towering a hefty six feet, two inches, writhed and slinked from side to side beneath the evening's purplish sky. It struck with a preternatural ability, slamming Mae to the ground.

"You know, Mae," a voice said, enveloping her, coming from all angles at once, "You had this coming. I want you to think about that. Think about it! This all could have been prevented if you weren't such a bitch!" The words seethed from the thing, forcing Mae to listen.

Mae fought to breathe but couldn't. She felt as if there was an anvil sitting on her chest, restrained and helpless, pitted against a force much stronger than she was. The stench of urine suffused with the ripe smell of pubic hair wafted into her nostrils as the meaty, bulbous head of a penis forced its way between her lips, over her tongue, and towards the back of her throat. Try as she might, she could not keep the intruder from gaining entry.

Mae tried to turn her head — nothing.

She tried to call out for her daddy, the only man she's ever counted on — nothing.

Mae just wanted to scream, but her mouth, the only orifice able to produce the sounds she needed, was stuffed with a disgusting foreign object.

"Mae! Mae! Mae! Wake up," Keyera said, shaking her sister.

Mae opened her mouth, straining to speak. Keyera leaned in. "Huh? What did you say?"

Mae tossed and turned, unable to form words.

"Wake up, Mae! You're having a nightmare again. You were screaming in your sleep. Are you ok?" Keyera asked, continuing to shake her sister. "I'm really worried about you."

Mae opened her eyes slowly, taking in her surroundings. *Yup, I'm still in my room. Yup, I'm covered in sweat, and triple yup, that's my sister standing over me and staring like I'm a basket case,* she thought. "I'm alright, sis. Just need some water." She rolled over, turning her back to her sister. She had the sudden urge to make herself small, to turn into an insignificant, unnoticeable being capable of being forgotten about, or better yet, never having been known at all. She wanted desperately to get away from the constant attention and worry and nonstop monitoring.

Sighing, Mae had a single thought. *If Mom was here, she would know what to do. She would rub my head, kiss my cheek, and fix this, all of it. Mom ...*

Keyera could tell her sister needed some time but didn't care. "Hey, you! Listen, you've been moping and stuck up here in your room since we brought you home from the hospital. You've been having nonstop night terrors, and all I want to do is help! So, I'm not leaving until you talk to me." Keyera found a plot of land on the end of Mae's bed, plopped down and curled up next to her sister.

"Suit yourself," Mae said over her shoulder. "I'm not talking, so you'll be here a long while."

"Whatever, sis. We're Daniels. That's what we do. We stick together. So, if sticking to you is what it takes, then so be it."

Mae ignored her sister, focusing instead on the smear of dirt on her windowsill. She drifted away, wrapped in her thoughts. *Mom. She was tough. Why can't I be more like her? Maybe If I was, this would have never happened to me.*

She laid still, thinking, questioning, and planning, her thoughts running rampant.

Since coming home from the hospital, a few of her classmates had swung by to check on her. Something she was — begrudgingly — glad for. Mae was in no mood to face her companions from school. How could she be? By now everyone there, if not the whole town, had undoubtedly found out what had happened to her. By who, maybe not, but what? Most definitely. She found solace in the knowledge that others cared about her.

Mae got up and decided she needed a little space. A few steps later, she found herself standing in front of her bedroom window, staring out in no particular direction. She allowed her eyes to roam and her thoughts to coalesce. She noticed Mr. and Mrs. Peters hadn't taken their trash out this week. The Finestine's were at each other's throats again. *God, when were they going to quit it and do what adults do when they're mad at each other — have makeup sex!* Mae scoffed, *after what happened, I don't think I'll ever willingly participate in it. I'll leave that to everyone else.*

The old spinster across the way was rocking on her porch with two of her many cats in her lap. *If I can't find a way to get rid of this darkness, these feelings of inadequacy, my desire to ... If I can't get my mind right, I just might end up like Ms. Taylor. Old and alone with a bunch of multicolored tabby cats to keep me company,* Mae thought. *Maybe life will be better that way. For me, at least.*

Her eyes traced the outline of the old oak tree in their front yard. The base was strong and sturdy. She remembered running around it as a kid. It's thick and hardy limbs swayed in the night's chilly breeze.

Mae's eyes narrowed and then widened as she saw the figure

of a man in the tree staring back at her. For a moment, she was terrified and full of rage. She had the sudden urge to hit him, to throw anything at him. She thought of chucking her heels under her bed at the perv but didn't want to ruin the leather. As Mae contemplated dethronement options, her eyes settled on her peeping Tom's eyes.

Those eyes, she thought.

The man's eyes were slightly hooded by the darkness and held Mae's gaze.

I've seen those eyes before. I'm sure of it. Mae ran her fingers through her hair, pulling it taut while she did. Keyera was asleep now, snoring.

Mae now stood wide awake, eyes transfixed on the man who seemed to defy all laws of physics. *How is he able to stand on that small branch the way that he is? He's keeping himself in place despite the howling winds and frigid temperatures. And yet, there he stands, shoulders square, feet firm with those odd eyes transfixed —on me.*

Mae could feel his gaze washing over her. The intensity of his stare was enough, for the briefest of moments, to make her feel faint. *I knew I saw those eyes before!* Mae said to herself, recognition dawning. *He was the man in the woods. The one carrying me!*

Several moments ago, Mae's mood was somber yet laced with intrigue. Her newfound recollection of the man now brought on a surge of fear and anger. *Either he was my attacker, or he was an opportunist looking to capitalize on a volatile situation. The question is, why is he here now, at this very moment, watching me?*

"*Mae, if you invite me in, I can explain everything,*" the man said, startling Mae as his voice crept into her head. She looked around the darkness, fumbled with her bedside lamp while almost dropping it, before holding it up, preparing herself to fight. "Who's there?" she said in a mild tone.

Keyera's voice, a whisper, sailed through the dimly lit room,

"Mae, go back to sleep. You're making too much noise, and I'm tired."

"Shut up and go back to sleep!" Mae retorted. "I'd hate to ruin your beauty rest." *God, she can be so insensitive at times!* Still looking around their dark room, she couldn't see where the voice might have originated from.

"Mae, I'm here, on the tree. There's no need to be scared. Let me in, and I'll explain why I'm following you. Trust me, I mean you no harm. If I did, I would not have tried to rescue you that night in the woods. I knew you were scared, just like you're scared now, but I was there to help then, as I am now. I assure you," the man said, bending at the knee and allowing one leg to dangle as he braced himself with a hand against the tree's trunk.

"God! How are you doing that?" Mae said, staring out of the window. "Is that really you speaking to me, the guy standing outside of my window like a creeper? You aren't showing on my active registry. No personal ID — nothing. How can you be speaking to me from this distance without an EMCD?"

"I don't need one … now can you please allow me to come in?"

"How come you keep asking if I'll let you in. You're a creeper. Why the hell would I do that!" Mae said, wondering why he hasn't tried to force his way in yet. "Why don't you need an EMCD? Everyone needs an EMCD. Those without it, they …"

The man sighed softly. Ignoring her last question, he said, *"Because I really would like your permission first."*

Mae wasn't quite sure if she should trust this guy, but as far as she could tell, he was sincere and seemed to be telling the truth. She wasn't sure what it was about this guy but felt compelled to trust him. "No! No, you aren't allowed in!" Mae said in direct conflict with what she was feeling. "I have a knife, and I will stab you and watch you bleed if you try anything. Your twig and berries will be the second thing to go too!"

The man could barely contain his chuckle and thought, *Despite all that she's been through, this girl is cute and has a spark to her that I doubt could ever be extinguished, no matter how bad her situation gets.*

"You're cute, you know that!" He blurted out without thinking.

Fuck! Mae thought, pulling the kitchen knife from her back pocket in one fluid motion.

Before Mae had a chance to blink or finish her last sentence, there he was, in all of his magnificent glory standing in front of her, six feet even — as far as she could tell — with the build of an action movie star. His masculine musk floated in behind him as if on a leash, politely making its way into Mae's nostrils.

She tried to use her EMCD to call the police but couldn't get a signal through. The air around her shimmered. Jax stood inside the bubble with her, away from her. Mae lunged towards him, knife in hand. He side-stepped, parrying her strike. Mae regained her balance and tried again. Jax knocked the blade from her hand and pushed her against the bubble's wall.

Tears streaked down Mae's face as Jax stepped away from her. He slid her knife towards her feet. "Here, you can have your weapon back. Like I told you, I'm not here to hurt you."

"You sure could have fooled me," Mae said, picking up her knife. "If you aren't going to hurt me, why are you here? What is this bubble?" She touched it, sending shimmering waves across its surface.

"It's a time dilation bubble. It slows down time inside, and nothing inside can escape unless I will it."

"Why the hell are you in my bedroom!"

"I don't want you! You're cute, sure, but not my type." That last bit was a lie, and he knew it, but so what. He wasn't going to blow this girl's head up any more than he'd have to. "I shouldn't have said what I said to set you off. I'm sorry. Now, please hear me out."

Mae's freckles were lightly glowing in the moon's pale light. Her face was scrunched up in distaste. "What do you want?"

"I wanted to tell you about that night. To tell you I

wasn't your attacker and that I will be here whenever you need me. I will never hurt you. I can't hurt you. You are important!"

"Why the hell would I need you?" Mae fired back. "I have my sister, my daddy, and the Sheriff's department on my side. I think I will manage. Is that all you came here to tell me? Prove to me you mean me no harm—leave!"

Taken slightly aback at Mae's abruptness, Jax said, "Well yea, that's what I came to tell you. Mainly that I will always be here when you need me. Just call my name."

"Who are you?" Mae demanded.

"I was sent by the man in charge. He had to bend some rules to make me and get me here, but I'm here. I'm so sorry about that night in the woods."

"What are you? Some sort of vampire?" Mae asked, half not expecting an answer, half praying he wasn't psycho. "And the man in charge, the one you mentioned, who's he?"

Her quizzical look and question about the First One confirm what I thought. This girl has no idea how very important she is. She would have never asked me that if she knew, Jax thought. He looked Mae square in the eyes and said, "He is the only one who can answer your question about who he is. In time he will provide you with answers. For now, I am all you have. I am the only one who can protect you from what's to come. From what's out there."

"And about the whole vampire thing, no, I'm not a vampire ... not in the traditional sense at least. My kind does not feed on blood but thrives on hope and experiences. And hope is a dying resource. Until you, that is. Look, I'm new at this so if you could cut me some slack, I'd appreciate it. I'm Jax, by the way."

Mae bust out in laughter, bending at the waist and slapping her thighs. She was flabbergasted at the very notion of what this man had said. Keyera stirred in the bed.

"You expect me to believe that some guy I've never met

will provide me with the answers to all of the questions I have and that somehow I'm supposed to be 'hope's' dying solution? Is that right? Ok, try this one … why me? Why did I have to endure such pain, humiliation, and torture! It's not fair, and I hate that guy from the woods for what he did to me. I hate myself for being too weak to fight back." Tears streamed down Mae's face. There was no sign of laughter, no evidence of joy. Just pure hate and sadness. The shards of dismay splayed across her distorted features in the dark shadowy room.

Jax stepped in to hug Mae, to bring her into his embrace and tell her everything was going to be ok. The truth was, everything wasn't going to be ok. She'd had something taken from her, and she could never get it back. To top it off, Jax was pretty sure the coming future wasn't as bright and cheery as he hoped.

Mae pushed Jax back, refusing his hug, still gripping her knife. She wasn't sure she was ready for physical contact … not yet. Turning her head, she continued to cry. The tears streamed down her face like a river flowing down a canal, searching for a way out, a way towards a bigger body of water. Jax stepped closer again. He never was one to take no for an answer. With gentle ease, he slid his arms around Mae and held her in a tight embrace.

Long moments passed until her weeping woke her sister.

Sitting up, Keyera called up the time in her mind's eye via her EMCD, frowned, and looked at her Mae, who was standing there, arms cradled around herself and sobbing.

"Hey, sis, are you alright? Why are you just standing there like that?" Swinging her legs off of the bed, Keyera made her way over to her sister and pulled her close. She moved Mae's head onto her chest and stared out of the window. There was a gentle breeze flowing in with a faint masculine scent, electrifying something within her.

After a short while, the girls found themselves lying in bed, eating ice cream, watching the news, and talking. Just talking.

Something they hadn't done much since the incident.

"I could use a drink," Mae casually informed her sister, rising to head out of the room.

Consternation showed on Keyera's face. "Since when did you start drinking? And where are you getting alcohol from? You aren't old enough to buy that stuff."

"Who needs to buy it when I can just take it? Dad has a ton of that stuff in his study. I haven't seen him drink in a long while. He won't notice his stash getting low. Trust me." Mae narrowed her eyes slightly as she impassively looked at her sister. "That is unless you're going to snitch on me."

"You know I would never rat you out, sis. Just that I don't think you should be doing that stuff." Keyera's eyes had a softness to them. This was not the badass, hard as nails sister Mae was used to. This sister was concerned and caring. Qualities Mae seldom saw in Keyera anymore. "I'll be fine, ok? I just need something to take the edge off. You, you don't know what it's like. I..."

Keyera interjected, cutting Mae off, "You're right, I don't know what it's like. But I do know what it's like to lose a mother, and I don't want to lose my sister too!" The loudness of Keyera's voice shocked her. She hadn't intended for it to come out the way it had, but what was said was said. Her concern now was for her sister.

Mae spoke, slowly this time, "God, would you..."

Again, Keyera cut in, less lenient in her use of a higher tone, "God has nothing to do with this!" She shouted, "I don't want you drinking!"

"Jesus, would you shut up for a second! You don't understand," Mae yelled.

Keyera rolled her eyes.

Releasing the doorknob and stepping closer to her sister, Mae continued to speak, softer this time.

Her eyes were downcast. "I did it for you."

Holding Mae at arm's length with both hands on her shoulders, confused, Keyera asked, "Did what? You did what for me?" Her eyes searched her sister's face.

Mae's mood evaporated as quickly as the ad on their view wall had come and gone. "I could have died that night. I am as sure of that as I am that you are my sister, but he whispered something to me, you know. Something I didn't tell the detective. Something that saved my life. He said if I didn't let him do ... everything that he did to me ... that he'd have his way with you before he left your corpse in the woods."

"I was scared," Mae continued. "I was so scared. Not for me, but for you! I did what he asked. He did what he wanted to me. I was powerless to stop him because of my love for you, Keyera! All I could do was think of you and what would become of you, and so I chose to sacrifice myself to his depraved desires in order to keep you safe. You don't understand! How could you understand! You will never understand!"

Keyera's face became a blur of mascara, foundation, and salty tears. She stood frozen in a state of dismay. Shaking and sobbing, she shrieked while embracing her sister for the second time that night, "I'm sorry! I'm so sorry!"

The stairs creaked beneath the gentle footfalls of Mae Daniels. She'd have her drink regardless of what her sister thought of her. *Not much to live for nowadays,* she thought. *Why not enjoy myself while I dull the pain.*

Halfway down the stairs, Mae heard several voices. *Since when did guests arrive? Whatever. Even Daddy needs company every now and again. Other adults he can be himself around. But why are they here so late?*

"David, the situation has changed! She should have never received that device. This could jeopardize everything."

"Jonathan, calm down. The situation isn't as bad as you think." Ryland tried to reassure the man.

David spoke with a slow, stern voice. "Does the girl know?"

"No. Not yet. I wasn't going to tell her until we knew it was safe." Ryland said.

Mae was hiding in the study. It provided a much better vantage point than the stairs. She wanted to know who her daddy was speaking to.

"Good. Keep it that way," said the stern man.

What are they talking about? Mae wondered. *What girl? Do they mean me? Know what? What should I know?*

Mae strained to see well. Craning her head ever so slightly out from behind the door frame, she could barely make out an emblem on the man's tunic. The holographic patch they wore over their left breast was that of a shooting star streaking upward from a crescent-shaped Earth. The star ascended through several multicolored layers.

Mae had seen that patch before on some documentary. *If I remember correctly, those multicolored layers represent another dimension. The spiritual realm, I believe.* Piecing it together, Mae understood what she was looking at. The holographic patch was representative of a soul transcending into the spiritual realm.

These people, they're Upgraders. But what are they doing here? With Dad!

Mae decided to try out her new device. She was plugged into the world now, and it was a better time than any to put it to work. Mae mentally toggled to the facial recognition feature as she took in each man's face. *How long is this supposed to take anyway? I thought this stuff was instantaneous. 'Information immediately at your fingertips.' Isn't that what they said in the hospital?*

Suddenly, the two men heads snapped towards where Mae was hiding, all conversation ceased. Mae immediately pulled her head back around the wall, out of sight of the men. Together, David and Jonathan walked past Ryland. Fueled with anticipation, they reached the location where their EMCDs notified them of an active ping, but they saw nothing. No one was there.

Spinning around to face Ryland, David spoke, "I believe it prudent that we reconvene this meeting another time. In the meantime, keep your daughter safe! We are all depending on you ... and more importantly — on her.

Mae climbed into her room through her bedroom window. She slumped against the wall, allowing herself a brief respite. Each breath she took was long and labored. She had the silliest of grins on her face.

Keyera pulled herself from the news broadcast on the view wall, startled as she faced Mae. "OMG, girl, you scared me. What are you doing climbing into our window like that?" she asked.

"I was trying to get away from those two Upgraders in the living room. The spotted me," Mae said between breaths.

"Do I even want to know what you mean by 'they spotted you'? And did you say Upgraders? You sure?"

"Yep, as sure as can be. They were Upgraders, alright. The question is what they were doing talking with Daddy." Mae said.

The current topic being reported on the view wall grabbed both sisters' attention.

GNN EARTH: NIGHTLY NEWS

Reporter: Did we hear you correctly, Mr. Mayor, that you do not know why there have been so many disappearances lately?

Mayor Blaxby: The Sheriff and I are working diligently to close these cases. I can assure the city that these few disappearances are isolated and unrelated.

Reporter: Mr. Mayor, sir, as much as we [the people] want to believe you, there is evidence that contradicts your previous statement. I have sources pretty high up that state there's a string of disappearances that date back hundreds of years, which no one has been able to link together until recent innovations in computing technology and big data analytics.

The ability to sort through both structured, semi-structured, and unstructured data has brought major breakthroughs in our ability to understand the big picture as it encompasses the global community. What do you have to say about that, sir?

Mayor Blaxby: As I said, my people are working on those cases as they relate to this city. I cannot comment on whether or not they are linked to any other case around the globe, and quite frankly, I find that very notion to be preposterous based on the information I've seen. Now, if you'll excuse me, I have matters to attend to. Thank you all. Many blessings to the people of South Boston, Virginia.

Several camera drones swirl about the mass of people angling for a story, casting their shadows at odd angles.

Reporter: As we watch the Mayor of our fair city depart, we can only wonder, what does he really know, and what isn't he telling us? Thank you for joining us for this evening's nightly news update. Marcus, back to you.

As the news report droned on about random acts of violence, one of the local high schools closing down, and an upcoming presidential address to the nation, Mae knew what she needed to do.

The thought had been gnawing at her subconscious for the last few hours.

Mae thought, recalling events from the previous night, *Yesterday, Grammy came to see me. Daddy had thanked her for coming.*

'She's upstairs,' Daddy said. 'I don't know how else to reach her.' Grammy thanked him for calling her before doing what grandmothers do best — comfort their grandchildren. When I asked her about Mommy, she said Mom was always a strong-willed little girl and always pushed herself to be the best, to be her best version of herself, which is why she was drawn to the Marine Corps. 'She was

tough as nails,' Grandma had said.

'There, in the Corps, is where she truly discovered she had no limits. That limitations are a construct of the human mind and act as safety buffers, as some kind of evolutionary process designed to extend our lives, which was a desirable trait for procreation. Who really knows?' Grandma said. 'What we do know, or rather what she figured out, is that in order to evolve — in this case, move beyond your perceived abilities — you have to be willing to risk pushing yourself past your breaking point. Only then will you achieve greatness.'

Mae took a swig from the bottle she swiped from her dad's liquor cabinet. *Grammy, thank you,* she thought. *I'm surrounded by darkness right now — lost; I wear it like a cloak and gods be honest, I'm scared, but you've given me hope — a way out. Thank you! I know what I need to do.*

CHAPTER 7

Course Correction

Beads of sweat trickled down Senior White House Aide Marious Lennard's pale face as he traversed the bustling passageways towards the Oval Office.

"Marious, hey, got a second?" Maria Condanova asked. A small, stocky press correspondent, always looking for the inside scoop. What she lacked in appearance, she more than made up for in passion and tenacity.

Marious had turned on his "do not disturb" settings earlier so he could focus on getting to the President free from distractions. Somehow, those settings never seemed to ward off the uninvited — mainly Maria Condanova. "No, Maria, I don't. Not right now at least. Had you paid any attention to my do not disturb settings, you would know that." A slight bit of tension crept into his voice.

Refocusing on his task, Marious continued to walk down the West Colonnade. *These correspondents are like leeches,* he thought. *Sleep with them one time, leak a small story or two as compensation, and presto, instant bloodsuckers. Normally I'd bypass the Press Corps Offices, but something tells me the old man should see this as soon as possible.*

◆ ◆ ◆

Marious had never felt more nervous than at this very moment. Not only had he jumped the chain of command, but he'd also done so blatantly. To top it off, he had just interrupted the President's lunch to hand him what? Information the man may or may not have already known?

He is the President of the Coalition — over half of Earth and several damned planets. Marious thought to himself, *Did I really think he wouldn't know about the information I'd just handed him? Stupid!*

President Branson sat back in his light brown nanogrown concord chair, an exact replica from the old continental United States, and stared evenly at Marious. "Son, where did you get this information?"

"Sir, it was in a pile of reports the Chief of Staff gave to me to either discard or file away to revisit in the future."

"And? Which one was this report?"

"Discard, sir. I believe the Chief thought there wasn't enough information to pay it much attention. However, I have a friend at SETI who tells me otherwise. Sir, you have to know that I'm taking a huge risk coming to you directly with this. If at all possible, please do not name me as your source."

President Branson walked around to position himself in front of his historic desk made from the timbers of the HMS Resolute, an old abandoned British ship from the post-industrial era. He leaned back, placed one hand on his hip, and continued to hold the data cube report with the other. He could see beads of sweat lining Marious's forehead and considered this man's position and predicament.

"Never mind the fact that you should have brought this information to your boss. The fact that you believed you couldn't do as much tells me more than I need to know. You have my word. Have Jannis assemble my special council on your way out."

"I've called you all here because I've recently come into some knowledge, knowledge which should have come across my desk a lot sooner. Ladies and gentlemen, what can you tell me about the string of disappearances around the globe?"

Each official in the situation room remained silent for a moment as they assessed the situation. Many of them had just been blindsided by the President's statement. However, they didn't get to their current positions by not being quick on the draw.

The report the President held in his hand was already abuzz with speculation among the science and intelligence communities; some rooted in facts, some not.

Clearing his throat, the SETI Director spoke up, "Sir, I'd like to begin."

"Alright, Bimala, please take the lead," Branson replied evenly. His mood was an unreadable mask of professional stoicism.

"Mr. President, I'll present the facts as I know them."

"Well, I'd hope that would be the case, son."

Bimala tried to hide his embarrassment and annoyance. "Back in 2017, the Arecibo Observatory in Puerto Rico discovered strange signals coming from one of our colony worlds around the Ross 128 star, only 11 light-years from Earth in the Virgo constellation. Since then, my guys at SETI have been running a background correlation program designed to cross-coordinate various points of data pertaining to that strange and unidentified signal with the signal that's coming from the Eskimo Nebula. The signals intensities vary slightly, but their modulations are the same. That has led us to believe the signals are one and the same, sir."

"Furthermore, the other information we discovered is staggering. I had my guys run another algorithm to determine if the string of mass disappearances around the globe were somehow related to the signals we detected, and well sir, they are. Every time there's a signal flare from the Eskimo Nebula, there's a disappearance associated with that same timeline. The dates we've been able to compile go back some time, sir."

"Lastly, at approximately 1100 hours on March 21st of this year, 2077 — little over a month ago — our boys over at the Atacama Large Millimeter/Submillimeter Array, or ALMA, located on the Chajnantor Plateau in Chile, discovered a strange artifact in deep space within the Eskimo Nebula. A closer look from the Hubble space telescope showed the object in all its glory. A magnificent sun-like sphere whose surface shimmered in rhythmic sequences. Sequences that could not be classified as a natural occurrence, Mr. President."

"Mr. President, if I may," Terrance Shaw, the President's Chief of Staff interjected, "the Office of Net Assessment seems to have some theories about what's going on. They sent me a report a day ago in regards to this phenomenon. At that time, I believed the report to be some self-indulgent sci-fi geek's chance at recognition and of little to no relevance, so I didn't bring it to your attention. But I was wrong. As you may or may not be aware, Mr. President, the ONA is a think tank at the Coalition Defense Force headquarters. They are read into every facet of information that comes through that building, and their AIs pieced it all together using more data points than I can fathom. That stuff is beyond me."

"A few of the main points of data used were numerous missing people cases that sprung up around the globe and at some of our colonies off-world, the thousands of previously unsolved missing persons' cases, and ultimately the strange signals emanating from deep in outer space, which the SETI team discovered. I now believe the ONA's report lends credence to Bimala's claims."

Kurt Carter, the President's Science Advisor, rotated to face Terrance. "Sir, all due respect, but how did the ONA come by that bit of information? Unless Dr. Aadrika cares to refute this, the SETI team never filed an official report with the Defense Force headquarters." Kurt's statement held an undertone of suspicion.

With a wave of his hand, Terrance said hastily, "No time for that now, Kurt, our focus should be on how we should proceed." Facing the President, the Chief of Staff continued, "Mr. President, I recommend we increase security at our military bases, major economic infrastructures, and for that of all major governing officials, on and off world."

A cacophony of noise erupted throughout the situation room. President Branson sat back for a moment, watching his staff's reaction before speaking.

"Everyone gathered here today, in this room, is here for a reason," Branson said, speaking as he'd done for the past ten years, evenly and coolly, intent behind every word. "You are the men and women I rely on to keep me abreast of such matters. Professionals. Craftsman of your trades. Advisors. And somehow, I find myself very disappointed in your abilities right now."

"Not only have we discovered the answer to the biggest question in Earth's history, 'Are we alone in the universe,' we, without a doubt, know where to find these beings who may or may not be hostile. And through all of that, no one thought to inform the one man who needed to know such information?"

Silence, like a dense fog on a cool autumn night, settled around the occupants of the situation room.

President Branson broke the silence, issuing rapid succinct orders, something he was known for. "Bimala, keep your programs running, the satellites listening in, and telescopes zeroed in on the Eskimo Nebula. How far is that nebula from Earth, anyway? Who has that information?"

"Sir, from our calculations, the Eskimo Nebula is some 5,000 light-years from us," Kellie Thompson, the Director of the Coalition Space Agency, said.

"Kellie, thank you for that. How prepared is your staff?

How's our newest flagship faring?"

Kellie's demeanor was that of a consummate professional —confident, courteous, and intelligent. "Mr. President," she said, "construction is all but complete. We are running systems tests as we speak, and soon we'll launch the first shakedown cruise. Mission parameters have us leaving for a trip around Sol within the month."

"Good. Just what I wanted to hear. Listen up, everyone. The information we've uncovered has presented us with an incredible opportunity, one I fully intend to capitalize on. These beings may be taking humans. One thing is for certain— we are not alone."

"This brings me to my plan. We will mount a reconnaissance mission to scout and report back on what is found within the Eskimo Nebula, and if possible, make a pit stop at Ross 128 colony before returning to Earth. Kellie, I want the new capital ship ready to launch within the next three weeks."

The Federation of Communist states will have to wait, Branson thought. "I'm dubbing this Operation Aurora-1, and it is a go, folks."

"Understood, sir," Kellie replied, half focused on the rest of the conversation, half issuing orders to her staff via her EMCD. Outside of those select few who were granted access, anyone entering the White House had their EMCDs blocked from being able to establish external communications. Kellie and the others seated in the situation room were among a handful of individuals who superseded that security protocol.

Branson turned to Ms. MacDonald. "Daniela, I want you to make sure the Coalition Intelligence Agency plays quarterback with any leakage of information pertaining to this mission. No one other than those in this room will know of the full extent of the mission and its parameters. I want all information on this kept classified, Top Secret Highly Compartmentalized Information, until we can get a handle on what's going on."

Branson felt at odds with the situation. He didn't know what he'd find by authorizing this mission, but he knew that he could not allow Earth and her colonies to continue to be blind participants in whatever was transpiring between them and these unknown beings.

Branson shifted his attention. "Kurt, get our Technologies Directorate working on a way to disrupt this signal. Assuming the worst, we need a way to combat whatever these beings are doing. Relay all findings to the Chairman of the Joint Chiefs, Tage Gunnerson."

Tage remained quiet and impassive as he nodded at the President's orders.

Kurt stared at the President; he was about to reply when his gaze betrayed that of a person engaged in a virtual meeting. A slight tinge of annoyance flashed across Branson's face before Kurt returned his attention to him. "Mr. President, my apologies, although I just received an urgent communique from my staff."

"Our boys over at Earth Station One, what used to be the old International Space Station, have detected anomalous subspace fissures which they're calling rifts. As far as we can tell, these rifts are giving off small amounts of tachyon particles. After running a trace program on the disappearance timelines that we've already identified, they found corresponding evidence of the presence of tachyon particles."

"Jesus, so let me get this straight. You're telling me, and everyone in this room, not only are we getting a signal from the Eskimo Nebula, but we're also detecting some kind of rift generated by those signals? Is that correct, Kurt?"

"Sir, that is partially correct. We aren't sure if the signals are creating the rifts, but we are sure that the rifts are being created at the same time as the signals." Kurt said before continuing, a hint of urgency in his voice, "Sir, I'm getting another notification — we're detecting one of those rifts now."

CHAPTER 8

The Cunningham's

John grabbed Charles's leg before pulling him, kicking and screaming, across the bed towards him.

Deflecting each of his 8-year-old son's swift kicks, John grabbed the pillow beside him, and with an even amount of force, brought it smashing down onto his son, who erupted with laughter. Trying to seize the moment, Daniel jumped onto his father's back. Laughing, they both went tumbling down onto the bed. Kimberly retracted her legs, and Charles rolled out of the way just in time as the force of John and Daniel's bodies came smashing down in a roar of laughter.

Kathleen was waiting just out of sight, two pillows in hand. As her dad and younger brothers caught their breath, she pounced. Pillows flailing, flying this way and that, Kathleen came charging into the room like a madwoman. Her girlish grin was replaced with a desire to dominate.

Not this time, Kathleen said to herself. *I will win, and they will eat pillow.* With a smirk, Kathleen launched the first pillow, which John easily deflected. He reached across the bed for a pillow of his own; his wife, Kimberly, quickly placed her foot on top of it. She waved her finger at John, giving him a grin, barely hiding her concealed desire for girl power, wishing for her daughter to win this round.

John pulled, "Babe ... get ... off ... of ..."

Kathleen struck. Her blow came swiftly and on target. The pillow connected with her dad's head hard enough to give him a slight headache. "... Ahh ... ok ... ok, I give," John chuckled. "Honey, I give." Kathleen launched herself on her dad, "Sure you do! You never just give!" Daniel and Charles joined in on the dogpile.

"Hey, watch it, you guys. Don't break anything." Kimberly shouted lightheartedly. Laughter came from all around. Whoops, hollers, and cheers echoed around the bedroom.

John laid there, huffing and puffing, with his three children panting on top of his collapsed body. "Ok guys, I'm going to get us something to drink ... any takers?"

Of course, three medium-sized hands shot into the air; in unison, they said, "I do."

John made his way out of the bedroom and down the hallway. He looked over his shoulder to check that the kids were still in the room and couldn't see him. Satisfied they weren't looking, John crept into the bathroom and hid behind the wall with the sonic resonators. A devilish grin plastered his face. They'll never see me coming, he thought, mentally shutting down his positional locator.

Sending his wife an e-message, John said, *"Kimberly, I want you to send the kids out of the room. Tell them I need their help downstairs."*

Instead of sending a direct message, Kimberly decided to pay John a visit via his virtual meeting space.

John Cunningham loved technology, and as far as the EMCD went, he loved fully utilizing its abilities. Mentally melting inward into his VMS, he found himself standing atop a fairly large, soft yet sturdy cloud, talking to his wife. She loved to use dramatic settings in nature for her virtual meetings.

Kimberly looked her husband in the eyes and flashed a smile

with a tinge of suspicion. "Babe, what are you doing?"

"Nothing, Hun," John said, looking around to remind himself this was just a virtual setting and not real, "just send the kids out."

"Why?" Kimberly said in her southernly sweet drawl. She maintained a girlish smile. "I will not send my babies out to get slaughtered. The bed is the safe zone, so as long as they are with me, they are safe." Stepping closer, Kimberly brought her lips within an inch of her husband's. The whiskers of his mustache tickled her lip, and she said, "Do I make myself clear, Mr?"

John loved his wife's southern belle accent. "Honey, it's all fun and games. I just want to talk to them," he said wryly.

How can I resist that handsome smile! He's lucky I love him, Kimberly thought to herself. *I'll send the kids but not without warning first!* "Fine, I'll send the kids, babe. You just better be nice to them."

The kids crept through the house as quietly as possible. Charles, the youngest at eight years old, followed closely on the heels of Kathleen with Daniel in tow.

"Darn it!" Kathleen said, attempting to ping her father's location but coming up empty.

"What is it?" Daniel said, his voice a low whisper.

"I tried to ping Dad's location but got nothing. He must have turned off his positional locator." *Of course he did, he's smart,* Kathleen thought. *What was it Dad always said? 'You don't make it as far as I have, doing the things I've done without having some smarts.'*

Kathleen stopped and took a knee with her brothers following suit. "Ok new plan, guys," she whispered. "Daniel, you're the bait. Charley ..."

"I told you I don't like that name," Charles said. "I want to be called Charles. You know I hate Charley!"

Kathleen, slightly annoyed at her little brother's timing to pitch a fit over a nickname, continued, "Whatever! Charles! Listen up. Dad's out there somewhere, and we need to find him before he finds us!"

Daniel whispered frantically, "Wait … why am I the bait! I don't want to be the bait."

Rolling her eyes, Kathleen said steadily, "Because one of us has to be the bait and Charley here …" tossing a side-eye at her little brother and rolling her eyes, "… Charles here is too dumb to be good bait. I need someone I can count on, and at the moment, that's you, pigs-for-brains. Now I want you to run down the stairs through the living room and back again as fast as you can. Don't worry, we'll be right behind you."

Screaming, "Ahhhhhhhhhh …" as he ran, Daniel charged through the living room, through the dining room, and veered left to head through the kitchen before turning around to go back the way he came. His legs moved as fast as he could pump them, fear and excitement coursing through him. He ran into the kitchen, around the island and out, past the archway separating the living room from the kitchen. As he passed a couple of pieces of furniture, Daniel caught a glimpse of something out of the corner of his eye.

John reached out and grabbed his middle son, snatching him off his feet and softly slamming him to the ground. He leaned in, with a hand over his son's mouth, and whispered, "Where are your siblings? I'm going to remove my hand from your mouth now. If you yell when I take my hand off of your mouth, I will tickle you to death! Do you understand me?" Daniel shook his head yes; he had a wild, excited look to him — his eyes darting from side to side, forehead glistening in sweat.

John removed his hand.

"Daddy, you don't want to know. If you let me go, I promise we'll go easy on you."

John tried to use his 'I'm Daddy, tell me what I want to

know' face, as he leaned closer again. "Daniel, at the count of three, my fingers will explode all over your belly in a dance native to the original peoples of this land. Trust me when I tell you, you'll be gasping for air in no time as you try to deal with a large number of tickles coming your way. Now, where are your siblings!"

Daniel's eyes slowed their flickering. He parted his lips in a sheepish grin, jerked his head slightly upward, and said, "They're right behind you."

Quickly, John spun around, releasing his grip on Daniel.

Charles and Kathleen simultaneously swung, smashing a couch pillow and a child's bouncy ball against their dad's head, catching him off guard. John fell backward onto his butt. Daniel rolled away and dashed out of the living room, making use of the distraction to make his getaway.

God, I taught the kids well, John thought. He reveled in this proud dad moment for a second before confessing, "Alright, you got me. I give. You guys win."

With the fun coming to an end, John got up and made his way upstairs to join his wife. His mind filled with thoughts about his family. *Kathleen is really picking up on strategy and tactics, and Charles and Daniel are learning how to follow directions and orders well. I love my kids. They make fine little warriors. Perhaps Kimberly will consider letting me send Kathleen to the new Joint Military Academy they're building on the moon. I hear it'll be state-of-the-art with the latest technologies humanity has to offer. I have no doubt she'll thrive there.*

John called out as he approached his bedroom, "Honey, are you ready to immerse into Galactic Siege III, Rise of the Delphines?"

"Why don't you come and see," Kimberly said, her gentle, sensual voice enticing him, spurring him on.

As John walked through the door to the bedroom, he noticed Kimberly in those new panties he'd brought her a few weeks back. The one with the missing crotch. She had nothing else on. With his excitement rising, John searched for the right words as he regained his composure.

"Honey, you look stunning!" He said, shutting the bedroom door. John slid into the bed, cozying up to his temptress and caressing her hair, "Let's knock out this immersion, and I promise I'll make the wait worth your while!"

Kimberly held John's gaze for a few moments. "Only if you do that thing with your tongue I adore so much?"

"Deal!"

Giddy with excitement, John and Kimberly settled back onto their bed for their real-life 45-minute immersion. They both thought-clicked through a series of steps to get to their favorite show and make the necessary bitcoin payment — unaware that their room door was opening.

"Mom, Dad," Kathleen said, poking her head in, "can I — OMG, I am so, so sorry you guys! I didn't mean to ..." she yelled, closing her eyes, her cheeks flashing rose-red. Her embarrassment passed almost as fast as it had come. Eyes still shut, with two clearly pissed-off parents, Kathleen spoke in a sweet, pleasing tone, "Can I join in and immerse with you two?" John and Kimberly looked at each other and back at Kathleen. Covers drew to their chest, they said in unison, "No! It's not for kids!"

Kathleen slammed the door.

Unable to control themselves, John and Kimberly broke out in laughter. Several seconds passed before they turned and whispered to each other, "Do we know each other or what?" Taking advantage of the moment, Kimberly leaned in, gently placing her lips on her husband's. She allowed his tongue to explore her mouth and dance with her own. Their foreheads touched while Kimberly pulled back, leaving behind a husband with a slightly nibbled bottom lip.

"God, that was a great episode! I really love how the Delphines can strategically attack their enemies on the Eastern front while gaining and forging new alliances on the Northern and Western frontiers of space. Nothing compares to this show," John exuberantly said to his wife. "I'll put the kids to bed and after ... well, you know what's about to happen!"

John and Kimberly's lovemaking went on for hours. They explored the depths of their sexuality with the additional software upgrade to their EMCD, allowing for a greater tactile interface in both the physical and mental worlds at the same time. By the time the two finished, both their minds and bodies were spent. The pair curled into each other's arms, allowing their minds to be swept away in the cool summer breeze.

The early morning rays shone through the dynamic, tempered glass windows. Kimberly sent a thought to the windows to filter out 50% more light as she gracefully rolled over. Rubbing the cold out of her eyes, she sent another thought to the replicator located on the room's far wall. After last night's shenanigans with her husband, she was going to need all the coffee she could get.

Kimberly blew into her hands, reeling from her offensive morning breath. She reached out over the covers to hold her husband's hand ... that wasn't there.

"John?" Kimberly called out. Frantically, she shot up when she didn't get a reply. John was a light sleeper. It wasn't like him not to answer. Looking over to his side of the bed, she saw it was empty, disheveled, and cold — with no John.

Kimberly activated the tactical settings on her EMCD, compliments of her husband — and which she wasn't supposed to have — to locate him within their house. The EMCD tactical setting was designed to pick up a target location's ping and relay that as a visual representation — or silhouette — in the requestor's visual feed. Effectively, Kimberly should have been able to see John's body anywhere within a 100-foot radius, through any wall or floor. Instead, she saw nothing. She felt it in her bones … something wasn't right. After several mental messages, numerous VMS requests, and more location pings than she cared to count, Kimberly resigned herself to the fact that she needed help; she called the CBI.

"Are you kidding me! My husband is missing and all you can tell me is to calm down and speak with the local police department? I don't want to speak to those incompetent asses. I want the Coalition Bureau of Investigation to get off their ass and do what they are designed to do. Investigate!"

"Ma'am, I'm sorry, but there is nothing we can do. This is a local matter. I am patching you through now," said the lonely CBI call center agent who had the pleasure of catering to all forms of irate and paranoid individuals daily.

A news report played in the background, as Kimberly sat, waiting to be connected to the local police department.

GNN: DAILY NEWS
"And in other news, the search continues for several missing people across the county. Our source at the CBI, who wishes to remain anonymous, has confirmed this case is bigger than previously believed." The news reporter, an apathetic rabble-rouser, said, "More to follow. Sandy, back to you."

The police operator finally came on, and Kimberly struggled to hold back her emotions. John would want her to remain strong.

"South Boston Police Department, what's your emergency?"

Kimberly told her story. As the words came out of her mouth, her emotional wall collapsed, and her tears began to fall. She knew then that she'd never stop searching for her husband, no matter the time it would take.

Thourn, invisible as he was, stood in the corner of the room, unnoticed by Mrs. Cunningham. Moments earlier, he phase-shifted to a quasi-state of reality where his physical body was no longer visible, but he maintained the ability to interact with the physical world.

He surveyed the room for a moment, noticing minute details imperceptible to human senses. Thourn and his Watchers surveyed every location where a culling happened. In every instance, there was a single constant — the stench of fear burned into the surrounding area. Culls always cause the flight-or-fight hormone adrenaline, better known as epinephrine, to be produced in mass, saturating everything as it's expelled from the body in bulk.

Thourn took in the hormone saturation pattern, the way it pooled on the bed before smearing on the floor like someone was dragged towards the open closet. He stared at the dangling clothes inside, sensing a second clue the thieves left behind: temporal chronitons — particles that aide in the slowing and manipulation of time. What Thourn couldn't figure out was what those particles had to do with the culls. *So ... they were here. Of that, there can be no doubt. Are the attackers coming from the future to alter the timeline?* he thought while considering thousands of other possibilities.

What he knew for sure was temporal chronitons pervaded the room he was standing in, and if he didn't figure out who was snatching humans and why, he might have to shut down this ride, send everyone home, and possibly destroy this pocket universe. His majesty would understand, or so he hoped.

Thourn set to work analyzing the unique signature associated with the temporal chronitons and tachyons the thieves were so kind to leave behind. If nothing else, Thourn saw such work as sloppy and amateur. He'd find them. He was confident of that.

Turning to leave, he said the words that came so natural to him, words he'd said countless times over the ages: *Your ride has undoubtedly ended, Mr. Cunningham. I trust your stay was ... memorable — and you do join us again.*

CHAPTER 9

Yellow Footprints

Mae rode on the bus in relative silence.

Everyone here, they look just as scared as I feel, she thought to herself.

The ride was bumpy, something which shouldn't have been possible with the new generation of motionless vehicles Tesla rolled out. But somehow, here she was bouncing up and down while sitting in a military transport vehicle heading towards God knows what.

Mae chuckled to herself as she laughed at the absurdity of her thoughts. Leave it to the military to use outdated technology compared to the civilian world. *I should have paid more attention when Mom shared her old sea stories.*

Looking up, Mae noticed a girl glancing in her direction from the seat across the aisle. *She's done that a few times now, what's her deal?* Mae thought. She was immediately rewarded with the girl's public profile and stats after activating the identification feature of her EMCD. The girl's name was Savanna Main, and she was 17 — the same age she was.

Ok, Mae thought, *so she's from the old San Diego area of the North American West Coast and doesn't seem to be that much of a social butterfly.*

Scrolling further down, Mae stopped on one interesting piece of information. After running the information through a customized search algorithm she'd downloaded a few days back while playing around with her EMCD, she made a connection that wasn't readily available on Savanna's profile. *This girl is loaded ... but what's she doing here? A girl like her could buy any life she wanted.*

"Hey, you," Mae said as she extended her hand. "My name is Mae, Mae Daniels."

Taking the invitation, Savanna leaned in and said, "I know who you are. I hope you don't mind, but I did a deep dive on you during the first few minutes of boarding the shuttle bus."

What's up with this girl? Mae thought to herself, an odd look growing on her face. "A deep dive?" she asked. "I thought only the military and civil authorities could do deep dives. Not average people like us."

Savanna knew this was coming and had what seemed like a pre-scripted spiel for Mae. "I like to know who's around me, and I like to know about those nuanced factors that reveal more about a person than they may have known themselves. You know, the minute details that you can gather, bread crumbs from across the spectrum of a person's online activities. You'd be surprised what you can find out."

Savanna continued, "So, I tend to automatically do deep dives on people by running a background program on my EMCD using facial recognition to identify those in my general vicinity. In my experience, terrible things happen when you aren't aware of those around you."

Mae's facial features lightened and hardened at the same time. *Does she know?* Mae thought. *No, she can't know, can she?*

Mae was slightly irritated at the moment and for good reason. This girl seemed too calm and collected, but more than that, it felt to Mae like she was holding her tongue about something. "Yes, but that doesn't explain how you managed to do that!" Mae said, "That's government and military-grade capabilities, so what gives?"

"If you must know, Papa is a defense contractor for the Coalition and stationed in Spain."

"Isn't that where EMCDs are ..."

"Developed and manufactured?" Savanna said, politely cutting off Mae with a slight grin. "Yes, you're correct. Do you understand now? I have one of the 2nd generation black EMCDs, while everyone else in society is still receiving the white 1st gen — minus those in authority who have the black 1st gen. My papa saw it fit to outfit me with next-level tech. A perk of working as the lead contractor on the EMCDs, I suppose. Just don't tell anyone. I don't think they would appreciate what I can do."

"Then why tell me? You don't know me." Mae said, taken aback. "We just met. Don't you think that's a little reckless of you?"

Savanna stared at Mae's almond-shaped brown eyes for a moment. Her own brown eyes flickered back and forth. After another brief period, she said, "As I told you, I did a deep dive on you. Based on the correlated data I've been able to compile, I believe you are a genuine person and, most importantly, trustworthy. You're someone I'd like to be friends with. I think we need to stick together if we plan on making it through boot camp. What do you say?"

Mae opened her mouth to speak but was interrupted when the bus came to an abrupt stop and the doors swung open.

An ungodly amount of yelling and screaming erupted in those few intervening moments. Confusion reigned as the men and women on the bus were quickly ushered off and herded onto yellow footprints painted on the sidewalk.

Mae knew Marines are not only heavily honor-bound but that they are deeply rooted in tradition almost to the point of fanaticism. They hold traditions to the highest value, above all else, and for some odd reason, stepping on a pair of yellow footprints at the start of your training was one of those traditions which had to be followed. Mae looked down and smiled at the sight of the same yellow footprints which bore Marines who served in every major battle that the old Continental United States had been in since 1915. Now those same footsteps, donated by the old United States Military, rested at the base of the Coalition Marine Corps intake facility for new recruits. The same yellow footprints her mother stood on all those years ago.

They ushered the new recruits through 'Receiving,' where they were issued their initial gear and simultaneously stripped of all remnants of their past lives. Now sitting cross-legged, cold and bald within their squad bays, each new recruit anxiously awaited their drill instructors.

Senior Drill Instructor (DI) Staff Sergeant (SSgt) Mike Vickers felt almost as giddy as a young schoolgirl anticipating her first day of school as he approached the squad bay hatches. His veins pulsed, and his heartbeat quickened. This was a dance he'd done many times before.

DI Vickers flexed his arms, cracked his neck, and stepped across the hatch threshold.

The newly deposited troops of platoon 7805 previous lives just ended as DI Vickers delivered verbal epithets coupled with the nonverbal body language of a menacing madman. The other two Drill Instructors were hot on DI Vickers' trail as he prepped the new recruits for what awaited them on their path to redemption.

These kids, they've spent the better part of their whole lives as civilians — and that civilian stench must be scrubbed from them! Vickers thought, before beginning their usual routine.

The recruits cowered where they sat, not sure if they should run or cry out for their parents.

Mae tried to send a mental message to Savanna.

Nothing.

What is going on here! she thought, trying again and again. Each time she got nothing but an error message.

If I can't send a message, I most likely won't be able to reach her via the virtual meeting space, either. They gotta be jamming us.

One thought permeated Mae's mind as she ran a hand across her freshly shaven head, *I hate this place already.*

Senior Drill Instructor SSgt Vickers stood in front of the platoon with his hands on his hips as a cloud of calm fury surrounded him.

"Sit up straight and look at me now," Vickers said.

"Aye aye, sir!" exclaimed the recruits of platoon 7805 in a mixed cacophony of voices.

"My name is Staff Sergeant Vickers, and I am assisted in my duties by Drill Instructor Sergeant Black and Drill Instructor Sergeant King. Our mission is to train each one of you to become a Coalition Marine. A Marine is characterized as one who possesses the highest of military virtues and never waivers from them. He or she obeys orders, respects their seniors, and constantly strives to be the best at everything they do. Killing and peacekeeping are the essential duties by which Marines serve the Coalition. To do this, a Marine needs two things — discipline and spirit! These attributes are the hallmarks of a Marine."

DI Vickers paused for dramatic impact as he looked the recruits directly in the eyes. "Each of you can become a Marine if you develop discipline and spirit. Then and only then will you earn the title of Coalition Marine!"

Now, "Ears!" Vickers spat.

"Aye, sir!" The recruits responded in unison this time.

Vickers answered the recruits' motivational yell with, "Eyeballs!"

Every head in the squad bay snapped in his direction, their eyes boring into him as they answered, "Snap, sir!"

"Whenever I say something, you will scream at the top of your lungs! Do you understand me?"

"Aye aye, sir!" platoon 7805 roared.

Not impressed in the least, Vickers said, "When I tell you to, and only when I tell you to, you'll stand in line in front of your gear."

Again, the platoon said in almost perfect unison, "Aye aye, sir!"

Vickers hollered to the motley group of recruits, "Get in line now!"

Each recruit bellowed out, "Aye sir!" as their bodies flew towards the brightly illuminated lines that ran neatly down the length of the metallic squad bay.

No one dared to talk or turn their heads. Those few who had done so attracted the attention of the two lesser DI's like flies to a fly trap. Mae wasn't sure what those symbols on the sleeves of the DI's meant; however, she knew the ones called Sergeant (Sgt) were beneath the one called Staff Sergeant. *I have a lot to learn,* she thought to herself. Mae had known that Marines were crazy, but this, this was something else entirely. Praying fate played in her favor, using only her eyeballs Mae risked a quick look to her right and her left.

The smaller DI, Sgt Black, is by all accounts beautiful. Too beautiful, Mae thought. *She looks like she could be on a magazine cover or something.* Mae pushed those thoughts aside. Something told her not to let DI Black's look fool her. The DI might have been beautiful, but there was something about her that frightened Mae. Perhaps it was the prosthetic hand and arm. They had developed the ability to fully regrow human skin in the labs years ago. Why this woman went without the skin upgrade for her bionics was beyond Mae.

The other drill instructor, Sgt King, was on the opposite side of the squad bay now, face to face with another recruit. *Oh God,* Mae thought, *was that a piece of lung that just flew out of his mouth? Or maybe it was food?* Whatever it was, it was now resting comfortably on the face of the recruit receiving the verbal beating.

Drill Instructor King towered over the recruit and looked as if he could devour him. He towered over almost everyone with an impressive height of six-feet, five inches. Had this been an end-of-the-world scenario, Mae didn't doubt DI King would eat the man.

The bus had dropped her and the other 36 recruits off at the pearly gates of hell less than two hours prior, and now she was bald, moving in a coordinated, almost mechanical motion, and currently awaiting her turn for verbal degradation.

The two DIs ran manically around the rigid recruits, yelling and slapping random body parts as they adjusted each one of them. DI Black's bionic arm and her mere presence intimidated the recruits. DI King was of a slightly beefier build and towered over the other Drill Instructors by a solid foot and a half.

With the dogs of war set loose on fresh meat, Vickers spoke calmly this time. "You will shed your current civilian clothes and don the black and gold Marine-issued running suits and undergarments you'll find within your new gear bags. Once that is done, you will form up on the sidewalk outside for the initial physical fitness test. You have little time to waste as the shuttles to transport you to Titan will leave within the next four hours."

"Am I understood?" Vickers yelled.

The recruits replied in a chorus, "Aye, sir!"

"Ready, move!"

Mae's running suit clung to her in places she cared not to think about. The air was humid and too stuffy for this time of the year. *One more mile,* she told herself, *just need to hang in there for one more mile. What did Aunt Lillie say that one time? 'Pain is as fleeting as life.' I think that fits here. All I have to do is en-*

dure this pain for one more mile.

"Whoever had the bright idea to have us run six miles should be shot!" Mae said aloud.

"I agree," said a male's voice.

Mae looked right and saw another recruit quickly gaining on her.

"Hey, I'm Garrett," he said. "I can't wait to get up to Titan myself! That's why I joined, you know, to get off of this darn rock." Mae noticed Garrett's breathing was controlled for having just run five miles. *Running at stride must come naturally to him,* she thought.

"That and to make connections for when I start my business," he continued.

"Nooo, say it isn't so. You want to leave this godforsaken place? Land of green pastures and plentiful harvest?" Mae said sarcastically. She didn't know the kid and wasn't in the best of moods. Her body ached, and her feet felt like lead. "I'm sorry," she immediately said. "I'm just not used to being held under someone's thumb and constantly told what to do. It's making me a bit irritable, ya know." Mae tried not to misstep as she turned slightly and said, "Hey, I'm Mae."

After Mae's attack of sarcasm, Garrett figured she would be better served focusing on her breathing than talking to him, so he tried to remain quiet. The two ran on in silence, except for the occasional joke or two.

The finish line was coming up. It was close enough that Mae felt she could touch it.

"Hey Mae, last one to the finish line has to give one of the drill instructors a hug." Mae's formal response to Garrett's challenge wasn't a witty retort or a sarcastic remark, but a small cloud of dust. Garrett let out a cough and picked up the pace.

Ok, Mae, he thought, *if that's how you want to do it. I thought you had nothing left, but I was wrong.* He worked to keep pace with Mae. *Wow, she's moving!*

Mae focused on the asphalt and the finish line ahead when

she thought she saw a familiar face off to the right. The boy in the distance was running faster than she was; most of his face was outside of her purview. *Don't I know him from somewhere?* she thought. *I think that's … Jamieson … from my hometown. I didn't know he'd joined too. I wish my EMCD worked! I'd just ping him and be done with this guesswork. I'll have to do this the old fashion way.*

One by one, the recruits crossed the finish line, hearing their times called out as they did.

"Excuse me, Sergeant. Hi, my name is …"

DI Sergeant Black flew off the handle, flinging the data pad she held while bringing her right hand up in as smooth a motion as Mae had ever seen. Fingers fully extended, Black jabbed her knife hand at Recruit Walker, an Asian kid from Chicago.

"Ahhhh … did I give you permission to talk, Recruit!"

Recruit Walker's body immediately went rigid. "No, ma'am!"

"No one told you to get out of line, Recruit. You'll wish you hadn't!" Sergeant Black smiled a feral grin. She had always found great pleasure in 'selective behavior modification.' Despite her diminutive stature and gorgeous young face, her talent for torturing recruits was one of her specialties.

"Ma'am, this recruit was just wondering why our EMCDs don't work here at Marine Corps Recruit Depot Duncan."

Oh man, that recruit is going to get us all fried if he can't keep his mouth shut! Mae thought as she worked her way through the horde of recruits, looking for the boy from her hometown. Several minutes went by before Mae realized she wouldn't find him.

DI Black continued railing Recruit Walker with the sort of vile words that would make even a sailor cringe. "Your EMCD will work when we want it to work! Is that clear, Recruit! Now get in my pit right now. Faster! Move! Move! Move!" Black commanded.

"Get down! Get up! Get down! Get up! Faster! High knees right now! Now get down ..."

While Walker endured his hazing, the mass of troops standing in the area began to put distance between them and the rampaging DI. No one chanced a look in his direction for fear of being associated with his blunder, which likely meant being hazed too. Eye contact was a sure-fire way to find yourself 'getting strong' right alongside whichever poor recruit found themselves at the wrong end of a drill instructor. Walker was just the first in a long line who will enjoy the throes of recruit training.

CHAPTER 10

Pick of the Litter

Sweat poured from Marious's pits after he'd gotten the message from Jannis, the President's personal assistant, to meet the President in the Oval Office at 1 p.m. Sweating was something he tried to avoid; so was not getting fired.

Marious's thoughts ran rampant with worry, *The old man promised me anonymity, and now he's probably calling to fire me. My bet, the Chief of Staff is pressuring him. What am I saying, it's probably nothing. I'm their aide after all. It's natural to get a random summons to one of their offices ...*

The door to the Oval Office slid open as Marious approached it. *He's definitely expecting me,* Marious thought. He came to a stop a few paces from the President's desk and exhaled, "Sir, what can I help you with?"

President Branson looked up from his desk and waved the holographic displays away with a slight flick of his wrist. Eyeballing the kid, he noted the large, mustard-yellow sweat puddles pooling beneath the aide's shirt.

What's with these aides? Branson thought. *They're always on the fence. You'd think they're all wild gazelles in a den of lions. At the slightest sign of trouble or displeasure, their fight-or-flight response kicks in. I'll have to remember to talk to Tag about remind-ing the aides to relax around here. Those sweat stains are unprofes-sional. At least the kid doesn't stink.*

Branson stood up and offered Marious a seat. He settled back into his and shot straight to the point, "Mr. Lennard, tell me again why you brought that report to my attention?"

"Mr. President, I, ah, I thought it wasn't right that you were being left in the dark. At least that was my initial assessment, and I had prayed to God that I wasn't right … hoped that I was wrong because had I been right and you decided to tell the Chief it was me that told you, I'd probably be in deep … ah, fired, sir."

Branson rubbed his chin. "Ah, I see. I figured as much. Son, let me tell you again that I appreciate you having the intestinal fortitude and moral courage to do what's right. I need more people like you, and that's why I called you here today."

Marious relaxed a bit but not entirely. He could not allow himself to completely drop his guard around the most power-ful man in the settled worlds.

"Have you heard of Operation Aurora-1?" The President asked, staring into Marious's eyes, looking for any sign of de-ceit.

"No sir, I can't say that I have."

"Good," Branson said. *That means the Coalition Intelligence Agency is doing its job — and my staff is keeping their lips sealed.*

"I want you to do something for me, Mr. Lennard. Some-thing that requires a bit of discretion. Can I count on you?"

Marious's Adam's apple heaved up and down. "Of course, sir. Whatever it is, I'm your man." His left heel bounced, shaking his leg as his right hand tapped at his thigh.

"Son, I want you to get me a list of Generals who aren't loyal to the Chief of Staff."

"Sir, you are aware the Chief and many of the top Generals came up through the ranks together, right, sir?"

"I'm aware of that. Just do your best, Mr. Lennard, and thank you. Remember, apply the same amount of discretion to this task as I did for you," Branson said with a knowing nod and wink.

"Sir, say no more," Marious said as he stood up. He focused on Branson's special task, giving him a bit more confidence than he had walking in. His leg was no longer shaking. "You'll have the report within the hour."

The familiar blue hue of the daytime sky was replete with deep smatterings of orange, red, and yellow, interspersed with a tinge of violet. The scent of coconut filled the air from the subtle, sweet-smelling flower, Plumeria Rubra.

Two people occupied the brown soft-top gazebo, perfectly perched above Hana Bay in Maui. Several red-crested cardinals sung their lullabies in the surrounding trees.

After completing the petrissage massage technique, the masseuse leaned into her client's lower back with her elbow. The reinforced kneading technique she used elicited a sound of satisfaction from the man.

"Ah … yes … yes … right there," he moaned, feeling his stress melt away.

A slim figure in oxford blue trousers and a matching blouse adorned with several military ribbons materialized several feet in front of the man atop the masseuse's table. Walking over, Major Salis stopped, saluted, and cleared her throat. Disregarding the naked masseuse, and more disconcertingly, the naked man on the table being rubbed on, she spoke, "General, sir, sorry for interrupting your mid-day virtual lunch break. I do believe you may want to put some clothes on. The President is calling. He's waiting for me to patch him into you."

General Sherman looked up, annoyed, and grumbled, "Major, I've told you not to interrupt me here."

Amazed at his cavalier attitude, Salis retorted, "But sir, it's the President!"

The General stood up and stretched, his flaccid penis swinging from side to side. "I heard you the first time. Inform the President I'm getting dressed, and I'll be right there."

With flushed cheeks, Major Salis turned about-face as fast as her feet would allow, stunned at the General's lack of chagrin. "Aye aye sir!" she said. It was all she could say without losing her mind.

"General Sherman, did I catch you at a bad time?" President Branson asked as Sherman turned about, stunned, still trying to wrap his towel around his waist.

"Sir, I wasn't expecting you to be tied in so soon. I would have dressed quicker if I'd known." Sherman sent a heated glare in the direction of his aide.

Without acknowledging his overt attempt at a passive-aggressive non-verbal scolding, Major Salis dematerialized from General Sherman's personally forged virtual world. "What can I do for you, Mr. President?" Sherman continued.

"General, I'm uploading the contents of a highly classified briefing to you as we speak. Long story short, I'm sending a manned mission, further than we've ever traveled before, on an information-gathering operation. I will need men, but I don't want to arouse the wrong kind of attention."

"You mean you don't want the Senate to know what you're up to, sir," Sherman said matter-of-factly.

Stepping closer, ignoring the General's insightful comment, Branson continued, "Robert, let me be frank. I am not sure what we'll find when we get to the Eskimo Nebula. It could be nothing, although I'd prefer to be ready for anything just in case. I don't have time to pussyfoot around with the Senate. More importantly, to ensure mission safety, I want troops who are highly flexible and well trained. Bear in mind that they will be heading into the outer reaches of human-explored space and beyond. So I want you to put together a group of very talented, well trained, and trustworthy Marines to be the Aurora's fighting contingent. Can you do that?"

Sherman scanned through the briefing notes in an info window floating in front of his face. A moment later, as the short, terse, melodic chirps of the red-crested cardinals subsided for the night, General Sherman looked up and smiled. "Sir, I will get you the Marines you need. Off the books, of course. In return, I'd like to be a part of the mission. I'll have overall command of the Marine element, but one of my old subordinates, Captain Alexander will command the troops directly."

Branson wasn't one for negotiating terms with what he perceived to be an order from him to one of his generals, although, due to the nature of his request, Branson felt more inclined to entertain it. "Agreed," he said. "They need to be ready to go in three weeks. I'll have my aide send you any other relevant data I deem necessary."

"Understood, Mr. President. Am I to understand I should deal directly with you or this aide of yours? Anyone else?"

"Just the two of us, General. I don't want anyone, even my Chief of Staff, knowing about this. Am I understood?"

"Completely, sir!"

CHAPTER 11

Boot Camp

Location:
Earth's Solar System
Titan, Saturn largest moon
Coalition Marine Base (CMB) Starfire

Eight long, grueling, and agonizing weeks passed since training began. Mae's body ached in places that were never meant to ache. From living in a constant state of exhaustion, her gaunt eyes no longer showed the hurt and depression that once threatened to consume her. This new type pain brought pleasure as she thought about graduation, about becoming a newly minted Coalition Marine, the tip of the spear of the Joint Special Operations Command.

Mae was a machine now, a number trained to do a job and be expendable. All the yelling, jumping, running, shooting, fighting, and screaming left no time for free-thought — Her heart thumped with excitement. The past eight weeks of recruit training was helpful to heal something that desperately needed healing. Her newfound friendships gave her hope; knowing they'd last a lifetime brought her comfort in an uncomfortable world.

Mae continued to push herself despite the enemies she began to make. She noticed many of her peers did not enjoy being outshined in an environment where being the best means everything.

◆ ◆ ◆

"Listen up, you sorry lot! I want one Fire Team on that ridge over there taking up overwatch positions and the other two Fire Teams on my six!" The Squad Leader's voice was firm and serious. Her face, indistinguishable from the surroundings as her helmet visor reflected the blue-green hue of the sky with wisps of white clouds strewn throughout.

Senior Recruit Raya Links continued, "The mission schematics should be coming through your EMCDs now. Don't foul this up. We need to capture 3rd Squad's flag if we want to progress on to the next phase of our training."

"Daniels, Beasley, Main, and Tall, you're taking the lead as the reconnoiter team. Your mission is to scout a path for the rest of the squad, and should your presence be made, harass and delay any enemy forces you encounter until the rest of the squad can make it to your position. As for the rest of the squad, split into your two respective Fire Teams and come with me towards the right flank. If my intel is right, we'll be able to outflank them."

What Recruit Links lacked in height she made up for in tactical prowess. The Senior Drill Instructor had made her the Squad Leader for the 2nd Squad after the platoon's last tactical evaluation scores were posted.

"How long do you think before recruit robot over there gets us killed?" Tall said over the tactical link, or tac-link as they soon learned to call it.

"Don't call her that," Daniels said. "She deserves respect, If for nothing else than because she's smarter than us tactically."

"If we fail this mission and don't get to move on to the next phase of training, I will ..." Tall continued.

"You will what?" Main interjected. "I bet you'll do nothing."

"I don't know what I'd do," Garrett Beasley joined in, "but I'll do something. I need to graduate. I need this job. I'm going to make millions one day, and this job, it's my stepping stone."

Daniels was moving at a steady pace now. The TALOS Mark 7 — 7th Generation SOCOM (Special Operations Command) combat armor suits the recruits wore — made movement easy. Their suits were virtually impervious to most weapons, gave the wearer strength 70 times that of a fully grown athletic male, and shot plasma bolts out of its arm cannons, garnering the nickname 'Zeus suits.' The power of the suits was constantly on the minds of the recruits. They knew what they were capable of but couldn't use a fraction of that destructive power. Neutered was the term the recruits tossed around. They all knew the powers that be turned on their suit's regulators, significantly dimming down their capabilities for this training environment, but it didn't mean they had to like it.

"Don't forget, we're on the same team here, Garrett," Mae reminded her friend. "We'll pass, you'll see. No need to go off of the deep end ... again." Laughter erupted over the Fire Team's private channel.

"Hey, don't remind me," Beasley said. "Falling off of a 700-foot cliff and surviving is no easy feat. Put me in the history books, folks. Put me in the history books."

Mae's Fire Team approached a narrow opening to a valley gorge. *Something isn't right. This place feels off,* Mae thought. Her tactical feed said 3rd Squad's position and flag should be about a mile ahead of them. They'd have to go through that massive narrow valley to get there.

"Team, hold up. Everyone, get low and take cover — now," Mae said.

"Yea sure, but what's up?" Main asked what they were all thinking.

"Savanna, I don't know just yet," Mae said, scanning the area ahead while simultaneously examining the data feed from her EMCD. "Something is off. Call it a feeling."

The Fire Team took up defensive positions 500 meters outside of the entrance of the valley gorge. "I don't think we can go around, Mae," Recruit Tall said. "The valley walls are steep and wide. It would take more time than we have to circumvent this entrance."

I think that might be the problem, Mae thought to herself. *If I were defending this position, I would have a lookout and or some sort of early warning system. There's nothing here.* "Guys, do you see the same feed I do? There's nothing on the electromagnetic spectrum or any other spectrum for that matter. That means there's no early warning system. Why?" Mae didn't expect anyone to answer that question as they could all see what she saw and most likely came to the same conclusion she did.

"It might be that they didn't have time to set their defenses yet," Recruit Beasley answered.

Chuckling, Mae thought, *Of course Garrett had something to say. When does he not.*

"No, this smells like a trap." Mae and Tall said almost in unison.

Recruit Main sent Mae a private message. "Ok, I'm going to try something."

Several moments passed before Savanna Main messaged Mae again. "I ran an administrative trace program on all EMCD active frequencies from the platoon's personnel roster, and nothing came up ... nothing, Mae. I don't like this. There is no way they wouldn't have been able to mask their EMCD responders unless someone on their team was hacking the platoon's database server."

Mae disregarded the fact that no recruit was supposed to have access to the platoon's personnel roster, which contained all sorts of private information about each recruit, yet somehow Savanna had gotten into that database in a matter of seconds. Mae thanked Savanna for the information then switched back to the Fire Team's channel. "Hey guys, listen up.

This is clearly a trap, but we have no other option right now. Move out and proceed with caution. Be advised. I think 3rd Squad is running black settings. Keep your eyes open and your arm cannons on a swivel."

Each member of Mae's Fire Team crept forward, on edge. The wide valley held a plethora of cliffs, boulders, and caves to hide in. The towering walls made it almost impossible to see more than a slice of the turquoise sky from their position.

Without warning, Black and gold silhouettes descended from the heavens, landing in the middle of the four members of 2nd Squad's first Fire Team. Mae was thrown into the nearest boulder. She keeled over from the force of the blow, gasping for air.

"Shit, they're on top of us!" Recruit Tall cried out as he parried a strike, returning one of his own. "I know, thanks for the insightful knowledge there, Tall," Savanna said. "Got my hands' full, guys!"

Mae looked up, watching her team fighting a handful of silhouettes in hand-to-hand combat. *They must have been cloaked, latched onto the valley walls. Shit! I should have thought of that.* Her mind was running multiple scenarios for a way out of this mess.

There was a deafening crack as an attacker's foot connected with her helmet. The bio-muscles in her suit absorbed most of the hit but not without consequence. Mae plunged into a rolling dive as her opponent sought to capitalize on his first strike with a follow-up straight jab. Coming out of her combat roll, Mae launched a right elbow strike to his rear. Twisting, Mae pounded the attacker with her knee; one hit after another landed in rapid succession. *This guy isn't going down!* she thought while keeping up the pressure.

The attacker hooked his arm under her leg and twisted his torso. Mae slammed into the valley wall with enough force to wedge her MK7 TALOS there for a few seconds.

Her attacker landed strike after strike to her mid-section.

Warnings flashed in her mind as her suit's integrity threatened to fail. Titan's toxic air would kill her in seconds if it was allowed to creep into her suit.

Savanna tapped into the tac-link. "Guys," she said, breathing heavily, "I don't know who these recruits are. Their shoulder identification holographics aren't displaying their names and platoon info. I can't access their transponder signals either."

Through gritted teeth, Garrett responded first, "I don't think they want to be known. If they did, why would they be running black! Is this another test?"

Mae caught her opponent's fist, wrapped her legs over his arms, and flipped backward. Anger and confusion surged through her as she fought to get her attacker into an armbar.

Sergeant King surveyed the battle from several thousand feet up with their eyes in the sky. "Staff Sergeant Vickers, you should see this. Something's going on with 2nd Squad's 1st Fire Team."

Vickers was slightly annoyed. These training missions were scripted and had been run a thousand times by thousands of recruits since the training facility's inception. There shouldn't be any problems, and yet, by the looks of the feed he was watching, there was. "Raise them on the comms and find out what the hell is going on over there, King. Send Black and some military police if need be."

"Aye, Staff Sergeant," King replied.

Mae's attacker drew a 20-inch obsidian K-blade from its sheath and flipped it end over end. Knife tip down, the attacker lunged at Mae.

Garrett, fighting his own attacker, noticed the glint of the blade as it slashed towards Mae. "Shit, shit, shit! Mae's in trouble, guys. That fucker actually pulled a knife on her. What in God's green hell does he think he's doing? This is just a war game, a freaking training mission."

Mae ducked under the third successive slash, pulling her own obsidian K-blade at the same time. Executing a high block, blade on blade, Mae kicked her attacker's right leg out from under him. In one fluid motion, she brought her knife down in a well-aimed strike towards her attacker's chest plate. Using his elbow to parry the blade, he blocked Mae's attempt to disable his suit.

Who is this guy! Mae thought. *What's his deal!* "Why are you hiding? What are you scared of? Show yourself ..." she demanded. Mae barely had time to react as she dove for cover. The air crackled and sizzled where she'd been standing a moment ago.

Everyone in the valley dropped, attackers and defenders alike, as warning signals wailed cautioning them of the superheated plasma bolt streaking through the air. The northwest valley wall exploded in a dazzling light show as the plasma bolt from Mae's attacker made impact.

"What the fuck is wrong with you?" Mae shouted over the general frequency. "You almost killed me!"

Mae, still crouching behind the boulder she sought refuge from, began building up enough pressure in her suit's biomuscles to propel her 200 feet in the air. She shot straight up in a blur, activated her suit's thrusters, and in a sharp arc, began hurling back towards to ground. A few seconds passed before impact. Both TALOS suits slammed into the ground with the force of a bullet train. Mae's attacker wrenched his arm free and jammed his K-blade into Mae's helmet. The blade stopped several inches from her skull as her arm blocked most of the blow. She screamed as her assailant tossed her several feet away.

Her attacker climbed out of the crater, and without warning, took off in a sprint. The rest of his team followed, shifting their camouflage platings to stealth mode.

"Mae's down," Savanna yelled, racing towards her friend.

CHAPTER 12

Aurora-1

Kellie Thompson leaned back in her seat and wiped the corners of her mouth. She neatly tucked her barf bag into the side receptacle of her seat and, for the seventh time, called out to the pilots, "What's our ETA?"

"Madam Director, we are 29 mikes, excuse me, I mean minutes, out from reaching the Coalition shipyards orbiting Mars. Please refrain from tying up this line as we need to focus our attention on flying. Thank you," came the smooth professional "fuck off" reply that only pilots could pull off.

Director Thompson was many things; a mother, a triathlon winner, and an avid foodie, but someone who enjoyed the thrills of space travel wasn't one of those things.

Hold on just a little longer, Kellie told herself. *By my count, we've been flying for approximately four and a half hours. Whoever invented space travel should be shot!*

"*Relax, ma'am,*" Director Thompson's assistant said to her via a mental link. "*Your vitals are off the chart. Maybe you should immerse yourself in one of those premium network shows to help pass the time. Galactic Siege III, Rise of the Delphines has some extraordinary reviews. My husband and I love it!*" The faintest hint of pained sadness creased the edges of her eyes at that thought.

"No, Kimberly, I'll pass. Thank you. Where do we stand on those new upgrades I authorized for the Aurora-1? We can't have our new symbol of unity between the members of the Coalition, its first flagship, to not be state-of-the-art in every fashion, now can we?"

Kimberly Cunningham leaned in and handed her boss a holo-data cube containing the progress reports she was asking about. *"Of course not, Madam Director. Last I checked, roughly three hours ago, we were right on track."*

"Good ..." Kellie began, her train of thought interrupted by a blinding flash of light. It encompassed the shuttle moments before a bow shock wave from an expanding ball of radiation slammed into it, flipping them end over end, tossing the passengers around the cabin like lettuce in a salad bowl.

Floating several thousand kilometers away from the now-ruined orbital shipyard, the lights of the shuttle flickered several times before coming back on. Kimberly wiped the blood from her head and called out to the pilots, "Situation report?"

The lead pilot's body movements were focused as his arms flew over various flight instruments and interactive photonic holo-displays. "Something hit us! Something big! Power's fluctuating but should stabilize. Our life support systems took a beating and could be better. We're drifting laterally from our previous position, but we're still space-worthy. We should have engine power within the hour."

"Yeah, I'll say. The view-ports are icing over," Thompson said. "Is everyone ok? Do we have any ideas on what caused the explosion?"

The second pilot swiveled around and walked to the rear of the passenger cabin. "The power couplings were fried in the blast. They'll need to be replaced. The only thing that could have fried the couplings is a massive gamma burst; they're in an unshielded part of the ship — known design flaw. So, either we received a gamma burst from the sun, which is unlikely considering our distance, or there was an explosion out here.

The reactors we use in our ships are the only other things that could have given off that level of gamma radiation in this region. And guess what we have plenty of around here?"

The Director's eyes widened as the implication began to hit her. "Oh god! Aurora-1. Kimberly, are we still receiving status reports from the Aurora? Is she still there?"

"That's a negative, ma'am!" The lead pilot shot back. "The Aurora is no longer on the plot! Telemetry says the explosion emanated from the Aurora's position — ah, where she used to be. Orders, ma'am?"

"Get us back Earth-side. The President will want to see me."

"Gentlemen, what we have here is a clusterfuck of epic proportions! Can someone please tell me what in Sam's hell happened up there?"

"Mr. President, we believe ..."

"I don't want to hear what you believe! I want facts. What happened?" President Branson fought to restrain his anger at the situation.

"Tage, my apologies. We lost good men and women up there. I want to know what happened. Sugarcoat nothing."

The Swedish man exhaled twice before regaining his professional persona and continued, "Sir, at 3:30 p.m. Earth's Eastern Standard Time, there was an explosion at the Phobos shipyards orbiting Mars. We lost several ships, including the Aurora-1. The other ships were of minor importance as they were primarily mining frigates and a few military-grade passenger shuttles. Our sources haven't confirmed if the explosion originated inside of the Aurora or the shipyard itself, although one thing is clear, Mr. President. The Aurora-1 was the intended target."

"How do we know the Aurora-1 was the target?" Branson asked.

"The blast forensics are undeniable, sir."

This isn't good. At all. Someone knows about our plans and doesn't want us to succeed. But why! It makes little sense. This mission is for the good of humanity. Branson refocused on his Chief of Staff and said, "What's the casualty count?"

Tage Gunnerson looked disturbed as he answered the President, "The shipyard personnel casualty list came in at a little under 600 men and women, sir. The blast happened in the middle of a shift change. Otherwise, the body count would have been a lot higher. The ships weren't fully staffed, so the body count of the Coalition military members was a little smaller with 146 dead or missing, presumed dead."

"Tage, do we have any leads yet? I need something to give the press. They are running rampant with the news reports."

"Sir, you're telling me. GNN is calling it a resurgence of hostilities from the Federation of Communist States, whereas several other news channels are calling it the precursor to Interplanetary War with Earth and all of its associated colonies. One of the news channels is saying that they have definitive proof that it was sabotage, but their voice is so small and their narrative isn't popular opinion, so they are being drowned out. It is only a matter of time before this completely spins out of control and irreparable damage is done."

Tea Buttler, the Director for Coalition Security, wrapped two knuckles on the nanowood, capturing everyone's attention. With the Chief of Staff talking, the President almost forgot she was there.

"Ms. Buttler, what do you have for me?" Branson asked.

"Sir, why not control the narrative by not only issuing a press statement but also by bringing in Regional News Network 9 into the fold? Their voice may be small, but they're on the right track. Let's let them run with the story, telling everyone they have the lead in our press release. In the process, we try to find the identity of their source. It has to be someone close to us because who else would have the information RNN9 is claiming their source has? If we have someone running around giving away information without proper clearance, then that's a problem for me. As you're well aware, Coalition Security is my responsibility, and I'd like very much to find out where our leaks are, Mr. President."

"Do it," Branson said after a moment. "Tea, I want actionable intel on this. I want you to find me someone I can prosecute! There's blood in the water, and the people demand justice. I want justice!"

Tea Buttler knew this was more than a witch hunt. If they couldn't get a suspect in hand and come up with a viable reason for the massive loss of life, there would be anarchy as the finger-pointing expanded to open hostilities again. Tea, resolute in her tasking, said, "Understood, Mr. President."

"Mr. President, we have one final matter to discuss: the mission itself. Do we move forward or scrap it altogether?" Tage said. "Considering the circumstances, I think it might be prudent to scrap the recon mission until we can get our heads around this situation — not to mention the time and resources it'll take to rebuild half of the shipyard and all the ships we lost."

The Chief of Staff's open opposition to continuing the mission was not a surprise. President Branson had been expecting as much.

No sense in answering right away, that'll make him think I have something up my sleeve. No, take a moment to show Tage and my staff I'm considering the situation and alternative options and then answer, Branson thought.

"Tage, you make some valid points. Points I would be remiss not to consider." President Branson turned to face his assembled staff and continued, "We've lost hundreds of men and women. Good men and women, citizens who put forth their best foot to advance the Coalition through their hard work and dedication. We've lost multiple ships, including the new capital ship for the Coalition, and more importantly, we've lost time. This sabotage has undoubtedly set us back. Which brings me to my decision. A decision I make with a heavy mind."

A few faces remained impassive. The Chief of Staff was not one of them. The edge of his mouth creased ever so slightly in anticipation of the President's next words. He'd tell them all it was over, that they could put this silly notion of deep space exploration in search of fictitious beings behind them and more on to more matters.

"In light of all that we know with theses strange rifts, signals, and artifacts both on planet and off, in our solar system, and out among our colonies light-years out and beyond, we must push ahead. We've been hit with a devastating setback, but I am beyond confident we will make a comeback," Branson said.

The smile threatening to form on Tage's face was eradicated by the President's statement; replaced instead by a tightening of his upper lip, effortlessly contorting his face in disgust.

"You all have my intent. Now people, go execute. We have a date with the Eskimo Nebula, and I intend to make that meeting. That is all."

CHAPTER 13

New Additions

Recruits bristled about under the watchful gaze of their drill instructors. Chow was the one time of the day the recruits were permitted to speak to one another about topics which didn't pertain to their training, and today was no different. CMB Starfire boasted a dining facility capable of holding an entire battalion of Marines at any one time. Today's complement of warm bodies within the dining facilities was slightly less than the 900-capacity limit for personnel.

Pulling up a seat alongside her friend, Mae said, "Hey girl."

"Hey, what's up? Are you going to eat that by the way," Savanna said, poking her fork into Mae's cornbread as she set her tray down.

Mae sighed and smirked, "What the heck, you already have your fork in it now. Please be my guest." She chuckled. Savanna Main was one of the smartest girls Mae knew, but her manners were slightly lacking, almost dudeish. *Hopefully by the time we graduate, her manners will be fixed,* she thought to herself.

"Some field op, huh guys?" Recruit Frankie Tall said as he made himself at home alongside his squad mates.

"Guys," Mae said, "I'm dumbfounded right now! I have so many questions that need answers! For instance, who were those guys, and where did they come from? Where the hell was 3rd Squad? Apparently, they were never in the Valley area ..."

"They were three klicks northeast of our position. So, Recruit Links was right to try to outflank them. She caught them completely off guard," Savanna said, offering up the tidbit of info she had managed to scrounge up earlier when she had run into a member of 3rd Squad.

Mae continued as if she wasn't interrupted, "... and since that wasn't them in the valley, who attacked us?"

Recruit Tall poked his rice pilaf, thinking to himself, *Did something just move in there? Never mind ...* "I don't know," he said, "but whoever they were, they caught us completely by surprise!"

"Yeah, did you see how they went no holds barred on us? Descending on us like demons, falling from the sky. Seriously, who does that?" Savanna said.

"Something didn't feel right from the beginning, and I should have never led you guys into that trap," Mae said, her features turned up in disgust. *I couldn't keep my Fire Team any safer than I could have kept myself safe that ... that night,* she thought.

In a low, barely discernible tone, Mae whispered, "I'm sorry, guys."

Savanna mentally pinged Frankie. *"She's blaming herself. It's typical behavior for someone who cares for those under their charge, but it won't help her or us. We have to help her out of this slump. There's a major field op coming up, and we need her head in the game."*

"Agreed, Savanna," Frankie said. *"Any suggestions? I'm not used to dealing with females' emotions."*

"Geez, haven't you had a girlfriend before?" Savanna asked, staring into Frankie's eyes. When Frankie didn't reply after a few seconds, Savanna continued, *"Forget it. Just follow my lead."*

"Listen, Mae," Savanna said, one hand on her friend's shoulder, "you were in charge, yes, but we chose to follow you. It was a group effort. I scanned the frequencies and various electromagnetic spectrums looking for signs of the enemies. Garrett and Frankie helped to survey the area we were in. You can't blame yourself. If you want to blame anyone, blame all of us because we all had a part to play in getting our asses kicked."

Tall, finding the perfect moment to interject, said, "You know, I can fix almost anything — ground cars, skimmers, hell I can even fix the TALOS suits if they'd let me. But when it comes to female emotions, I understand them as much as I understand quantum mechanics and string theory. So, all I have to say about all of this is you'll be fine, Mae. Buck up."

"Jesus Christ, Frankie! How could you be so insensitive? Jerk!" Savanna exclaimed, growing flush from anger. She slid closer to Mae to comfort her more. "What Mae's feeling isn't relegated to just the female gender by any means. It is perfectly natural to feel this way. Mae is our Fire Team leader, and because those ass-hats ambushed us, we never got to finish our mission."

"You two trying to comfort me is comforting in itself. I'm just glad to know I have good friends like you guys," Mae said with a genuine smile on her face.

"Yea, what they said," Garrett Beasley said as he plopped down in between Mae and Frankie, giving her a warm hug.

Mae's laugh startled her montage of friends. "You too, Garrett. I'm glad to know all of you."

Mae allowed her friends' conversation to fall into the endless background noise of the dining facility. "You know, when I first met you, I wasn't sure I could trust you — fully," she said, facing Savanna. "You seemed too intrusive."

"I get that a lot," Savanna said as she continued scarfing down her meal.

Trying to ignore the interruption, Mae went on, "But over the past few weeks, I have grown to feel I can trust you." Her soft honey-colored eyes settled on Savanna's raven black buzz cut and back down to her face. "This place — the drill instructors, the recruits, the countless hours of physical pain and mental anguish — it all comes together to make up our new lives now, which has afforded me the opportunity to forget. To forget because the pain was too great. I was seeking a way to lose myself and not be accountable to my emotions, but being a recruit has taught me that to change, I needed to let go of the past and embrace the future."

Curious as to what Mae was alluding to, Savanna decided it was best to stop eating and just listen.

"Something happened to me before coming to boot camp. Back home in Virginia, something … bad … happened. If I ever find the guy who attacked me, well, he better watch his back!"

Savanna, thinking back to the day she and Mae first met, knew now what Mae was talking about. She didn't need it to, but one of her algorithms within her next-gen EMCD had discovered as much about her, but she decided it was best not to reveal this to Mae just yet. A wave of compassion came over her, and she said, "What happened, Mae?"

"I …," Mae looked away for a second and then continued, "I was raped, Savanna. They never caught the guy, and honestly, I don't know what I would do if I ever found him. How do you get closure from something like that?"

Savanna tried to look shocked and upset as if this was the first she heard about this. "Oh my God! I would ask if you are ok, but I feel like at this point its moot. My words won't help, and nothing I can say will take back what happened to you." With a downtrodden gaze, Savanna labored over her tofu, thinking about her friend's pain.

Mae stared intently at Savanna. "No, I'm not alright. I've moved past what happened to me, but how could I ever get over it? How could I ever truly be alright?" A shiver ran down Mae's spine, and she squeezed her orange tight enough to form a small rip on its surface. The scent of citrus filled the air as a few beads of juice trickled down the side of the orange, through Mae's fingers and onto the table's self-cleaning surface.

"Revenge," Savanna muttered, jamming her fork in the center of the tofu.

"Revenge?" Mae repeated questioningly, pondering the thought. "You're right, that would make me feel better," she said with a maniacal laugh.

Savanna said, "Just imagine getting the creep and doing terrible things to him ... like shoving a pipe up his ..."

"Savanna!" Mae said, eyes wide with shock but with a smirk on her face. "I would have never taken you as the sinister type."

"I'm not," Savanna said. "But let's face it, if they can do terrible things to us, why can't we do the same to them?"

"And I knew I liked you from the day we met on that bus that brought us here, to hell. So, carry on, tell me more of what I should do. That is if I'm ever able to get my hands on that assjack that took what he wanted from me."

Savanna went on to describe several horrid ways to exact retribution, and Mae smile grew bigger as she did. The two were deeply engrossed in conversation when a commotion erupted around them as recruit after recruit trotted past, trying to get outside into formation before their allotted chow time was up.

"Come on, let's go. We can finish up this wholesome talk later," Mae said as the two girls vacated the premises.

The squad bay was abuzz with activity as the recruits used various cleaning techniques to get their home squared away. Of course, their actions were unnecessary as the advent of nanotechnology made cleaning an antiquated concept. The recruits were required to clean not because of a current lack of technology, but to teach them hard-learned lessons about discipline, attention to detail, and instant obedience to orders. Lessons which, under normal circumstances, took far too long to impress upon someone.

DI Mike Vickers walked down the center of the squad bay and back towards the front of it, which was effectively coined the quarter-deck, and stopped. Vickers eyed the chaos for a few moments before saying, "Zero," in a loud stern voice.

"Freeze, Recruit, freeze," was the coherent and tonally aligned response from Platoon 7805. Each recruit stood statuesque; no one moved for fear of retribution from the drill instructors.

"Recruit Schneiderman, front and center!" DI Vickers said in a clean, crisp tone. He radiated control and discipline.

Schneiderman screamed, "Aye aye, sir!" as he ran to Vickers, stopping one arm's length away from him. The recruits knew better than to get too close.

"Did you do the buddy system with someone?" Vickers asked.

"Yes, sir," Schneiderman said. "His name is Jamieson Burgess, sir!"

Vickers nodded to the recruit standing just out of sight, and Jamieson walked through the threshold of the squad bay's entryway. As he made his entrance, Vickers continued speaking, "Listen up, Marines! We have a transfer from another platoon, Recruit Jamieson Burgess. Treat him as you would any other recruit of platoon 7805. Now, as you were."

The recruits returned to cleaning.

Mae knocked on her friend's mental door, *"Savanna ... Savanna, you there?"*

"Yeah Mae, what's up?" Savanna asked as she bent down to scrub the metallic baseboard. Mae was swabbing the deck on her side of the squad bay.

"I know that kid, Jamieson. He went to my school," Mae told her friend. *"It's kinda cool that I have someone here that I know from back home,"* she said, trying not to smile for fear of drawing the drill instructors' wrath.

"*He's kind of cute too,*" Savanna said, chuckling. "*How well do you know this Jamieson character — if you know what I mean?*"

Mae stood straight up and tried to bore a hole into the back of Savanna's head with her eyes. It seemed to each recruit that they would be better off if they moved out of her line of sight. Savanna turned and caught Mae's stare as Mae said to her mentally, "*Are you crazy? You don't know him like I do. He's cute, yes, but uber-arrogant and believes he's God's gift to women. Those qualities are a turn-off to me. Do you have any idea how many times I've turned him down?*"

Savanna shot back, "*No, why don't you educate me?*"

"*More than I care to recount,*" Mae said. "*He's just a guy I know from back home, and that's all he'll ever be.*"

CHAPTER 14

Idle Threats

Jamieson made himself at home with his new squad. The platoon was broken up by squads, with 1st Squad being closest to the squad bay's entry hatch. The squad leader had given Jamieson the bunk next to Mark Schneiderman, his recruitment buddy.

"Hey man, glad to see you," Mark said. "Nice of you to finally join the party, man. What took so long anyway?"

"Back at you, bro," Jamieson replied. "You know how it is — the Drill Instructors do everything on their time, not ours."

Jamieson's face contorted into a faint expression of contempt and guilt wrapped in a tinge of worry as he looked beyond Mark, straight to Recruit Daniels. *What's she doing here? She shouldn't be here! Does she know?*

Mark followed his buddy's stare. "What's up? You know her?" Jamieson broke his gaze and looked back at his friend. "Yeah, I do. She and I went to school together."

"Oh sweet, open a chat with her, or better yet, a virtual meeting place. We're on our Senior Drill Instructor Square Away Time anyway. So, we have 30 more minutes before lights out and they turn the EMCD blockers back on and block things like that."

"No!" Jamieson shouted mentally to Mark. *"I don't want to talk to her just yet. Set up the VMS, but only invite me. Encrypt it; I have something I want to talk to you about."*

Mark compiled, and both boys' eyes shone hollow as their consciousness delved into a shared virtual world known only to its creator and whoever they invited. Normally, this sort of EMCD use was prohibited; however, since the recruits were on their Senior Drill Instructor Square Away Time, also known as Personal Time, to get their military uniforms in order and compose messages home, Mark and Jamieson decided to take a chance.

◆ ◆ ◆

The recruit on fire watch knew she should have been patrolling the squad bay right now, but her bowels were calling. Sharing an open living space with members of the opposite sex had its challenges and pooping in public was chiefly among them as far as Recruit Lisa Sanchez was concerned. With any luck, she'd be able to enjoy her time on the commode without any interruptions, and by the time she'd finished, it would be time to wake the next sap for fire watch.

"Mark, Mark, wake up," Jamieson whispered, lightly shaking his buddy on the shoulder. Mark, comfortable in the ergonomic, self-adjusting bed, rolled over and continued to drool, oblivious to his friend's attempt to wake him. "Mark, seriously, man, wake up," Jamieson said. "I need you, bro."

Sliding one hand over Mark's mouth and the other under his arm, Jamieson twisted Mark out of bed and onto the floor. Mark floundered about, searching for his assailant while trying to get free. "Mark, dude, it's me!" Jamieson whispered as he gently and slowly released his friend. Beginning to wake up, Mark regained his composure, whispering back, "Dude, what the fuck! You could have woken me up like a normal person."

Jamieson rolled his eyes as he pulled on a tactical balaclava. "Listen, I need you to come with me. It's time."

Together the two boys lurked down the squad bay, passing row after row of sleeping recruits until they found who they were looking for. They wore their combat overalls with non-slip noise-canceling socks attached, making their movement go virtually unheard.

Jamieson placed a hand on his buddy's shoulder. Through his EMCD, he said, *"Mark, grab her arm in three seconds."*

Together, the pair grabbed Mae. They leaned over her, applying their combined pressure to hold her down. She struggled. To her dismay, her assailants were strong. Jamieson climbed on top of her, pinning her arms to the bed. Mark pulled off one of his socks and shoved it into Mae's mouth. Through his mental link with Jamieson, he asked, *"What are we doing here?"*

"We're here because ..." *Fuck!* Jamieson said to himself, cringing at his mistake. Through their mental link, he continued, *"... Because I said so. Now shut up for a second!"*

Mae was trying not to panic. She'd been in this situation before. She knew what to expect and dreaded what might happen. She refused to let it happen again, but that's when she heard it.

I know that voice, she thought, *but ... that's Jamieson!*

As Mae's mind began to put the pieces into place, the guy above her used his EMCD to mask his virtual voice, *"You know, Mae, you had this coming. I want you to think about that. This all could have been prevented if you weren't such a bitch!"*

Mae's head began to spin as she considered the implications of what she'd just pieced together. *No! No! It can't be him! What the fuck!*

Jamieson leaned in, continuing his diatribe, *"If you tell anyone, I'll kill you!"* The words seethed from his mind.

Mark looked indignant, furious at him for dragging him into the middle of what he thought was a lovers' quarrel.

Mae's eyes boiled over with controlled rage. *"It's you who should be scared. Death no longer scares me. The torment I've gone through has changed me — hardened me. I see you for what you are. A deeply disturbed, sad little boy who wants so desperately to be seen and loved. Was it your father? Was he the one who emasculated you?"*

Jamieson furiously fought to control his anger. No, it wouldn't serve him well to lose it here where there were potential witnesses.

Mae stared deeper into his eyes. She saw it. She saw where his hurt stemmed from. *"No. There it is. It was your mother. She tortured you, turning you into this sad excuse of a boy. No wonder you don't handle rejection well. Especially from a female. Frankly, I'm surprised you aren't batting for the other team."*

Mae leaned her face closer to Jamieson's deep brown eyes, her arms still pinned to her sides. His eyes were almost akin to the blackness she saw within him.

"I know what you are, and you do not scare me. You should run because the tide has turned," Mae said.

Jamieson, startled at her jarring psychoanalysis of him, let go of her and backed away slowly. He wore a mask of hatred.

Turning, Jamieson crept his way back towards his side of the squad bay, not waiting on his crony. *"Give her one for me and come on,"* he mentally said to Mark.

Mark rose to follow his buddy. Without warning, he slammed one home into Mae's gut. *"Think on that,"* he said before turning to catch up to his buddy.

Mae's arms flew around her aching stomach as she gasped slowly, letting out what little breath remained. Hastily, Mae drank down more air, filling her body with what it so desperately sought. She watched the two hooded boys make their way back towards their bunks with careful ease.

Mae's body was shaking from an overload of adrenaline, and her heart thudded rhythmically. *What am I going to do! Dammit, this shouldn't be happening. This can't be happening. If this is someone's version of a sick joke, I'm not laughing,* she thought to herself as she slumped back into her bed. A single tear trickled from her eye, falling onto her pillow.

CHAPTER 15

Shadow Men

"Senator, as you requested, the mark has been eliminated."

"Eliminated! Is that what you call eliminated?" The short, slightly plump mixed-race Asian man allowed his agitation to overtake him for the quickest of moments as he said, "Over 800 dead, several ships destroyed, and half a shipyard now in pieces floating around Mars. My German friend said you were efficient. Perhaps he was a bit overzealous in his assessment of you!"

The mercenary stood impassively. His suit tunic had not a stray strand of fiber remotely out of place, a long-standing habit from his military days.

"I wanted a quiet job. All you had to do was take out the Admiral assigned to lead the recon mission and sabotage the ship. Instead, you left death and destruction in your wake. Assuming you left no clues tying this back to me, I believe I should at least commend you on the part of the mission you did manage to carry out to my specifications. You aren't all that worthless."

"Mr. Senator, if you wanted subtle, perhaps you should have specified such. You get what you ask for. In the absence of dir-

ect and specific orders, I improvise. I'm something of an art-
ist," Cassius Lowell said with no hint of humor in his voice.
*I'd love to show you firsthand just how artistic I can be, my portly
friend,* Cassius thought to himself.

Senator Malloy never heard the noiseless click of the wrist
dagger as Cassius gradually granted the weapon freedom from
its sheath. He ignored Cassius's flagrant and bumptious attitude. Instead focusing his attention on his chess set, Malloy's
mind went to work.

When he spoke next, Malloy's voice was even, deliberate,
and devoid of emotions. In a barely perceptible accent, he
whispered, "What are you hiding, Branson?" Malloy's question
wasn't aimed at anyone in particular.

Cassius thought better than to interrupt his employer while
he was thinking.

Malloy turned to face the mercenary. "I've known for some
time he's been funneling money into a secret project, but even
with the destruction of the Aurora-1, the financial records
still do not add up. There is still money being funneled into
something. Something I have yet to figure out. My contact in-
forms me the President still intends on sending a reconnaissance mission out to the Eskimo Nebula. I must hand it to the
man. If nothing else, he is brazen."

Cassius continued to stare impassively at the senator. He
was bored of his speeches but knew Malloy well enough by
now. The man was not done speaking. His type never was.

Malloy's bushy brows furrowed as he leaned in, fingers extended with the tips pressed hard against the mahogany wood
desk. These days, for most citizens of the Coalition and many
people in the FSC, such items of elegance were hard to come
by. Cassius suspected the Senator kept such opulence in his
office as a display of his superiority, power and abilities.

*For men like Malloy, power is everything. He comes from
old money and is hell-bent on bringing back the old status
quo, pre-coalition era.*

President Branson has been in office for the last ten years now.

He's united most of the planet, making us global citizens vice na-tional one's determined to hold on to the national ideologies that threatened the very survival of our species.

Under Branson, we've expanded out past our solar system, colon-izing a handful of planets and moons, ensuring humanity survives should there be another world war. Guess now it would be con-sidered an interstellar war. Either way, the man has done well for humanity. Too bad his successes are the very problem that's caus-ing a disgruntled undertone among the aristocrats.

The Senator trots around publicly praising the President, getting in good with him, while in the shadows, he's plotting his downfall. Keep your enemies close — smart. Either way, I don't care, Cassius thought. *So long as Malloy is paying, I'll continue to kill for him.*

It seems, for now, the senator will have to continue to work in the shadows to bend the powers that be to his inevitable will, which means more money in my pocket ... unless he forces me to kill him. Within his mind, the mercenary smiled hard at that last thought.

Cassius continued calmly standing in his signature stance with his arms behind him. *Senator Malloy doesn't need to try to seem imposing with this overly extravagant office,* he continued. *It's distasteful — the man has plenty of wealth, power, and posi-tion. Why flaunt it. Not to mention, with unfettered access to the most advanced medical technologies, the Malloy family is known for their longevity. What more could he need? I suppose it is all a part of the act. Wants and needs are two separate things, and this man will never be happy until he's acquired all of the power he pos-sibly can. They are all the same in that way. Disgusting.*

Finishing his sentence, Senator Malloy went on to say, "No ... no ... I want you to get close to him. Infiltrate his inner circle somehow, find out what he's doing, and then end him. Do I make myself clear, soldier? Branson dies! No loose ends either!"

These damned military types always need things repeated, Malloy thought as he set his 1,100-carat emerald pawn down on the d3 square of frosted glass embedded in the Indian emerald-and-ruby mahogany chess set adorning his desk. *That's something I do not have the time for.*

His chess set was one of but a handful of magnificent ancient, hand-crafted, Mongol-style chess sets to ever be made. No one created handmade chess pieces anymore. Everything was either nanogrown or manufactured in the almost obsolete mega factories.

Cassius stared at the Senator for a brief moment while twisting the blade in his sleeve a few times before sheathing it. He turned on his heel and strode off. His footsteps were light as he walked towards the office's metallic doors overlaid with genuine African blackwood. "You'll receive a data diamond when I know something. Until then, do not contact me."

The door slid open and closed, leaving Senator Malloy standing there, narrow-eyed and visibly perturbed. *Why did I hire such a damned loose cannon? I should have been wary of his high recommendation; subtlety is most certainly not one of his fortes. That's fine. When I am finished with Branson, I will see to it that Cassius Lowell is nothing more than an insignificant footnote in time.*

CHAPTER 16

Ah, What?

The training platoon came to a halt after hiking 150 miles across the Herschel Plains, aptly named after the explorer to first trek across it. Located just five kilometers south of CMB Starfire, the Herschel Plains afforded the Marines excellent training grounds for the recruits to continue acclimating to their TALOS suits, as the plains extended over 300 miles and were relatively flat compared to its surroundings.

The recruits' nano-created exomuscles and exoskeletons were designed to absorb the majority of their 300-pound load, which came in handy as they hiked the Herschel Plains. They were little more than barely fatigued by the hike's end. Mae shouldn't have been moving as sluggishly as she was; however, the bruised ribs she sustained during the ambush two days ago were causing her problems again. Mae's ribs had been without pain and almost healed until Jamieson had thrown his full weight atop of her. His actions stressed the capabilities of the microscopic medical bots coursing through Mae's bloodstream, causing a relapse in her injuries.

Having Jamieson around ruined everything, and now Mae had fallen behind during their forced march, chiefly due to the amount of pain she was in. This, in turn, caused her to become the singular focus of the attention of Drill Instructor Sergeant Black. The other two drill instructors were too busy with the rest of the platoon to bother with Mae, but Sergeant Black now had a special place in her heart for her with what appeared to be a genuine level of hatred.

The platoon had come to a halt outside of their squad bay. That's when the fun began.

"Recruit Daniels, get on my quarterdeck right now!" Drill Instructor Sergeant Black ordered. Mae moved as fast as she could, considering the circumstances.

"Faster! Move it, Recruit!"

Mae complied with the Drill Instructor's torrent of demands, making her way to the quarterdeck. *This is stupid—it's not my fault I fell behind. But of course, I can't say that. I can't tell anyone. Who would believe me? They would probably think I was making it up so I could get out of trouble. No, I will take this punishment and every one thereafter. I don't want handouts for real or perceived misconceptions. I'll get them to respect me for what I can do and who I am as a person on my own right.*

Drill Instructor Sergeant Black was akin to a berserk show poodle — beautiful and elegant yet ferociously deviant. As Black screamed at her, Mae couldn't help but picture her on the cover of a holo-mag or adorning the side of some building's view wall advertising something. "You think you can just fall out of my forced march and get away with it, huh!" Black yelled. Mae continued doing side straddle hops, pushups, and mountain climbers at the Drill Instructor's behest.

"Oh, well, I got something for that! Get up!"

Mae quickly stood. "Get down," Black said with Mae promptly following suit. "Get up! Get up now!" Black reiterated as her voice screeched and saliva spewed everywhere. The Drill Instructor's intensity translated into speed of movement for Recruit Daniels. Once Mae was halfway up, Drill Instructor Black was awash with fury and ordered Mae to get back down.

I wish she would make up her freaking mind, thought Mae, exhaustion settling in. *I don't think I can take much more of this.*

Drill Instructor Black continued to scream, "Faster! Up, down ... up, down ... up, down ..." Mae's legs shook and her arms trembled. She worked feverishly to push herself away from the ground. Without warning, she collapsed on the quarterdeck.

"Recruit Daniels, who the hell gave you permission to rest on my quarterdeck!" Black, with flailing arms, bellowed into Mae's ear.

Drill Instructor King's attention had been drawn to the quarterdeck by a few of the recruit's gasps and reactions to Mae collapsing. King dashed to the other side of the squad bay, jump boots clinging on the metal as he made way towards Mae's limp body.

Friggin' recruits always want to be weak, never want to put in the work to become a Marine and earn their place. I got something for her, King thought. His knife hand swung into action, hollering as his neck muscles twitched, "You sorry excuse for a recruit! Get your lazy ass up and get back to work!" Mae didn't move. Both Drill Instructors launched several more verbal attacks at her before realizing something was seriously wrong. "Fuck, Sergeant Black, I don't think she's playing," King said in a low, raspy voice. *"Me either,"* Black shot back via her implanted EMCD.

"Senior Drill Instructor Vickers, this is Drill Instructor Sergeant Black. I need a med-drone over here stat. Daniels is down."

Vickers' reply came through fast, with a speed and intensity that only the EMCDs could provide. One would have thought the other was in their head — literally. *"Dispatching a med-drone to your position now. What happened?"* Vickers demanded.

The med-drone arrived within a minute of the request going out. In those intervening moments, Sergeant Black filled Staff Sergeant Vickers in on the sequence of events leading up to Mae's collapse. Paperwork was going to need to be filed, and depending on what happened with Daniels, one of them might end up on the receiving end of an ax, figuratively speaking.

Oh God, it's bright, Mae thought as she cracked her eyes open, one lid at a time. Squinting, she took in her surroundings and fought back a feeling of confusion. *How did I get here? I was just on the quarterdeck getting "strong" as the Drill Instructors called it. More like getting hazed.*

It had been a long-standing tradition of the Marine Corps to use specifically-approved hazing techniques, along with some non-approved ones, to break down potential Marines, aka recruits, and build them back up into something remotely resembling a Marine — a warfighter, a citizen. Traditions died hard with Marines, and Recruit Daniels was one in a long line of recruits who just had the honor of upholding one of those long-standing traditions.

Mae wrapped one arm around her upper torso as she used the other for purchase while attempting to sit up. "I must have passed out or something," she mumbled to herself. "I'm sure someone recorded my face plant and shared it with everyone on the base by now." She said, a bit resigned to that fact, knowing this stage of their training came with relaxed security blocks on their EMCD's. Things tended to go viral if they warranted enough attention. Once something became virulent, the only thing able to kill it off was a lack of interest from the attending masses.

The advent of the EMCDs made instant recording and spontaneous memory recollection a part of everyday society. Anything you didn't care enough about, you allowed to be uploaded into the cloud for quick and easy access. If you considered it too private for safekeeping on a public domain, the old-fashioned method of committing it to gray-matter memory was the option of choice. Instant recollection was a Godsend for many but a disaster for a large handful. Under Coalition law, the government had the right to download and use in a court of law any and all memories stored in the cloud by any persons falling under the purview of the Coalition.

"Nope, I don't think you're famous or anything," a voice said from behind the thin biowall separating the two. "Your face plant was gracefully executed. So much so that I hear those two Drill Instructors are being investigated for negligence." *No need to tell her I initiated that investigation*, Liam thought. "Of course, I don't need to tell you this, but I kinda feel sorry for you."

"Who are you?" Mae asked, slightly taken aback at this man's response to her self-directed question. "Forgive my lack of formalities," she continued, "although this biowall makes it hard to see the person on the other side."

"No, no, I like the lack of formalities and the level of anonymity the biowall provides. For now, just call me Liam. So ... what should I call you? Or do you prefer 'girl on the other side of wall'?"

"What, who came up with that name? 'Girl on other side of wall.' That's the silliest name ever." Mae chuckled, allowing herself a small smile. Something she hadn't genuinely done since before the incident.

Liam laid in his medical bed with one foot on the mattress and the other dangling off, his folded hands behind his head. "I did, and if you aren't careful, I'll bore you to death with my innate ability to come up with more random nicknames that'll make you gag."

"Alright, alright, I'll bite, Liam. Where am I? I take it I'm in a hospital room but which one and give me specifics if you have them."

Liam considered her request for a second before replying, "You are in the main hab facility of CMB Starfire. You seemed to have experienced some sort of blackout. The doctors think it's due to the level of pain you were in. Apparently, you have some pretty nasty bruises from another incident. Wanna tell me what happened?"

"Ok, 'guy on the other side of the wall' ..."

"Nope, you can't do that," Liam interjected.

Chuckling again, Mae said, "I can and I will. You aren't the only one who gets to make up the rules around here ..."

If she only knew, Liam thought.

"... and since you asked, I got pretty banged up a couple of days ago when I was attacked by an unknown assailant. My squad and I were doing a training exercise, and my Fire Team was ambushed. Wait ... how did you know about my bruises and whatnot?" *Creeper much?* Mae thought as she paced around her medi-bed.

"That's an easy one. C'mon, I thought you could do better than that. Alright, so I overheard the nurse talking to the doctor about your condition shortly after they brought you in, and your case interested me. So I did some digging and bam, your info was there for me to indulge in at will."

"What is it with this place? You people! Is there such a thing as privacy anymore?" Mae thought inwardly, *first Savanna and now you.*

"Um, nope. Ever since the advent of our lovely little implants, real privacy, at least the kind you crave, is a thing of the past. For the most part, the little bit of privacy you see is nothing more than a thin veil of deception. Privacy is antiquated."

"Right. So, Liam, what's your deal? Why are you here?"

As Liam and Mae spoke, she felt herself becoming more and more comfortable with him. His voice and the calm, confident way he presented himself interested Mae, like he had everything figured out, but he didn't sound like brass. *I suppose it would be my luck to wake up and have an interesting, hot-sounding guy in the adjacent room who has the uncanny ability to make me laugh.*

"Hey, Mae," Liam said.

Mae walked towards the biowall and replied, "Yes?"

"Set your VMS status to accept, and I'll send you a meeting request. As much as I enjoy talking to you through this biowall and all, maybe we should chat face to face."

The two were interrupted as Mae's nurse walked in. "Hello, dear. How are we feeling?" This last question was redundant as Mae's EMCD had the capability to, and had been, broadcasting Mae's vital functions to the medical staff.

"I'm doing alright. My sides are a little stiff, but I'm managing. How long will I be in here?" Mae asked.

"Well, that's dependent on you at this point. We need to run additional test, but I'm optimistic," the nurse said.

Mae let out a gentle breath and ran her fingers over her thighs. "I'm not sure I understand. What other test do you need to run? I'd really like to just get back to training." Mae never cared for the sterile feel and smell of hospitals.

This place is making my skin crawl, she thought to herself.

If Mae's nurse was annoyed by her, she did not let on. She continued the conversation with a warm, motherly smile and said, "Darling, when was your last period?"

"Huh?" Mae looked up at the nurse, perplexed, and in a low tone, she said, "My period has been irregular of late, but that's due to training. I read that intense physical fitness can sometimes cause women to have periods that do not follow their normal cycle."

Mae's nurse's smile was a bit warmer this time, although her eyes told a different story. They broadcasted a tale of pity and sadness, all of which were directed towards her. "Sweetie, I'm afraid you are correct and yet wrong."

Liam Alexander was listening intently now, not sure what to make of what he was hearing. He was a weapons expert, tactician, technical expert, and legal killer, so listening to a conversation about women's menstrual cycles and how they worked was a bit beyond him. Had the conversation been about any other woman, Liam would have paid it no mind, but there was something about Mae that drew him to her.

The nurse rubbed Mae's shoulder, causing her to slump back a bit. She felt slightly uncomfortable. Mae knew now but did not want to believe it. *The slight curvature of my belly ... guess I was in denial. But this can't be; it just can't. I don't want this. All I want is to be a Marine — to forget.*

As Mae's nurse began to speak the words aloud, which somehow made real the thing growing in her belly, the alarm began to blare in everyone's heads, 'EMERGENCY, EMERGENCY! ACTIVE SHOOTER ALERT. REMAIN CALM AND IN PLACE. BARRICADE ALL DOORS. MILITARY POLICE ARE ON THE WAY.'

CHAPTER 17

Savage Returns

"Sweetie, listen to me. Everything will be ok. Just stay here and, and remain calm," the nurse said as she frantically looked about; for what, Mae wasn't sure.

I'm sure that last bit was more for her than for me. I. Am. Calm. Why am I so calm? There's a killer on the loose and I'm calm. A fine time to be relaxed, Mae. Somewhere deep down, Mae was happy for the gunmen's presence, for the distraction from her new reality. *I hate my life,* she admitted to herself.

"Ah, there it is," Mae's nurse said as she picked up her tranquilizer and medical injector gun. Turning back towards Mae, she said, "I'll be right back. I am going to see if I can provide some help out there. Perhaps secure a door or two or help the wounded."

The nurse turned to leave as Mae blurted out, "Are you fucking nuts! Did you not hear the emergency message? We are to remain in place and barricade the doors."

The door to their small medical room slid open. Two strong hands gripped the arms of the nurse, shoving her back into the room. The door slid shut behind the man.

Mae stared in wide-eyed disbelief and thought to herself, *Oh my god—he—is—hot. I knew it!*

"Who, who are you? Listen, I can help you escape if that's what you want." The nurse fumbled over her words, speaking faster than Mae had previously heard, a look of shock and confusion radiating from her. "I promise I will not say a thing. Please just let me live."

Liam released the woman he was forcefully holding, "Listen, I'm not here to hurt you. I just wanted to keep you from making a huge mistake. Nurse, you do realize that there is an armed gunman outside of these doors, roaming the halls. He may or may not be trained, and you were going to do what exactly? Go fumble around, trying to save everyone. Ma'am, I have news for you. I think you have a death wish, and maybe, just maybe, you should seek immediate medical attention."

Mae busted out laughing and quickly realized she should have laughed inwardly. "Oops," she said, covering her mouth. She was still trying not to laugh at Liam's crass and emotionless sense of humor.

Liam caught Mae's gaze and gave her the slightest of winks as the corner of his mouth curled into a tiny smile just a bit before he became serious again.

Mae's nurse was still staring in disbelief as she realized she wasn't going to die when Liam spoke again. Looking between the two women, he said, "I'm Liam. If you want to live, follow me. If not, stay here. Either way, I'm leaving in favor of a better defensible position."

The three began making their way down the long, spacious corridor amidst a flurry of recruits, civilians, and permanent staff seeking shelter. *Does no one follow directions around here?* Liam thought to himself.

The trio was busy navigating the chaos-filled corridor, heading towards the lab on the right side at the end of the hall when madness erupted.

The gunman turned the corner behind them and opened fire. His magnetic rail gun spit out thousands of rounds per minute as its powerful magnetic coils sped up the armature rounds to incredible speeds as they left the weapon. Those rounds didn't carry any explosives as the wielder of the weapon depended on the speed of the rounds themselves to cause the desired damage.

The speed of the rail gun rounds caused massive bodily destruction to anyone who was unlucky enough to be in its path. Accuracy was a tradeoff for the high firing rate the gun brought to bear.

Bodies were blown apart indiscriminately, causing random appendages to litter the walls and floor in a gory mess. Horrifying cries for help rang out as agonized people, many clinging to life by a thread, pleaded for assistance or mercy — neither of which came.

Mae's nurse screamed as her left leg was blown off of her body, followed closely by part of her right shoulder. She was propelled forward several feet and hit the wall at an angle before collapsing to the ground.

A bullet grazed Mae's forearm as she sought cover. "Stay low!" Liam yelled at Mae as they low-crawled. "Quick, help me with her."

Shrapnel struck Liam in the thigh, but he continued on, ignoring the pain as best he could. Their hearts were pounding. Racing forward, the two each grabbed one of the nurse's remaining limbs — Liam taking an arm and Mae a leg. "Hurry, get her into the lab."

After they managed to get into the laboratory and out of that death trap of a corridor, Mae and Liam pushed furniture against the door. "Help me with her wounds," Liam said, pulling off his belt.

"You're familiar with combat medicine, right?"

"Yeah, but I haven't had to actually use that bit of training."

"It's alright, just follow my lead."

Mae watched Liam work and tied her own belt around her nurse's arm. The field-expedient tourniquets weren't pretty, but they'd do for now; with any luck, they may even save her life.

"He can't keep that rate of fire up forever," Liam told Mae through a mental message, partly due to exhaustion and partly to keep the gunman from hearing them. Mae shot back, *"What do we do now? We can't stay in here forever."* She looked around as she checked herself for holes, *"And by the looks of it, we're stuck in here. I don't see a way out."*

Mae considered her position. *Things could be worst. I'm trapped in a medical facility not designed for this type of damage, on a planet where the atmosphere is unbreathable, with bruised ribs and a smoking hot man who I'm sure is my superior. He's different — to say the least.*

Liam looked at Mae, this woman he found himself attracted to and couldn't explain why. *We need a way out of here,* he thought. *This woman — no — this recruit is right; we're stuck, and about to get our shit punched in. If I can get Sara here, maybe we'll be able to get out of this alive. We can't get out, but she can get in.*

"Listen," Liam said, *"I have a plan. We need to batten down and hold out until my associate can get here. I just sent her a message, and she's on her way. She isn't too far from this facility, so that works in our favor."*

Captain Sara Marsh's EMCD pinged with an incoming message. She swore, *I thought I set that thing to 'do not disturb.'*

"Listen up, gents. We hit planet fall in five minutes, vector up .4 degrees, to the right .2 degrees, after which let the AI take over the landing sequence. There's nothing worse than a multimillion-dollar Zeus suit becoming slag because you lot forgot to sync your AIs!" Captain Marsh said as she paused her own auto-landing sequence amidst the incoming message. Checking the ID, she noted it was from Liam and immediately opened it.

"Shit!" Sara spat out, forgetting her comms were still set to the platoon frequency.

"What is it, Captain?" Staff Sergeant Samuels asked.

"The medical facility is being attacked by an unknown assailant. The skipper just requested I pay the threat a visit."

A few thought clicks later, Captain Marsh was vectoring away from her landing group, heading towards the medical facility.

She noted the jovial tone in the Staff Sergeant's voice as he replied, "So in other words, the Skipper got himself in some hot water and needs you to bail him out. Got it, Captain. Happy hunting."

◆ ◆ ◆

"Liam Alexander! Where are you?" The gunman bellowed out between rounds.

Liam and Mae listened as the thump, thump, thump, sounds of automated fire reverberated through the facilities nanofabricated, metallic-like structure. The planetary engineers had used nanites, delivered to the surface of the plant via interplanetary ballistic missiles, to seed various surfaces on Titan to begin growing the infrastructure locally — a cost-effective solution to a costly problem. A few months after seeding, the hard part was done. Facilities of various sizes erected themselves using bits of the local geology and metallurgical components found in the ground.

Mae rubbed her hair, noting it was a bit longer now, almost curly again. *At least I don't look like a boy anymore. Well actually, that's probably left up to interpretation.*

Liam's head movements caught Mae's attention. *"What are you doing?"*

She watched him; he was efficient as he scanned from side to side. *"I'm looking for the gunman. Maybe If I can find his exact position, I can time my attack just right."*

"You aren't seriously considering going out there. You saw what he did to Nurse Ellie here — and everyone else, didn't you?" Mae's

nurse laid on the floor a couple of feet away from them, uncon-scious and barely breathing. The two tourniquets struggled to stave off death.

Liam continued to scan through the wall. He picked up a number of human outlines and froze as he locked eyes with the gunman standing on the other side of their door. *Shit,* he thought. Mae was still speaking when Liam dove into her — shoulder first, driving them both several feet to the right. A loud rhythmic beat resounded in their ears. The entire front wall erupted in an intense and unrestrained fury as the furni-ture barricade and the nano-grown metal wall exploded into thousands of pieces. Liam laid atop of Mae, shielding her with his body.

Debris rained down, pelting the laboratory's three refugees.

Adam Shigley, gunman extraordinaire, stepped into the doorway he'd just created for himself. The settling dust slightly obscured his view of the room. He paused, checked his internal chronometer, and estimated he had less than five minutes before the authorities arrived. That was fine. He'd found who he was looking for, and once he took care of him, he would help himself to eternity in the afterlife, comforted with the thought that he finally got his revenge.

The assailant dropped the now-emptied rail gun. He walked towards the two conjoined bodies on the floor, coming within striking distance. Liam looked back over his shoulder and rolled to his feet.

The man snapped out a hard-right jab towards Liam's head. Liam watched the man's shoulders and parried the blow to his right while catching the man's wrist at eye level. Simultan-eously, he launched his right knee into the man's diaphragm while connecting his fist to the man's jaw with his free hand. The man snapped back but stopped short. Liam still had his wrist in his grasp.

Adam used his reverse momentum to drop his weight,

bringing his boots to bear on Liam's abdomen. He kicked hard, sending him flipping head over feet.

Liam flung his leg in a wide arc, allowing his heel to connect with the gunman's shoulder as he attempted to dodge the attack. Before Liam's leg hit the ground, Adam slid in close, hooked an arm under Liam's leg, and executed a sweeping leg throw.

Liam could taste the blood in his mouth as he hit the ground hard. *"This man is clearly a pro, Mae. Stay behind that table and out of the way ..."* The two men threw a series of strikes and counter-strikes at each other. *"I'd. Hate. For. You. To. Get ..."* he continued, through heavy breathing while trying to focus on finding an opening to gain the upper hand and end this fight.

"Hurt." Liam finished while connecting a series of hammer fists to the assailant's ribs.

Mae watched the battle unfolding before her. *I've never seen anything like this. Liam is swift and agile, yet the other man has him almost evenly matched. If I don't do something fast, we both might not walk out of here.*

Liam noted with a bit of satisfaction that Mae was making her way towards the lab tables, which were obstructed from the gunman's view. They afforded her a straight shot towards freedom. *Good, at least one of us will make it out of here,* he thought.

Adam Shigley grinned mirthlessly while blocking a number of blows and returning a few of his own, "You don't remember me, do you?"

A bead of sweat began to trickle down Liam's temple. *What? So, I know this psychopath! Ok, think. Where would I have seen him before?*

"No?" Adam said as he blocked two successive blows from Liam, managing to wrap both of his arms around his. Pulling Liam in close, Adam continued, "You killed my brother, my best friend — my only friend. And now it's your turn to visit hell."

Liam considered what he'd just heard. *This guy's brother probably died on some obscure mission on some equally obscure moon in some unforgiving and unrelenting location.* Because that's what guys like Liam did. They get sent off to frolic in the underbelly of hell to bring back the heads of Satan's minions — discontents unwilling to conform to the political agenda of their governments.

Before getting assigned to CMB Starfire, Captain Liam Alexander, a Marine Raider, operated under the guise and authority of the Coalition's Joint Special Operations Command.

This deranged man's brother must have served with me in some fashion, on one of those missions so black the members of the teams weren't allowed to know the real identities of each other. But somehow, this asshole found out my identity. I'm gonna have to 'talk' to someone about that, Liam thought.

Another thought flashed through Liam's mind. *This man came here to kill me. Not a problem — I will deal with that accordingly, but I can't allow Mae to be injured in the process, at least not before I get to know her better.* Liam was a snake eater, bred for war. He'd survived worse, and there wasn't much he feared, with the exception of one thing — not having any children to call his own, children to carry on his genes and teach the finer skills of survival.

Mae broke up the two men's trip down memory lane as she yelled violently, swinging a chair in their direction.

Shit! Liam thought. *Seriously!*

Adam released Liam from his clutches and dropped to the ground. Liam attempted to dodge the attack as well, but the chair flew through the air and connected with Liam's side. Mae squeezed her eyes tight as she swung her blunt-force instrument.

Liam staggered backward, tripped, and fell. Mae's momentum carried her forward, following Liam's trajectory, landing on top of him.

"Pathetic," Adam said as he drew his SpecOps-issued K-bar from his leg holster while standing. "You call yourself an Operator. You are a disgrace. No wonder my brother died serving with you!" Adam began to move closer towards Liam and Mae. "See you in Valhalla, you son of a bitch."

Liam was sure now was not the time for his smart-ass mouth but decided what the hell. "I'm sure men of your, um, colorful caliber don't get to partake in the glories of Valhalla. Sorry, try again."

Adam surged forward, bellowing out a deep guttural sound before his body exploded outward, peppering the room and its occupants with entrails, blood, and bits of various body parts.

Mae wiped what might have been part of a lung from her face and spat out remnants of the gunman to her side.

The pair looked past the spot that only a few seconds prior held the maniacal madman intent on killing Liam only to see a massive black shape standing where the door should have been.

Standing in the massive hole where Adam Shigley had been minutes before was a Marine in Zeus armor, scanning the room with an outstretched arm, seeking more targets of opportunity. Satisfied there were none, Captain Sara Marsh sent the appropriate mental commands to her suit to unseal and partially retract the helmet's faceplate.

"Hey, Captain Alexander, heard you needed help," Marsh said with a mix of humor and concern.

Captain? Mae thought in dismay, looking at Liam, the guy who a part of her was hoping to get to know. *He never mentioned he was an officer! I'm good with it if he is, but I wonder how he feels. Am I imagining our attraction, or is it real ...*

"Sara, it took you long enough," Liam said, helping himself up and extending a hand to do the same for Mae.

"Sir, you're getting rusty. You should have been able to handle this man way before I showed up. I saw the way he fought.

He's had Spec Ops training. Any ideas on who he was?"

Liam raised an eyebrow at his companion. "Wait, so you're telling me you were there the entire time and you just now jumped in?"

Sara didn't flinch at the unspoken reprimand carried in Liam's tone, "You looked like you had everything in hand, regardless of how slow you were moving. Sir." She didn't have to use the 'sir' title when addressing him since they were both Captains, but Liam was in command, plus she knew he hated it.

"I'm not making excuses, but you are aware I was in medical for a reason, aren't you, XO? It's not as easy as you think to take out an armed assailant with a partially torn rotator cuff," Liam said.

Mae stared at the exchange and realized a few things.

I'm way out of my depth here, and honestly, I don't belong. These two are Spec Ops, and I'm not even halfway through recruit training. On the other hand, this guy is like — a complete badass. He not only protected me, but he did it while injured and managed to hold his own. But what about her? They seem overly familiar. Is there something between them, or am I reaching? Reaching for sure! Get a grip, girl!

Mae walked towards Captain Marsh, extended a hand, and introduced herself, "Recruit Mae Daniels, ma'am. Thank you for the save."

CHAPTER 18

Forging Ahead

President Branson stepped out of the sonic shower and into the drying rack. Within 30 seconds, his body was devoid of moisture, and he was slipping on his robe.

Standing in front of his mirror, Branson turned from side to side admiringly. *Not bad for 55. That Medical Tissue Nanotransfection technology the science division is working on is out of this world. What did they call it? M-TNT? Doesn't matter, the stuff works — well! I don't feel a day over 25. It slowed down my aging, but it's a shame this stuff isn't able to truly reverse it. That and the fact that it gave me my vitality back is still a win in my book. A hearty 'thank you' to my STEM advisor is in order.*

Branson rubbed his hands across his chest, reveling in how strong he felt. He gazed down to the slow-rising bulge beneath his towel, feeling as virile as ever. *I seriously could have used this stuff back in my Force Recon days. If my military guys don't have this yet, I'll have to fix that. Will come in handy where we're going.*

Speaking of fixing, I know who needs a good ... Branson's thoughts trailed off as he approached his wife. "I have something for you, hun," he said with a wink. "Shut down your EMCD and come here," he instructed, motioning for Sophia to get on top of him as he sat on the edge of the bed. "Last thing we need is one of my agents accessing your feed and watching us get nasty."

Sophia Branson rested her arms around the neck of her husband as she straddled him. He began caressing her hips, tracing the curvature of her body with the tips of his cold fingers. Sophia leaned in closer, positioning his face between her chest.

The heat between the two was palpable. Sophia was more than ready to feel her husband inside of her, his body against hers and, most importantly, an orgasm! It had been so long since she was intimate with her husband that she'd almost forgotten what it had felt like.

Sophia contemplated her needs, weighing them against her duties as a wife. *I need this. I want this. I don't know what's gotten into him, but I'm happy something did. I'm going to sleep so good tonight!*

But something's been bothering Johnny, and if he doesn't get it under control, it'll consume him. Shut up and take it, Sophia. You can worry about everything else later. Sophia's thoughts betrayed her as her mind raced in all directions except the one she so desperately wanted it to head in. *But I know my Johnny, and there's something weighing on him. We'll talk first, and then I will take care of him.*

"Johnny, wait a minute," Sophia said, between ragged breaths. "I need to know what's wrong. You've been very preoccupied, more so than you normally are. What's going on?"

"Well, sugar plum, since you asked," Branson said, wrapping his big hands around his wife's waist, pulling her in closer. He locked eyes with her for a moment, gathering his thoughts.

"We have a problem, and I'm attempting to rectify it."

"What's that?"

Branson reached up and swiped a few strands of golden blond hair away from his wife's face, groaning. "Do we have to right now? Let's finish this talk later?"

"Lovebug, as enticing as that is, I'm doing this for you. Now spill."

Branson closed his eyes for a second before continuing, "I've recently come into some knowledge — knowledge that has the potential to shake humanity to the core, change the very fabric of our society and how we see ourselves in this universe. Imagine how the world and colony planets will react when they discover we are not only *not alone* in the universe, but that we believe those aliens are currently and have been stealing humans for their own nefarious or benevolent reasons. No one really knows that last part."

Most people would be shocked, maybe even scared, by the revelation President Branson just dropped. The First Lady is not one of those people. Since an early age, Sophia always believed there was more to life and the universe than what was directly in front of her. She always had a deep affinity and fascination with the unexplained and the potential for extraterrestrial life.

So, the news her husband just delivered did little more than jumpstart her childlike curiosity again.

"Go on," she said, excitement plastered across her face.

"I wish I could say that that was the extent of the problem. However, I was briefed a few hours ago that several hundred Mars shipyard workers and Space Force crew were killed through an act of sabotage. The target was the Aurora-1, the new Capital ship I was having commissioned for the Coalition. Now — gone, all of it."

"I thought about it, and despite what happened, I've decided to continue the mission. On the surface, it'll appear that the Aurora-1 is being rebuilt, but this is only a ruse designed to keep our enemy's attention while my other plan is coming online."

"Other plan? You aren't talking about that project you hinted at a while back? What did you call it? Ares something-or-another?"

"Close, hun. The Archimedes project is its name, and it has been operating in secret since I took office. An entire fleet of warships has been built over the past 15 years at my behest. I had anticipated using those ships against the Russo-Asian alliance, better known as the FCS nowadays. However, now they are needed for another reason."

"Sugarplum, listen. This mission is of the gravest importance. Our people are being stolen, and I have to find out why. I need to see if I can stop this, which is why you may not like what I have to say next."

"Go."

"What?"

"You heard me, Johnny, GO. I would love to cry and get upset and tell you how much you need to stay, how much I need you and absolutely miss you, but that would be selfish. When I married you, I knew you were destined for greatness, and I still believe that. I will not stand in your way, my love." Sophia leaned in and gave her husband a small peck on the lips. She lingered for a second, taking in his scent.

This woman is phenomenal! Branson thought. "Thank you, hun. I love you more now than ever, darling. Thank you! Truly."

"As you suspected, I do plan on leading the Archimedes Task Force, with General Sherman serving as the leader of the ground force contingent I'm bringing."

In Sophia's heart, she knew she made the right decision, but she still wanted to scream. Instead, she asked, "So, what are you going to call them? Your ships, that is."

"I have thought up a few names, but I am stuck on the last two. Consider this," Branson said, "in 1520 AD, the Portuguese navigator Ferdinand Magellan discovered the Strait of Magellan. At that time, Ferdinand had a small complement of ships in his employ, five to be exact. Those ships were named The Trinidad, The San Antonio, The Conception, The Victoria, and The Santiago. Fitting names for the task at hand."

"Just like that great Portuguese explorer who set out from his homeland on an expedition of discovery, we too are heading into the black depths of space to do the same. I don't know what we will find, but I know that this is important and needs to be done."

"That's why for this expedition, I find it fitting to adopt the same names Magellan used. Do you have any suggestions for the other two ships?"

"I'm not overtly creative, Mr. President. You knew that when you married me," Sophia said before being interrupted by the President's playful yet sensual touches.

"Oh, say that again, Mrs. First Lady," Branson said, nibbling on his wife's collarbone.

Sophia let out a yelp followed by a low moan.

"Mr. President!" she exclaimed, his hands tracing a path along the inner edges of her thighs. "Johnny ... oh — Johnny ... wait, wait, let ... let me speak." Sophia said, easing out of Branson's grips, pushing him away and forcing him back onto the bed. She hovered over him, her hands resting on his chest.

Half intent on hearing Sophia out, half intent on other things, Branson's groping only marginally slowed down.

Several quick wraps on his stateroom door brought a frown to his wife's face. "Honey, I should probably take this," Branson said begrudgingly.

Sophia rolled off of her husband. Letting out a slow and lengthy exhale, she said, "Go ahead. I'll finish without you." *So close!* She thought. *So close!*

CHAPTER 19

Shower

Mae pulled off her last article of clothing, tossed it into the squad bay's laundry facilitator, and padded naked into the shared showers. A glance left revealed Savanna showering with what looked to be the bulk of the other recruits.

I can't. I need to find a spot that isn't crowded, Mae thought. *Savanna seems unusually quiet. What's her deal?*

Opening a channel, Mae sent Savanna a private message. *"Hey girl, no matter how hard you stare, they won't grow... the powers that be put something in our food to prevent that sort of thing, you know,"* she said, chuckling out loud.

"Screw you, Mae!" Recruit Johnson said as he cupped his stout meaty penis, turning his back to her. "I can't help it! Growing up on Proxima Centauri b stunts your growth, you know!"

"Oh hey, sorry. That laugh wasn't meant for you and your little buddy there," Mae said, this time actually snickering at Johnson's johnson as she walked by.

Savanna's eyes followed Mae's sultry form walking towards the far back corner of the shower room. Each successive step

Mae took sent shivers through Savanna's body, as the gentle jiggles of Mae's petite butt drew on her basic desires. Savanna's breathing increased, and there was a moistness between her legs. Moistness, she noticed, that didn't come from the shower water. *I'll never get used to that,* she thought.

"*Girl, you're funny,*" Savanna replied. "*These boys wouldn't know what to do with me if they had an instructional manual. Besides, I'm not interested in any of them here; not my cup of tea.*"

"*Ha! Something tells me you're right. Hey, find me later and let's talk, ok?*"

"*Ok, will do,*" Savanna replied.

Mae turned her attention to the slightly unreserved Garrett Beasley as she said, "Mind if I shower next to you?" *You're safe,* she thought.

"No, of course not. Need some soap? There's some in that corner right over there," Garrett said with a sly smirk on his face, pointing down and away from him towards an empty spot on the ground. Funny things about smirks, a solid hit to its wearer usually eradicated all traces of such things. "Ouch, I was only kidding," Garrett said, holding his hand where Mae had punched him.

Mae glanced left in Garrett's direction, watching him apply shampoo to his hair. "I didn't take you for the religious type," she said.

"I'm not," Garrett said, lowering his arm, blushing slightly. "I mean, yeah, ok, a little. What's it to you anyway?"

The emblem etched into him was the same she'd seen before, that night at her dad's house with those two Upgraders in her living room. It was a shooting star streaking upward from a crescent Earth, traversing through several multicolored layers. The star is said to be representative of a soul transcending into the spiritual realm.

Mae washed her chest and stomach, allowing the sonic water jets to sweep over her as she replied, "Nothing, I just noticed the tattoo under your arm. I wouldn't have taken you as an Upgrader. Our society thrives on technology, and they, well, they stand against it."

Garrett's eyes swept over his friend. He felt dirty for ogling over Mae's body as they showered next to each other. She was a perfect specimen and deserved to be worshiped, but by who, he wasn't sure. He'd wanted it to be him, but not at the expense of their friendship. Despite what the brass put in their food and water to prevent erections, he could feel his member struggling to fight off the incapacitating effects.

Stop it! Garrett thought to himself. *Mae is a friend. Don't embarrass yourself, man!*

"*You're wrong, you know,*" he shot back to Mae mentally. "*About Upgraders. They stand for so much more. Upgraders are your shamans of old, Mae. Our claim to fame is our ability to access and influence the world of benevolent and malevolent spirits. To do this, we believe in purity of mind and body, so yeah, no technology. We Upgraders hold firm to the belief that the merging of technology with the human body will bring about the technological singularity, and for humanity, that, my friend would be bad ... very bad.*"

Garrett continued, "*Did you know that shamans have been around for a very, very long time? It's said that Shamanism was founded by a lover of someone called Thourn many ages ago. He confided in her the secrets of the cosmos and the meaning of life itself. Love, you see, is blind. We all know that, but I guess Thourn had to learn that lesson the hard way. His only request of his lover was that she tell no one of the secrets he bestowed upon her, and you know what she did?*"

Mae thought this was comical. "*Let me guess, she broke her oath and told someone?*" Garrett affirmed her answer, prompting another response from Mae. "*This Thourn guy should have known better. Most women like to talk, duh. We are verbal creatures, you know.*"

Garrett couldn't help but chuckle at that statement as he continued, "*After they split, Thourn's lover went on to spread her word, which eventually metastasized like roots to a tree, giving birth to the majority of the world's religions. Through this woman,*" *whom we believe to be the first shaman, we have gained knowledge of the spiritual world and, more importantly, how to project our astral-selves there."*

Mae considered Garrett's words. *"Well then, why do you have implants? Doesn't that go against your beliefs? And about the spirit world projection thing ... can you talk to them too?"* Mae's quizzical look almost made Garrett feel a bit defensive.

"Mae, I can see where you would be confused," Garrett said aloud. "But to clarify, I'm a non-practicing Upgrader. I hold close to many of their beliefs, but some don't. I do believe our copious use of technology will eventually lead our species to a point where we are indistinguishable from technology and vice versa, but I've grown too reliant on my EMCD to ever give it up. Horrible, I know. Oh and no, I can't talk to spirits. I haven't reached that level of shaman mastery to be able to do that. I'll never get there — not so long as I embrace the heavy use of technology."

Garrett shifted, turning his back to Mae as he continued to scrub himself. "I mean, look at all of the good technology has done for us. Major wars, famine, most diseases, they're all a thing of the past. Technology has brought humanity out of the Stone Age and thrust us forward, giving us hope for a better future. At least that's how I see it. How can I not embrace that?"

Everything Garrett was saying made sense to her, but one word stood out above all else: hope. *That guy, Jax, he had mentioned something about hope,* Mae thought, something she had forgotten until now. *"My kind do not feed on blood but on hope. And hope is a dying resource; until you, that is."*

"What was that, Mae? Sounds deep."

Mae shot back, *"It's nothing, Garrett. I was just thinking out loud. Hey, mind getting my back?"*

Garrett stepped closer to Mae's rear, soap in hand, and languidly obliged her request. *This is major friend zone,* he thought, *but I'd rather it be me than anyone else.*

CHAPTER 20

Night Wing One

Cassius Lowell worked the flight controls of Night Wing One, an oblong black shuttle with sharp, soft contours, a keen nose, no visible windows, and short half-wings ending with a pylon of various weaponry, in preparation for the President's arrival. The Night Wing was more of an Intersolar vehicle than a shuttle, although the inelegant euphemism stuck.

Night Wings were designed as flying fortresses, capable of travel through both atmosphere and space. Their flight range was their only real weakness, maxing out at a top distance of four Astronomical Units—coming in just shy of Jupiter's orbit from Earth.

When it comes to transportation for the highest-ranking VIPs, it is no contest. Everyone wants to get their hands on a Night Wing — as a handful have. The President's Night Wing was the exception. The shuttle was twice the size of the old Air Force One bird with ten times the armor along with offensive and defensive capabilities rivaling most fighter jets.

The call came through to Hugo's EMCD with crystal clarity. *"Do you have eyes on the target?"* The merc, known as Kilo-1, asked.

Cassius listened to Hugo's heavily accented Latin voice, "*I have eyes on but no shot; the Archies are here in force, I know it.*"

"*Kilo-2, what am I payin' you for! Sight in and kill the man, and let's be done with this. It's simple.*"

"*That's a negative Kilo-1. The target is too well protected. I don't have a shot. Their leader's polychromatic Zeus armor is shifting in and out of the visible spectrum. I've run enough ops to know that is a subtle sign. The Guardians want potential enemies to focus on the leader while their stealth compadres do the clean-up work. The moment I fire, those Archies will be on me before I have time to extract.*"

Cassius stood and walked to the adjacent bulkhead, accessed atmospherics, and entered several rapid commands before he said, "Very well. Switching to plan bravo. Your pay just got cut by two-thirds. I do not tolerate fear nor failure. Proceed to the extraction point. If there's a problem, come see me and we'll discuss."

Three Night Wings lifted off from the presidential airfield, rapidly gaining altitude. Within moments of ascending into the sky, the Night Wings reached cruising altitude.

President Branson unbuckled his seat restraints and made his way from the middle of the shuttle up to the third deck at the rear of Night Wing One. "Marious, keep up. Stay by my side at all times. Do you understand?"

The President smiled curtly as he passed one of several stewardesses.

"Yes sir, Mr. President." Hesitating for a moment, Marious decided to speak up, "Sir, if I may, what are we doing?"

Branson stopped before a pair of blue security doors. He waited several seconds to allow the biometrics system to do its business. A faint hissing sound preceded the opening of the security doors. He took a seat on the only piece of furniture in the secure meeting room and spoke in the open now. "Young man, we're getting ready for a secure video message. We need the relay systems of the Night Wing for that."

"No sir, that's not what I meant. What are we doing? You had your Personal Security Detachment pull me out of my quarters in the middle of the night. And now we're in your personal spaceship ripping through the sky at insane speeds. Sir, I don't mean to question your decisions. I just would like to know what's going on — if that's ok, sir."

"Son, we're heading to Kourou. It's in French Guiana. We should be there in about a few hours. First, we need to stop off at a midway point in the southern Rocky Mountains. You should consider getting some rest. You're going to need it." President Branson wasn't used to his junior subordinates questioning him, which was something he liked about Marious.

The young man questioned everything and had an indomitable sense of honor about him. Branson saw a lot of himself in the man, and for that, among other things, he decided to keep him close. Marious was one of a handful of people he felt he could actually trust.

"Sir, thank you for that, but I don't understand the need for all of the cloak and dagger. Why not leave during the day? And where are all of your staff? It just seems odd that no one else is on this ship besides you, me, your wife, your PSD, several stewardesses, and the Secretary of Defense."

"I have all of the staff I need at the moment, sitting right in front of me — everyone else I can reach instantly via my EMCD. Now, sit there and say nothing else. Observe but say nothing. Understood?"

"Yes, sir," Marious replied, feeling moderately satisfied.

The security room doors slid open to welcome John Herrington, the Secretary of Defense for the Coalition. Captain Gomez shifted to the visible spectrum and did another security sweep of Mr. Herrington.

"Holy cow! Where did he come from?" Marious said to no one in particular, his eyes stuck on the spot Captain Gomez had materialized. "The PSD members combat coveralls even have stealth technology! What else are they hiding?"

"Mr. President, what is this? I understand the need to be cautious, but I'm the Secretary of Defense for Christ's sake!"

"John, welcome. Have a seat. Apologies for the added security, but I have it on good authority that these measures are required. Now put your pride away and let's get down to business."

The view wall adjacent to the President came to life. A person in their mid-forties with heavily androgynous features came on. It wasn't until after their voice rang throughout the room that they could discern the person to be male.

"Mr. President, staff, good morning. We are expecting your arrival and are very excited. Landing platform 7 will be ready for your ships. The products are just about done, and no one outside of my immediate staff knows you're inbound, as you requested."

The President leaned in, with a slight glint in his eye and said, "Yes, Director Gibson, let's talk about the products…"

Walking out of the security room after the meeting belied a situation very different from what the President expected. Several bodies laid motionless throughout the cabin — a few were stewardesses, the others were the Guardians that made up his PSD.

The President and his companions stood for a moment, taking in the scene before reacting. The Secretary of Defense ran to an adjacent bulkhead which housed an arms locker. Frantically, he punched in code after code, each one wrong.

President Branson turned to head back into the security room. The doors shut quickly in front of him. Captain Gomez dove for the President and yelled, "Get down!" He looked down at Branson, lying on the floor. "Sir, my apologies, but I need to keep you safe."

Cassius strolled out of the cockpit and through the ship before entering into the room that held the President and his staff. He liberated his blades from the sheaths attached to his arms.

Captain Gomez unholstered his sidearm and stood, whirling in the direction of the pilot walking towards them. "You, what's going on here? Did you see what happened?"

In his best Southern accent, Cassius said, "Captain, there was a malfunction with the ship's atmospherics. Since the cabin is sealed, we have our own atmospherics. I'm not entirely sure what's going on. I was coming to see if everyone was alright, but as we both can see, that's not the case."

The President rose from his hiding spot and said, "My wife? Where's my wife?"

Cassius continued to walk closer. "Mr. President, I'm afraid she's gone. They all are. My co-pilot and I were the only ones left until I found you guys. Thank God I found you two. There has to be a lunatic on board. I've already called the two trailing Night Wings and informed them of the situation. They will have men on board to secure the ship as soon as we land."

Captain Gomez kept his gun trained on the man in the pilot's uniform, the trigger slightly depressed from the pressure of his pointer finger.

Cassius inched his way closer, now within arm's length of the Guardian. The Archie was devoid of his armor, which gave Cassius a modicum of hope that his plan would work after all.

Captain Gomez's commanding voice demanded Cassius to stop.

Cassius did as instructed. He was in position now, so it didn't matter either way.

Branson used the seat in front of him to hold himself up. "No, no, no! Not my Sophia! She can't be ..." he said, visibly distraught. Deep imprints formed in the seat cushion around his hands. "I won't accept that!"

Captain Gomez's eyes darted to the left in a brief attempt to measure the President's state of mind.

Cassius leapt in, blades in hand, and attacked. A shot rang out. It was too late. One of the blades connected with the polycarbon gun, screeching on impact. Gomez parried the knife to the left. Cassius swung low with his other knife. Two successive thrusts to the thigh brought Captain Gomez to one knee.

Gomez retracted his gun arm, extended it again, and fired several shots in the spot Cassius's head had just been in. Cassius moved fast, anticipating Gomez's every move. He dodged Gomez's aim, leaning in and biting the Captain's hand, causing him to release his grip on the weapon.

Gomez screamed in agony as he landed several right jabs to the man's face. He blocked two more quick knife blows, kicking Cassius's foot out from under him.

Cassius landed on his hands, flipped over, and drove his heels into Gomez's chin. The Captain went sprawling backward. Rising, he wiped the blood from his mouth and lunged forward. Cassius dodged left, then right, twisting flawlessly to come around Gomez's backside.

Gomez's liver collapsed as the first of Cassius's blades punctured the back of the man's combat overalls in through his fifth and sixth rib on his right side. Cassius drove his second blade deep into Gomez's stomach, riding the man's body to the deck before withdrawing and wiping his blades clean.

"I'll deal with you in a minute," Cassius said pointedly at John Herrington, who was hiding behind a table on the right. "Mr. President, someone has paid me a great deal to pave your way to the afterlife. We wouldn't want to disappoint."

Cassius lunged. Branson dove out of the way and regained his balance. Blocking a knife strike from up high, both Branson's and Cassius's forearms were locked in a dance of power and will. Branson sent a punch with his free hand to Cassius's face, followed with a blow to the man's solar plexus. Anticipating the latter, Cassius withdrew slightly to lessen the effects of the President's second strike.

Shit, the President is strong for an old guy — too strong, Cassius thought briefly.

Branson managed to dislodge his attacker's second knife while he was focused on avoiding the blow to his own solar plexus. With his free hand, Cassius jabbed Branson's throat. The impact from the webbing between his thumb and pointer finger caused Branson to cough suddenly. Cassius dropped the second knife to his other hand, flipped it end over end, and buried it deep into Branson's left shoulder.

Cassius was aiming for the man's heart, but Branson had shifted his position slightly, changing the impact point by several inches.

Branson crashed into the view wall behind him, shoulder first, slumped over and smiling.

This old man is enjoying this! He's seriously fucking enjoying it? It doesn't matter. He'll be done in a minute, and then I'll deal with that other old fool. No witnesses, Cassius thought.

Marious inched closer and closer to Cassius, gun in hand, careful not to move too fast for fear of being discovered. His body odor overwhelmed the stench inlaid on the carpet. He thought he almost felt the vibrations of the engine in the tips of his fingers, but he knew better. Night Wings were quiet as a whisper.

He realized it was his blood pressure he felt. His vitals were beeping rapidly in his mind's eye. His EMCD assessed every aspect of his body and relayed that data back to him. From what he gathered, if he didn't get his fear and breathing under control, he would pass out from fright.

Crouching about five paces behind Cassius, Marious stood and shakily pointed his weapon towards the man attacking the President. He closed one eye and sighted in. The gun swayed. "Freeze!" he yelled.

That's my boy, Branson thought to himself.

Cassius never took his attention off Branson. He considered his options.

"*Sir, what do I do? He's just standing there. Do I shoot?*" Marious asked Branson.

"Yes!" Branson shouted.

Cassius dove right, rolled, and dashed through the hatch leading to the hanger bay.

Marious fired once, twice, a third time, tracing Cassius's path. Each shot rang out in the small room like a sonic boom.

Not today, Branson — not today, Cassius thought, making his way towards a small, sleek twin-jet fast-mover.

"Should I go after him, sir? I've never been in a situation like this."

"No. Seal the hatch and help me up. Without the codes, he's not getting off of this bird.

The plane shuttered. The overhead fluorescent lighting changed, bathing Branson and Marious in amber. The pair perked up as the emergency klaxon blared in their heads on repeat, WARNING — WARNING — UNSCHEDULED DECOMPRESSION OF HANGER BAY IN PROGRESS.

Branson scowled, "He's blown the damn hatch. Must have used an evac pod to make his escape. Just help me up and get me to the cockpit. We need to see who's flying this bird and figure out if we can track him."

Branson tried to keep it together, but his mind continued to return to his wife. If she was on board, he'd find her. She couldn't be gone, she just couldn't. Sophia was larger than life. He needed her to be alive. As illogical as it was, he forced himself not to believe anything less. He would find his wife.

The trip from the landing platform to the hyper-train took only a few minutes. Everything had been planned out over a decade ago to include the need for economy of movement should the day arise to use this facility. That need was today.

Branson leaned back in his seat, the plush cushions conforming to his body. The hyper-train pod occupants were all looking at him. The Secretary of Defense cleared his throat, breaking the tension. "Mr. President, I think we should reconsider not moving forward with this plan. Clearly, the threat here is more serious than either you or I previously thought. I don't feel comfortable with the idea of continuing on while there is someone out there trying to end our lives. Trying to end your life, over what? We still don't know!"

Branson opened his eyes slightly and peered at the man. He mentally double-checked the time to their destination, *four hours until we reach Kourou. Good.* "John, you're on the team, right?"

"Yes sir, you shouldn't have to ask that."

"Then act like it. The plan will move ahead accordingly. If you truly understood the stakes here, you wouldn't even consider going back now."

"Sir, no one seems to truly understand the stakes here, except for you."

Marious watched the exchange with stark interest. If he was going to be by the President from now on, he supposed he'd better learn how to play the game better.

"John, there's a threat to our species, and I intend to find out what that threat is. Now, relax. We should be at the launch site soon."

CHAPTER 21

Transformation

"I'm not who I was one year ago, and maybe, just this once, change is good."

— E. GRIN

Savanna looked at Mae as she always did, warmly and intently. "Hey girl, how you feeling?"

For a moment, Mae didn't answer as she prepped the simulator for her Fire Team's turn. It had only been a day since the incident, and she was back with her team.

The medical staff was overly appreciative of Mae and Liam's actions, and as a parting gift, they managed to slip Mae some combat-rated medi-bots, which had her back to full health in a matter of hours.

Liam had pulled some strings at her behest as well. What Mae had gone through had been traumatic. However, she was training to become a Marine, and she didn't want to let a madman with a gun keep her from her from that. At least that was what she had told Liam, and to Mae's surprise, he had agreed with her.

"I'm good," Mae said, typing away on the holo-projected interface. "Never better, thanks for asking."

"Mae, you sure? You seem slightly colder than normal." Savanna said via her EMCD.

"Sorry. Just, just that I have so much on my mind. Like where was Jax during all of this? And will Liam ever truly be interested in someone like me — a recruit, I mean," Mae replied.

"Jax? Who's that? You've never mentioned him before. Is he hot? I bet he's hot, huh?" Savanna flashed her friend a sly grin and chuckled a bit.

What's with this girl? Mae thought. *"Jax is, no, was, my protector,"* she said.

"Your protector? Nice, I wish I had one of those," Savanna said.

She finalized the data input for the training scenario that her team was tagged with running.

"Yeah, my protector, or at least that's what he said. Some protector. He wasn't there when I needed him that night in the woods, and he wasn't there the other day with the gunman. If life has taught me anything, it's that I can't rely on anyone but myself."

Mae's Fire Team entered the battle pit, dropped their gear, and de-bloused, remaining in olive drab tank tops and their midnight black combat jumpsuit bottoms.

Savanna's gaze slid from Mae's tight curly red hair down to her bronzed honey shoulders. Mae turned around while placing her hair in a bun. "What? Do I have a bug on me?"

"Huh? What, no. I mean, not exactly. I thought I saw something, but it's gone now," Savanna said with a slight flush.

"Ok, great," Mae said. "Shall we begin? Garrett Beasley and Savanna Main, you two will go first. Frankie Tall and I will go next."

Taking their positions in the virtual training simulator, recruits Beasley and Main prepared themselves for an unfair fight. Several attackers were scheduled to engage the recruits at once, testing their teamwork and physical prowess.

There are multiple training zones that utilize photonic projection simulators with biofeedback looped into the Marines' and recruits' EMCDs spread throughout the base. The photonic projections, coupled with the biofeedback, made for a form of tangible simulated reality. Not nearly as visually appealing as the immersion technology in the civilian sector, which wasn't designed for the level of taxation the military would place on it, but nearly ten times more effective at giving users a realistic training experience.

"Hey guys, I'll be back in a few. Gotta use the restroom," Mae said. This drew a few stares as the majority of her fellow recruits were engaged in deeply strenuous hand-to-hand combat.

Emerging into the hallway, Mae gave the appropriate greeting of the day to several permanent staff and a few drill instructors from adjacent platoons walking about, who looked like they wanted nothing more than to rip her a new one. Looking down the hallway, Mae spotted Jamieson heading into an access corridor and decided to skip the restroom break and keep pace with him instead. She kept back 20 feet or so; it wouldn't do to let him know she was following him.

What is he up to? Mae wondered as Jamieson disappeared behind a nondescript door. She yelled, "Good afternoon, sir!" as a drill instructor came within her personal bubble and continued on his way. The drill instructors were everywhere, allowing for little breathing room.

Arriving at the door Jamieson went through, Mae paused, checked her surroundings, and then slipped inside. She trekked down the long corridor as silently as she could. Unlike the rest of the training facility, this space was narrower and felt constricting, barely three feet wide and six feet high. The air had a sour taste to it and smelled of rotten eggs.

Holding back the urge to vomit, Mae considered turning back. *The smell is giving me a headache and making my stomach turn,* she thought, *but I'm not leaving until I find out what this prick is up to.*

Mae approached an opening, which gave way to what appeared to be some kind of engineering room. The room's single occupant was Jamieson.

Jamieson Blackum leaned back in the engineer's chair, exhaling in gratification as the methylphenidate penetrated his skin and permeated each nerve ending of his central nervous system. The stimulant patch he'd just applied was one of several he'd acquired a day ago during the aftermath of the gunman's foray through the medical facility. Now, after several weeks without, Jamieson was finally able to quiet his out-of-control impulses and gain a bit of mental clarity. *God, that feels good*, he thought.

Something glinted out of the corner of his eye, causing him to turn around. A metal tube connected with Jamieson's temple before he had time to register the face set on the small frame wielding the instrument.

"Wake up!" Mae commanded, slapping Jamieson across the face. His eyes were blank in confusion as he regained consciousness.

With his mental faculties returning to him and feeling the restrictive force of his bonds, Jamieson said, "Look who it is, little Mae came to play. I guess I should be scared, huh? Beg for forgiveness. Maybe plead for mercy? Is that what you want, bitch?" Jamieson spat out the gentle trickle of blood flowing from his swollen lip.

"Quite to the contrary, Jamieson. I don't want your begging or your pleading, or even to hear your sickening voice," Mae said as she set her metal weapon down in favor of a piece of dirt cloth she'd found on the far wall's workbench.

Jamieson twisted and contorted his body in a feeble effort to free himself.

Scream, Jamieson, scream. Don't let her get away with whatever she plans on doing here, Jamieson thought to himself.

Mae was out of sight now. Turning his head around, Jamieson franticly sought to find out what she was up to. The rancid smell and taste of grease, sweat, and something else Jamieson couldn't quite make out assaulted his taste buds and olfactory receptors as Mae tied the cloth she was holding around his mouth.

The dim lighting accentuated Mae's curves. She stood in front of her captive and straddled his lap. The subtle bronze glow of her cheeks reflected in Jamieson's eyes as she spoke, "Not every form of pain is the physical kind. But what I have come to know is that pain serves multiple purposes. Thank you for that," she said calmly.

"Through pain we learn to change and survive. Pain even leads some of us down a path of retribution and retaliation. Should we cower and take the pain, horde it and allow it to consume us, or do we shape our pain to our will and use it for our ends?" Grabbing Jamieson's head by the hair and yanking it back, Mae spoke quietly in his ear, "Answer me."

Jamieson continued to struggle against his bonds.

"You know what, I'll just go ahead and tell you. Well, I've learned to use it — pain — as a person uses an appendage." For the first time, Jamieson had fear in his eyes. He could see the rage boiling under the surface of Mae's face and how much restraint she was using to keep herself in check.

Mae pulled a medium-sized blade from her combat jumpsuit and raised it to Jamieson's throat. "You sneaking into this room like this presented the perfect opportunity, you know. I considered just killing you but decided I'd have fun with you first, you know, like you did with me. You can thank my friend for that. It was her idea. If it were up to me, you'd burn! But before we begin, I'll give you the chance to tell me why, why you did what you did. I should warn you, you only get one chance. Make it count!"

"I, I wanted you," Jamieson said via his EMCD. "*The countless rejections — I had enough! You needed to be taught a lesson. I wasn't sure if I was going to go through with it. But then, you were there, in front of me. I couldn't believe my luck. I had come too far to turn back, so I gave you what you deserved. I took what should have been mine. I would have treated you right, you know, if you had only given me a chance!*"

"A chance? Luck!" Mae's words seethed out through clench teeth. "What I deserved! So, someone rejects you, and you take that as a sign to force yourself on them? To violate them!"

The heat from Mae's glare made Jamieson's blood run cold. She thought of what was growing in her belly as she took in every inch of his face, the face she'd never stop hating.

Without another moment's hesitation she stood up, removing herself from Jamieson's lap. She dropped to her knees and smiled. Rubbing his inner thighs, Mae brought the tip of her combat knife to a point right beneath his scrotum. "Enjoy!" she said.

The combat uniform took a few moments to cut through, but once Mae had broken through, she took Jamieson's manhood in her hand, feeling his girth and length. She paused for dramatic flair and smiled. Her thumb caressed the pearly penile papules, the extremely sensitive border between the head and the shaft of the penis. Jamieson tried to yell but only muffled sounds escaped.

I think I'm going to be sick, Mae confessed to herself as she brought the knife to Jamieson's now swollen manhood, allowing the serrated edge to pierce the skin of his penis and began to rip across the somatic nerve. Jamieson twitched, bucked, and screamed into his dirty gag as he tried anything to escape his sadistic captor.

Oh God, oh God ... I don't know if I can do this, Mae thought, fighting back bile as she tried to keep a serious face. She looked into Jamieson's eyes, her one-time tormentor, and steeled herself to keep going. Blood began squirting faster now as trabecular smooth muscles and helicine arteries were severed by Mae's assiduous cutting motions.

Stroke after stroke, Mae worked.

The smell was enough to cause the toughest of men to succumb to the grotesque scene playing out in the small engineering room, positioned some 50 feet off from the main corridor.

As the knife severed the last remnants of penis from Jamieson's body, Mae allowed the girthy tool to fall to the floor. It reminded her of a deflated underwater tube worm.

I need to stop his bleeding if I want him to last for what's next.

Jamieson buckled over in agony, and with a violent shudder, disgorged bits and chunks of puke into his mouth. His stomach's discharge seeped through the dirty rag still restraining his ability to speak and spilled out of its sides. Hot tears streaked down his cheeks.

Jamieson's skin was clammy, and his eyes were gaunt.

"*Please ...*" Jamieson managed to convey to Mae through their implant, "*please ... stop ... please ... have ... mercy ...*" Consciousness threatened to leave him.

"Like you did me, Jamieson!" Furious, Mae grabbed a small plasma torch from the workbench and resumed her previous position. "Don't worry, I won't let you die. No, not yet. You don't deserve that luxury." Mae put the plasma torch in front of the gaping wound above his testicles. She turned it on. Jamieson bucked and screamed into his puke-filled gag as the flames cauterized the wound she'd created when she severed his penis, terminating the flow of blood.

After filleting Jamieson's penis into a half dozen bits, Mae picked up each piece and forced them into Jamieson's semiconscious mouth. She immediately tied the rag back around his mouth, ensuring there was no way he'd be able to spit any of it out.

"Now be a good boy. Chew and swallow. You don't want to waste any," Mae said.

She held Jamieson's head up with one hand while she grabbed his scrotum, rotating his testicles between her fingers. "No one will ever be your victim again! But just in case, I will save these for a rainy day!" she said, clenching down on her new toys. She tugged hard, brought her knife to bear and severed Jamieson's testicles in two rough slices. Again, Mae stemmed the flow of blood. She had zero intentions of allowing Jamieson to die — only to suffer.

As Mae walked away from Jamieson, she could feel herself letting go of much of the hatred she had been harboring until now. She would never forget that night in the woods, but she no longer allowed it to control her, to dictate her actions. She found herself in that moment, and she was happy with who she had become.

CHAPTER 22

She's a Beauty

President Branson stepped out of the bullet pod he'd just spent the last six hours traveling in. Strengthening his neutral-toned blue suit, he surveyed his surroundings. Worry lines began to crease his eyes.

The Kourou facility was nondescript from where he was standing, but he knew better than to judge a book by its cover. The walls were the color of cork. They shimmered with that same reflective light seen on most facilities grown out of the very ground they were constructed on (or within, in this case) due to the microscopic nanotechnology used to eat the local geography and reshape it into humanity's will.

Within the Kourou facility, various flags representing each nation of the Coalition lined the corridor in honor of the President's arrival. The facilities director and several of his staff waited in attendance at the opposite end of the lengthy hall to render formal greetings to the President.

When the President approached, the lead man identified himself as the director, extended a hand, and greeted him, "Mr. President, it's a pleasure to have you here. Should I have your suite prepared for you or would you like to get right down to business? As you already know, we don't get very many visitors ... in fact, no visitors. Your orders."

The President consulted his internal timekeeper and saw it was the wee hours of the morning. *No rest for the weary,* he thought. "No, Director, please just take my staff and me directly to the hanger bay. I'd like to see the Archimedes project now. We can discuss some things along the way."

"Yes, Mr. President. As you wish."

John Herrington and Marious Lennard followed quietly, both men exhausted from the morning activities. Marious's senses were still on end from having fired a gun for the first time. Somewhere in the back of his mind, he worried the guy he'd almost shot would come back and finish the job.

Branson stood in a vast man-made cave, the largest ever built. The cavern was over 4,500 feet in length, 1,000 feet wide, and another 1,000 feet in height. The Aurora-2 stood in the middle, a vessel which was larger, faster and stronger than its predecessor. This ship was the brainchild of his forethought and imagination made real.

"She's a beauty!" Branson said, almost singing the words. His eyes were transfixed on the mammoth 1,900-foot space combat vessel before him. It was the length of five and a half football fields and stood equally impressive. Similar in shape to a long — almost rectangular — crystal, with multiple armor platings jutting out at various angles.

The bow of the ship resembled a snout, with dozens of different weapon systems protruding from it, many of which Branson had no idea what they did. The other weapon systems were hidden along the ship's hull. Its aft section gave way to the ship's propulsion systems, which took on a honeycomb pattern.

The Archimedes project, another first of its kind, was designed as a military space program with aims to protect the Coalition from outside threats.

Branson never thought those threats would be nonhuman. The Aurora-2, along with several ships of various classes, from destroyers to heavy cruisers, were constructed and designed with the intent to unite and form one singular ship known as the Interstellar-1.

The anticipation in the air was heavy for the crew of the Aurora-2. The majority tried to go about their duties just as they'd always done, continuing to prepare the ship for its maiden test flight. Techs bustled back and forth, hurriedly making their way through the spacious ship, testing one system after another. Staff members reviewed hundreds of performance reports while the command staff ran dozens of simulations, both routine and battle-related, something President Branson insisted on.

The President's arrival aboard the Aurora-2 had been something of a surprise. The command deck was taken aback when the arrival of the President, his staff, and several guardians was announced.

"Ma'am, the sentries guarding the main boarding hatch on the starboard side just relayed to tactical that the President is boarding the ship!" Commander Zane Ode, the ship's executive officer, XO for short, said to Alessandra Daa`e, the ship's captain.

Hot coffee spewed a few feet across the bridge from Captain Daa`es' mouth as she mentally replied, *"Commander, are you kidding me!"* Several officers manning their stations turned around to see what was going on, looking at their captain in bewilderment. Each one of the bridge crew, in turn, quickly returned to their duties when they noticed the captain was sternly glaring at the XO in what they took to be an intense mental conversation.

Regaining her composure, Captain Daa`e continued, *"Now is not the time for games. We're expecting our new admiral, not the President! And for that matter, if that is, in fact, the President who just boarded our ship, why weren't we informed ahead of time?"*

"Never mind that. Follow me. We should get down there and greet the President."

Few people within the Coalition were unaware of Branson's accomplishments. His reputation preceded him as he was all but credited with bringing the Coalition together. Branson was widely revered, and that reverence shone on each crew member who passed him while he and his entourage made their way to the bridge.

"Captain, what a pleasure," Branson said, extending a hand as he and Captain Daa`e's paths met in the wide, brightly lit corridor. Daa`e, a career Naval officer, was accustomed to and prided herself on being in complete control, something the President managed to throw into disarray within a few minutes of his arrival.

"Mr. President," Captain Daa`e said, taking the offered hand, "welcome aboard the Aurora-2. Your presence here was ... is something of a surprise. What can we do for you?"

Daa`e looked at the President, taking him in appraisingly before stopping at his eyes. *Those eyes, so much sadness rests in those eyes,* she thought. *The man radiates an air of calm confidence belied by his slightly disheveled clothing and besieged eyes. Something's — wrong.*

Looking at the Captain and then the XO in turn, President Branson turned his attention back towards Daa`e. "Captain, I know you were expecting Admiral Bahati. However, he will not be coming. Come, let's talk."

"Yes, sir, would my ready room be sufficient, or would you like more formal settings for your staff to sit in as well?

"Your ready room will do," Branson said before facing the SecDef and his aide, shadowed by the guardian cadre of

Marines in TALOS Mk8 armor. "Gentlemen, why don't you all head off with the XO here while Captain Daa`e and I talk. We'll catch up shortly."

Branson turned back towards Daa`e. "I'm afraid you'll have to lead the way. I may have commissioned these ships. but I am not 100% familiar with the ships layout … yet."

The meeting between Captain Daa`e and President Branson didn't take long. He found he rather liked the captain as he saw a bit of himself in her with her professionalism and keen intelligence, but it was her love of space that touch him. His wife loved the cold blackness of space more than anyone he'd known, and now he wasn't sure if he would ever see her again.

The thought of his wife caused a tear to liberate itself from its duct.

Daa`e had assumed something was wrong, although Branson had assured her it was his allergies. Any self-respecting ship's captain, or junior crewman for that matter, knew the ship atmospherics kept pollen and other irritants out of the air they breathed. Captain Daa`e decided to go with it for good measure. She was sure the President had his reasons for lying to her. She just wasn't sure what they were yet.

The bridge buzzed with activity.

"The crews of the cruisers and destroyers are being shuttled in now, sir. We should be able to lift within the hour," Daa`e said.

"Good. Make the preparations and let me know once we are ready to leave atmo and transit SOL."

Turning to his Defense Secretary, Branson asked, "Any news on Sherman? The General should have been here by now."

"General Sherman is 45 minutes out, sir."

Damn that man, Branson thought. He's cutting it close. "Ok John. Thank you. I have a job for you."

John focused intently on the President's words. His body language revealed nothing more than a confident yet wary man. *The President looks ragged. I supposed I would too if I had just lost my wife to a brutal assassin. Well, we don't know for sure what her status is, but what reason would the killer have to keep her alive?* "What is it, sir? What do you need of me?"

President Branson sent John Herrington a pre-recorded compressed virtual message, similar in nature to the old voicemails. In the message, Branson laid out his plan and John's role to play.

It took the SecDef a matter of moments to download the message and assimilate the information. Virtual messages weren't the preferred method of passing information back and forth as they weren't designed to hold a large amount of information, and they removed the ability for instantaneous feedback, save for various instances such as this current moment.

Branson led men and women on missions in some of the most hostile environments known to man, battled politicians and corporations in the political arena, and now he found himself seated on the bridge of the most advanced combat spaceship built by man, to head out into God only knows what.

The President felt slightly out of place aboard the command deck of the Aurora-2. He had been a ground-pounder during his military days, spending the majority of that time as a Recon Marine — he enjoyed his fights up close and personal. So, he always found being on a ship a bit odd and restricting.

The command chair Branson sat in had manifested itself directly out of the deck of the ship, as did all of the furniture within the ships that made up the Interstellar-1. As Branson shifted from one side to the other, the nanites within his seat measured several variables and further adjusted to fully conform to his body. He ran his fingers through his close-cropped sandy brown hair and strained under the weight of heavy thoughts. *Sophia's gone. My beautiful Sophia, the woman who'd always propped me up when life had beat me down, when all I wanted to do was fall, who gave me counsel, and never faltered in her love of me.*

He let out a sigh under his breath. *Loving me isn't easy at times, I know that, and Sophia knew that. And now ... and now, I don't know if I'll ever have the chance to tell her how much I love and value her again.*

Branson's left eye glinted with tears in the overly bright command suit. *I want to yell, holler, and break something! But I can't. Thousands of men and women on these ships are counting on me. Duty has stripped away my right to feel anything. Damn, does it piss me off! As much as it pains me to say this, I'm not ready to push my duties aside, because if I do, who would carry out this mission?* he thought. After several moments of mental silence, Branson steeled himself against a single thought. *Sophia would want me to finish this.*

Branson's soul felt weighted down with an inordinate amount of responsibility to the human species and to their daunting mission. In this moment, he decided to do what he'd always done in the face of adversity, to meet it head-on and overcome ... somehow.

"The eye of the storm is ten minutes away from completely encompassing this facility, Captain," the Major at Tactical Command announced.

Captain Daa`e studied the readouts at her command station. "XO, what is the status of the ships in the Task Force?" Daa`e could have accessed that information with ease, but her attention was better suited to focus on more important matters. It was the XO's job to manage and coordinate all of the staff within the Aurora-2, and ultimately the Interstellar-1 once each ship was attached to, and became a part of, the Aurora.

"Ma'am, all ships and departments report back green status. The Interstellar is ready for liftoff. Optimal window for acceleration out of earth's atmo is 4 minutes 15 seconds."

"Good, thank you, XO," Captain Daa`e replied. Swiftly turning in her command chair, Daa`e faced Branson and asked, "Sir, would you like to give the command?"

"Thank you, Captain," Branson said, loud enough for the entire bridge to hear. "I'm appreciative of the gesture. The honor is mine. However, since this is the maiden liftoff for the new Coalition fleet, I think the honor should be my flagship's captain. Give the order. My time will come."

Branson appreciated the gesture Daa`e just offered him. The command to launch was reserved for the commander of the flagship. However, he'd thrown a wrench in that system with his arrival aboard the ship. By nature of his title and position as the President of the Coalition, he was now the highest-ranking person aboard any of his ships.

Daa`e nodded in approval and swiveled her seat to face the front again. Wanting to confirm her calculations, Daa`e asked, "Helm, once we take off, how long until we reach the heliopause?"

Lieutenant Richardson replied immediately, "Ma'am, it'll take eight days to traverse the Sol System and reach the heliopause, but ma'am, with the stop-off at Titan you requested, we estimate a total of almost nine days."

Ensign Smith called out, "Captain, the eye of the storm is now directly over the facility we're in. We'll lose our window of opportunity to launch and leave atmo undetected within ten minutes if we do not leave now."

Daa`e's response was swift. "Do it," she said, hands working various visible and nonvisible holo-displays arrayed around her command chair. The holo-screens which displayed some of the more sensitive data was visible only to her through her EMCD implant.

The roaring of the ship's engines seemed to have been a direct manifestation of the anger, despair, and sorrow President Branson felt at the loss of his wife. He maintained an outward appearance of strength because he needed to.

Deep within me, he thought, *down in the depths of my emotional well, a dangerous storm is brewing. Fight as I might to keep it all at bay, I fear one of these days it may get the better of me. I have a duty to my people, which is what matters now. Lock the rest away, Jimmy. How can I set the example for everyone if they see me moping around like a four-year-old abandoned child? Regardless of my own personal turmoil, I must see this through.*

A ship the size of a grain of sand arose from the eye of the Category 4 hurricane, which was now localized over French Guiana, a semi-desolate wasteland save for the industries that built there after the war. The hurricane arms extended for 100 miles in all directions, obscuring the launch of the Interstellar-1.

John Herrington mentally kissed the ground he stood on. He was grateful he wasn't in the Interstellar-1 right now. After he had opened the compressed virtual message President Branson had given him, he learned that his mission was never to head out of Sol with the rest of them, but instead to learn and understand the full extent of the President's plan and then relay that to the Vice President once he returned from Venus. Modern civilizations thrived on order, something that would be desperately needed in the President's absence, although order was nothing without willing and able-bodied men and women capable of enforcing it.

"There is no one more suited to ensuring order is maintained throughout the colonies than me. It's no wonder Branson woke me in the middle of the night and dragged me south of the equator. He needed me to see the stakes. Well, Mr. President, I have, and based on what you've told me, I'll play ball. If not for you, then for my six-year-old daughter. I cannot imagine her being taken by one of those beings," the SecDef said, murmuring to himself.

The SecDef's moment of reflection passed fleetingly. He focused inwardly and instructed his avatar to compose a message to be given to the Vice President the moment his electronic signature was detected entering Earth's atmo. John was careful to remember to add that the official story they were going to release to the press would be that Branson's on a tour of the outermost colonies. The citizens would be fed the narrative they wanted them to know. After all, the election crested the horizon, and Branson wanted to secure himself another 20-year term.

CHAPTER 23

Stolen Treasures

Adam spread his wings, caught the wind, and sailed. Unneeded at the moment, and without much thought, his two lesser wings relaxed, folding back behind him.

Descending from the sky at a steady pace, Adam whirled his long massive frame around a few passersby before coming to rest on the central landing platform for this work section.

Mara, Adams' assistant, stood on the platform several feet back from where he'd landed. Mara stepped closer as she spoke, "My Lord, all continues as planned. The troops are ready for the next incursion into the human realm."

The dark energy comprising Adam's wings dispersed into the ether. As Adam walked, he folded the four meaty protrusions on his back that focused the energy to form his wings behind him as the dark energy faded.

"Mara, tell me how successful the last mission was?"

"Very successful, my Lord. We retrieved several hundred prime candidates. I believe the Council will be pleased with our stats. The Reapers have been standing by for another incursion, my Lord; I must add that they are anxious. I think they get some kind of rush out of traversing the veil and eliciting fear from the humans of Mantheia."

Adam thought about the current state of affairs. "The Chancellor, not the Council."

Mara paused near her console. "Sorry, my Lord, what was that?"

Adam, taking no offense at Mara's lack of focus on his words, replied, "The Chancellor would be pleased, Mara, not the Council. He gave us our orders. I cannot say with certainty the Council knows what we are doing here."

Maintaining her composure, Mara said, "My Lord, I do not think the chancellor would act without the authority of the Council. To consider such is — blasphemy — my Lord. You should mind your thoughts." After pulling up the appropriate screens and commands, Mara turned to face Adam, her semi-featureless face level with his. "I've generated another veil opening. The dispersion pattern is inputted and the command to execute is ready to be given, my Lord. Your authorization is all that is needed."

Let's hope you're right, Mara, Adam thought to himself, scanning the data displayed in front of him before finally giving the command, "Execute!"

The pair looked down from their perch at the command deck as they watched the activity below. With steady beats of shimmering purple wings, nearly 200 Voltari lifted themselves off of the ground.

Their wings shone in stark contrast to the charcoal-gray skin of their bodies as one by one, the Voltari, also known as Reapers, anxiously crossed the veil to descend upon an unsuspecting human race.

◆ ◆ ◆

The engineering room's light gave off a soft incandescent glow. Each photon of light was momentarily frozen in time as a wake of temporal chronitons and tachyons blasted outward a dozen feet in all directions. Those exotic particles emanated from a point in space now occupied by a newly formed portal from which several Reapers spilled out. Dark beings, responsible for countless disappearances, set loose upon humanity to continue their abductions unabated.

Gorgon, Paragon commander for this flight of Reapers, spread his talons, allowing each corresponding appendage the opportunity to take in the artificial metallic feel of his new surroundings. His well-hidden nasal cavity was assaulted by the acidic air. Each successful visit to this realm brought Gorgon closer and closer to revulsion. But he'd continue his trips through the veil due to the abilities the veil afforded the Reapers.

I will never get used to this, having the ability to create small zones of frozen time. These humans, Gorgon slowly thought — with great disdain, *are defenseless against such a weapon. They are rather pathetic creatures. The inability of their feeble minds to comprehend the sight of my kind, it's almost laughable. They cower in fear when they see us — something I've never seen in Aletheia. We'll use that fear to aid in obtaining our goals,* Gorgon thought to himself.

The main hallway lay just ahead. As Mae walked, she allowed herself to continue contemplating what she had just done when she noticed a soft blue glow perforating the edges of her vision. She turned around to look for the source of this new light.

My God! Mae thought. *What are those things! Where the hell did they come from?* She ducked behind some tubing and attempted to remain as still as possible. Several creatures occupied the spot she'd been not moments before. Their dark gray bodies held no form in particular yet looked to be fairly solid. Their oval-shaped heads rendered no indication of eyes or ears, only a very large mouth filled with several rows of jagged teeth.

"Savanna, Savanna, come in. Are you there?" Mae's attempt to contact her friend resulted in failure. *Damnit. Those things must be using some sort of jamming field. I have to get out of here somehow before they spot me. I need to warn the others.* Mae began to move when she suddenly stopped in her tracks.

The faceless creatures that had stepped through the portal had hovered in the area, at first seemingly taking it all in before closing in on Jamieson. What was even stranger was that the immediate area surrounding those wraith-like creatures rippled with waves that threatened to reflect all of the light around it. Jamieson's stiff body was lifted by one of the creatures with relative ease and was taken towards the portal. The last thing Mae saw of Jamieson was his eyes locking onto hers. A plea for help emanating from his eyes before being snuffed out as his body crossed the portal's event horizon.

I don't know what I just saw, but whatever these beings, these wraith-like creatures are doing — it can't be good. Mae stumbled to her feet, catching the attention of one of the wraiths, and began to run as fast as her non-augmented legs could carry her.

Savanna caught the roundhouse kick directed at her head, rotated her feet and hips, allowing her momentum to carry her body around before letting go of the Federation spec ops soldier, sending him crashing to the mat. *Simulated soldiers are too easy,* she thought. She widened her stance, loosened her shoulders, and watched the soldier's body language to anticipate the next strike.

Savanna's vision blurred for a moment. She fought vertigo as a very weak tachyon pulse hit her. As fast as the sensation came, it was gone.

Realization sunk in faster than she could think. *Reapers!*

Where's Mae! She looked around. *Shit!* She exclaimed as she stood, dodged her simulated opponent's attack with a speed the other recruits had never seen and blurred into motion towards the hatch leading to the main hallway.

"Savanna, you alright?" Tall called after her with hands cupped around his mouth. Savanna maintained a singular focus, ignoring all attempts to communicate with her.

Save Mae!

She was gone before any of the Drill Instructors noticed she had moved.

Less than five feet from the hatch that promised salvation, Mae's body began to cramp up as she became enveloped by the strange faint blue light that preceded the wraiths. She screamed as her body betrayed her, refusing to move. Each movement was harder than the last. The sounds escaping her were whittled down from a high-pitched scream to an imperceptible whisper before her immobile body was picked up and carried towards the portal.

Mae thought of her dad and wished he was here to protect her. Her mind drifted towards the strange guy who kept trying to help her, Jax. Where was he now? Where was he when she needed him? Of all of the people in the world, Mae's thoughts always brought her back to her mother and her strength. *She wouldn't have gotten caught,* Mae thought.

One by one, the wraiths returned back through their portal. Mae's stiff body began traversing the portal's event horizon when the hatch she was trying to get to was blown inward. As her mind and body traversed realms, the last image Mae saw was of Jax lunging through the open hatch towards her and her captors — late again.

CHAPTER 24

Eskimo

Winds buffeted Titan's upper atmospheric layer, whipping around the planet at 250 miles per hour while orbiting Saturn at a distance of 760,000 miles. The inhabitants of Titan, predominately military, continued with their daily routines — training, studying, researching, terraforming, and exploring — oblivious to their coming visitors.

The tranquil and picturesque scene of Saturn's yoke-colored moon, Titan, was disturbed by the sudden appearance of several Coalition warships; their Alcubierre drives ceased the folding of space, transitioning them back into normal space. The battleship Aurora was the first to appear, followed closely by the two heavy cruisers, Trinidad and Tollbooth.

The light cruisers, San Antonio and Conception, along with the two destroyers, Victoria and Santiago, appeared a fraction of a second later.

◆ ◆ ◆

Captain Daa`e thought-clicked the appropriate screen and

released the command code needed to send a message, tight beamed and directionally aimed at a single location on the planet's surface, the Command and Control node for CMB Starfire.

"Sir," Captain Daa`e said, "the connection is established and ready for your broadcast."

Branson attempted to straighten in his seat a bit more. Even if he didn't feel 100% up to it, he would fake it until he made it. "Thank you, Captain," he said, giving his own command, sending their consciousness spiraling into a generously spacious office adorned with local fauna and strange-looking geological formations. Branson and Daa`e were now standing in front of the chiseled chin of a man, an air of seriousness radiating from him.

"Colonel Arcain," Branson said as he took up a seated position at the only desk within the space, "we are pressed for time so I will get right down to it."

Colonel Arcain stood rigidly — in a cool military sort of way, eyes transfixed on the virtual presence of the President of the Coalition, the man that ended the war and brought about a new era of peace and cooperation for the human race.

Arcain's mouth moved slightly ... slowly ... wordlessly. It was only after Captain Daa`e lightly tapped him on the elbow that he realized he wasn't speaking. "Sir, I ah ... was not expecting you. Is there something I can do for you?" he asked.

"Yes, there is a theoretical physicist specializing in exotic particles on this moon, and from what I was told, he is on this specific base. The man is the premier expert on Alcubierre drives, and more importantly, our experimental hyperspace drive systems. I'm heading out of the system for a bit to begin the campaign tour. It's that time, and I want to make this tour go by rather quickly. For that I've decided to incorporate the new hyperspace drives into my fleet. So, I'll need Dr. Castor Grosbeak to accompany us to ensure nothing out of the ordinary happens while using those drives."

Colonel Arcain risked a fleeting glance at the captain accompanying the President. Daa`e's face was impassive and revealed little. *All of this seems too strange. Why would the President visit me, via direct mental link of all things, just to ask for some scientist? I'm sure there's more to this that I'm missing,* Salvador thought to himself.

"Yes sir, Mr. President. I will get the transfer paperwork started. When would you like him to report to your ship?"

"Now," replied the President.

"Ah — yes, yes, sir. Of course. Is there anything else I can assist you with, sir?"

Captain Daa`e remained impassive, no doubt wondering why she'd been brought along on this call.

Branson sniffed the virtual brandy present on the corner of Colonel Arcain's desk before replying, "Yes. General Sherman will be in touch with you shortly to facilitate the transfer of some of your Marines to my ships." He set the brandy down.

"Sir, I'm afraid I don't understand."

"Colonel, you do not have to understand. I require troops during my campaign tour, and your facility is best suited to provide them."

The air felt a few degrees colder than before. Perhaps it was his imagination — after all, they were in a virtual environment. Carefully considering his next words, Arcain continued, "But sir, you are the President, the man who pieced together much of the world's nation-states and ended that damned horrific war. Why would you, of all people, require Coalition Marines to protect you — if you do not mind my asking? Coalition Marines aren't trained for light forays. The firepower they pack is enough to level city blocks — depending on how many you have, possibly even a small megacity or larger."

The President mentally sighed. *Why is it that senior officers always feel the need to question orders when they're in a closed-door setting? That attribute has its benefits; however, at a time like this, I'd prefer if it wasn't present. Get a grip, Johnny, we haven't even begun most of our journey, and you're already agitated.* Branson ended his internal thoughts and self-pep-talk and consulted his internal clock. He thought of Sophia and how she'd want him to remain strong and said, "Listen, Colonel, I'd love to continue to entertain your questions, but to be frank, I currently do not have the time nor the inclination. So, begin the paperwork for the troop transfer and ensure you give General Sherman your full support."

Colonel Arcain remained in place, his service uniform's adaptive nanostructure, programmed to match the surrounding environment of the orange moon-haze with flecks of moss green and orchid blue, randomly intermixed, forming and reforming patterns. His military bearing was never one to be called into question, which is why the Corps decided to give him this premier posting as the Commander for Recruit Training. In a crisp tone underlain with a bit of subservience, Colonel Arcain said, "Understood, sir. Apologies for the inquisition. I'll see to the transfer right away. I must add, sir, that an unscheduled transfer of this nature must be logged with Coalition Training Command. If there are no objections from you, that log might encounter some ... digital degradation. Sir."

Captain Daa`e narrowed her eyes at Colonel Arcain. *Did that Marine officer just blatantly admit to the President he lacked integrity? No wonder he's stationed out here, so far away from Earth. Shameful. The Coalition's Space Force would never allow such men in its ranks.*

Now he's getting it, Branson thought. *Sometimes, rule bending can be a necessity, maybe even the most viable option for successful mission completion.* "Colonel Arcain, your cooperation in this matter is noted," Branson said as he stood and shook the man's hand before ending the virtual meeting.

Back on the bridge of the Aurora, Daa`e's jawline was rigid, a sign of her disapproval of what just transpired. Her eyebrow ridges furrowed in distaste.

Her expression clearly shows she doesn't approve of my methods, Branson thought, *or maybe it's politics all together*

Daa`e dislikes? 'Why not tell the man the truth?' she probably wondered.

Branson made eye contact with Daa`e. She quickly turned away towards her display, flushing slightly for giving the President such a scolding look.

Marious sat in his seat, observing the curious exchange of body language between the two as he'd been instructed to a day earlier. He shook his head inwardly and returned to the data feed streaming across his holo-displays.

The bridge doors slid open, allowing General Sherman entry as the man strolled down the gantry towards the command alcove. A cluster of holo-screens floated in the alcove's immediate vicinity, displaying everything from star charts to atmospherics within the ship, and framed the trio of seats nestled there.

"General, please take a seat. We were just discussing the upcoming flight. How are our troops?" Branson asked.

Captain Daa`e was intuitively aware of the General's presence the moment he approached the bridge. The ship's Tactical Officer had given her a link where she could monitor any camera feed she desired within the ship without having to constantly ask — Captain's prerogative. The particular feed she was just watching in her mind was from the camera positioned outside of the bridge, which had just recorded the General's approach. Daa`e never believed in not being aware of one's surroundings.

"Mr. President," Sherman began, taking a seat in the newly formed chair that arose out of the deck as he spoke. "The troops are adjusting alright. When we got them, they were just about to graduate boot camp. Their training will not be complete until they complete the Marine Combat Training Course and then, for some, go through the recently formed Space Warfare School."

"Well, if my hunches are correct, we might solve that problem."

"I'm sorry, sir?"

"The combat issue, General. My gut tells me our cadre of Marines held up below decks won't need to attend the Marine Combat Training Course. They may very well receive all the combat training they'll ever need when we get to where we're going."

"And where is that, sir?"

Captain Daa`e swiped a floating display screen over to Sherman as she spoke. "Here, General. We are going right here," she said, pointing to a spot within the display screen with her mind. "The Eskimo Nebula."

"Sir," Sherman began before looking to his side and thanking Daa`e, "I read the mission briefing you sent over. What do you expect we'll find over there?"

The Helmsman, Lieutenant Richardson, broke their concentration with her update to the command staff and the bridge crew. "Approaching Sol's heliopause now. Orders, ma'am?"

Captain Daa`e smiled slightly. "Sir, would you like the honors?"

Branson surveyed the crew. Tension was high with anticipation. No one knew what they were doing outside of the command crew. Regardless of the task, each crew member was ready to execute their jobs. Branson said with a smile, "Thank you, Captain."

He entered a series of mental commands, and the ship's communication node began broadcasting both in head and overhead. "All hands, this is the President. For purposes unbeknownst to you, I've kept the mission parameters a secret. I've heard the scuttlebutt, all of the unofficial rumors swirling around the ships about what we are actually doing out here, and I will tell you, if there's nothing else I've missed from my time in the military, it's the scuttlebutt." Tensions died down a bit as light laughter sounded around the Task Force's ships.

"Several days ago, I learned of a potentially grave threat to the human species, and we are here to confront that potential threat. There is an alien race out there that is sending signals to Earth and her surrounding colony worlds. Many of the disappearances we've recorded over the years that have fallen into the category of unexplainable and for many became cold case files are actually linked to these alien signals."

Low murmurs began spreading amongst the crew, exponentially picking up volume and intensity.

Ignoring the affable growing chorus, Branson continued, "In light of the evidence I've presented to you, I've decided to activate the Archimedes Project, which are the very ships you stand in now. Originally intended as a secret military fleet to defend the Coalition from threats, these ships now stand as the only vessels which will present humankind with the answers to some of our greatest mysteries."

"We will meet these beings and attempt to engage in peaceful negotiations. We still do not know if they are friend or foe, and because of that, we will not fire unless fired upon. We are not going there to wage war but to gather as much information as possible, and if feasible, open peaceful diplomatic talks. I have faith in each and every one of you. Now let's find out what's been happening to our people. Branson out."

"Captain Daa`e, signal the other ships to initiate convergence. We'll need to make the transition as the Interstellar-1."

"Aye, sir," Daa`e replied as she began to send the appropriate messages and codes for the ships to come together as one. "Sir, I didn't see anything relating to the Interstellar-1's unusual design anywhere in the mission briefing," Daa`e said, as nonchalantly as possibly, probing for answers she didn't have. As she was the ship's captain, she should have been aware of every detail surrounding her ships. She was knowledgeable and well-informed when it came to the Aurora, her ship, her baby, but the Interstellar-1 was another thing entirely.

Branson slid his command chair closer to Captain Daa`e's. An action that was unnecessary, but Branson always found it comforting to speak to someone face to face. He said mentally, *"Captain, there is a file in your mental queue titled Specs.*

Please read at your leisure. You should have had that file sent to you prior to lift-off. I'll give you the short of it. Dr. Grosbeak theorized that the hyperspace drives will not only move us at incredible speeds through the substrate of normal space but that the movement will generate a large buildup of exotic particles directly ahead of the ships. Now, we could negate the effects by making small short jaunts through hyperspace, but that method would take us far too long to reach our destination."

"What about just using the Alcubierre drives, sir? They are highly effective and have worked for us thus far. I'm not entirely sure I understand the need to use experimental drives, especially ones that, like a lot in this Task Force, haven't been tested out before."

"Those drives would work, but they would take even longer than the small jaunts through hyperspace would take to get to our destination using the hyperspace drives. If we want to get to where we are going and back in any reasonable amount of time, we need the hyperspace drives. And if we want to defeat that buildup of exotic particles so we can stay in hyperspace longer without having to frequently stop, we need the Interstellar-1. When the ships come together, they create a singular mass, a conglomerate of interstellar warships designed to withstand the stresses placed on them by the buildup of exotic particles while traveling through hyperspace."

"Can you elaborate, sir?"

"Yes, somewhat. The Interstellar-1 creates a kind of bow shockwave, which acts as a deflector bubble. That is all I have. The science of how that all works is a little beyond me, Captain. If you want a more in-depth answer, I am sure Dr. Grosbeak would be beyond happy to give you a crash course in interstellar quantum physics along with the exciting world of quarks, gluons, excitons, and the like. I hear the study of exotic particles is a riveting topic."

Captain Daa`e's cheeks flushed, and she couldn't help but chuckle a bit. "Sir, I'll pass," she said aloud. "Thank you for that bit of information. I think I now know all I need to," Daa`e said reassuringly to Branson.

"Good. Helm, the ships are formed for maneuver. You may

engage the hyperspace drives. Destination: the Eskimo Nebula."

CHAPTER 25

Breakthroughs

The Interstellar-1 plowed through a majestic cloudy haze of various colors and intensities, stretched across either side of the ship, forming two walls. Scarlet red streaks infused with magenta, violet, and cyan blue passed on one side. Lemon yellow clouds suffused with a brownish-orange and turquoise color speed past on the other.

The silence on the bridge was so intense, it wrapped each crewman in the tightest of embraces, leaving only their jaws slack in their positioning and movement.

"It's beautiful!" one crewman noted.

"What do we call it?" another whispered.

"Should I be scanning this, Captain?" the XO asked.

"Yes!" Daa`e said in a long-exasperated reply.

Branson allowed himself this one moment of respite from the pressures of the last few days. A small glint of salty liquid slipped from his right eye. *Sophia, my love, if you were here to witness this, you would be on cloud nine, grinning from ear to ear. Hyperspace is everything we thought it would be and more. I'm not sure what to call this substance that we're flying through, but whatever it is, it's breathtaking!*

After storing the last few moments in his personal in-head enhanced storage, Branson spoke up, "Captain, see to it that each ship is ready for emergence from hyperspace in ..." consulting the data displayed in-head, he continued, "... five days.

"Sir!" Daa`e exclaimed. "That's, that's not right. It can't be. What you're saying is, I think, impossible! At our best speed, with the folding of space using the Alcubierre drives, it would have taken us almost two months to reach the Eskimo Nebula — which is 5,000 light-years away. What kind of tech do these new drives ... these ... these Grosbeak drives have? Is their tech that much more superior than the Alcubierre drives, or is it the fact that we are traveling through a substrate of normal space — hyperspace?"

"Ma'am, I think you just came up with a great name for the new, and apparently magical, drives we're using," Commander Zane Ode said, eliciting chuckles from General Sherman and the rest of the bridge crew.

Branson ran his fingers through his neatly cut brown hair. "Captain, as I told you, Dr. Grosbeak is something of a quantum physics genius. I found him buried under a rock, literally buried under a rock — well, more like living in a cave in the Balkans. Either way, the man had been laughed out of academia for some of his more radical ideas, to say the least.

So, when my avatar came across his resumé, I couldn't pass up the chance. I commissioned him to build our new star drives, or what did you call them ... Grosbeak drives ... not really sure if he would succeed or not. However, I wanted every conceivable advantage over our adversaries. I understand we are at peace, but it would have been foolish to wholeheartedly believe no one is out there with designs on our society. Either way, outside of Dr. Grosbeak and the team he employed to get the job done, the tech involved is widely unknown."

The rest of the bridge crew shook off the overwhelming feeling of awe they felt and returned to work.

Dr. Castor Grosbeak internally measured every step he took, ensuring exactly 26-inch intervals between each footstep. His thumb and forefinger tapped against each other every time his heal struck the deck. On most days, he was able to overcome the urge to correct everything, to fix it all and to have everything just right. His perfectionism always screaming at him, clawing and fighting to gain control. Other days he caved to his demons and did just enough to quench their thirst. Counting steps and ensuring their exact interval measurement was one of a hundred ways he maintained his sanity.

Grosbeak came to a stop outside of the enlisted Marine berthing area. His presence caused the hatch to slide open. He stood there, breathing heavily several times in an attempt to calm his nerves. He closed his eyes and quickly tapped his thumb to the tips of each finger over and over and over again before finally stepping across the entryway.

"Ah, Gunnery Sergeant. Hello," Grosbeak said, in as much of a conversational tone as he could muster, speaking loud enough for the Marine to hear him.

Gunny Jones turned around, vaguely confused for a fraction of a moment. Consulting the ship's neural net, he ran through the stats associated with the stout man coming towards him, waving to him as though they knew each other.

"Dr. Grosbeak," Jones said in a husky voice, "what can I do for you?" He removed his hands from the tactile interface that required his DNA code to activate, pausing the diagnostic he was running on his TALOS Mk7 suit.

Grosbeak flashed a crooked smile. "Gunny, I was hoping you or one of your Marines could, uh, assist me with something."

With a raised eyebrow, Gunny Jones eyed the man. "What kind of assistance can my Marines or I provide?"

"I'm in need of your unique talents ... and armor. I need a

TALOS suit and someone who can operate it."

"For what!" Gunny Jones said with more emphasis than he'd intended.

"Gunny, I'm working on something which will take your God complex to the next level. I understand you Marines like to believe you are invincible or something. Akin to Zeus himself, I hear."

Jones stood still for a moment, clearly assessing the short man along with what he'd just said. He eyed the man skeptically. The offer was enticing. *The TALOS already provide us with near invincibility to most weapons, along with the ability to fire plasma from our hands like Zeus and his lightning bolts. Invisibility is standard, and our suits' enhanced speed and strength are unmatched throughout the Coalition. Heck, some of our armor can even fly, like the TALOS Aegis with the Valkyrie add-ons. What more could this man do to enhance those capabilities?* Jones thought.

"Tell you what, Doc ..." Jones began.

"That's uh, Doctor, Gunny. Just Doctor."

Jones furrowed his brows as he continued, "Yeah, sure. Tell you what, Doctor. I will volunteer to help you, provided you can convince me why I should."

That's doable. Easily so! Dr. Grosbeak considered.

"Do you have a weapon on you? Any type will do."

Jones scoffed. *Questioning if a Marine had a weapon on him was like asking a person if they breathed, if their heart beats, or even if their mind produces thought. Of course, I have weapons on me.*

The black obsidian blade Gunny Jones now wielded seemed to materialize out of thin air. He lifted the large combat knife, flipping it several times in his hand before saying, "You mean like this, Doctor?"

"Yes, yes ... that'll do. May I see it?" Grosbeak said with an outstretched hand.

Gunny Jones narrowed his eyes at the squat man. "Sure, what would it hurt. Here."

Grosbeak handled the weapon in an awkward fashion.

I'm on a secret class of warships heading to an unknown destination on drive systems that seem to defy the laws of the physical universe, Jones thought to himself. *And now I'm handing over my combat blade to a goddamn civi. Shit ... I've seen it all. Strange times these are.*

Jones's train of thought was swiftly cut off. He watched, bewildered, not quite believing his eyes. As soon as he'd handed the knife to the doctor, the man slapped a patch of nano onto it and thrust it straight into his chest. Only the doctor's hand, which was wrapped around the knife's hilt, was visible and resting against Jones's chest.

Frozen in disbelief, Gunny Jones forced several words out of his mouth slowly and tainted with astonishment, "What in the ... how am I not dead ..."

The doctor didn't respond. Instead, four seconds later, he withdrew the knife, all but invisible save for the hilt and knuckle bow, and held it up. Placing a finger to his mouth, he said, "Shh. Give it a second."

"Ah, there we are," Grosbeak murmured aloud as the knife blade rematerialized before the Gunny's eyes.

"How in the ... how ... just how. That is — impossible."

"I take it I have your attention now, Gunny? Was that convincing enough?"

"Shit, Doc. I mean, Doctor. When do I start?"

Gunny Jones whistled as he ran his fingers across various surfaces. "I don't know what half of this stuff is, but it sure looks important." Jones picked up several items of interest and placed them back down in different spots as he walked around Grosbeak's lab.

Dr. Grosbeak closed his eyes and began counting to twenty, slowly exhaling with each count. The rhythmic tapping of his forefinger and thumb was barely audible as it kept pace with each breath he drew and exhaled.

"What's wrong with you, Doc?" Jones said, leaning in close to a containment field of some kind. From the best Jones could tell, it looked as if a whole galaxy was being contained within the field. "Doc, hey Doc-doctor, what is this?"

Grosbeak cracked one eye open as he took his meditative breaths. *The man is a barbarian. He knows nothing, and for Pete's sake, would he stop moving things! Just breathe,* Grosbeak thought, closing his eye again.

With his meditative technique now finished, Grosbeak spoke. "That is a scaled-down model of the Milky Way."

"You mean like some sort of hologram?"

"No, I mean like a replica of the Milky Way. I used particles of various quantum states, and with the help of the containment field, I was able to position them in such a manner that the final product is a scaled-down replica of the galaxy. And before you ask, no, it isn't a real galaxy ... just a replica of one. The power it contains is immense and should be handled with care. Never mind. It is unimportant. Can you go ahead and don your armor, please? I'd like to get started."

"I don't see the rush, but yeah, sure. I'll suit up."

Gunny Jones began the intricate dance of suiting up, easing into his combat armor by relaxing his mind, allowing it to absorb him through the back of it. It was something he'd done hundreds of times, and each time it still creeped him out.

There was something eerie about stepping up to the back of the armor and waiting for thousands of microfilament fibers to jet out, grab you, and suck you into absolute blackness, leaving you deaf and blind until all of the connections were established and the biomech senses came online. Those intervening moments, devoid of sight and sound, were enough to make anyone without the proper level of training go mad.

"Ok Gunny, please hold still," Grosbeak said. He stood several feet away, visually monitoring the area while mentally manipulating the loading bay arms, which were now coating the Marine in new nanoparticulates.

"What are you doing to me?"

"Please keep still. I'm going to make you walk through walls," Grosbeak said unemphatically.

"No, really, what are you doing?"

"I'm going to make you walk through walls. I could explain the science, but something tells me I'd be wasting my time."

"But that's impossible!" Jones exclaimed.

"Not impossible, just highly improbable — until now. Do you not remember your combat knife, Gunny?"

Jones's face shone with understanding.

"You see, 150,000 years ago had you told cavemen that they could one day pick up something called a telephone and speak to people far away, that they could transfer the resonate waves generated by their vocal cords over vast distances only to be absorbed and reconstituted by our brains into a discernible speech pattern; had you told them that in 100 years after the invention of the telephone, you would be able to link minds together, control machinery, furniture, and even your perception of reality with your thoughts and still be able to do so, so, so much more, all through a device the size of a grain of rice called an EMCD, they'd think you were mad.

You see, technology is growing at an exponential rate. It has been since the development of fire, and it was, is, a matter of time before new technologies will be developed faster than we can keep up with them. We are on the cusp of the technological singularity, you know. It just so happens that I intend to help get us there."

"What is this singularity you speak of, and just how do you intend on taking us there?" Jones asked, trying not to move. He asked more to keep his mind busy than out of curiosity at Grosbeak's scientific babble. His disembodied voice resonated throughout the medium-sized cargo bay recently converted to meet the doctor's needs.

"I intend to be a tool, a mechanism, to help our species along to biotechnological greatness by advancing my ideas, of course. The technological singularity is another term for transcendence, which is the moment where biology and technology merge and become indistinguishable from each other. We become something more, something greater than what we are. Whether that is a good thing or a bad thing remains to be seen. One thing is for certain. We are speeding down this evolutionary highway, and there is nothing we can do to stop it, just shy of shutting off everyone's minds all at once.

Now, enough chit-chatting. Do you see that 20x20 cargo crate over there? Yeah? Good. I want you to run through it."

"Doc, I'd rather not be responsible for the destruction of Coalition property."

"Doctor! It's doctor. Now, trust me. All will be fine."

"If all is fine, why do you need me," Jones mumbled to himself.

"I will set the dimensional shifting to last for thirty seconds," Grosbeak announced from his workstation. "You may begin... now."

Gunny Jones stepped down from the platform. His footfalls fell silent as the material the armor was made of absorbed the soundwaves it produced. Bit by bit, Jones began to shift out of sync with this reality. Squaring himself on the cargo container, Jones took off at a moderate trot, which, due to his enhanced power and augmented strength, meant he crossed the 20-meter distance between him and the cargo crate in a little less than three seconds.

At the last moment, as Jones's armor emerged from the container, his suit began phase-shifting back into normal reality. Something caught his foot, causing him to slip and fall.

Jones' voice boomed throughout the cargo room with a loud, guttural sound. "Shit! Shit! My fucking arm!"

Of course, he would be the one to scream from a little fall. Isn't he supposed to be a Marine? Good help is hard to find, Grosbeak thought. He strolled over to the gunny's position, ensuring he took his steps in exactly 26-inch increments.

"Oh, my," Grosbeak said as he surveyed the scene. "That wasn't supposed to happen."

Jones continued to moan, holding a slowly rematerializing stump, a smoothly severed remnant of what was once his arm. The armor's built-in anesthesia began to kick in, easing him into euphoria while aggressively numbing his pain.

Grosbeak's awareness splintered as he was made aware of a pending call from the President. He tried not to look too flustered as he answered, "Mr. President, what can I do for you?"

"Dr. Grosbeak, we are in the middle of testing various operational plans, and I don't like how things are going."

"How so, Mr. President?"

"The variables we've fed the AIs are all based on what we know about ourselves — our capabilities and limitations and the minuscule amount of data we have on our potential foes. What bothers me is the fact that the aliens have been studying us for years and we, we have next to no data on them. I need something that'll change things. Something the enemy doesn't know about, which doesn't seem like much. Any ideas?"

Grosbeak looked at the sprawled-out Marine in full combat armor currently missing an arm and sighed. "Sir, I had something for your dilemma, although I don't think it's ready."

"That's excellent news. I didn't think you would have been able to come up with anything, but I wanted to exhaust all options. Well, what is it? What do you have?"

Grosbeak sent the mental commands needed to share his current visuals. The president gasped at the sight of the one-armed Marine sprawled out at his feet. "What happened!" Branson barked. "What in Sam's hell is going on in your lab, Doctor!"

"Dimensional phase-shifting, sir. There was an … unfortunate accident. I believe it was a timing issue, something I plan to have fixed in short order."

"Doctor, your first order of business is to ensure that Marine makes it to the infirmary. After that I want you to dedicate every waking moment to perfecting that technology. We need every advantage we can get where we're going."

"Understood, Mr. President," Grosbeak said, thumb and forefinger rhythmically tapping against each other to calm his nerves. Outwardly, his expression was impassive, a look he perfected over the past twenty years working with peers who struggled to see his greatness. His inward emotional state was another story altogether. Grosbeak's thoughts trailed off as he uttered emotionless words to the President.

I understand, Mr. President, Grosbeak repeated to himself. *Do I? Can I really perfect phase-shifting and not cause injury to any more subjects? This. His injury. It's something I did not anticipate. Gunny Jones was not supposed to get injured. My math should have been perfect.*

Goosebumps sprouted on the back of Grosbeak's neck. Eying the clean cut of the Marine's bloody stump across muscle, arteries, and bone, partially encased in a layer of black armor, Grosbeak could feel a bit of his confidence waning.

I threw out the conventional method of scientific research and adopted a more cavalier approach to it, he thought. *In return, my bravado cost someone their arm.*

Progress, Dr. Grosbeak considered, *no matter how small and insignificant, or large and grandiose, comes at a cost — the bill is sometimes paid in standard currency and sometimes in blood. I cannot afford to dwell on this Marine's accident. Besides, the infirmary should be able to grow the man a new arm using recycled biomass without too much of a problem.*

Using the cargo bay's mechanical loading arms to help the Marine to his feet, Grosbeak said, "Come on, up you go. Let's get you down to med bay and get you all patched up."

◆ ◆ ◆

"Say, you're pretty good at this. How long did you say you've been wrangling Arqualian saddle worms?" Petty Officer Third

Class Baker asked. Turquoise trees swayed around the pair, foreshadowing the impending storm looming on the horizon. The heavy scent of cinnamon hung in the air, bringing with it the warning that the two were not alone.

Seaman Nickles spoke as he jumped down from atop the saddle worm, "Dude, you know, a while. I've been around, from Tau Ceti to Epsilon Eridi. There isn't a part of the Coalition I haven't seen. I ran into the Arqualian saddle worms on an excursion to Beta Centauri and been hooked ever since. The way they ride like horses after you mount them ... I've never felt anything like it."

Baker paused long enough to sniff the air. "We should mount back up. I smell cinnamon, man!"

"Shit!" Nickles said, readying himself to mount the worm again. "The Tasselled Ursidae are close, probably coming our way. We should get out of here, maybe head towards that settlement a few klicks from here."

Baker nodded in agreement. "Yeah, I hear those beasts are carnivorous and have superb vision, even at night. They'll see us before we ever see them. Since they migrate inland from their seaside caves when they sense a storm coming, I would say it's a safe bet we're on the menu while they're seeking shelter."

"Agreed," Nickles said. "You ever see one up close?"

"No, and thank the stars! Most people don't live to tell their tale after an encounter with a Tasselled Ursidae."

"Ha, I heard they have fleshy ganglia that dangle from their skin like the beards of the old Tasselled Wobbegong shark of Earth's southwest Pacific Ocean. Something about a fleshy beard gives me the heebie-jeebies."

The pair laughed as their worm moved at a galloping pace.

A chime resounded in both sailors' heads, temporarily freezing them in place. The noise seemed to come from every direction at once, cutting through the simulated environment the two crewmen were immersed in.

"Sorry, Mateo, but we need to get back to work. Our chow break is over," Nickles said, allowing his avatar to fade away from their jungle excursion, returning his consciousness back into his prefrontal cortex.

Petty Officer Baker, an E-4, outranked Nickles, an E-3 or Seaman, by one pay grade and should have been the one telling Nickles what to do, but that didn't matter anymore. Something as trivial as proper rank protocol didn't seem to matter that much with the junior enlisted on the lower decks, so far away from the flagpole.

Nickles sat up straight and his eyes refocused from his abrupt return to reality. He found his uniform tucked away in a small alcove within their dark corner and pulled on his coveralls.

"What's the rush?" Baker said cajolingly. Bits of his green hair were still matted to his scalp. "It's not like you're going to get in trouble for being late. I'm your team leader. It's all good — you're good. Come back over here," he said, padding the makeshift bed the two had erected beneath a couple of shelves. The cargo hold was absent of any authority figures due to its status as the secondary backup storage location for this deck, making it an ideal discrete junior-enlisted love grotto.

Nickles worked to mask his look of annoyance. Try as he might, the corner of his right eye twitched a few times as he said in as jovial a tone as he could muster, "Sorry, but I don't want anyone to notice I'm absent at the same time as you, with no good excuse as to why, so I'm going." Before walking out, Nickles looked back. "We'll see each other later, ok."

Baker sat back, allowing an expression of glee to wash over him. He didn't know what changed with Nickles, but he didn't care. He had developed a hard-on for Nickles ever since the older-looking junior sailor was assigned to his team. Nickles, however, rejected him at every turn — until now. Out of the blue, he'd suggested they'd come to the grotto for lunch. Everyone knows what lunch on the 3rd deck's cargo hold means, so Baker had washed and paid extra attention to his private parts.

Rolling over, Baker noticed that Nickles had forgotten his data pad in his haste to be a good little Seaman.

"Jordon, hey Jordon, you left your data pad," Baker said to Nickles in-head via his EMCD. *"Want me to bring it to you?"*

"No," came the terse reply. *"Don't bring it to our work section. I'm not there. I was sent on an assignment to the upper decks, so if you wouldn't mind swingin' by and bringing it to the section I'm working out of — I just might swing something for you later."*

Petty Officer Baker hastily sat up, excited now. Forgetting he was under a shelf, he knocked his head into the metal support strut holding the shelving in place.

"I'll ... meet ... you ... there," Baker barely managed to get out as he held his hand to his head. *Maybe in time, this fling can become something more,* he considered while putting on his coveralls.

"Ok, good. I'm on Deck 7, C-wing. The last cargo bay is where you want to go."

Baker's steps were light and perky, betraying his serious facade. He was elated with the recent dalliance between him and Nickles. How could he not be? The man was scrumptious. "Excuse me," he said when he bumped into a stout man in a white tunic walking beside a fully-armored Marine with a missing arm. *What's a civvy doing on this boat?* Baker thought as he looked back. *Whatever, as long as he stays out of the way, what's the harm. Ah, here we are, Cargo Bay 7-C-12. Where's Jordan? Place looks empty.*

Baker tried to raise his new friend on in-head comms. Nothing. He tried to signal his work section ... maybe they had a lock on him. Nothing. *What's going on! Comms on ships never go down, not like that crap they give those dumb Devil Dogs,* Baker thought. Cupping his hands together, he called out, "Seaman Nickles, you in here?"

Nickles walked past the Combat Information Center, also known as the CIC, on 2nd deck tipping his head in respect to the guard who was paying particular attention to anyone coming remotely close to the CIC's entrance. Nickles turned into a maintenance room and took up residence at the nearest workstation. His demeanor denoted someone who belonged. Two crewmen walked past him without second-guessing his presence.

Nickles splintered his consciousness for a moment to check his internal timekeeper. The time on deck was 1805. If he timed things correctly, Baker and his tablet were about to enter the cargo bay on deck 7. Nickles's eyes glossed over as he mentally entered the necessary codes into the cipher he had created for this very moment. Codes inputted, Nickles sat back, smiled, and waited to watch the whole thing play out as he tapped into internal sensor feeds.

The Interstellar-1 rocked violently. Several decks bucked, shook, and blew apart under the tremendous stress and kinetic force exuded on to it. Almost a hundred dead, many others wounded. Those who weren't killed in the initial explosion were tossed about the ship by a violent torrent of energy.

"Tactical, what the hell was that!" Captain Daa`e demanded. "Captain, it was an explosion. A portion of deck 7 is ..." Major Yutu paused before speaking again, not exactly sure he was reading the sensors correctly, "... gone! The ship's AI is feeding me data now. Nearest we can tell, Cargo Bay 7-C-12 was the focal point of the blast radius, making it the epicenter."

Captain Daa`e maintained her cool demeanor as she issued orders, "XO, get damage control on it. I'm going to speak with the President." *Someone has to do it,* Daa`e thought. "Let me know once we find out the cause and how many are dead or wounded."

"I'm on it, Captain. The system is updating now. I'll send you the data once it's all compiled."

"Thanks," Daa`e said before she got up and headed for the President's stateroom.

The doors slid open for her as she approached. *Was he waiting for me?* Daa`e thought. She stood still waiting on the President to finish his holographic call with Dr. Grosbeak.

"Sir, I take it you already know what's going on?" Daa`e said.

"Sit down, Captain, please. Yes, I know what's going on. My aide, Marious Lennard, ensured I was tapped into the systems aboard this ship before I got settled in for the night."

Flushing, Daa`e said, "My tech crew should have ensured you had access. My mistake, sir."

"No worries, Captain. My guy is just quicker than most. It's one of the reasons I keep him around. He anticipates my needs. Never mind that, though. We have a security problem, and you need to get to the bottom of it before we exit hyperspace."

"How so, sir? Tactical and the ship's AI are still sorting through the data. I wouldn't be so quick to call it sabotage."

"Figured you say that. Here, take a look." Branson swiped a holographic video recording over towards the Captain.

"Do you see that crewmen?"

"Which one, sir?"

"There," Branson said, highlighting the figure with a thought. "He was seen at 1803 bumping into Dr. Grosbeak, who was escorting Gunny Jones to the infirmary. And at 1805, he was picked up by internal sensors entering cargo bay 7-C-12."

"Ok, sir, I'll bite. I don't see the need to bomb that cargo bay, though. Nothing of value is down there, just back up supplies — which can be remade over time. That cargo bay isn't attached to any vital ship areas. I don't get it, sir. Why would the bomber want to bomb there of all places?"

"Captain, what I am about to share with you must not leave

this room." Branson stood up and took a seat closer to Daa`e. "Dr. Grosbeak may have been the intended target. However, it was more likely his work that was the target. Ever hear of phase-shifting?"

"Sir, I can't say that I have. What is it?"

"Grosbeak is a genius. Plain and simple. He is the goose that laid the golden egg, and he just created something that will give us an edge wherever we are going. That is why I think he or his work was targeted. Dimensional phase-shifting, as Grosbeak says, is a way to shift our quantum state from one reality to the next but for brief moments at a time. Thirty seconds to be exact with a recharge time of a couple of minutes. The science is still a little iffy, as you can see," Branson said, zooming in on Gunny Jones' arm. "Gunny Jones was testing the tech when he phase-shifted back into this dimension too soon, losing an arm in the process."

Daa`e jaw went slack. "Your bread crumbs line up. I'm compelled to believe you, but I thought that kind of tech was impossible?"

Branson replied, "So did I. Listen, I spoke with Grosbeak, and he backed up his data onto DNA-encoded cells he's placed on his chest for safekeeping. The saboteur probably thinks they destroyed the research. It's imperative that he or she continues to think as much."

"I see," Daa`e said. "I'll issue the necessary commands. Grosbeak will be kept safe. No one outside of you and I know will know of the DNA-encoded cells he's carrying. That is, unless someone else on your staff knows?"

"No one besides you, I, and Grosbeak know. Let's keep it that way," Branson said.

CHAPTER 26

Turbulent Departures

The Interstellar-1 exited hyperspace engulfed in a dazzling display of billions of multi-spectral energetic particulates springing to life, flooding outward in concentric circles. From afar, the sight could have been mistaken as a rainbow-colored glitter cloud bursting, rippling, and illuminating the darkness it once held tight.

Daa`e came to a standstill outside the President's quarters. Marious Lennard, flustered, was hot on her heels the entire way.

"Marious, unless you have the President's password to his quarters, I do not need you. You can go."

"Ma'am, I don't think he should be disturbed right now."

"Why?" A look of annoyance peppered Daa`e's face. "We just left hyperspace. The next order to give is the President's. Now, if you have nothing to add, you can go. Or do I need to have you escorted away?"

Marious narrowed his eyes a twinge. "Very well, ma'am." Turning, a sweat-stained Marious strolled back towards the bridge.

Captain Daa`e resumed her efforts to rouse the President.

"Mr. President, it's time to wake up. Sir, open your eyes, your people are waiting on you. Shall I get the sonic shower all ready?"

"No," Branson said in a gruff voice.

Eyes still shut, the memories of his sweet Sophia flooded his mind like a gentle flow of water on the beach. *"What's the point, Lucinda? What is the point anymore? Without Sophia, I'm nothing."* He stretched out his arm, allowing the empty bottle of brandy to roll out of his hand and crash into carbon fiber deck plating. Each shard of glass, a physical manifestation of the state of his heart, danced across the ground.

Nanoparticulates rose from the deck, ensnaring and devouring dozens of pieces of glass into its structure. Within minutes, all traces of the bottle's existence were wiped away, save for the sweet odor of alcohol exuding from Branson's pores and mouth.

"Sir, Sophia is gone only as much as you allow her to be. She is here," Lucinda, the AI avatar of Branson's Earth-side aide, said as she stimulated a part of his brain. *"And here,"* she repeated, making a small part of Branson's tunic above his heart vibrate slightly.

"Sir, you should know Captain Daa`e is outside your hatch, and I estimate if she doesn't contact you soon — 37 seconds to be exact — she will have your hatch opened by force. I would advise you not to allow the masses to see you in this state."

Branson grumbled before triggering the release of Mephedrone, a major stimulant, through his tunic's nanoconnectors. "Let her in," he whispered.

The doors to Branson's quarters slid open, spilling a flustered ship's captain onto the area rug in front of the hatch. Daa`e landed on her hands and knees as gracefully as a drunken cat.

Smirking, Branson chided, "Captain, that's a fine way to greet your President."

Daa`e's cheeks burned fire-engine red, "Sir! I've been trying to reach you for six minutes now. I was beginning to believe something might have happened to you. Wait, sir ... that smell? Is that you?" Daa`e instructed her EMCD to send the necessary signals needed to change her smell receptors in her brain's parietal lobe, freeing her from the President's stench.

Branson let out a husky laugh wrapped in intoxication, the Mephedrone not fully taking effect yet. "Yeah, it's me. What of it. Better yet, forget you saw anything. I'll be better in a few minutes anyway."

Daa`e stepped closer, crouching near Branson's legs. The door, long since closed, gave the two an unusual level of privacy — something the crew would no doubt begin to speculate on. "Sir, what's going on with you? Since coming aboard, I've noticed your behavior deviate from what we know of you — the sadness behind your eyes, the darkness clouding your essence, and now this. I'm worried about you." Her palm reached up to frame Branson's handsome, stately-like features. He peered down at her.

Daa`e's mind began to roam while waiting on Branson's reply. *I'm allowing my professionalism to take a back seat, for what? A fallen president? No, he's more than that. This man is the only one to see the threat no one else did ... and still hasn't. His leadership and guidance has saved billions of lives before. There is no reason to doubt him now. We need him. Do I need him? No! Do I want him? Don't know ... he is ... stop! Stop! Stop! Remain professional ... as much as possible.*

"Alessandra, I'm sorry. You shouldn't have seen me like this. I'm rather embarrassed. A part of me cares, but another part of me, a part swimming in a well of misery, doesn't. Something you don't know is that I lost my wife before coming here. There was an assassination attempt on my life. It wasn't successful, but there were other victims. My wife was among them. We didn't find her body, and I don't know if she's alive or dead at this point. I chose the mission over my wife, and it's tearing me up inside."

Daa`e held his gaze for a moment. "Sir, I cannot imagine your loss, your grief. I don't know how to mend a broken heart, but I do know your wife probably wouldn't have wanted you to wallow in self-pity and put the entire mission in jeopardy. She would want you to lead, like the man you are. Wouldn't she?" Standing, Daa`e said, "Let's get to the bridge. You have orders to give."

Daa`e studied her holographs and screens for several moments. "Sir, the anomaly is off to port 17 degrees. It does not appear to be defended. It's just there, stationary. Should we proceed?" Her voice was cold, professional, and exuded authority. She stood the tallest when she felt her weakest. The anomaly positioned directly in front of their warship was little less than awe-inspiring and made her tremble slightly.

The creatures which created that — thing — must be light-years ahead of us in tech, Daa`e considered, closing her eyes briefly to mouth a small prayer to those she'll soon join in the hereafter — the realm where spirits dwelled.

Most days, her religious preference took a back seat to her command. She worked hard to stay religiously neutral in front of the crew. Today, she'd made an exception.

The anomaly appeared to be a giant two-dimensional oval, neither reflecting nor absorbing light, existing in a state of quantum flux. The computer systems and AIs were having a hard time analyzing it.

Branson looked at Daa`e and flashed her his 'I'm your best friend, vote for me smile,' before saying, "We've come this far, Captain. No point in getting cold feet now." Opening a comm circuit to everyone tied into the ship's net, he said, "All hands. This is the President. We've reached our final transition point. We do not know what to expect on the other side, although I am confident that whatever it is, we are ready to face it and will do so together. A team, a people, which is unified, is far more prepared for what comes before them than that of a disjointed citizenry. Whatever happens here today, know that I am proud of each and every one of you. Your First Lady would be proud. Take your stations. Ship captains, prepare your crews for transition. Branson out."

"Helm, you heard the President. Make for that anomaly, top thrust." Beaming a mental thought to her right, Daa`e addressed her tactical officer, *"Ensure every ship is prepared for battle. I do not want to be caught off guard once we emerge from whatever ... whatever that is."*

"We're through the portal, ma'am," Lieutenant Richardson at helm control call out. "The Interstellar-1 is disbanding. All ships are uncoupling in their preplanned sequences as directed."

"Good. Thank you, Lieutenant." Captain Daa`e said. "XO, scan the vicinity for any sign of life. And find out what's wrong with optics. The display screen should not be that bright."

Commander Ode looked perplexed. "I don't understand this, ma'am. According to the readings the science station is recording, what we are seeing is correct! Optics is working just fine. The entirety of space —this space — is, in fact, bright. Our instruments can't explain it. There is light everywhere. Its brightness isn't absolute, but nonetheless, it is golden yellow delight. The brightness is pockmarked with planetary bodies and interstellar gases as best as we can tell. And look at these," Commander Ode mentally highlighted several dark bodies sporadically spaced throughout the region.

"What are those?" Branson and Daa`e asked in unison. "There are thousands of them, hundreds of thousands of them," Daa`e continued.

"They appear to be some sort of dark stars ... not exactly black holes but something else. We are still analyzing everything now. From what we can tell, those dark stars are a variable hub of dark matter and dark energy combined. Sir, ma'am, I think we've stepped through some inverse to the universe we know. Our instruments are going wild with the amount of dark matter and dark energy we're detecting."

President Branson focused on his screens in an attempt to make sense of what he was seeing. Still nursing a headache, he decided to opt for the verbal explanation of what he was witnessing instead of trying to download data on the topics. "Someone, please give me the long and short of what's going on." A few beads of sweat permeated his dirty brown Ivy League haircut, a classic crew cut and side part.

The young science officer spoke up, her voice a low whisper at first, "Sir, I believe what the commander is saying is that we are in a different universe our own. Our universe, the one we know, the, ah, dark one, is made up of only five percent of what we know the universe to be. The rest of the universe is 25% dark matter and 70% dark energy. We know this because gravity itself is too weak a force to not only create and hold galaxies together but to be responsible for the continued expansion of the universe."

"Those forces, the exotic matter and energy we don't see, is dark matter and dark energy. We actually know next to nothing about the stuff. We seem to have crossed some kind of rift, or doorway, to the other side of the universe. The side where this stuff exists. Perhaps another realm would be a more accurate term for where we are."

"Well. Lieutenant ..." Branson called up her name in-head, "... Brown. Thank you for that. I think I understand. The observable universe we know is comparable to what, a speck of sand I think would be the right analogy, when compared to ... this ... side ... of the universe ... this realm?" Branson said those last words as he splayed out his hands, turning several degrees to emphasize the space they were just in.

"Sir, that is ..."

Lieutenant Brown's voice was abruptly cut off when the ship shuddered. Explosions ruptured from several locations around the bridge. One explosion, emanating from the science station, flung Brown several feet backward. Her head cracked against the raised dais the command crew sat atop. The sound was reminiscent of a cantaloupe being smashed open on a warm summer day.

Daa`e's eyes grew wide. She took in the damage and rested her sights on her downed crewman. Brown's vitals read as flatlined in Daa`e's in-head display. *No time to linger on her. Need to figure out what's going on,* she thought.

Three more explosions violently rocked the ship. The warning klaxon wailed its cry in everyone's head as crew members fought to regain control of the situation. Several of the crew were strewn about, injured from the internal blast, falls, or bangs.

"Report!" shouted Branson.

"Sir, we are under attack!" Daa`e half yelled, half relayed in a tone suggesting she didn't have time to answer obvious questions. Her body tensed, every movement well-coordinated. Returning her attention to her console, her hands began flying across the spatial displays glowing and hovering before her face.

"Have we identified who or what is attacking us?"

"No, sir. Not yet. We are working on it." Daa`e's attempt to hide her frustration was failing.

Not my ship! she thought.

"Tactical, raise shields. Where's that firing solution?"

"Working on it, ma'am. Their fire is coming from everywhere and yet nowhere. We can't get a lock on their ships. They're ... blending in with the light of space. I believe there are dozens of small ships out there, perhaps a quarter the size of our light cruisers. To compound the issue, we don't know what it is they are shooting at us."

"Not good enough. Get that solution, Major — and I mean now."

"Helm, contact the light cruiser Conception and tell them to swing to port ahead, maximum thrust, and use the Aurora-2 as a shield. They're taking the brunt of the attack."

From the science station, Chief Bassard flung the data he had compiled at the captain. The information populated across Daa`e's display several microseconds later. "Ma'am," Bassard called out in a calm and even voice. His tone had a calming effect on those crew members in his immediate area. "It looks like our attackers are using a kind of focused 'mass' weapon, rubidium lasers. The lasers themselves are relatively harmless. It is only when they interact with something, anything of mass, that they turn deadly. All matter that comes into contact with the laser has its mass sped up to near-c before disintegrating. Very effective weapons. Our scientists have postulated the creation of such weapons, but they haven't been able to create them."

"Well, looks like someone has! What effect are our shields having? Can we defend against a weapon like this?"

"The shields are slowing down the lasers, ma'am. Only our outer hulls are being ablated away. But ma'am, if we lose the shields, we will be destroyed. That is a certainty. Until we know more, I'd recommend steering clear of their weapons engagement envelopes."

Major Yutu's posture perked up a bit. "Ma'am, fresh intel! The computer extrapolated best guesses on probable firing points based on the regions of space their shots are coming from and the strike angles against our hulls. Sending data to the command deck now."

"Got it. Helm, execute evasive maneuvers. Tactical, widespread firing solution. Use the dragnet. Until we know where they are, this is our best option for striking back."

"FIRE!"

Like a shotgun firing buckshot, thousands of soccer ball-sized metallic rounds shot out from the Aurora traveling in the general direction of where the bulk of the enemy fire was coming from.

Major Yutu held the cursor over the cloud of metal balls traveling in the direction of the enemy. "Time it just right,

Major," Daa`e said through gritted teeth. "I don't want to show our hand just yet." The bridge crew continued to be jostled about as the Aurora was peppered with shot after shot from the unknown assailants.

"Now!" screamed Daa`e.

A bead of plasma screeched through space, ripping a trail of destruction as it sought its target. Moments later the plasma bolt struck home, hitting the middle of the cloud of metal balls. The point of impact glowed intensely as it absorbed the energy from the plasma bolt. Using that same energy, it intensified it and redistributed it to its friends, forming an interconnected web of plasma and metal.

Six enemy ships were caught in the dragnet, interlaced plasma cutting through their ships, leaving a field of debris hurtling towards the Aurora-2. The debris smashed into the Aurora's shields, disintegrating on impact.

A few of the more junior crew members cheered while everyone else remained quiet, working on their piece of the pie.

"Captain, the enemy fire is waning, although the Conception is drifting off course. Their comm chatter must be malfunctioning," Lieutenant Richardson said.

"What are they saying?" Branson asked.

"It's a garbled mess, sir. Through the static I've only been able to pick up partial phrases. I'm going to work to clean it up a bit now. It sounds like they are saying something about crewmen taken. Probably a misinterpretation from the garbled mess of communications spewing from that ship. We'd know if we were missing crewmen ... right, sir? Ma'am?"

"With what we've seen so far, I'm a little reluctant to say we would know anything at this point," Branson said.

Commander Ode struggled to speak as the ship continued to shake and shudder under the hail of enemy fire. "Captain, I don't think they've taken to us killing their comrades. The light cruiser Conception and the destroyer Santiago are registering an increase in hits along their shields. We're getting hammered. There's a massive amount of damage along our starboard side. I'm not sure we can take much more of this."

Captain Daa`e gripped the banister surrounding her workstation until her knuckles were white. "Tactical, zero in on the fire we're receiving and launch another round of soccer balls. The dragnet seems to be our most effective weapon against our little invisible friends. Don't wait for my command — just fire."

Chief Bassard shouted, his calm temperament waning, "Damn! Starboard shields have failed. We're taking heavy damage. Multiple bulkheads are collapsing."

A deep groaning shudder echoed throughout the Aurora as several sections of hull plating were obliterated under the next cascade of fire. Explosions erupted across the bridge. The secondary communications console blew free of its couplings. Comms Technician Salisbury dove for cover, the console flying within inches of his head. Another crewman was struck in the knee by the communications console, crushing his patella and fracturing his tibia. The communications console continued its flight across the bridge, striking a fourth crewman center mass before careening off and smashing into the President's left arm.

A sickening crunch trailed the console's impact into the fourth crewman's chest — Captain Daa`e; killing her instantly. Her body collapsed like a rag doll, as though a child got tired of playing with her and tossed her aside.

Screams echoed throughout the bridge. Fits of coughing dominated the sounds as a light fog of smoke, coming from a handful of small electrical fires, enveloped the bridge crew, assaulting their nostrils and lungs.

The Aurora pumped hundreds of soccer balls into the surrounding space. Plasma dragnets activated, making contact with several more enemy ships and destroying them on impact. The Aurora's alarm klaxon changed from imminent danger to possible danger as the heavy hail of enemy fire lessened.

Their devastating attack weaned down after the two dragnet shots took out a sizable portion of the enemies' numbers.

Major Yutu, at Tactical, called out between several heavy breaths, "Ma'am, I think that did it. The enemies' attack is dying down. They might be in retreat."

President Branson stumbled to his knees, holding his left arm, the part below the elbow twisted and bent at an odd angle. "Major, the Captain is ... no longer with us. Report to me now." Branson's eyes never left Daa`e's. The deep crevice in her chest left by the comms console was too much for him to look at. *I was on the brink, and you brought me back, reminded me who I was and why I'm out here. Your steadfast devotion inspired me, Alessandra. This ship needs you, not me, not a broken man struggling to keep it together. First my wife and now you. I'm going to resign myself to the fact that the universe hates me.*

The XO gave the President a weary, skeptical glance before sending him a private message that interrupted his thoughts. *"Sir, all due respect, but I think it may be best if I take charge of the Aurora-2. No one knows this ship — no one knows these ships — better than I do. That is, other than the late Captain, sir. And from the looks of it, you're in no shape to command."*

"Commander, I understand your stance, but now is not the time. I'm taking control of the flagship. I will command both the fleet and the Aurora-2. Fall in line or step aside," Branson said, replying promptly.

"Aye sir, you have the con." The commander said with cool professionalism.

Branson's executive-style tunic injected him with a healthy dose of nanites and M-TNT; they worked in tandem to slowly heal his wounds. He spoke up, loud enough for the entire bridge crew to hear, intending to stomp out discontent before giving it the chance to take hold.

"Let's take advantage of this lull in fighting. XO, please get our wounded and dead off the bridge and collect them from around the ship. Make sure damaged decks are closed off and we get all systems back online."

"Sir, should we try to pursue?" The major at Tactical asked through gritted teeth, no doubt upset at the loss of Captain Daa`e.

"Pursue what?" Branson asked. "You heard our boys over at the science station. We can't track them, and we can barely see them through optics. No, we'll stand down for now, collect our wounded, and fix our ships. Find us someplace where we can get raw materials to regrow our damaged sections. You have your orders."

"Aye, aye, sir. Relaying those orders to the fleet now," Commander Ode said matter-of-factly.

"Ah, sir?" Chief Brassard sounded unsure of himself for the first time. "I'm not exactly sure if the instruments are reading this right, but we have a ship approaching. I say again, we have a ship we can track!"

"What? Put it on display in everyone's in-head. We need to see it." *What else are we going to have to contend with*, Branson thought. *My decisions brought us here, and I'm starting to question what I was thinking.*

The fleet's sensors registered the sleek, smooth design of the alien vessel. The ship's hull resembled a stingray bisected by a large slit from its head down to its center, almost cutting the ship in half. Only blackness could be seen trailing in this wake.

"What in Sam Hell are we looking at, Major?" Branson demanded.

Unsure of what he was seeing, Major Yutu replied, "Some sort of ship, sir. Their approach is slow and steady, and they are very visible. Almost like they want us to know they are non-hostile."

Chief Bassard chimed in, "Sir, spectral analysis suggests that ship is organic. Not sure that is possible, is it? Lieutenant Brown would know better than any of us."

"Son, we are on a ship that just sailed through dimensional space. A part of space no human has ever traveled. We've crossed through some sort of portal that brought us to a parallel universe, an inversion of everything we know, and you're questioning whether or not a ship can be made out of organics?" A couple of crew members chuckled. "I'm still trying to wrap my head around these dark energy stars that are populating 'light' space. Tell you what, we find out who or what is on that ship and we make it out of here alive, then I'll tell you what's possible and what's not."

Bassard nodded at the President with rose-colored cheeks and said, "Sir, you have a deal. So long as you get me home so I can celebrate my little girl's birthday, I'll believe anything is possible."

"They're hailing us," Commander Ode said in disbelief. "Their call is on all channels and all frequencies."

"Put them through, Commander, on the all-hands channel. I think we've all earned the right to see and hear what these beings have to say. Arm the RTD rounds just in case. Don't fire unless I give you the command."

CHAPTER 27

Enjoy the Show

Mae fought a shiver as a cold breeze caressed her skin. The muscles on the back of her neck contracted, causing a field of goosebumps to sprout. She opened one eye and then the other. It took a minute to fully open both eyes and bring them into focus. She felt the carpet beneath her, pressed firm against her head and side, and struggled to think of where she was.

Mae scraped her dry tongue against the roof of her mouth. It was a chore and she thought her mouth had been stuffed with cotton. Pain spiked in her head with each beat of her heart. The world shifted as she sat upright; the bed no longer resided on the wall. The distinct smell of carpet and dust stopped assailing her nose.

Her eyes adjusted to the dim light bathing the spacious room. She could see an oversized stuffed giraffe in the corner of the room, its familiarity tickling the recesses of her mind. A hologram of a uniformed woman projected itself inches off the far wall. In it, sun-kissed auburn hair draped a milky white face framed by soft round cheeks and wise blue eyes. Her complexion stood in stark contrast to the midnight black tunic she wore. It was inlaid with gold trim and bore a rank insignia above the right shoulder blade. The name below the picture read 'Master Gunnery Sergeant Anise Daniels, Coalition Marines.' Mae gasped. Recognition took over her features; she knew that woman. She stared at the holographic projection, and her mother stared back.

She continued to take in the room bathed in low light. She racked her mind, searching for possibilities for how she could have ended up back in her room. *This is my room! But that picture, it's out of place,* she thought. *How in the world did I get back here? The last thing I remember was Jax's eyes staring back at me apologetically.*

She stood, fighting the pounding in her head, and began to make her way to the door. A small part of the wall flickered in the corner of her eye. She paused for a moment, looking for the source of the light. She knelt down for a closer look but couldn't find anything; the wall looked fine, no flickers, nothing amiss, nothing. Mae stood, blinked, and wiped her eye before continuing on. *It was probably nothing,* she thought.

Exiting her room, Mae stepped out onto the second-floor landing and called out in a scratchy voice, "Dad? Keyera?"

Silence ensued. "Anybody?" she said, making her way down the stairs. Mae needed water to soothe the dryness of her throat and started for the kitchen but found herself frozen in place at the base of the stairs. Her jaw dropped at the sight she was taking in. To her right, she was staring at what should have been the side of her house. Instead, a large opening framing the living room greeted her. Mae walked towards the wall, trepidation in each step. Something was there — some kind of barrier made of energy — just in front of her.

Mae touched the soft glowing energy field and recoiled in pain. Her attention shifted abruptly from the blisters forming on her hand to the beings on the other side of the energy barrier. Muscular creatures hovered outside of her house. From her vantage point, their exact height was hard to pinpoint, but Mae figured the creatures were taller than an average man, possibly six foot tall or so. Their shimmering purple forewings beat too fast for her eyes to follow, while their aft wings flapped gracefully, keeping them aloft with precise movements. The creatures' faces lacked any features, save for a mouth and vertical ridges where the rest of its facial features should have been. Their movements reminded her of hummingbirds. One of them was facing her; its ridged faceplate seemed to have detected Mae's presence without the use of eyes. The color drained from Mae's face. She heard a series of high-pitched clicks interspersed with low ones. The other five creatures all turned their heads in unison, their attention now solely on her.

Mae recoiled backward, stumbling over a side table. She scrambled to her feet and raced towards her father's study. Mae dashed through the French doors and came to a sliding halt near his desk. She scrambled to tuck herself underneath it, disregarding the clattering of desk ornaments smashing to the ground around her. Her breathing came and went faster than her thoughts did. She looked down at her moist palms and vigorously rubbed them against her legs, trying to calm herself. She thought about what she'd just saw. Creatures were hovering in the darkness. Her home was not her home but something else. Beyond the creatures, Mae remembered glimpsing shapes in the distance, each with a flowing energy screen in front of them, like her own.

"*Where am I!*" she thought. Her freckles sparkled in the low light. She looked down and noticed her uniform was gone, replaced by her old civilian attire. Mae no longer wore her drab olive tank top with her midnight black combat jumpsuit bottoms she had on when she was taken. She was now in an orange-red plaid shirt with blue jeans. The shirt's sleeves were rolled up to her elbows, revealing her honey brown skin. Her curly red hair was pulled back into a ponytail. The small scar at the base of her skull where, a few months earlier, she'd received her EMCD was visible now. She ran her finger along the incision. The procedure was risky, and she had been forced to undergo it much later in life instead of the required age of five. She shut her eyes at the memory.

Mae sat rigid as a thump, thump, thump sound slowly tapped against the house. "Alright, stay calm. There's nothing to be scared of. This time of year, there are always chestnuts falling on the house," she mumbled to herself. "But am I really home? Because if not, those can't be chestnuts, can they?"

The rapping sounds stop. "They are not," whispered a faint, disembodied feminine voice.

"Excuse me?" Mae said, her voice barely perceptible. "Who's there?" Wary of leaving the protection of her hiding space, Mae tempted a glance around the side of the desk, checking one side and then the other. *I need a weapon,* she admitted to herself, thinking of what she could use to defend herself against those ... things.

"They are not chestnuts," the distant voice repeated.

Satisfied those things weren't in the room with her, Mae said a bit louder, "What are they then?"

"My fragile bones knocking on your wall. It has been a long time since I've had new company. Your cell has been empty for many months.

Cell! Mae said to herself.

"Do you know where we are?"

"I've been able to piece together bits and pieces here and there from others. I believe we're far from home, you and I, on a planet the Voltari call Taranzu. They consider themselves to be an enlightened species, although they still have barbaric traditions, such as the imprisonment of other species for their viewing pleasure."

"So why am I in my house?" Mae asked. She thought she knew the answer but needed to ask anyway. She chuckled inwardly. Was it her fate to always find a mysterious person to have random conversations with while separated by a wall?

The woman's frail voice came back after a moment, "They scanned your memories and placed you in a setting, one you have the greatest emotional connection to. I guess it's their way of giving you more natural surroundings. Don't you see, girl," the old woman coughed, "we're on a preserve. We're nothing more than animals to them."

"And my clothes?"

"Same," replied the old lady. "You can expect to find whatever memories hold the strongest emotional ties to you in your cell."

Though the woman couldn't see, Mae nodded in understanding. *That explains the picture of my mother too,* she thought.

"Others?" Mae stammered. "You mentioned others? Who are they and where are they now?"

"I grow tired, girl. We can talk later."

"Please," Mae called out, "I need to know."

A tired sigh preceded the old lady's reply. "The others are those who came but have since left this place behind. They were culled."

Horror resonated in Mae's voice when she said, "Culled!" *That sounds horrible, and it's something I want no part of!* "Hey, hey, lady. How do I get out of here?"

Mae sat listening to her own breath, waiting on a reply that never came.

Mae didn't have a watch and her EMCD wasn't working. *Probably jammed,* she thought. *It must have been half a day since I've spoken to the lady next door. I need to get out of this place!* Hesitant to leave the comfort of her hiding spot, Mae grabbed the jar full of pens off of her daddy's desk and emptied it. She stayed beneath the desk, wary of prying eyes, and pulled down her pants. The relief that followed was satisfying. She tried not to become too consumed with how good it felt to let it all out, paying particular attention not to spray urine onto the floor where she had to sit. She set the jar aside and settled down for a nap to help pass the time.

When Mae woke, the same dim light from earlier clouded the room. It came from nowhere in particular yet pervaded the house unopposed. She closed her eyes and focused, listening intently. It was quiet. She felt a little safer knowing she was alone, that those things weren't in her house-cell with her. Mae crept out from beneath her hiding place and eyed the dimly-lit room. Shadows were cast at odd angles. Her dad's old-style Barska solid brass telescope stood next to the window, its sheen glinting even in the low light. She smiled, remembering the time her dad had finally let her peer through it.

Breaking her reverie, Mae made her way to the study's entrance, each step slow and methodical. She'd grown up in this house and knew the floorboards intimately. If the aliens did replicate it based on her memories, they would have made it the way she remembered it, with creaking floorboards and all. Satisfied she was quiet, she continued into the foyer where the stairs led upstairs. She remembered how she'd only saw the forcefield downstairs and thought she was bound to be safer upstairs where she wasn't being watched.

Mae crept into her room, turned, and eased her door closed. She noticed a flashing section of wall and crouched to take a closer look.

This wall must be malfunctioning. It's probably their photonic projectors. I guess human tech isn't the only one susceptible to flaws. I can use that, I think. Maybe I can smash through this wall and see if I can make it out of here through the crawl spaces, Mae thought. She reached down to grab it when a reflection in her bedroom window gave her pause.

Her blood ran cold.

In the corner of her eye, she spied movement in the window. Her pulse quickened. Mae turned around and found herself standing face to face with one of them, a Voltari. Its faceplate was inches from her. She could make out individual rivulets in the grooves of each vertical ridge. Its charcoal skin was pulled taut by wiry muscles rippling just beneath the surface. Its head was almost twice the size of Mae's but still proportional to its own slender body.

As it stood to its full height, almost eight feet tall, Mae noticed four meaty protrusions, double the length of its arms, standing in the place where its wings once were. Mae eyed each protrusion, gasping in both fear and surprise, as each one folded in on itself and tucked behind its back.

Steeling herself, Mae narrowed her gaze in defiant opposition to her imminent culling, which she figured must end in death, and said, "Who are you?"

A number of clicks and chirps bellowed from the massive Voltari. As quickly as the sound began, it was gone.

"I like you — human," the Voltari said as two more decloaked on either side of it. "You do not have fear in your veins. I smell your strength. You are a warrior and will be my new Totem."

There were three of them now. The threat of fear crept into Mae's mind. She redoubled her efforts to keep it at bay.

"*Piayoc, are you sure this is the human you want?*" Malmat asked. "*There are so many other humans here. This one is frail. Pick one of the males of her species — a young one. I saw a human male with fine muscle tone and good posture several cells over. That one would be sure to win us favor with the Counsel of Three.*"

Piayoc stared at the scrawny human standing tall before her. The human's bravery intrigued her. *Most humans do not shine like we do, but this one does. Her sheen is dimmer, but it is there. No, Father has it wrong. This human will be the one to help us gain a higher social position and favor with the Counsel.* "*Father, this is the one. I am sure of it. This human is the one we should get. Look closer, Father. Do you see that? She shines.*"

Malmat tilted his head and focused, intensifying the theta

waves he projected towards Mae. His aging faceplate came to rest two feet from Mae's face. *Yes, I can see it,* he thought to himself. *She does shine — but only my people and the 'others' — the abhorrent Quintessence — shine! No, this is a trick. The 'others' technology must be interfering with my abilities.*

Malmat watched as the human narrowed the slits surrounding the beady orbs they called eyes. She brought her hand up to her face orbs, blocking them from his sight and focusing her attention towards the corner over Adam's shoulder. She spoke but to no one in particular. *"This one is defective,"* Malmat said. *"She talks to herself. We need to bolster our clan's standing. Only a new Totem can do that. This human has no use as a symbol of our means when her mind does not work right!"*

◆ ◆ ◆

Mae raised her hand to her eyes to shield them from a violent burst of radiant white light. From her right, the figure of a man began walking out of the shimmering light towards her. "Who are you?" Mae asked, her expression a mix of surprise and shock.

Thourn's ethereal image wavered, his will to project breaking, pulling, and incrementally drawing him back to his body. Leveling his gaze at Mae, he spoke evenly but with an air of urgency, "Listen, Oralee, we do not have enough time to explain everything. Even now, my astral form is being pulled back to its vessel."

"My name is Mae, not Oralee," Mae interrupted. She asked hesitantly, "You're some kind of ghost? Like a — spirit?" Thourn let out a soft chuckle, "No, not a spirit. What you see is my true self. My body, our bodies, can only contain us for a finite amount of time. They were never designed for longer than that." Mae cast a fleeting look towards the Voltari still in the room, their presence drowned out by the light silhouetting Thourn. Maintaining his gaze on Mae, his mood steady,

Thourn put Mae's uneasiness at rest as he said, "Do not worry. Only those I wish to see me may lay eyes upon me. My name is Thourn, and I do not have long here, so I will be brief. Your situation is not what was planned for you. Your father will not be happy when he learns of your fate." Again, Mae interjected, hope and sadness welling across her face as she spoke, "My father? You've spoken to him? Please tell him I'm sorry, that I should never have run away and joined the military."

"No, Oralee, I do not speak of the man you've known in *this* life as your father. Ryland is not your true father." Mae took a couple of steps backward and sat on the bed. She was now oblivious to the three domineering creatures standing in the room with her. The admission that Ryland Daniels was not her father made her feel weak, uncertain of herself or anything else. Pushing those thoughts aside, Mae said, "My ... true ... father. I don't understand."

"You have no idea who you are, and I do not have time to explain, young one."

"What does that mean?" Mae blurted out in consternation.

Thourn's image became a loose shell of its former self. With each passing moment his likeness became harder and harder to make out. His commanding voice spoke one final time before winking out, "Survive, Mae! We'll speak again, but you must survive at all costs. Help is on the way."

CHAPTER 28

Greetings

"Sir, all laser banks, missiles, and RTD — Rapid Target Disintegration — rounds are armed. We have a solid target lock."

"Thank you, Major."

A window appeared within Branson's mind that corresponded to the one hovering in front of the bridge crew. The transmission came through audio only.

"Leader of the human vessels. I am the Apotheosis for this region of Infinity. We would be honored to have you as our guests." The voice said, mechanical in its machinations, eliciting an eerie feeling from Branson.

"Mr. — Apotheosis," Branson said the word with emphasis, tasting it, rolling it around in his head before continuing, "I am President Branson, commander of this fleet. Do you have a name? Something I can call you? That is assuming 'Apotheosis' is a title and not your name." *Who are you?* Branson thought.

Activating a link to his tactical officer, Branson said, *"Major Yutu, how're our weapons lock?"*

"It's solid, sir. The enemy ships are holding steady, 7,000 meters off of our port side."

"Copy, maintain that lock. If you see any hostile action, any-thing that you believe would take too long to get a clear order to fire from me, take the shot. We will not be caught off guard again."

"Solid copy, sir."

Branson rubbed his arm where his tunic had injected him with Mephedrone, a synthetic stimulant. His fingers lingered over the location long enough to be noticed by a few of the crew. Thoughts of his wife, Sophia, filled him, followed by an overwhelming flood of remorse for Captain Daa`e.

Marious's eyes narrowed as he and the other bridge crew watched the President's every move. Every action and broad-casted mental thought he made were absorbed by those around him, recorded through their optic nerves and relayed to the rest of the fleet via the semi-instant link of their EMCDs.

Members of the fleet watched Branson while listening to the thoughts he shared.

"Chief Bassard."

"Yes, sir?"

"Continue scanning the surrounding area. See what you can dis-cover. I want to know if the enemy is coming back around for an-other sneak attack. Check for gravitational displacement and any sort of spike in dark matter or dark energy readings in our vicin-ity. Lieutenant Brown provided us with valuable insight before her passing, and I think it's safe to assume they would be using tech closely based on those exotic particles, considering we're in a region of space filled with it.

"Got it, sir. Already on it."

"Good, Chief. Keep me informed."

"President Branson," the Apotheosis continued, "our lan-guage is eons old in comparison to yours. You will not be able to understand nor speak my true name. My kind has taken a liking to human names recently, it's what you would call a trend. I have never done as such, however, for our interactions, you may call me ... Peter."

"Alright, Apotheosis Peter. What can we do for you? Who are you, and why have you chosen now of all times to present yourselves? Are you part of the group that attacked us when we first arrived here, in … in light-space?"

The audio-only comm connection continued as the mechanical male voice said, "President Branson, thank you for entertaining us. All will be explained once we are aboard your ship."

"No! Apotheosis Peter, I am sorry, but that is not an option until we are satisfied with the answers we get."

"We understand, President," Peter said with no further explanation. A deafening silence passed by in what felt like an eternity before he continued, "we were not your attackers. Those who attacked you are the Forsaken, what you would call outsiders, castaways. They lurk on the periphery of our dominion and disrupt our way of life. We are … sorry you had to encounter them."

"So, you're telling me we were just attacked by alien pirates? Some of your kind?"

"Yes, President. As I have told you, the Forsaken are of the Voltari but not of my people. You were attacked and robbed. They've taken your most valuable commodity — some of your crew. The Forsaken specialize in genetic trading, and you presented them with a 'fat' target when you entered their territory with so many vessels filled with humans — Originals."

To Branson, it almost sounded like there was a bit of excitement in the mechanical voice as it said the word Originals. He knew actionable intel when he saw it. *"XO,"* Branson said mentally, *"get with all of the ships. I want an updated ship manifest uploaded to the Aurora's AI stat. Verify what the Apotheosis just said. If I'm missing crew, I want to know about it!"*

Not waiting for a reply, he returned his attention back to the audio communication between him and the Apotheosis.

"Why are you here, Apotheosis?"

"President Branson. Your vessels have taken a considerable amount of damage. You are missing crewmembers, and you are a very long way from home. You must be scared. Allow me to resolve your fears."

Soft chirps and beeps of various lengths and intensity replaced the conversation as Apotheosis Peter broke the audio connection.

"Apotheosis? Are you there?" Branson said. Several moments passed before the Apotheosis responded. "Apothe ..."

"Yes, President. Check your sensors. You can now see the Forsaken the same as we can."

Branson accessed his EMCD, *"Science, Helm, Tactical, confirm! Can our ship see the pirates?"*

"Sir, I can't explain it," Major Yutu said, responding first. *"That alien somehow hacked our AI and rewrote some of the software controlling our sensors. We can now see the enemy vessels, or vessel, should I say. We've spotted one of them, trailing some sort of organic debris, 2 AU out. They're making a run for it."*

"Verify the other ships have the same capabilities now as well. Next, find out how this is possible. How did the Apotheosis hack our top-of-the-line systems — and as fast as they did!"

Apotheosis Peter's voice broke through the chatter on the bridge, "Would you like me to tell you where they are most likely taking your crew members?"

"What will that bit of information cost us?" Branson replied with caution in his voice.

"We seek an audience, faceplate to faceplate."

What in Sam Hell is he saying? Faceplate to faceplate? Linking to Lieutenant Richardson, Branson said, *"Helm, can we extrapolate where those ships might have gone based on the trajectory of that limping one? They don't know we can see them, so it might be a good idea to follow that train of thought."*

"Sir, there is a good bet that they've seen us talking to our little friend here. If they are smart, they will assume our new friends have given us the means to detect them and at least agreed to assist us in finding our comrades. I don't think we have a choice here, sir. You should accept the Apotheosis's offer."

Branson cracked his knuckles and twisted each of his wrists before speaking. "Apotheosis, I will grant your wish. Under one condition. If you are willing to submit to a scan and an armed escort the entire time you are aboard my ship, I will grant you passage."

"President, we have no reason to fear your security measures, we ... what is the correct term? Come in peace."

◆ ◆ ◆

"Mr. President, sir," Commander Ode said, "spectral analysis says the small planetoid off of our port side, the same one we believe the pirates were hiding behind before they attacked us, is rich in the elements we need to regrow the damaged sections of our ships. The Conception suffered major damage and is holding together by a miracle. We should be able to tow her to the planetoid without risk of her falling apart. That would allow us to get all of the ships operational quickly."

Branson eyed the XO appraisingly and weighed his options. "What is the risk of leaving the Conception in place and sending the material she needs to her?"

"Sir, that would add almost a day to our refit time. Current estimates put us at little under six hours to mine that planetoid and regrow the parts needed for our ships. We incur increased risk to our captured crew the longer we delay getting to them."

"Very well, Commander Ode. Execute the first course of action. While you relay the necessary orders, would you please accompany me to the primary airlock on Loading Deck 1?"

Branson looked at Commander Ode and raised an eyebrow. "It's time we meet our ... friend." Feeling the hairs on his arms rise, he tried to shake off the odd feeling that something was off about all of this as he and the Commander made their way towards Loading Deck 1.

◆ ◆ ◆

The President, along with five other senior officers and

various enlisted crew members, stood in the loading bay of Deck 1, primarily used for crew member passage. Branson's presidential guard, Marines in TALOS MK8 'Zeus' suits — more commonly referred to as Archies among the general military — shifted about the large cavern, positioning for the greatest field of fire. The airlock cycled through, releasing a low hiss indicating the inner hatch was ready to be opened. The Archies shifted their polychromatic Zeus armor out of the visible spectrum, rendering themselves invisible.

Gasp and low murmurs of disbelief escaped a few of the men and women standing in the loading bay. The first being to appear, standing almost eight feet tall, was charcoal gray with a massive muscular frame. Its presence elicited fear and disbelief from the humans around it.

Two more of the powerful beings stepped through the hatch, causing a few of the crew members to stumble backward, tripping over their feet and clattering to the deck.

"Everyone, calm down, now!" the XO bellowed. "You are Coalition Military. Act like it!"

Two half-nude humanoid beings emerged from the airlock behind the aliens. The humanoids' complexion was a shade similar to Brazilian gray suffused with rich ombré brown hues. Their eyes were less almond-shaped, like that of a human. Instead, they were rounder with wide dark pupils and prominent brow ridges. Each of the humanoids had black and silver-gray hair and was almost physically indistinguishable in shape and form from the humans from earth.

Marious crept close to the President and whispered, "Sir, your mouth, it's open."

"Thank you, Marious," Branson thought back.

Extending a hand, Branson spoke loud enough for everyone present to hear as he approached the first of the beings. "Welcome aboard the Aurora-2. I am President Branson."

The first Voltari to come through the airlock stepped closer, his talons click-clacking on the deck. *"President Branson, I am Apotheosis Peter,"* his voice resounded within the heads of the people in the immediate vicinity. It was soft and smooth, ripe and enticing. His slightly sublime tone was vastly different from the neutral, almost-artificial mechanical one from the earlier conversation. *"Thank you for welcoming us aboard your vessel."* Apotheosis Peter swiveled his head from side to side as he projected his words into the minds of the humans assembled to greet him. *"As I told you before, there is no need to have security present. You may tell your armored men to leave."*

General Sherman cursed aloud before sending a mental message to Branson, *"Sir, how in the world did he spot your Archies? There's no way! And for God's sake, where are these things' eyes?"*

"General, what is and isn't possible in this realm seems to continue to elude us. Until further notice, I think it's safe to assume anything is possible here. Perhaps their faceplate emits some kind of signal ... maybe a form of echolocation that allows them to see in spectrums we can't. I'm just guessing here, at least until we know more about them. General, keep our forces alert while these beings are on board."

"Apotheosis, if you will, you and your party can come this way to my conference room. There, we can discuss matters that need addressing."

"Yes, President, that would be most acceptable."

The air within the conference room felt thick to Branson. On the left, sat his military staff, and on the right, the Voltari and their humanoid companions. The three Voltari each had four long, meaty appendages sprouting from their backs that occupied a space that would have normally held twice as many humans.

Branson considered that their long muscular protrusions were some sort of antenna designed to aid in the being's navigation of their environment.

"Apotheosis," Branson said, breaking the tension, "tell me,

why have you come here and more importantly ... what do you want? When do you intend to inform us of the supposed location where the pirates, excuse me, the Forsaken, took my people?"

Apotheosis Peter's faceplate vibrated visibly for a moment then he let out several clicks and chirps. *"President Branson, the location of your missing crew is within your database now. Satisfaction is yours now, yes?"*

Branson found he was staring in disbelief. "Yes," he said, not quite understanding what just happened.

"Our Supreme Chancellor wishes to meet with you, President Branson. This is why we are here. He detached me from my duties as Apotheosis of this region of Infinity to be your guide to Taranzu, our planet of origin. The Supreme Chancellor is most pleased that you have finally come to him. Tell me, President, do you enjoy the flesh? The cold hard reality that one day soon you will die and the feebleness of your body will not be enough to stop you from perishing?"

"My flesh is fine. Thanks for asking, Apotheosis. As for death, I haven't feared that beast for a very long time," Branson said with an edge to his voice he'd forgotten he'd had.

◆ ◆ ◆

Branson paced the office within his stateroom. The rooms spartan-like accoutrements, devoid of anything other than the bare necessities to function, accentuated his emotional state.

"Sir, aren't you the least bit concerned with what that thing said?"

Branson paused by the view-wall, the bright golden glow from light-space reflecting off his worry-lined face. He twisted the glass in his hand. The reflection he focused on — a twisted and marred version of the man doing the staring — peered back at him. "I am, Marious, but I can't allow it to show," he said. "I want you to monitor our friends. See what you can pick up."

"You got it, sir. Anything else?" Marious felt a pang of excitement as he thought about the prospect of spying on their alien guests. A few beads of sweat glistened on the right side of his hairline.

The lines on Branson's forehead creased tighter as he thought. He took a sip of his tonic and said, "No, that's it for now."

Marious's presence faded and was immediately replaced by that of General Sherman and Major Yutu.

"Mr. President," the two men said in a slightly discordant greeting.

"Gents, at ease. Where are we with the tactical situation? Are we ready for launch?"

Sherman spoke first, "Our boys and girls are getting suited up now. Once the XO finishes maneuvering the fleet in the system towards that colony bubble floating just beyond the second gas giant, we'll be able to line the ship up for launch and send them in."

Major Yutu, a man less crass than the General, spoke formally and professionally to the President. "Sir, the ships' AI should have a targeting solution for the spot on that bubble we picked within the next few minutes. Our boy's insertion point will limit flight time and detection. It's as optimal of a location as we're going to get under the circumstances."

"What's the holdup, Major? I thought tactical would have had that solution by now," Branson asked, setting his now-empty glass on the table.

Sherman scoffed under his breath at the sight. Major Yutu pretended he hadn't noticed the empty glass and bottle of bourbon being absorbed back into the ship, one nanoparticle at a time. "Subluminal targeting acquisition is something we are still refining, sir."

"Understood, Major," Branson said after blowing out a breath.

From the bridge, Commander Ode monitored the conversation via his EMCD while directing the Task Force ships' captains.

Branson eyed each man in the room before speaking one last time. "What we are about to do here will gain us no friends in this sector of space. They attacked us, and I'll be damned if we leave a crew member behind. Gents, we are a go for Operation Phantom Mamba."

CHAPTER 29

I'm Coming, Mae

"Yeah, this idea might not have been the best," Jax thought, falling through the air. The luster of his plan began to peel away with each passing second. His dread increased as the ground grew closer. Staring up at the newly destroyed windows of the cliffside house he was just thrown out of, Jax watched the shattering of more windowpane glass as, one by one, two Voltari squeezed their massive gray frames through the hole, launching themselves at him. Looking over his shoulder at the ground looming below, Jax figured he had at least a minute before impact.

Those Voltari will catch me way before then, he thought. *I could use my abilities to slow down, but then they'd be on me even sooner. Life was so much easier when I was just a model. No one tried to kill me then. Yeah, they wanted my body but never my life. I need a serious plan! Too late to change professions now. Think, Jax, think! Hell, what would Savanna do?* Jax said, chuckling at his own reference to his previous persona.

20 minutes prior ...

Several dwellings lined the lip of the cliff, overlooking a turquoise sea framed by mountains touching the sky. Maneuvering closer to the house Thourn guided him to, Jax paused, opening his ears to take in all the sounds surrounding the geometric cliffside villa. Listening to the lapping of the waves far below the cliff where the primary portion of the villa rested, Jax lowered himself closer to the ground. The blades of violet-blue bioengineered grass crunched beneath his feet as he eased closer to the villa's entrance. The low luminosity of the two imposing neighboring moons provided Jax additional cover.

Thourn had better be right, Jax thought, pulling himself through a small thicket of bushes, several feet from the protruding entrance to the villa. *I can't believe this is the only way to get to Mae! That's assuming they haven't killed her, or worse, added her to their damned dinner menu!*

Creeping out of his hiding space, Jax raced across the grounds until he reached the front door of the sharply-shaped villa. Testing the locking mechanism and seeing that the doors were unlocked, Jax slipped inside. Walking down the main hall, he ducked from room to room until he found himself at a set of stairs.

"*Thourn, hey Thourn, you there?*" Jax called out in his mind.

A moment passed by before Thourn's answer rang in Jax's head. "*I'm here, young one. What can I do for you?*"

"*Which room did you say the culling would happen in again?*"

"*You really should learn to pay better attention. How else do you expect to rescue Mae?*"

"*I pay attention — it's just that the layout of this house is confusing.*"

"*You need to find the room with the small pink ribbon framing a hand-drawn picture on the door. Then you'll be where you need to be.*"

"*Got it. Thanks, old man.*"

"*Old is a relative term, Jax. It is a human concept and does not affect us.*"

"*Don't take everything so literal, Thourn. You'll never get a girl that way,*" Jax said jokingly as he ascended the stairs and approached the door with the pink ribbon.

"*Romance for Watchers is forbidden! That rule now includes you, Jax.*"

Speak for yourself, old man, Jax thought to himself. *I'm gonna get some* ... "*Uh-huh, sure. Whatever you say, boss,*" he replied mentally. "*Just remember, I never asked to be 'awakened,' Thourn ...*"

The sound of a weapon being primed and pointed at the base of Jax's head made him pause, his hand inches from a door's access panel. "*Uh, old man, I'mma have to finish this conversation in a bit, something's ... come up.*"

"Don't move!" the voice behind Jax said grittily.

Jax slowly raised his hands and said, "Alright, alright. I can see what this looks like, but you should hear me —" The butt of the weapon smashed into the back of Jax's head, cutting off his words.

"I don't need to do nothing but see you out and pull this trigger! You picked the wrong house to rob! What, you thought you'd come in here and have your way with my little girl or something! You tweakers, you're all good for one thing — dying! You won't be the first one I throw off this cliff and probably not the last."

Steadying himself, Jax began to stand, careful not to give this guy another reason to pull the trigger. "Listen, sir, I am not here for you, your daughter, or your belongings. I know what this looks like, but you should believe me. I am here for the things that are coming to take your daughter — and most likely, you too."

"Yeah, sure. You can take that lie to your grave, tweaker! Head back the way you came — slowly. You move the wrong way, I will disintegrate your head."

Jax focused on his breathing. The man behind him maintained steady pressure on the back of his head.

Rookie move, Jax thought.

As the pair rounded the corner, Jax morphed the color spectrum around him to match that of the gray-brown hue of the nanogrown walls and the blue glint coming from the overhead translucent infinity pool. Slowing down time around them, Jax whirled and pinned the man to the wall with one hand while snatching the long-barreled home defense laser scatter gun, also known as an L-Rad, from him.

After several moments of silence, Jax spoke, "Listen to me, sir. I am not here to take anything from you, your daughter, or otherwise." Drool pooled beside the man's mouth on the spot of the wall where his face was pressed.

With rising anger, the man spat out, "And how am I supposed to believe you. Show yourself!"

Jax stopped shifting the visible light around him. His face appeared first, followed by the rest of his body. "Next time, do not hold the weapon so close to a person's head," Jax said. "You do that and you've lost the battle before it's begun."

The man pinned against the wall in Jax's grasp eyed the faint shimmer from the corner of his vision as it transformed into a man. His own feet were dangling above the ground. He shifted his eyes, looking around for a way out, but he felt gripped by hesitation and fear. He did nothing. Bits of Jax's exposed brown skin, the parts his black burglar's outfit didn't cover, glowed lightly from the pale moonlight shining through the above-head translucent infinity pool.

"I'm right here," Jax said, lowering the man down to his feet. "Listen, any moment now, there will be ... beings from, well, it's hard to describe. Just know that things are coming to take your little girl, and I'm here to stop them."

The man's struggles against Jax's grasp lessened a bit.

A little girl's ear-piercing scream split the air. Its frailty was felt more than heard — fear surfing on each sound wave crashed on the rocks of their hearing. A sense of urgency surged into their veins as the shrill cry for help permeated the air.

◆ ◆ ◆

The door with the pink ribbon framing a small hand-drawn picture began to bow, rippling multiple times before shattering. Shards of teak blew inward, pelting the room's occupants. Through the smoke-filled haze, a figure dove into the room and rolled forward. A massive taloned hand flew past his head. Several strands of Jax's hair, cut free from his head, floated towards the floor. Coming out of his roll, he stood, bracing himself in a warrior's stance.

Sarah watched on in terrifying agony as the three faceless creatures swiveled their attention from her to the medium-sized man clad in black who'd just burst through her door.

Without pause, the man cloaked in darkness lunged toward the trio of tall, muscular creatures with four long appendages sticking out from their backs, framed by the shadows. The man ducked under the swipe of a hand, with long, razor-sharp nails, of one of those creatures. Rising to his feet, he spun around, pointing the same gun her daddy owned at the first monster. Sarah screamed louder then she'd done previously as the L-Rad barked with enough force to be felt in her bones. "Daddy!" she wailed.

Beyond the threshold of the room's missing door stood Sarah's dad, frozen in shock at the maelstrom of violence in his daughter's room. A slow trickle of liquid began pooling at his feet.

A bright flash accompanied several dozen plasma shots fired from the L-Rad and provided enough light to frame the room's occupants in a moment in time: the man with the gun pointed at a monster flying backward, two other creatures lunging for the man from his side, and his little girl cradling herself, wrapped in immobilizing fright.

Sarah squeezed herself deeper into her corner. Cupping her hands over her ears, she placed her head between her legs, salt-stained cheeks nestled tightly between small, thin arms. She could not stop herself from shaking.

Sarah continuously rocked forward and backward on her bottom, saying, "This isn't real. This isn't real. This isn't real!" in a small, shaky voice. She squeezed her eyes tighter. The loud commotion in her room continued. The boom, boom, boom from the L-Rad made her ears rang. After each shot, the loud thump of a body could be heard slamming into a wall, the bed, and breaking and scattering dollhouses and other toys across the room.

Breaking the seal between her arms, Sarah peeked out. Her corner no longer felt safe. The creatures weren't dying!

The man fighting the creatures kicked one, sending him staggering backward, before flipping over and bringing his knees up and down on the top of another one's head, driving him to the ground. The third monster grabbed the shadow man, tossing him into the ceiling. The room shook with the force of the impact.

From the corner she sat in, Sarah could see the monster closest to the shadow man slow down, muscles writhing beneath its charcoal gray skin, struggling against whatever held him in place. The shadow man cocked his arm back and then jumped into the air. He struck the closest creature's faceless head with enough kinetic energy to break its neck. The man dove past the falling limp body of the monster, and over his shoulder, he yelled, "Run!" while throwing his weight into the two remaining creatures.

Sarah's body was moving before she'd fully processed the command. She scrambled to her feet and ran past the shadow man and creatures he fought. Jumping over the head of the one dead monster and out of the hole in the wall where her door used to be, she continued on, almost slipping on a puddle of liquid, past her daddy and down the hallway. Her father turned and hustled after her. As Sarah ran, a big, meaty arm jutted out of the wall and reached for her. A scream left her mouth before she realized it had come out. She fell backward, her momentum carrying her forward several feet past the arm. She rolled to her side and back to her feet again. Sarah chanced a glance back at the arm, but it was gone now, replaced by the wild-eyed man she called Daddy. As the pair hit every corner harder than intended, they regained their balance and continued on towards the home's main entrance. In the distance, the sound of loud, shattering glass added to the crescendo of their footfalls.

◆ ◆ ◆

The present …

Jax's mind whirled, *Thirty seconds. That's all I have, and those two Voltari aren't making this any easier. I hardly slowed them down back there. They're tough, I'll give them that. At least I managed to kill one.*

Sighing, Jax focused his abilities on slowing down. He twisted his body, making it as flat as he could, right before passing between the two Voltari. They'd narrowly missed grabbing him. Reaching out, he snagged one of each of their meaty appendages and held on tight. Planting his feet behind their shoulder blades, Jax rode the Voltari's towards the ground.

A thrill coursed through Jax as death raced up to greet him. *Here we go. Either this half-cocked plan is going to work, or we're all going to die.*

"Listen up!" Jax howled. "I know you can hear me! Open a rift now, or we all die! You and me. No do-overs! You want me gone, open a rift!" The wind whipped past him, stinging his eyes and stealing his tears. He wasn't sure if these beings understood him, but he sure hoped to Abnar they did.

The ground was closer now. Jax gritted his teeth, closed his eyes, and said a prayer. He could live with not seeing his modeling career through to the end. He was almost willing to accept the fact that he'd failed Mae; he was forced into the position as her protector anyway. But what he couldn't live with was the idea that his Earth mother would never know what happened to him. She'd given him the best experiences of this life. He'd just hoped the ride wasn't over yet.

The larger of the two Voltari fumbled with something, its clawed hands shielded by its heavy frame. They were two breaths away from becoming a smear on the shoreline rocks, when a shimmering misshapen circle of light materialized, swallowing the three occupants.

CHAPTER 30

Friend? Maybe ...

Mae's stomach churned. She pulled at the tight, organic collar-like device around her throat as she fought back another bout of overwhelming nausea.

It was all wrong, so very wrong.

From the twenty-foot-high alcove, her three captors had placed her in, she had an ideal vantage point. She could see the entire expanse of the aerie they called home, to include their current eating place. Had it not been for their unusual meal choice, she might have regarded the scene as beautiful.

The inside of the aerie contained shimmering walls that changed colors depending on the angle you observed them from. All around her, within the entirety of the spacious apartment, there were arching cathedral ceilings that curved down to enclose massively oversized windows giving way to interconnected skywalks from one treescraper to another.

Mae watched as her three Voltari captors hovered over a pit, which doubled as their eating area. The larger one, Malmat, held a severed arm between two razor-sharp talons as he lowered it into his mouth. His semi-featureless ridge-lined face smiled, revealing rows of sharp black teeth stained with blood. Mae shuddered at the sight, wondering if she was to be next. Piayoc, the Voltari Mae identified as the one to thank for being culled, or picked, was using her foreclaw to peel the skin away from the skull she held. Mae did not know the servant her captors were eating, but she'd known he was human and that was enough for her.

Mae's mouth tasted of bile. She turned and excised the contents of her stomach over the side of the ledge, looking away as the bile struck the ground and splattered all over. She felt a cold stare and looked back at the three Voltari. The one they called Adam stood near the far exit, close to their eating pit, with his large gray shoulder resting against the wall. His long, loose-fitting blue kilt flowed in the breeze beneath a thin brown utility pouch, as his bare chest seemed not to notice the cold. His ridge-lined faceplate was pointed in her direction. It sat like a mask atop his face. Their lack of eyes made Mae uncomfortable. She knew he was staring at her, yet nothing on his face could tell her that, aside from its angle.

She stopped moving.

"I'm not cleaning that up," Adam said to Piayoc, while focusing intently on Mae.

"I know, I know. It's my responsibility," Piayoc said between bites.

"We will all take part in caring for this human until she no longer suits our needs ... like this one," Malmat interjected as he slivered his long tongue across his lips, wiping away the remnants of their last Totem's blood. *"Piayoc, you're up first. Clean her mess, and then the two of you will take her around the main aerie and the land. Ensure our contemporaries are able to see the human."*

"Progenitor, we understand," Adam said.

"Do you?" Malmat questioned.

"It's simple politics and posturing, Progenitor. I understand that better than most. Having an original human, not one of these do-

mesticated ones, will bolster our standing once we undergo the next review for clan ascension."

Adam pushed off the wall and leapt into the air, his four wings alight with energy, shimmered as the rainbow light from the walls reflected off of them. He soared across the room until he drew up near Mae. *"Can you hear me, human girl?"*

"My name is Mae, Mae Daniels. And yes," Mae replied back in her mind, disdain in her voice, *"I can hear you."* She slunk further back into her alcove until her back touched its wall.

"Why do you cower like that? I know what type of person you are. You are stronger than you let on. I smell it—your strength. Its odor is heady and pungent. Perhaps, you do not realize your own power; human minds are strange that way. You all fester in lies, deceit, and ambition as you try to gain power from external sources, from someone and somewhere else, but you fail to realize the power within yourselves. You should be glad we came, that we culled you! We've taken away your need for ambition. As our Totem, you will desire nothing except our love and attention."

"What do you get from this? From taking me against my will. I do not want to be here." Mae changed her tone to see if she could appeal to him on a different level. Despite her inner self screaming at her not to, Mae began edging closer to Adam and said, *"Listen, Adam ... I would like it very much if you would release me. If you would allow me to go back to my unit on Titan, or even back to my home on Earth. I will not tell anyone you exist, I swear it!"*

Adam's faceplate visibly shuddered and several small vibrations permeated the air between him and Mae.

"You cannot leave. Originals as Totems are rare. Those who are not used in service to the Genetic Preeminence are sent to the observatories for our viewing pleasure. To own one of you is a symbol of great means. For this reason you cannot leave. We do not fear your kind knowing of us; in fact, they already do. We exist throughout your lore as fictitious creatures of the night because, on the other side of the veil, your minds refuse to accept the possibility of our

existence."

Mae's mouth hung slack as she tried to process the possibility of never leaving this place, never earning the title of Coalition Marine and honoring her mother's memory. Above all else, Mae's heart sank at the possibility of never having free will again and experiencing life on her own terms.

Adam extended his large hand, simultaneously retracting his talons so he wouldn't injure Mae. "*Come. We must get you cleaned up. We cannot have you in our presence in such a state.*"

"*I don't want to go with you. I don't want anything from you except to be returned home,*" Mae said defiantly through gritted teeth and glistening eyes.

"*You are our Totem now. Humans of this world would kill for this position. It is the highest and most coveted position your kind could wish to seek. Do not fear me or my clan. If we wanted to harm you, we would have. Tell me, have you been harmed in some way, Mae?*" Adam asked.

Mae's thoughts betrayed her.

"*Ahh ... there it is. You do agree — no harm has come to you yet. You see that. Now, enough of this. Come to me,*" Adam said.

Mae considered her position, *I'm an ... what did he call me? An original human trapped on an alien planet, amidst these giant flying creatures, with no perceivable way to escape. I could try to escape, but if I did, I'd stick out like a sore thumb. The indigenous humans here all have the same features and don't look like me, with their brownish-silver skin tones. Even their eyes are off! Almost fully black and rounder than normal humans. And then there's my curly red hair, which is completely opposite of their off-black hair color. I'm not sure I'll be able to hide amongst them. I need more information and I need resources ... and allies. I definitely need to find some allies.*

Mae strengthened her resolve. She raised her head and met Adam's invisible gaze as she extended her hand.

The ledge Mae stood on provided a grand view of the valley that housed this Voltari city, known as the main aerie by her captors. She was high up, which is likely why they were unconcerned about her trying to escape. On the platform Mae stood on, she spied an arching skywalk off in the distance. She considered using it but thought better of it. The lack of railings terrified her. Without her armor, she knew she couldn't survive a fall from this height. She estimated she was about fifty stories from the ground.

Mae's eyes sparkled in amazement as she turned her gaze higher. The tree-like skyscraper she was in, and the ones all around her, were beyond enormous. Their towers extended skywards, well beyond the limit of her sight.

For all of their terrifying qualities, the Voltari are magnificent builders, Mae thought. The magnitude of their abilities set her nerves on edge. How could her people ever hope to compete against beings that built things on such grand scales?

Mae sought solace in the quietness around her. Taking it all in, she had only one question, "Where am I?"

From across the spacious ledge, Piayoc made herself visible. Pointing her faceplate towards Mae, she said, *"You are within the Home Crater on Taranzu, our planet of origin."* Piayoc tilted her head. *"Curious. Do you miss your home, human?"*

"My name is Mae Daniels, and you may not be able to comprehend being stolen from everything that you know and then being dumped in a zoo only to be picked as some sort of token human to a group of alien beings who are grotesquely ugly, hauntingly scary, and eat humans, so I'll be blunt — yes!" Mae's breathing intensified as she was keenly aware she'd just mouthed off to her captors, who, not hours earlier, had been eating her predecessor.

Shit, shit, shit, Mae thought. The following moment of silence between her and Piayoc felt like an eternity. A small crease began to form on the edges of Piayoc's toothy mouth.

Is she smiling at me? Mae thought.

"We are very far from the planet in Mantheia where you were

culled from."

"Wait, what did you just say?" Mae asked. *"Ok, I'm just a feeble human girl, so … help me out here, What's Mantheia? How far are we in human terms?"*

"I cannot put it into terms you will understand—of how far you are. The distance is beyond your comprehension. Instead of thinking of how far we are, think of where we are. Mantheia is a portion of Infinity that is but a grain of sand in comparison to Infinity, what all of the species of this realm call Aletheia, which is where we are. You were plucked from your realm to serve our needs. You should not fight this."

"I fight it because no one should be forced to serve another's needs. Maybe if you'd asked, I would have come willingly …"

"Would you have?" Piayoc interjected.

"No, but that's beside the point."

"No, Mae, that is the point. We need you and so we took you. That is our right. Your presence, your genes, brings us closer to achieving Genetic Preeminence."

Mae wondered how much Piayoc would be willing to share. *"What's Genetic Preeminence?"* she asked.

"Climb on," Adam said, strolling in front of her and stopping to take a knee at the crest of the ledge. He smelled like the caffeine-containing kola nuts from Africa, sweet and rose-like. His aroma reminded her of breakfasts with dad and the perfect cups of coffee he would make.

Despite his smell, the sight of the Voltari sent shivers down her spine. Their very presence affected her on a subconscious level. She was scared, and at the moment, there didn't seem to be anything to be scared of. The Voltari's actions left Mae perplexed. She'd been told to stand on this ledge and she did as she was instructed for fear of retribution. She was not, however, expecting to go for a ride on the back of one of her captors.

"I will not say it again," Adam said.

Mae did not move right away. Fear held her in place. She stared at Adam's large frame and equally large energy wings. She noted that they were able to summon the energy for their wings at will, using the four meaty appendages on their backs as some sort of mast to channel the energy. Her eyes moved over his charcoal gray muscular body and clawed hands and feet. He looked like he could break her in half without much effort.

Adam turned his head in Mae's direction and, with a thought, summoned her forward through the organic collar she wore around her neck. Mae felt an overwhelming compulsion to obey him. She took one step and then another before climbing onto his back as he had directed. Mae closed her eyes and shuddered in revulsion at the thought of her lack of control.

I will get my will back, Mae thought, as she felt Adam's mass beneath her, his muscles roiling between her legs as he stood and leapt off of the ledge.

◆ ◆ ◆

Mae closed her eyes and allowed the serenity of the land to wash over her. The warmth of the day's air enveloped her as she and her new owners soared through the aerie filled with thousands of biotreescrapers and their interconnected latticework of free-hanging skywalks; over the giant mushroom capped forest to the northwest; near the southern face of the horizon at the base of the home crater wall; over massive rolling hills and valleys before angling upward through the clouds.

"Hold on," Adam said directly into her mind as he banked hard right, flying over Piayoc and knocking his sister on the forehead before diving past her, fleeing her retribution. The trio sped towards a landmass filled with hundreds of towering sandstone-like structures jutting out of the ground, reaching for the brim of the home crater. Each mass of sandstone towers presented the group with dozens of cascading waterfalls lined with fauna, which reached out and snatched

smaller, cat-sized creatures out of the air.

As he flew, Adam ducked, rose, and ducked again while trying to evade his sister. Mae felt something hit her back. She looked over her shoulder and saw a slimy greenish-blue creature, with long eye stalks and a rippled body, sitting on her shoulder blade. Another slimy creature came hurtling towards her head, and she ducked hard to the side. The harmless slug flew past them, falling to its death. Piayoc continued hurling slugs at Mae and Adam as they evaded her.

Noticing a waterfall approaching on the left, Adam dove through it, righted his body, and jutted out all four of his wings to brake hard before hitting the rock face. He pushed off the sandstone rock with his large, powerful clawed legs and flew straight up. As Adam and Mae rotated mid-flight, Mae peered through the waterfall's flowing water to see Piayoc's shimmering image gaining on them. A moment passed before the pair broke through the crest of the waterfall, angling straight towards the twin dark stars orbiting overhead. Mae stared at the two roiling dark masses, amazed at their function and design. Unlike normal stars from her realm, these stars did not burn her eyes but instead held her in a mesmerizing stance.

The trio pierced the layer of mist that hung suspended below the clouds of the Home Crater before soaring higher than Mae had ever dreamed. The walls of the Home Crater blotted out the horizon in all directions. At this moment, Mae was freer than she'd been in a very long time. Thoughts of her dad crossed her mind. She thought of her sister's stubbornness and silly laugh before the memory of her mother crept in. Her mother's sternness was always followed by an almost imperceptible softness in her eyes when she looked at Mae or her sister. She thought of her grandmother and how persuasive she could be, which contributed in part to her finding her way into the Coalition Marine Corps. As the cool mist of the Home Crater continued to fall away from her, Mae considered her friends, Savannah Main, Garrett Beasley, Lisa Sanchez, and the other members of her squad. *Were they enjoying their new units? They had to have graduated by now,* she thought. *Did Garrett find his claim to fame and strike it rich?* Mae's thoughts drifted to 'that boy' and what he'd done to her. Jamieson had stolen what was hers and left her with the cruelest gift of all, a seed born of pure evil. It took everything in Mae not to claw at her stomach.

Mae raked her fingers across the small outward curve of her stomach. She thought about what transpired between them and how he had tried to kill her during training to keep his secret. A secret she was now responsible for. She remembered, with every detail, how she held his helpless manhood in her hand, witnessing the fear on his face before she severed it and made him eat it.

He will never harm another girl the way he harmed me, Mae thought. She looked down at her belly while Adam continued to rise. Glancing over her shoulder, Mae noticed Piayoc was still on their trail. She could no longer make out the details of the continental landmass they ascended from. *This world is bigger than anything I've ever seen,* she thought, *but it's no place for me or my unborn baby.*

Mae released her white-knuckle grip on Adam's back, falling backward, past Piayoc, hurtling towards the ground at speed. She closed her eyes, waiting for the end to come.

She welcomed it.

CHAPTER 31

Unlikely Arrival

Startled, Mae cringed, before wrangling beneath the massive hands gripping her body as she was wrenched out of the sky, her fall arrested. She opened her eyes to find Piayoc's slightly smaller frame by Voltari standards and narrower featureless face staring at her.

"*Why would you do that?*" Piayoc demanded. "*You will never do that again. Do you understand, human!*" Fury seethed through Piayoc's mind into Mae's.

Adam reached them several seconds later. He hovered close, in a nonthreatening manner. "*If you do not wish to live, Mae, you should tell us now. Because we need an Original that is willing to serve us. If not, what use are you to us?*" Adam said in a placating tone. "*Mae, I will be honest with you. I think you are special and for that, I will give you another chance to prove your worth to us. Although you must know, this chance will not come without cost. If you understand me, say so now.*"

"*It may be beyond her comprehension, Adam. Humans notoriously lack the intellectual capacity needed for true intelligence,*" Piayoc said.

"*No. She's different, Piayoc. Smell her. Do you smell that?*"

"*Yes, it's the stench of a human. We will have to bath her ourselves when we get back to the aerie. It is plain to see that she can't be trusted with such a task.*"

"*You are not using your senses, Piayoc,*" Adam said. "*I can smell her intelligence from here. She's ... special.*"

They never shifted their faceplates from Mae's direction. As they hovered a dozen miles above the ground, the warm air sailed over her skin, causing a slight trickle of perspiration to creep from Mae's hairline. Her heart pumped twice as fast, adrenaline coursing through her veins.

Mae's insides were a jumbled mess of emotions. She had just tried to kill herself. That was a moment of weakness, one she had no intention of doing again — at least she hoped. She was lost to an alien species that fed on the weak and those they no longer needed. She saw that firsthand when she arrived at their home, their aerie. On the outside, Mae's face was stoically devoid of emotion. She would not show fear or give these beings any kind of satisfaction.

She nodded her head in reply to Adam's question.

Mae noticed a slight change in Adam's and Piayoc's body language. The pair weren't as rigid as they were a moment ago.

"*Come on, you two,*" Adam said. "*We should continue our flight and then return back to the aerie.*"

The trio flew on towards the Eastern Gates, a ring of mountains that made a natural barrier, holding back a large body of water. Piayoc took the lead, angling towards the large lake basin jutting out from the rim of the mountains' center. They flew under the lake's basin and through the waterfalls veiling what lay beyond.

I'm glad I didn't eat much, Mae thought as she attempted to keep her nausea from Piayoc's wild flying at bay. She held her head close to Piayoc's back as she weaved in and out of stalactites the size of suburban houses growing from the underside of the massive lake basin connected to a large archway set into the mountainside.

As the trio emerged from the city of stalactites, Mae gasped. An amphitheater, miles wide, framed one side of a large, smooth parade ground hidden in the shadow of the jagged underside of the lake basin. It stretched from the middle of the Eastern Gates for several miles.

The Coalition would definitely be envious of this parade ground, Mae thought. *If I'm guessing right, it can house hundreds of thousands of troops. What could they possibly need that much space for?* Mae eyed the few hundred Voltari engaged in both aerial and ground battles over the parade grounds. She tried to keep pace with some of them but found they moved too fast for her eyes. Mae shifted her attention beyond the amphitheater, the massive concrete-like parade ground, and small forest city to the massive archway embedded in the mountain. Its eroding entrance warned of impending collapse, yet its wide opening beckoned for any brave soul willing to gamble their lives away to enter.

"*Piayoc, where are we?*" Mae asked.

Piayoc and Adam dove in spiraling circles towards the large training grounds. "*We're in the border city, Garoth,*" Piayoc said.

"*What's beyond that large archway? Where does it lead?*" Mae asked, pointing.

"*Beyond the arch of the Eastern Gates are ruins, memories of our past. It's an ancient place. It is said that no one has visited there in … what you would fathom as thousands of years. Beyond those ruins is a desert wasteland with more ruins. Those ruins and the ones within the mountain all used to be one vast, interconnected city. Our ancestors lived there before they learned to harness the power that is ever-present all around us and take flight. Now those ruins are nothing more than relics of the past. They're triggers for memories we no longer hold, lives we no longer live.*"

"*What's beyond the desert ruins?*" Mae probed, not sure if

Piayoc would continue to tolerate her questions.

"*Nothing*," Piayoc said. "*Beyond the desert is the wall of the Home Crater.*"

Interesting, Mae thought. *A city, maybe more, lies beyond those gates ... and they haven't been there in centuries? If I can figure out where it leads, maybe I can get away from them and hide there until I can figure out a way off this damn planet!*

After landing, Mae began climbing off of Piayoc's back when she froze at Piayoc's low guttural sound. "*Do not get down! We are not staying long. We are only here for our kin to witness you.*"

Mae narrowed her eyes at the back of Piayoc's head, pausing for a moment. She took several deep breaths, then climbed back up Piayoc's back.

Through gritted teeth, Mae asked, "*What are they doing, all of those Voltari that are fighting each other?*"

Piayoc seemed to take no notice of Mae's agitation and replied, "*It's a test of strength, will, and cunning. The victor ascends the rank ladder, gaining more prestige for their clan. The overall victor is granted the right to sojourn with The Keeper of the Code for a genetic blessing.*"

"*Our progenitor, Malmat, got our clan out of the trials by footing the bill for an Original Human — you, Mae Daniels,*" Piayoc said, briefly turning her head over her shoulder in Mae's direction before continuing. "*Everyone participates in the annual battles unless they've recently acquired an Original, then they get a ten-cycle pass. That is almost twenty years in human terms. The population disparity between Originals and Voltari is large. On Taranzu, my people vastly outnumber Original Humans, so the majority of people are subject to the trials. We were lucky to have found you.*"

Mae considered what she'd just learned. *These beings are just as much of a warrior race as they are master artisans and builders. Incredible.* As her thoughts swirled, she almost missed the large, slender Voltari that landed not far from where they stood. *She's got to be a female,* Mae thought, her ability to notice minute differences between the sexes was growing. The Voltari female's charcoal gray visage increased in size as she grew closer.

"*Adam!*" the female called, stopping a few paces in front of the trio.

"*Is that how you greet your superior! On your knee, Marah. Beg your Lord forgiveness, and I may forget your lack of protocol,*" Adam said, his voice booming into the minds of those around him.

Mae thought she noticed a moment of hesitation on the female's part before she bowed slightly. "*That is why I am here ... my Lord.*" Raising her head defiantly, she said, "*I challenge you to a match for succession.*"

"*Marah, you do not want that to happen. I will not grant you mercy for this request. Your insolence will not be forgiven, and thus, you will not succeed. My cost imposed on you — when you lose — is death.*" Adam said, as his wing arms unfurled and blazed to life. Shimmering purple energy sizzled in the air as they coalesced into four distinct wings.

Gust after gust of air assaulted Mae's face as Adam lifted himself several feet above them. Mae partially covered her face, but she watched as he continued to speak for all to hear with his taloned hands spread wide, "*If you're brazen enough to pay the high price I have set, challenge me now — and die.*"

With dizzying speed, Marah lunged off the ground into the air towards Adam, her clawed hands outstretched.

"*Hold on,*" Piayoc said to Mae as she sped away from the ground, retreating to a safe distance. Piayoc landed between the edge of the massive parade ground and the outskirts of the forest city near the black market.

"*What's happening?*" Mae demanded. Her attitude never seemed to have much effect on her masters.

Piayoc turned, lowering her faceplate until she was eye level with Mae. "*My Totem, you are a curious one. Perhaps Adam was right about you. Maybe there is some intelligence hidden in you.*"

Mae felt an uneasiness grip her body at the proximity of Piayoc's razor-sharp teeth to her face. She stared for a long moment at the black gums wrapped around Piayoc's serrated teeth, the coarse ridges lining her faceplate, and the small slits where her nose should be. Mae steeled herself against a shiver that made its way through her body. She stepped closer, refusing to show these creatures her fear. Mae locked her eyes on Piayoc's faceplate with a ferocity that matched her will.

Piayoc smiled at Mae's gesture. *"Marah works for Adam, and if she can best him in a trial by combat, what we call a match for succession, then she has the right to assume his mantle as Herald of Special Projects or to mate with him."*

Perplexed, Mae asked, *"Does he have a choice?"*

"No," Piayoc replied.

Like hundreds of other Voltari and human servants in the area were already doing, Mae and Piayoc turned their attention back towards Adam and Marah. The pair were heavily engaged in aerial combat. Marah sent a series of strikes and kicks towards Adam; each one was deflected.

Marah's left leg flew towards Adam's cranium. He shifted his weight, spun on his axis, and emerged behind Marah before she could react. Grabbing her two lead wings, Adam planted his taloned foot behind the much more slender Voltari and yanked back hard while simultaneously kicking with enough force to send Marah crashing into the ground below.

Marah's wing arms, now broken, hung limply from her body, draping the ground as she rose. Her two lesser wings shone with half the luminosity as before. She watched for what seemed like an eternity as Adam descended from the sky until his faceplate was level with hers.

Marah rapidly threw a hail of kicks, slashes, and strikes. Adam met each blow with greater speed and power — except one. Marah's arm shot past Adam's faceplate. He leaned to the left, shooting a straight jab towards Marah's larynx, grabbed her chin and yanked, pulling her to her knees again. At the same time Marah pulled her arm back to her side, raking Adam's face with her talons.

"Marah, I expected so much more from you," Adam said, ignor-

ing the warm sticky blood dripping down his faceplate.

"*Expectations are designed to disappoint,*" Marah said, slumped on the ground.

"*This was unnecessary,*" Adam said, taking both of Marah's arms in his grasp. "*I was going to make you my mate. Now I will have to find another or reproduce alone.*"

"*My Lord, I needed to! My clan's been in the lower rankings long enough. Besting you would have been the easiest path for me to boost our standing. You have to understand.*"

"*Except you didn't best me. In fact, ...*" Adam said, clamping down on Marah's biceps, applying more and more pressure until the sound of ripping muscle and breaking bones could be heard, "*... this challenge was a joke and a waste of my time. You bit off more than you can chew, Marah.*" Adam grabbed Marah by the throat, raising her above his head.

"*My Lord,*" Marah managed to gargle, the pressure on her throat heavy and restrictive, "*allow me one request. Consume me. If I am to die, allow my genetic code to give you strength through my weakness. Grant me this one request, my Lord.*"

"*No,*" Adam replied, "*you do not deserve it.*"

Marah writhed in Adam's grip as he reached down and pulled a small creature from the satchel hanging off his waist. She struggled more as realization set in. Adam raised the creature and placed it on her face before dropping her. The surrounding area was quiet with curious Voltari. Marah's body lay on the ground, the life force draining from her. The creature worked fast, withering her down to a lifeless pile of exoskeleton and bones.

Mae's stare swept over the grotesque scene, taking in every detail with her EMCD. She watched as Adam slipped the creature back into his satchel before flying off.

"*Let's return home,*" Piayoc said. "*The challenge here is over.*"

"*Piayoc, what's that?*" Mae said, pointing behind them towards a small jungle of low-lying, open-air apartments adorning thousands of massively squat trees. Markets lined the dirt paths between trees. Mae noticed Voltari everywhere wearing bones around their necks or freshly chopped and still rotting human body parts. Some Voltari had one or two human eyes embedded in their faceplates, while human ears dangled at odd angles off of others.

"That is the black market. You do not want to go there, Mae. This section of the continent is where some of the less reputable clans reside. They've taken to debased acts of savagery and unsanctioned genetic splicing. Some of them even try to mate with their humans," Piayoc said in Mae's mind. *"Their debased acts typically go unchallenged so long as it doesn't spill into the rest of the aerie."*

Piayoc rose into the air, flapping her wings twice as hard to compensate for Mae's weight.

A loud crashing sound caused Mae to look back. Below her a man and two Voltari tumbled out of a portal and through a handful of vendor stands and markets before coming to a rest. Several Voltari were visibly perturbed by the intruders. The man got to his feet, shifted his clothing to match the indigenous humans around him, and looked up.

Mae's eyes met his and tried to contain herself. *Jax — it's Jax! What in the world!*

CHAPTER 32

Operation Phantom Mamba

Liam Alexander closed his eyes as their launch clock wined down.

... 50 seconds.

His light breath, muffled and hot, was the only sound he heard amidst the darkness of his Aegis armor. To increase structural integrity, the Aegis armor systems lacked any openings for ocular vision, save for emergencies. He thought-clicked the appropriate sequence of mental buttons to bring up the external camera feeds in his mind.

Two techs stood near a handful of floating displays, their fingers tapping across each display in well-rehearsed patterns. The lead tech signaled to the other. They prepared to press the launch button.

... 30 seconds.

"Team, listen up," Major Alexander said. "Once we're space-born, double-check your telemetry. Make sure you're on target. Remember, this is a snatch and grab. Our objective is to get our people out, not wage an all-out war. If we can avoid it, belay engagement in favor of finding our guys and gals. The transport ships, launched ahead of us, will conduct exfil. Our job is to get a homing beacon to the location where they're holding our people and hold the pirates off long enough to get them out."

"Now, double-check your readouts and standby for deployment."

… Launch.

Liam noted a slight jolt as his TALOS Aegis, cocooned within the insertion pod, was accelerated to near the speed of light as it was fired from the Aurora's central spine-mounted rail gun. The Valkyrie add-ons made it a tight fit within each insertion pod. Their hawk-like wings stealing the last bit of wiggle room not taken by the TALOS's bulky armor.

"Team, T-minus four minutes until we hit our mark. One minute of acceleration with three minutes of decel. Be ready!"

The extremely fast-moving cluster of Coalition insertion pods was lost in the backdrop of the looming colony bubble — a technological marvel.

"Anyone else suddenly have to use the head?" Private First Class (PFC) Walker stammered. "I think I just pissed myself. Look at that thing. A species built that, and we're going in there?"

Several other Marines murmured their own words of astonishment.

"Can the shit talk, Walker! All of you, shut it!" Despite the vast distance between the two, Gunny Jones's stern voice boomed within PFC Walker's ear.

"Come on, Guns! I'm just saying, maybe it'd be better to turn around while we can. Cut our losses."

"Walker, one more word out of you like that, and I'll personally see that you're left on that thing, whatever the fuck it is.

Understood?"

"Aye, Gunnery Sergeant!" Walker said resignedly, "Understood."

After having bled off almost all of their speed, one by one, twenty insertion pods slammed into the side of the colony bubble. The nanotechnic matrix of their hulls began eating their way through the colony bubble's strange hull.

PFC Raya Links emerged feet first, bursting into an open space full of darkness and began tumbling towards the ground several thousand kilometers below.

"*Guys,*" Links said over the mental tac-link as her body flipped end over end. "*We're in a cavern of some type. I'm falling. Activate your Valkyrie's as soon as you emerge from the pods.*"

She loosed her mechanical wings from their resting position on her back. They flared to life, slowing her as she regained control of her tumbling freefall.

"Turn on your camouflage, Marines. We don't need to be seen if we don't have to," Gunny Jones said.

"Belay that," Major Alexander said, immediately countering Jones's order. "During the mission briefing, the general said these beings have a method of seeing in spectrums outside of what we consider visible —which happens to be in the same spectrum we shift into for camouflage. That means they can see us when we go stealth, Marines, so conserve your power."

"*What are we going to do without our stealth?*" Sanchez asked Walker mentally through her EMCD. "*I dunno,*" he replied, "*but I don't want to be here. This place doesn't seem right. They should have left me back on CMB Starfire. I didn't ask to be here.*"

"*Walker, we're Coalition Marines now. We don't ask for none of this, but we will happily take it,*" Sanchez said. "*Remember that, Now let's go, buddy.*"

The Marines descended head first from the heavens on powerful obsidian wings. They streaked towards the ground like mad hellions loosed from their leashes besieged on the lands of the enemy. Their entry point receded from view at mind-numbing speeds. In the blink of an eye, it was no longer visible. Using the thruster packs on their backs, each Marine crossed the vast distance from insertion point to ground in a matter of minutes.

Following the coordinates they'd been given, they touched down on the outer edge of a continent-sized forest housing biotechnic tree-like skyscrapers three thousand feet tall and inundated with massive perches, gravity-defying free-hanging skybridges, and cathedral-like rooms. The skybridges were interwoven into the biotreescrapers in patterns of three.

"It's kind of hard to remain hidden when dozens of large armored men with wings just descended from the sky and landed in your backyard," Major Alexander said to no one in particular.

"On me, Marines. Intel suggests we're close. Several hundred meters in that direction," Alexander said to his strike force, while mentally highlighting and sharing a route which would take them four degrees starboard of their current position.

"Liam, what do you suppose this place is?" Captain Marsh asked over a private line.

"Not sure, Sarah. Intel suggests it's possibly a piece of a Dyson Sphere. The pirates must have done some sort of terraforming to it. Besides that, carbon dating suggests it's pretty old. They aren't sure how old, but they date it at around 600 million years old. Could be older."

"There's no fucking way. Liam, the implications alone ..."

"I know, Sarah. It means our universe had intelligent life long before humanity evolved on Earth."

"Technically, we aren't in our universe, Liam."

Major Alexander extended a portion of his consciousness into Sarah's mind, waited for a mental version of her to coalesce, then he pulled her in close and tapped her on her bottom. His mental avatar grinned before releasing her. She'd been by his side a long time and she never had a problem telling him when he was wrong. He really liked that about her. *"Depends on who you ask,"* Liam continued, withdrawing his consciousness. *"The word on the street is that we are in our universe. Just that we left a small portion of that universe behind, the universe we know — you know, with normal matter and regular space — the dark stuff."*

His gentle husky voice, preceded by a light chuckle, filled Sarah's head, warming her from the inside out. Within the claustrophobic confines of her TALOS Aegis, Sarah smiled as she leapt over a small obstacle and took up temporary cover on the edge of a large tree.

"Where is everyone, sir?" Gunny Jones asked over the tac-link, a channel he knew everyone was monitoring. His pace was moderate and deliberate as he navigated between the bio-treescrapers and redwood-sized undergrowth, towards the spot on the map Liam had highlighted.

"Guns, to be honest, I'm not too sure. We still know next to nothing about these beings. We don't know their habits, how they live, how they sleep, how they eat, and most importantly, how they think. To defeat an enemy, we must master how they think to anticipate their moves. When the enemy is unknown to us, we tend to spend more time fighting ourselves than them while we figure out how best to defeat them. I think we are in the latter situation right now, Guns."

"Yes, sir," Jones replied, more out of habit than anything. "But I'm reading no signs of life within our immediate area. Shouldn't there be something, someone, you know — some kind of activity here?" Gunnery Sergeant Jones asked.

"Guns, the size of the colony bubble we're on is on par with the size of a small planetoid. Most likely a broken-off part of a Dyson Sphere. Maybe these pirates are like hermit crabs, and they moved in and renovated the place to suit their needs. We don't know their strength in numbers, but based on the size of this place, there could be more of them here than there are people on Titan, or maybe there's just a couple hundred. Either way, stay sharp! All of you! This is no time for complacency."

Captain Marsh held up a hand, signaling to the other nineteen Marines — what constituted a platoon reinforced — to halt. At the same time, she sent several commands to the Platoon Sergeant, Gunny Jones, and each of the four squad leaders to fan out and form a defensive perimeter. "Captain Marsh," Major Alexander called over the tac-link. "What is it? What do you have?"

"Not sure yet, sir. I thought I saw something flash by that biotreescraper several hundred feet ahead. The spot on the map we're heading for." Marsh activated her enhanced visual perception display, giving her limited ranged x-ray vision. She slowly and meticulously scanned her surroundings from left to right. The atmosphere was twice a thick as the troposphere on Earth, and the local fauna seemed to respond to their presence. She peered through much of the purple and orange vegetation at ground level. Her vision came to settle on something a little less than four hundred feet from their current position.

"Look alive. I got something," Marsh called out over the tac-link.

"What is it?" Alexander asked. His suit lacked the 'snoop and poop' suite of hardware the scouts were so accustomed to operating. Captain Marsh was one of a handful of Marines within the Task Force with this specific loadout. Alexander's TALOS was primarily and optimally designed as a command and control, or C2, suit of armor.

"Two heat signatures. They appear to be moving in this direction — slowly. I think they're trying to sneak up on us, sir."

"They're blocking the path we need to take to get to our stolen shipmates," Liam Alexander uttered, studying the tactical display in his mind.

An explosion rocked the center of the Marines' position. Private First Class Walker and Links were the closest to the explosion. Their bodies were heaved into the air on arching trajectories. Walker crashed into two Marines nearest him, hammering them to the ground with his armor's weight, while Links was blown into a tree twenty feet from her previous position. Her TALOS slammed sideways into the tree, hard enough to rattle her brain and cause momentary paralysis. Her body, a slumped pile of obsidian armor embossed with gold trim, slid ten feet down before hitting the ground. The other four Marines within the outer edge of the blast were forced back a couple of feet but remained standing.

While the intruding Marines had been scanning the horizontal plane, they left themselves vulnerable to attack from above. At the epicenter of the explosion stood three Voltari pirates, talons open and poised to attack. Their four shimmering purple wings, extending on meaty protrusions, shone in stark contrast to their charcoal gray bodies and faceless heads in the dead of night.

Several other Voltari descended from the darkness above on four massive wings made of energy, their glow exasperated by the intense darkness around them. Their faceless energy-infused bodies were almost majestic, aside from the primal fear they elicited. Liam found himself momentarily stunned by their radiance before springing into action.

His armored legs pushed off from the ground, propelling him several feet to the closest Voltari, taking full advantage of the winged pirate's close proximity and the extra-human strength his TALOS armor provided him. He drew his arm back and felt the buildup of kinetic energy. In one swift motion, he connected his fist with the closest pirate's faceplate. The being's neck snapped back from the tremendous force of the strike, leaving his head hanging at an awkward angle.

Liam sent several mental commands to his Marines, who were now engaging the enemy on both land and in the air, dashing about at incredible speeds. Not waiting to watch his pirate's body slump to the ground, he activated his thrusters in conjunction with a powered jump, throwing himself into a sharp parabolic arc. On the downward trajectory, Liam pulled his 20-inch obsidian K-blade and drove it down towards a Voltari engaged in mid-air combat with PFC Sanchez. The blade struck its target but was deflected, not quite scratching the being.

Sanchez blocked a clawed attack at her armored face with her left arm while bringing her right arm cannon to bear. The pirate caught Sanchez's right arm at the elbow joint. He bore down, releasing a sickening crunch as Sanchez's armor tore into her flesh, crushing tendons and bones. Through gritted teeth and searing pain, Sanchez thought, *his strength is off the charts. He shouldn't have been able to do that!*

"Sanchez, duck!!" Liam screamed through the mental-link. Bringing his arm cannon level with the pirate's neck, he loosed a short burst of superheated plasma, disintegrating its head. Sanchez raised her head and saw her attacker's now-headless body fall away towards the city-forest floor. She nodded at Liam to show her appreciation.

Bolts of plasma streaked about the orgy of bodies, intermingled in a deadly dance of life and death playing out in the sky and on the ground. Plasma shots filled the dense air with superheated electrified bolts of ionized gas. The Voltari were quick and nimble in the air, dodging many of the shots hurled their way.

Liam surveyed the carnage. The Voltari's dominance of the sky was quickly becoming apparent. Large craters were made in the biotech superstructures as plasma bolts found solid matter to destroy. The skybridge over Captain Marsh collapsed, narrowly missing her as she zoomed away.

PFCs Houston and Beasley managed to take down one of the Voltari pirates after trapping him in a small rocky outcropping and pummeling his hard exoskeleton with blow after blow of their armored fists, delivering almost four thousand pounds of force in each of their one hundred lightning-quick moves. Each blow depressed the Voltari's exoskeleton a bit more than the last until it finally cracked. "Guys, their bodies are as hard as rock," Houston said in her usual lazy drawl, the previous moment of battle having no effect on her inflection.

"Graphene!" Beasley corrected. "If they were as hard as a rock, we would have been able to take them down a lot easier," he said. "I'd say their exoskeletons are closer to graphene. That stuff is 100 times stronger than steel."

The pair droned on as they sought their next target.

Chaos reigned.

Four targets remained, two of which were almost double the size and width of the previous ones.

"Captain Marsh, grab a squad and take that big one buzzing around on the left. I want this one," Major Alexander said as he mentally tagged the Voltari pirate ahead of him as his designated target.

Liam's blood pumped harder. Faster. His Aegis worked double-time to counteract his metabolic functions. Something in him stirred, the darkness he tried so hard to suppress rising from the depths of his essence. Liam's veins pulsed on the surface of his skin just beneath his protective armor. The darkness attached to his soul screamed for life. It needed to feed; Liam was obliged to let it.

The Voltari watched the curious human stalking towards him. *So confident these humans,* Brytac thought to himself. He reached out with his mind and called his commander, *"Paragon, the humans have overcome this volley of our probing attacks. Are our brothers ready to repel them from this aerie?"*

"We are en route now, Brytac. Hold them off until we arrive. I know of a particular merchant who would be delighted to receive a fresh stock of genetic material from Originals."

Brytac spread his taloned feet wide enough to anchor himself. He leaned forward and began vibrating his faceplate. Two nearby Marines began moving towards the Voltari but were waved off by the advancing major. Brytac's faceplate shook with increasing intensity. He sent a focused beam of oscillating theta waves towards Alexander's helmet.

Alexander stumbled, gripped his helmet, and screamed. His left leg buckled. He caught his fall before looking up. His anger rose while fighting a wave of intense mental pain and nausea. Through his blurring vision, he raised his free arm, pointing his plasma cannon at the Voltari in front of him.

Brytac launched himself towards the human, his mental on-slaught continuing.

PFC Links broke away from her engagement and sent a torrent of plasma blasts Brytac's way, the ground around his feet exploding into millions of pieces. Brytac dashed left, then right, and left again, skimming the ground and avoiding each blast while gaining on Major Alexander. Noticing his human target pointing a weapon at him, Brytac dug his talons into the ground, bringing him to a skidding halt before he thrust himself into the darkness above.

Liam managed to level his arm cannon. He fired into the spot the Voltari had occupied seconds before. The mental assault had ended. His head throbbed. His in-head display showed his armor was working quickly to bring his cardiovascular and neurological systems under control.

PFC Links's scream rang in his mind through his EMCD as if she was beside him. Liam turned left and saw her. Thirty feet away, she was engaged in combat with one of the pirates. No, that wasn't quite right. It was the same ginormous pirate that had just assailed him.

"Captain Marsh!" Liam called over the tac-link. Her acknowledgment was immediate yet labored. "Sir? What is it?

"I need a distraction. Something to draw the pirate's attention away for a moment."

"Got it, sir. We're a little busy trying to take this other one down, but I'll get it done," Marsh said, before ending the connection.

Liam watched as Captain Marsh and PFC Marcus peeled off from their fight, leaving several others to deal with the second obscenely large pirate. They rushed to remove their Valkyrie wings and placed them together in predetermined patterns. The nanotech inside each wing registered the patterns and begun tying each piece together with tendrils of nanoparticulates that blossomed from each wing. The resultant combination was a car-sized variant of the plasma cannon each TALOS Aegis carried.

"Captain Marsh, fire the cannon towards the pirate attacking Links. Draw him away from her. I'll do the rest."

Marsh mounted the single-seat cannon. She allowed her hands to hover mere inches above the controls, maneuvering the bulky cannon with gestures of her fingers. Marcus, acting as Marsh's spotter, fed her grid coordinates for their firing solution.

Marsh curled her fingers, sending the signal for the cannon to loose its rounds. Bolts of superheated ionized plasma, wrapped in a magnetic casing, left the muzzle of the cannon, whizzing through the air until they struck matter. The front-facing wall of the biotreescraper behind Links exploded in a violent torrent of energy.

"Jesus Christ, guys! You almost took my head off!" Links screamed into her comm as debris rained down on her prostrate body held aloft against the biotreescraper by Brytac. The wall above Brytac and Links, now gone, revealed a floor full of human captives.

In route to PFC Links, Alexander, fully intent on taking advantage of the situation, bellowed, "Get me a fucking beacon on that building—now!" He was close to reaching Links.

Liam watched on in horror as the pirate held each one of Links's limbs in his taloned hands and feet. He had her pinned to the wall of that biotreescraper. Ripples of orange, yellow, and green fanned out across the face of the building from the spot where Links's body was held. The living building reacting to the presence of life. Through the darkness, Liam watched as those ripples changed from light to dark colors. Purple and dark blue hues began to replace the orange, yellow, and green patterns as the pirate tore each limb from PFC Links in slow succession.

The screams that echoed throughout the Marines comms were unnerving.

Liam armed his cannon and pointed it towards the pirate. Several dozen more feet and he'd be on him.

He sighted in on the Voltari, but it was too late. He was

forced to bank hard right as a bloody limb streaked past his faceplate, severed muscles and ligaments flapping as it passed. Each of Links's other limbs flew past Liam before he reached the Pirate.

Liam closed the distance. His fist slammed into the building, sending shimmering orange waves out in concentric circles. Brytac danced around Liam's onslaught, his massive form belied a swiftness and agility that Liam was hard-pressed to match.

Liam fired once, twice, a third time. Each shot struggled to find Brytac as the huge Voltari worked his wings to keep him out of Liam's line of sight. Seeing an opening, Brytac brought his wings together, dropping his body from the sky until he was directly in front of Liam before flaring them out again to arrest his speed. A taloned hand shot out and embedded itself in Liam's shoulder, pinning him to the wall. Liam planted his feet, pushing the huge pirate back. He held the pirate's free arm, his enhanced strength waning. He listened to the screeching sound of the alien's razor-sharp talons embedded in his shoulder, tearing through his armor and flesh. He fought the waves of nausea threatening to overtake him as he struggled to free himself.

Captain Marsh gritted her teeth silently, saying a prayer as she ended the call with Dr. Grosbeak. *That doctor better be right, or Liam might not make it out of this alive,* she thought.

Marsh eyed Gunny Jones as he withdrew his armored arms from the inside of the field cannon. "She's ready for you, ma'am," Jones said in his gruff voice. Marsh nodded her appreciation.

Captain Marsh watched as Liam and the pirate he fought disappeared behind a biotreescraper.

She swiveled the massive land cannon, mentally maneuvering the targeting reticle in her mind's eye until she found her mark. Marsh watched through her enhanced vision as the pulsating outline of two figures fought in hand-to-hand combat on the other side of a biotreescraper. With outstretched arms hovering over two plain circular patches, Marsh made last-minute maneuvering adjustments to the cannon. She focused the mental targeting reticle, found her mark, then fired.

The battlefield stood still as the plasma round whorled across the intervening distance from barrel to target in the blink of an eye. It phase-shifted milliseconds before hitting the outer wall of the living building, rematerializing on the opposite side. A split second later, the round struck home.

Liam ran up the side of the building with the Voltari flying behind him, closing the distance with each of Liam's steps. Liam pushed off the biotreescraper, intending on flipping behind the pirate. The top of his helmet was three meters above the Voltari's when an explosion followed by a brilliant flash of light flung Liam head over feet, perpendicular to his original arc. He tumbled fifteen stories towards the ground.

PFCs Sanchez and Beasley swooped up from the surface, catching Liam twenty meters before he made impact. "We got you, sir!" Garrett Beasley said, ignoring the debris pelting his armor.

"Thanks, Marines, I got it from here," Liam shot back. Beasley and Sanchez heard the gratitude in their boss's voice and smiled behind their faceplates.

Liam stood on solid ground, now staring up at the massive crater in the side of the building. Smoke, ash, and debris were everywhere. *Where's that damned pirate?* Liam thought to himself as he scanned the area. "Anyone got eyes on that pirate I was facing?" he asked over the platoon's tac-link.

"Yeah, he's wherever the rest of that wall went," Captain Marsh replied, allowing a sigh of relief to escape her lips. "You're welcome, sir," she added as a wry smile crested her face. Accessing his private channel Marsh chided him, *"How many times have I saved your life now?"*

"Not nearly as many times as I've saved yours. Now coordinate the rescue of our shipmates," Liam said, not feeling very jovial.

She'd robbed him of his kill. He needed that kill. His appetite for blood screamed to be fed. He'd have his fill soon enough.

Liam watched as four Komodo drop ships descended from the sky towards their position. Four aft wings framed the drop ships' stalky V-shaped bodies. Several exposed gun positions around the front fuselage gave the ships the appearance of ominous, frilled-neck dragons.

The first of the Komodos decelerated while turning its sleek, stout bow away from the biotreescraper that housed the stolen sailors. As it arrested its speed, the stern doors opened, bringing its edge to rest along the freshly made crumbling hole of the biotreescraper.

Sailors coughed, waving away smoke and debris from the recent explosion as they were transferred into the belly of the Komodo from the back by the tall, steely-eyed Loadmaster.

"Sir, we have a situation," Gunny Jones reported. "Send it, Guns," Liam said. "We have a massive horde of those winged creatures heading our way. They're skirting the horizon, probably hoping we wouldn't notice them until it's too late."

Liam swore under his breath. "ETA on their arrival?"

"In about eight minutes, we're going to be overrun, sir!"

"Solid copy."

Liam switched comm channels, hailing their rides. "Lead Komodo pilot, this is the Ground Recon Commander Major Alexander. We have hostiles inbound. What's the ETA on getting our people out of here?"

"Major, this is Lieutenant Commander Barnet. We see them. Inbound track has those bogies arriving too late. Dust off in four mikes, how copy?"

"Lieutenant Commander, solid copy. We're oscar mike in four minutes."

Liam mentally toggled the channel to send an all-hands message to his Marines. "Listen up, you lot. Complete egress is in little less than four mikes. I want our asses out of here before that horde reaches us! Understood?"

Uniform acknowledgments populated in his in-head display as he made his way to the closest drop ship.

From the back of the Komodo, Liam stood and stared into the horizon. Captain Marsh took up position on his left. Using his EMCD, Liam accessed the link with his second-in-command and allowed a small portion of his mind to drift into hers. *"Sarah, I've seen a lot of things in my time, but that mass coming towards us gives me the chills."*

"Same, sir," Sarah said, focusing on the mass of creatures highlighted by their shimmering purple wings. Their faceless bodies filled the sky now as they angled towards the fleeing Komodos.

Together Major Alexander and Captain Marsh turned and shut the hatch in preparation to fly through light-space.

CHAPTER 33

Accidents Happen

Mae worked hard to keep her footing as she climbed out of the living chamber and into the corridor leading to the atrium using the slope her captors fashioned for her. Once she was in the expansive corridor, Mae walked, taking in the surrounding artwork and vast array of weaponry, some of which appeared aged, others newer. Since the time she and her captors spent flying around the continent, Mae noticed that the pieces of technology dispersed throughout the home weren't based in biology like the rest of Voltari technology she'd seen. She strode on, passing several openings on either side of the corridor. Each opening gave way to various rooms, their purposes beyond her understanding. Mae felt like an ant amongst giants. The few pieces of furniture that littered either side of the hall were disproportionately larger than she was.

The beating of heavy wings brought Mae out of her ruminations and amazement. As she stepped closer to the third opening on the left, her mind picked up the voices of Adam and Piayoc.

Mae crept closer, knowing any information she could gather

would help her eventually escape this place. She flattened her body against the wall, sliding close enough to peek into the chamber without being seen.

Just like old times, Mae thought, thinking about the night she eavesdropped on her dad's secret meeting with the Upgraders. *Except for this time, I'm stuck light-years from home with no way out. So, yup, definitely not like old times,* she mused.

Piayoc's voice rang out in Mae's mind, *"Adam, our Totem must be in heat. There can be no other explanation."*

"No, I don't think she is, Piayoc. I don't sense it."

"Did you not say she was different, Adam? Did you not say there was something off about her? That she wreaked havoc on your senses? Then how could you sense it if your senses are out of whack because of her?"

"Ok, let's assume you are right. What difference does it make? We do not have a male Original she can mate with."

"Could we use one of the ones in the Special Projects lab?"

"Maybe. It would be risky. Without direct guidance from the Chancellor, I cannot just pull one of the Originals out of the pods. If I did, I'd be found and dealt with accordingly, even as Herald."

"That limits our options then."

"No, it doesn't. I don't think this is very important."

"Adam, you know it is. Human psychology and biology are tied to their reproductive systems. They are not like us. They cannot reproduce at will. They copulate because they have a physical and mental need to. From what we know, their mental states become a bit unstable when they go long periods without copulation. Didn't you read the instructions when we purchased her?"

"Ok, so we have a problem then. We need her in good health, at least for a bit longer."

"You do it," Piayoc said, floating down near a large ottoman. *"Mate with her."*

"No, are you out of your mind! Malmat will not allow it, not to mention it is illegal." Mae thought she heard genuine revulsion in his voice. *"Only the Forsaken do such things. They have no morals. Their debased devotion to our beliefs is warped and*

twisted and have led them down a separate path from us," Adam continued.

"This is how it must be, Adam. You have to."

"Piayoc, listen. The Chancellor and the Council of Three tolerate the Forsaken and their existence as a social experiment. He's curious if they might be onto something. He wants to reach Genetic Preeminence just as badly as we do. Do you know what the Chancellor would do if he found out there were Voltari outside of the Forsaken practicing that method of procreation? He would add my genetic code to his own."

"No. He won't. You said it. He wants to reach Genetic Preeminence more than any one of us. What if this human, Mae, is as special as you think she is? What do you think would happen if you added your genetic code to hers through procreation? Shouldn't we at least try and see what happens?"

"You make an enticing argument, sister. I am curious. I can smell her intelligence and aura, and they are greater than any other Original our Reapers have culled."

Adam fell silent, his thoughts no longer broadcasting. Mae's heart thumped in her chest and she began to perspire. When Adam spoke again, it startled Mae and she almost made a noise.

"If I do this, it will need to be at my lab. There I can monitor her properly and make the necessary preparations for the coupling. No one will suspect anything since that is where experiments on humans are sanctioned. There is one thing you should know."

Mae couldn't tell if Piayoc was happy about Adam's decision, but she noticed a slight change in Piayoc's body language. She seemed less tense now.

Piayoc placed her head to Adams and said, "Thank you. Now, what should I know?"

"I thought I sensed it before but was unsure. As I said, she is different. But after having her in such close proximity as we flew around the continent, I could tell. Our human is with child. It will need to be removed before I copulate with her. We can offer it to the Chancellor. With such an offering of genetic material, our clan will *most certainly ascend to the top tier of society. He may very well grant us a bountiful genetic blessing."*

Piayoc and Adam both turned their heads towards the chamber's opening. A loud crash came from the hall beyond, followed by quick, scampering steps. Human steps.

"Leave her to me," Adam said, taking off after Mae.

◆ ◆ ◆

The shimmering light from the sun beckoned Mae. The urge to reach out and touch the single pinprick of refracting light, etching out in all directions like a star swallowed by the water, engulfed her.

Each attempt to move her arms failed. She bit her lip, straining beneath the surface to reach out and touch the light.

Nothing.

Her arms did not respond. Her legs bore the weight of a thousand anvils. Panic swelled inside her.

Her body began to convulse.

The light grew in size, threatening to blot out her vision.

The water surrounding her became more and more viscous, restricting her movements.

The light began to overtake her.

Mae's body hit the floor; water splashed around her as searing light stung her eyes before receding. A pair of strong arms gripped her beneath the armpits and slung her onto a sticky surface, a table of some sort.

"What ... are ... you ... doing ... with ... me," Mae half-mumbled, half-slurred. The drugs in her system beginning to dissipate.

The Voltari in the dimly-lit lab continued to work, ignoring Mae's words. They were smaller than the ones she'd previously seen. The green light from several other fluid-filled chambers bathed the room, casting dark, misshapen shadows.

A violent burst of radiant white light filled the room. Each of the Voltari in the lab continued working, seemingly un-affected. Beside Mae, the figure of a man stepped out of the shimmering light.

"Mae, focus. You have to focus now," Thourn said.

Mae's mind struggled to put together coherent thoughts. "It's you again," she mumbled.

Thourn looked at Mae from head to toe. "You are in a precarious situation, but it does not need to be this way."

"Why?"

"Listen to me. I was given two charges from your father. The first was to see to the internal workings of life on Earth and throughout the universe, Mantheia. The second was to see to your protection. I'm afraid I've failed on the second account. I sent Jax to protect you, but he got to you too late. I'm sorry for what happened to you. It spurred a chain of events that ultimately led to this single point in time."

"My father? You mean my true father? He gave you all of those tasks? How can one man manage the universe? And now that I know you should have watched over me, I am undecided if I should hate you as much as I hate Jamieson or not."

"When your father created the Mantheia universe, you, Oralee, were born. You are not like the others of our kind. You are special. The first of your kind, in fact. You were born of the universe itself. The rest of us simply manipulate it to our will. Do you understand?"

Mae couldn't believe what she was hearing.

"You have great power coursing through you, Mae."

"How? I feel no power! Only meekness. Where was this power when I needed it? Tell me, where was it?" Mae yelled. The corner of her eye glistened.

"When your father created Mantheia for us to experience life, to know what it means to be human again, he created a gate. Our people call it the Infinity Gate. Once our kind leaves Infinity and passes through this gate, their memories and powers are stripped. They are born again in their mortal form. We regain our non-corporeal form, memories, and abilities when we die and pass through the Infinity Gate again. But now, that you're in Infinity in mortal form. Should you die here, you will not pass through the Infinity Gate. You will not be restored to your true essence. You will be lost to us forever, Oralee."

A handful of Voltari workers and lab technicians in Mae's vicinity continued working, impervious to her verbal outburst. One of the Voltari pulled a long, wide black tube down over Mae's small swollen belly.

"My time here is coming to an end, Mae. If I was here in a corporeal form, I'd be able to awaken you, bring a small number of your latent abilities to the surface along with your true memories, but I can't while in this form. I need you to awaken yourself."

"Has that ever been done?"

"No," Thourn said. His gaze rested on Mae's amber-colored eyes before studying every cyan-gold freckle loitering her cheeks. He continued, "But I believe in you."

More drugs began coursing into Mae's body. She could feel her faculties slipping away.

Thourn's light dimmed as his image faded.

"Remember, Oralee, the power is within you. You have to find it."

Mae looked down at her prostrate body and screamed in horror. The part of her belly engulfed by the black tube turned translucent. Dozens of organic arms sliced into her abdomen, separating her skin, stomach muscles, intestines, and other organs.

Darkness crept into Mae's vision, chasing Thourn's receding light as her fetus was pulled from her body.

Thourn's image disappeared, followed by Mae's consciousness.

◆ ◆ ◆

Mae opened her eyes to a modestly-sized room. Vague familiarity coursed through her psyche. The room was spacious enough to walk seven or eight feet in either direction, yet abstract enough to remind her this wasn't her world. She laid on a bed in the center of the room. The porous walls glistened. Unlike the beauty of the biotreescrapers she'd been residing in, Mae now found herself in a dank residence that smelled of bile and excrement. Everything about the room was aesthetically unpleasing.

Mae trembled as she pushed up on her elbows. The muscles in her arms shook, weakened from whatever drugs were in her system. The buckling of her elbows marked her failed attempt to sit up before plopping back down. Her head spun. She was still adjusting as the medication they'd given her earlier was leaving her body. Raising her head a bit, she looked down at her belly. Her foggy mind worked overtime to process what she was seeing. Her toes were clearly visible, past the place where her baby bump was supposed to be. She grabbed the sheets and yanked them back.

I'm naked? she thought, groaning as she ran the flat, smooth surface of her palm across her abdomen. Her skin felt as smooth as it always did. *No scar, no pain. Only emptiness*, she thought.

Mae felt the coolness of tears flowing down her face. They peppered her pillow as she leaned her head back, no longer willing to keep her emotions at bay. All of the agony, pain, and despair from the past several weeks cascaded through her, causing her to question her existence. This moment surprised her. She had wanted nothing to do with the baby. Every day it grew in her womb, her hatred towards Jamieson grew, but how could she hate something whose only sin was being conceived.

She'd done everything she could to avoid admitting to herself that it was real, that she had a real live thing inside of her that would one day grow to become a person. A person made of part her and part of … him! A rapist. Despite how it was conceived, he or she would have been capable of either good or evil. Regardless, she had wanted nothing to do with it because it reminded her of such a traumatic time in her life.

And now it was gone. The tiny human she had been growing. Someone she could teach to love deeply and be nothing like its DNA donor. It was gone, and she didn't know how to feel. Tears flooded her face, matting the hair behind her head. The cacophony of emotions welling within her was too much to bear.

Mae turned over, brought her knees to her stomach, and hugged them tightly.

"*It was for your own good,*" the voice from the shadows said.

Mae turned over and peered into the darkness. Adam stepped forward, decloaking as he did so. "*You could not have been allowed to carry that baby to term. Other Voltari would have found out an Original was pregnant and would have come for the baby. In this, I did you a favor.*"

CHAPTER 34

Run

The drumbeat of Mae's heart was drowned out by the clicking and screeching coming from behind her. At the edge of her awareness, she knew her arms were swinging and pushing, her legs pumping and stretching; each step a distant feeling; every breath a ragged gasp. The scene shifted past her in a blur as she fought to run past the bulky furniture and oblong protrusions extending from the floors and walls to supply the many laboratories.

Shadows danced along the wall before rotating 90 degrees to the right, stretching down the same hot, dank cylindrical corridor Mae fought to escape.

Beads of sweat dribbled into her eyes. She squeezed them shut tight a dozen times, blinking hard, to rid herself of the stinging, salt-induced pain.

With the end of the corridor in sight, Mae hoped and pleaded there was refuge on the other side of that door. *Come on, girl, make it! Just make it!* she thought to herself. Her mind trailed back to moments before when she'd did the one thing she thought she'd never be able to do. He had loomed over her.

He was going to force her ...

"*I had to do it,*" she thought. "*There wasn't any other way, was there?*" Mae's thoughts drifted back to the moment she had reached into Adam's satchel, pulled out the same small creature he'd used on Marah, and placed it on his face — wilting him to a mummified corpse as it sucked his lifeforce from him.

As she neared the door, the screeching from behind grew in pitch and volume. The dancing shadows now bathed the corridor around her.

The impact to Mae's side came with enough force to cast a cloud of confusion over her. Tackled from the shadows, she flew sideways, through a sticky, circular doorway. The pervasive darkness engulfed Mae and her attacker as the doorway melded around them.

"Get ... off ... of ... me!" Mae stammered out between heavy breaths. Her elbow connected with the man's face, knocking him off balance. The tightness of the pod's interior allowed enough room for Mae to shift her weight as she rammed her knee into the man's side. Her two rapid strikes caught the man off guard, leaving him momentarily shocked and vulnerable. The confined space did little to aid him as he defended himself from Mae's onslaught. In an effort to salvage the remaining bits of his pride, he called out, "Alright! Alright! I give. Stop, would you!"

Mae relented her attack. "Who are you, and what are you doing here?"

The man rubbed his side. "You're welcome!" His back leaned against a slick jelly-like wall. "I just saved your life! You could be a little more thankful!"

Within the dark confined space, vertigo swept over the pair. Up became down, down became up.

The twisting and turning motion of the small pod-room they occupied reminded Mae of a roller coaster.

"I didn't need saving! I had everything under control."

"Yea. No. That's about ... wrong. You were a hair-split away from dying. I saw how close you were to getting caught. Don't play tough with me, kid."

The pod lurched sideways, causing Mae to feign an upchuck. Wiping the saliva from the tips of her mouth, she asked, "Again, who are you?" Then she reluctantly uttered, "And ... thank you."

"I'm just a man trying to get home, not unlike yourself."

"How do you know I'm trying to get home? This place is lovely. Was thinking of staying."

"They sent me here to collect you and bring you back to the Oasis — to the only group of humans willing to do anything around here. To the resistance."

"Who sent ..." Mae's voice trailed off as the pod came to an abrupt stop. The circular doorway retracted, revealing a bustling marketplace.

The man stepped out of the pod, sidestepped two indigenous humans pulling a cart laden with a hodgepodge of body parts and biomechanical bits and pieces of various sizes. Mae leapt over the trail of fluid leaking from the cart. "Listen," she said, "this place, I don't know it. We made it out of that facility, but I'll bet my ass we'll have company any minute now. You don't know what I did. You're here to rescue me, right? So, rescue. Which way out of here?"

"We're somewhere in the black market on the outskirts of the capitol aerie. That pod put us several dozen miles closer to the transit point we need to reach which'll get us to the Oasis. Come on, this way."

"You sure?"

"You seem like a nice girl, so I'll entertain your questions while we're attempting to run for our lives. First, I'm John. John Cunningham. Nice to finally meet you," he said, grabbing a ledge and swinging his legs over. John hit the ground and tucked and rolled forward before ducking and weaving around assorted mammals hanging from sticks and elaborate fabrics strewn overhead. "She hasn't shut up about you since your ID pinged on her in-head map," he said, running at a light trot.

Mae kept pace. The humans who made up the bulk of the occupants on the street paid little attention to the pair darting between carts, buildings, and other people. Several Voltari flew overhead, although their attention was on other matters. Two of them sported what appeared to be human eyes; another had a human rib cage inlaid on its chest.

Do they know we're on the run? Ridiculous ... they can't know ... can they? Mae's thoughts ran on.

Her mouth creased to form a word when John interjected, "Before you ask, tell me what happened back there, and I'll tell you who I'm referring to."

His EMCDs active status bleeped in Mae's mind, displaying on her in-head map. She leapt over several tables before projecting a portion of her memory into John's head.

They ran on, stopping every couple hundred meters to gather their bearings. It had been almost 20 minutes since Mae showed John what happened to her back in that facility, and she couldn't help but wonder what he was thinking.

John's words were gentle. *"I'm sorry!"* He broke the silence yet commanded attention. *"Your baby! Jesus! What you had to endure — what they did to you — no one should have had to endure it. I have ... had kids. If something like this happened to them ..."*

"I don't want pity, John. I don't need it. The only thing that matters now is getting off this planet and as far away from the Voltari as possible. Can you help with that?"

John opened another channel from his EMCD to Mae's. Through it he projected his emotions as he felt them. Raw. Unkempt. Intense. Mae held back any sign that she felt what he felt. With a thought, he said, *"I can. That is why I'm here. But ... they'll keep coming. They have the means to, don't forget that. Don't drop your guard. Ever! Not until they're all dead."*

Mae crouched beneath a thicket of lavender-colored flowers clustered together in a two-story-high brush, two hundred meters long as it was wide. *"Let me get off this planet first, and then I'll worry about the rest,"* she thought back.

"*Get low!*" Mae yelled into John's mind. "*That's the third pair of Voltari I've seen circling overhead. Something about that doesn't sit well with me.*"

John crept forward and waved Mae on. "*We can rest up in that building before taking on the last leg of our journey.*"

◆ ◆ ◆

Mae and John slowed their approach. They reached a towering tree sporting a latticework of spiral steps partitioned every couple hundred feet or more by circular enclosures with angular roofs. The flowers and foliage etched into the walls of the wide steps made them appear inviting.

John eyed several shops lining the base of the tree. "That one," he said, pointing. "We need to get off the streets and under some cover. That shop looks decent enough."

The pair walked past a handful of Taranzu-born humans and into a shop whose sign sported the sigil of a butcher's market. The grayish hair and chestnut eyes of the indigenous humans were a constant reminder of how out of place they really were. The humans brought to this world within the last few hundred years, who weren't put into zoos, sold as slaves, or kept as pets, were handed over for food processing.

No bell rung, no special chime went off, nothing of note happened when the two entered the shop. "That's weird," Mae said in a low whisper.

John raised an eyebrow, "What?"

"This place looks quaint from the outside. I expected something to happen, some kind of chime to go off, politely announcing our arrival."

The pair eyed their surroundings. The inside of the cavernous store was vastly misleading from the small-town feel portrayed on its facade.

The two slinked between rows and rows of hanging carcasses, human and animal alike, each one with their arms and legs missing. A buzzing sound came from a room up ahead to the right — the only room in the building as best as they could tell.

Mae crouched by the oversized opening while John leaned over her to steal a peek at what was being worked on.

Within the room beyond, an eight-foot Voltari, covered in red blood, turned to put down what looked like a meat cleaver in favor of a bone saw. Each massive utensil had a formidable appearance in the Voltari's large hands.

Mae shot John a mental thought via her EMCD. *"Can you see what that is wiggling on the table? What's he got there?"*

"No — I can't get a clear picture," John said as he leaned his head in further than Mae's.

His hand slipped on the wall; before falling into Mae, John caught his grip again. The Voltari stopped working and partially turned his head in their direction. His faceplate vibrated, simultaneously releasing a loud clattering sound. Alien words sounded in their minds. "If you'd like to acquire something, please pick your meat. I'm on my way," the Voltari said. He placed his utensils down, turned, and walked towards the door.

Ice ran through Mae's veins. She pushed John back as they scurried to find a hiding place among the many racks of meat.

The Voltari paused several dozen feet into the store amidst the hanging meat. He looked from left to right, continuing the search for his customer. The human skull dangling from his neck reminded Mae of a keychain.

Mae and John crept into the room the Voltari came from, careful not to make any noises. The table the Voltari left was saturated in blood, guts, and excrement. A human tongue hung by a clip overhead. Mae's eyes examined the poor soul strapped down. They locked eyes, and he bucked and wiggled. His body, devoid of appendages, was a physical reminder of the brutal, savage nature of the Voltari. Half of the person's face was peeled away, and the muscles and tendons underneath were no longer attached. They laid in a heap on the table beside the man with other cuts of meat.

The look of fear, defeat, and resignation washed across the half of the man's face still remaining.

Mae stood motionless as she took in the scene.

"You stare as if you know him," John said, failing to hide his look of revulsion. *"Let's go, there's nothing more we can do here. We all die, but this ... his ending isn't one I'd wish on any man; God bless his soul,"* John said, pulling on Mae's arm.

"Wait," she said, taking her arm back and pulling her combat knife out of her utilities. *"There's something I need to do first."*

"What are you ..." John's words trailed off. He watched in contemptuous surprise as Mae slid her combat knife, tip first, into the tortured quadriplegic's throat. She pushed until the hilt met skin, waited a few seconds, and then withdrew the knife.

"What was that?" John asked.

Mae pulled a bag out of her cargo pocket with what looked like two rotten eggs in them and placed it on the table beside the body. *"A debt was owed. I paid it."*

"Oh, good, because for a minute there, I thought you were making a mercy kill. Who was he?"

"In a previous life he went by Jamieson. Now, he's no one. Let's go."

◆ ◆ ◆

"This way," John said, pointing towards another doorway leading out of the back of the butcher's market.

The pair climbed a few thousand steps, pausing only to catch their breath and check to see if they were being followed. The wind billowed, bringing with it a cool, crisp air, the kind normally reserved for mountaintops. A six-legged teal horse sporting a red boney, fin-like mane, trotted by with two Taranzu-evolved humans on its back. Its shimmering tail reminded Mae of the glittering streamers on a little girl's bike.

Mae and John came to a spacious landing where more quaint shops lined the edges of the platform. John paused next to a table of exotic fruit manned by a rather small Voltari — by their standards. Her six-foot-tall frame wasn't what caught Mae by surprise. It was the blond shoulder-length human hair framing her featureless face — the scalp beneath the hair clearly visible. "John, maybe we should keep moving," Mae urged.

"In a second ... I just need one second. I'm not as young or as in shape as I used to be.

The water fountain in the middle of the platform had a handful of human kids playing around it, splashing water at one another. Some of the water splashed at the feet of a towering statue of a Voltari warrior wielding two weapons of glory, swords forged in the relic city of Oasis. John noticed Mae's adoration of the statue and said, "He looks like a Voltari of old. They whisper about them in the Oasis. How their weapons, their blades, were the only known material capable of cutting through their insanely tough exterior."

"Hmm ... do we know where we can get some of that metal?" Mae asked half-jokingly. "I wish I did," John said. "We think they were all destroyed, but who knows. If I was on the path of genetic perfection and there was something out there that threatened that, I'd do all I could to get rid of it too. Maybe they did the same as they continued their forced evolution."

A shadow steadily replaced the sun, its darkness slinking along the fountain towards Mae. Her gut clenched.

She looked up. A clawed foot reached down, clamping around John's shoulder. He shot Mae a look that seemed to last a lifetime before his body flew into the doors of the closest shop. His glare said everything all at once: *Run! Save yourself! Fuck! Help me!*

The anger inside of Mae began to swell. Images of the Voltari's hand swinging at her preceded a moment of intense pain. The buildings, ground, and sky all swirled around her before she tumbled to a halt near the edge of the stairs.

She watched through her eye that wasn't swollen shut as a Voltari landed and began to walk toward her. From the side of the Voltari, she saw the vague outline of a man leap towards it. A shadow, moving with brutal effectiveness, loosed a spinning heel kick, sending the Voltari staggering backward a few steps.

Wings of intense purple plasma jutted outwards from the Voltari's back in a blinding display of power. Mae blinked a few times to try to clear her mind. She fought back her dread and struggled to get to her knees.

The air wavered slightly, coalescing around the form of a man — the shadow man. He ran towards the Voltari before it could take flight. A massive fist connected with the obscure figure, followed by another, and then another. The figure grunted in pain as the air wavered all around the Voltari, taking hits of his own. *Who is this guy?* Mae thought, watching through her one open eye.

The Voltari buckled, his knee joint taking a crushing blow from the obscured figure. Mae gasped as the Voltari's head snapped back. Decloaking, Jax smiled at Mae as he grabbed the Voltari's head, yanking back hard, connecting his knee to the base of its skull and crushing its spine. The sickening crunch echoed across the courtyard before the Voltari's body hit the floor.

Mae's eye glistened as she waved and smiled back at the one man who was supposed to protect her yet always managed to be too late. *Not this time,* she thought. *He kept his word. When I needed him the most, he was there.* "Thank you," Mae mouthed at Jax while taking steady steps towards him.

Jax began walking towards Mae when he suddenly stopped.

Shadows danced on the ground all around them. Three of the shadows began to shrink to the size of a pothole as their owners descended from the heavens, taking up residence around Jax.

He looked at Mae with sorrowful eyes before disappearing. Wavering air, almost imperceptible, moved with speed towards the fountain, dodging left and then right. The first of the three Voltari warriors, Reapers, swung his massive clawed hand before impacting the ground with enough force to shake the windowpanes of the quaint shops lining the treetop plaza.

The figure shrouded by wavering air leapt onto the Voltari's hand, taking two steps up his arm before using its shoulder as a springboard and launching himself onto the fountain's warrior of old.

"*This had better work*," Jax half said to himself, half to Thourn. He reached down, taking each of the old statue's weapons in his hands — two blades similar to ancient Earth's broad sword.

His heart raced while he watched the three Voltari lunge for him.

With grunting effort, Jax pulled each sword free. He focused, forcing his powers to flow through him and into his hands. Beads of sweat ran down his head.

A distant voice played in the background beneath the thumping of his temples, "*Clear. Your. Mind.*"

"*Clear it, young one. Focus on what you perceive to be true and it will be,*" the voice said. Jax smiled with recognition. He leapt towards impending doom.

The Voltari's gangly appendages flailed about as the trio approached. They looked like a horde of meaty gray tarantulas fighting for the fly in their web.

Jax's stolen weapons of glory began morphing into human-sized black battle axes with gold runes and trim etched into them.

Mae watched in shocked horror as the combatants converged. It looked to her as though all time had stopped. The sounds were gone — all of them — insects chirping, billowing winds, birds' tweeting, and the horrified screams of people running for cover all ceased. Nothing moved, save for Mae and her protector.

Jax's time in the air was short-lived. Flying through the formation of Voltari, Jax swung hard left, forcing himself into a spin. His ax went through the lead Voltari's tough, thick neck before embedding itself into the chest of the Voltari on his left as he completed his spin. Before striking the ground, Jax turned and chucked his last remaining ax. Mae listened to the crunching sound his ax made when it buried itself halfway into the skull of the third Voltari.

The world around Mae came crashing back into her senses as time returned to normal. Jax struck the ground shoulder first, rolling and coming up in a warrior's stance — ready for the next fight. Behind him, the lead Voltari's body crashed into the fountain, his head rolling beside it. The Voltari with Jax's ax lodged in his chest landed on his feet. He stood erect, flared out his blazing wings of violet energy, and pulled the ax free, flinging it back at Jax.

The ax slammed into the spot Jax occupied moments before. The Voltari took several steps before collapsing to the ground. The third Voltari Jax had dispatched laid face down in the fountain, black battle axe cleaved its skull and protruded above the fountain's lip.

A dozen Voltari descended from the sky, surrounding Jax. Strong winds whipped about the platform as they heaved and thrust their larger-than-life wings. Jax held a hand up, squinting his eyes while struggling to stay on his feet; he dropped to one knee, and then another. Within a blink of an eye, the Voltari were on him — all of them.

Mae screamed, "Nooo!" as her mind raced and pulse quickened. Circumstances threatened to consume her. The Voltari took her life away, and now they were going to take away the one person who has been dedicated to her, despite having received nothing for it.

She felt hot; a volcano roiled beneath her skin. Her unkempt emotions caused her breath to come in ragged gasps. The air around Mae pulsated and shimmered as she yelled again with unmatched ferocity, "No!"

The surrounding buildings shook.

A pair of Voltari lunged at Mae. As they crossed into the

shimmering air around her, their bodies began to crumple, imploding into billions of molecules.

Balling her fists, Mae took a step towards the deadly dog pile, and then another, and another. The power she felt coursing through her scared and excited her at the same time, overwhelming the irritation she felt at her throbbing headache.

For a brief moment, the world disappeared, replaced by a violent explosion of cosmic energy. Mae watched her creation with interest, the creation of Mantheia and the infinity gate, and felt the flow of time and quantum energies of the universe surge through her.

Mae's consciousness returned to the present. She'd never felt more alive, more invincible than at this very moment. But the pain — her body ached with indescribable pain.

"Get. Off. Of. My. Friend!" Mae hollered, her determination solidified the closer she got to the dogpile. The magnitude of her powers threatened to escape. Her thoughts were of a singular focus: Save Jax.

One Voltari body after another was flung away from Jax's battered form as if God himself reached down from the heavens and plucked them off, their bodies bending, breaking, and crumpling before finally imploding in a destructive torrent of deconstructed molecules.

Whatever abilities Jax possesses is all that's keeping him from this life and the next, Mae thought, her vision swimming as she looked down at her protector, her friend. She reached down to stroke his face.

Fatigue overtook her as a pervasive darkness engulfed her mind.

◆ ◆ ◆

Thourn's voice called out, following Mae into the void, *"Mae, you have to rein your powers in. Your mortal form was never designed to harness the full extent of your celestial abilities. If you don't, you'll die."*

CHAPTER 35

Revelations

Mae sat on the boulder's edge overlooking Lake Tahoe in old California.

The serenity of the semi-arid landscape, a mirror-still lake bordered by a gentle smattering of sugar pines and quaking aspens, filled her with a sense of calm she hadn't felt since before the Voltari and Taranzu, before the Marines, before that night ...

Mae's torchlight cut a swath through the night's sky, its output strong enough to give her the sense that the torch's light touched the sky filled with orange clouds and celestial nebula. Mae reached up and traced a smiley face in the nebula, her finger trailing a ribbon of light.

She heard footsteps approach and stop behind her. "May I sit with you?" the familiar voice said.

"I've wanted nothing more than to get to this point in my life — to see you again," Mae said, admiring her artwork in the majestic stellar mass, holding back a flood of emotions. "Sit or stand, I don't care. Just don't leave me again ... please ... Mom." Mae's voice cracked.

Anise Daniels took a seat beside Mae, her hiking boots swung over the edge, dangling dozens of feet above the still lake. "That wasn't by choice, Tadpole," Anise said, wrapping her arm around her little girl, their heads resting on each other.

"They told us you were dead. You're supposed to be dead," Mae whispered. "I didn't believe them … I couldn't believe them. You were supposed to teach me how to talk to boys, apply makeup, how not to freak out when I have my first kiss, and then you were gone. Can you imagine Dad trying to teach Keyera and me to apply makeup and what to do during our time of the month?"

Anise simultaneously chuckled and cried.

"It took so long to accept it, you know. Your unexplained disappearance never felt right. You're a climber! 'How could she die on such a small mountain!' I'd told myself. You'd climbed Fuji a dozen times. But that last time was different. You never came back. Mom, you never came back! You were supposed to come back," Mae said, wiping away the line of snot pooling on her upper lip.

"They took me. I never stood a chance. The closer they got to me, the more I couldn't move. I was immobilized, and they knew it. The hike had already drained me of my energy, and then they came, the Reapers. Once they grabbed me and brought me here, I thought I'd never see my family again. You, your dad, and your sister. I had given up hope a rotation ago." Anise looked at Mae's expression and corrected herself, "I'm sorry, ten years ago."

"This isn't real, is it?"

"It's as real as you need it to be. You're not supposed to be able to tell the difference, though."

"Ever since Jax needed saving, I've felt different, more in-tune with the world around me. I don't feel anything here, in this world, so this must be fake, it must all be in my head."

"You have been in a coma for five days, but with the detection of more EMCDs, however weak, I thought it was time to make contact and try to wake you."

"They will pay for what they did to you, Mom. For what they did to our family and so many others," Mae said with confidence, casting aside any doubts in Anise's mind.

Mae smiled while looking her mom in the eyes. "I suppose I should call you Master Gunnery Sergeant now, huh, Mom."

"Recruit, if you come back to the present, I'll let you call me whatever you'd like, so long as it begins and ends with Mom," Anise said, chuckling. "Come on, let's go. There's someone waiting on you."

Anise stood, shook off the dust, and extended a hand towards Mae. She took it. The world around them swirled into a van Gogh-esque rendition of Starry Night before winking out of existence, leaving the darkness to come crashing in.

◆ ◆ ◆

"Where am I?" Mae's raspy voice came out as more of a croak than a question. Her eyes adjusted to the nominal lighting as she attempted to sit up.

"Take your time," Jax and Anise said in chorus, each one of them standing beside Mae. Jax was in his red and midnight blue jacket with the cowl pulled back. His jacket's blackened buckles prevented light from glinting from their surfaces. His face was bruised and one of his arms was in a sling. *Broken?* Mae thought.

Anise stood clad in a brown leather jacket, left open to reveal an all-black bodysuit framing her muscular body. The leather jacket was of a quality Mae had never seen before. Her eyes raked over her mother's boots for a moment longer taking in their appeal. *I need to get me a pair of those,* she thought.

"Welcome back, Tadpole," Anise said. "When you are back on your feet, we will talk." Turning, Anise walked away with a handful of men and women in tow; two remained behind, taking post by the open archway.

"What's going on here, Jax?" Mae said. "Everything seems ... off."

Jax handed Mae a glass of water.

"There's a lot you don't know, Mae. There's a war coming. With the arrival of the human fleet in high orbit, this merry band of free people, colloquially calling themselves 'The Resistance,' feels there's no better time to strike at the heart of Taranzu, the Voltari, then now. If they can destroy their main *genetic blessing* production plant, they can slow down — even stall — the slaughter of humans long enough to get a large number of us to safety through the underground."

"There's a resistance? How come no one ever hears about them? Why haven't I seen them until now?"

"If they were so easily seen or found, they wouldn't be much of a secret resistance now, would they? But yeah, there's a resistance — and your mom's their leader! Cool huh? But yeah, they're mainly just a bunch of humans who managed to escape the grasp of the Voltari and hide out in this old abandoned city."

Mae suppressed a choke as she worked on finishing swallowing her gulp of water.

Jax pulled the sling off of his arm, flexing it, testing its range of motion. "Get up," he said, extending a hand, "there's something I want to show you before the world comes crashing down."

"Um, don't you need that?"

"Nope. It did its job. I heal fast. One of the perks of being awakened. Now, come on. I really want to show you something."

"Wait. My EMCD has been recording everything through my eyes. I need to get a message to the humans overhead. I don't know when there'll be another chance."

"I'll transfer the codes you'll need to link into this city's comma ray. You can send your message en route to our destination."

"How do you know so much?" Mae asked as they walked

past the pair of guards, who turned and began following them. "I saw you when you came through that portal, you know. I thought we'd never see each other again."

Jax playfully tapped Mae's arm. "Now you're concerned about me. Wait," he said, grabbing her hand and pulling her back, "we're here." A bulbous part of the wall flowered opened, revealing a circular entrance. It slid open. "Our ride has arrived," Jax said, taking Mae by the hand and guiding her inside. The pod's iris slid shut, leaving the occupants momentarily blinded by darkness. A soft iridescent black light swept up the sides of the pod, pulsating rhythmically. The occupants fought back a wave of vertigo as the pod transported them from the old underground city the Rebels had coined The Oasis.

The dizzying motion stopped, and flower-like petals peeled back, followed by the iris opening. Mae and Jax stepped out onto light foliage. They stood at the outer limit of a towering jungle whose leading edges rested a couple hundred meters from a cliff drop-off, overlooking a secluded beach. Bioluminescent blue waves lapped at the shoreline, leaving a gentle ocean spray behind.

The solar system's dark star umbra rays bathed this side of the planet, bringing with it a feeling of night. Jax took Mae by the hand and led her to a predetermined spot on the beach. Mae reached down to swoop up a fistful of sand. Spreading her arms, she twirled gently in several circles, releasing the sand as she did.

Jax smiled. "I never gave you credit for managing to stay alive all of this time and out of one of these creature's bellies. I wouldn't know what it feels like, but I hear soup bowls are a horrible way to go."

"Thanks," Mae said, pausing to examine an opal seashell. She ran her fingers over the smooth cotton-colored protective covering of the strange mollusk living inside. "The secret is to kill them first," she said dryly, never taking her eyes off of the shell. Her newly somber mood took Jax off guard.

"Huh?"

"Nothing, Jax. What I said was the secret is not to let your hope burst."

Jax changed the subject to lighten the mood. "I think this looks like a good spot," he said, waving at the two chairs, fire pit, and beach towel laid out.

"If I didn't know better, I'd say this was planned," Mae said, taking a seat on the towel and folding her legs behind her. Jax started the fire and took a spot opposite Mae on the towel. She stared into the fire's impossibly deep blue flames, "Want to tell me about what you did with those swords? I've never seen anything like that, morphing those swords into axes — badass."

"No, not particularly," Jax said. "Want to tell me about what happened back in that plaza?"

"No. I mean, I don't know." The cool breeze from the lapping waves raised goosebumps on Mae's arms. Jax motioned for her to sit closer to the flames, closer to him — she did. "I couldn't stand there and watch you die. I didn't know what to do. One minute I was walking towards you, the next, I was waking up in that bed with you and my mom hovering. That's all I remember. That and an intense need to save you. Looks like I succeeded somehow."

"Let me fill in the gaps for you," Jax said, beginning his recap. As he spoke, Mae listened and watched him, really noticing him for the first time. Not the random guy who'd found her battered in the woods or the man who pretended to be someone else in an attempt to remain close, even if it meant going through recruit training with her, but the protector who finally saved her when she needed it most.

Mae thought it over one more time and then sat up onto her knees. Looking down at Jax, she motioned for him to come a bit closer.

Jax stopped talking. Focusing on Mae's request, he drew nearer with a small smile on his face. He stared at her scintillating lips and hazel-brown eyes, accentuated by the golden freckles on her cheeks. He drew in closer, drawn to her, dying to taste her lips.

Mae drew back a fist and connected it with the cheekbone of her companion.

"Ow," Jax yelped. "That hurt."

"Oh please, that didn't hurt. I saw you fight almost 20 Voltari and come out alive. Any normal human would have died in the first 30 seconds."

Jax rubbed his cheek. "Emotionally. It hurt emotionally." His heterochromatic eyes changed from two different colors to dark brown. His body morphed from a six-foot-tall athletic man to a slightly shorter teenage female. The smiling face staring back at Mae brought back a flood of emotions, some bad, yet many great. "You gonna hit me again, Mae? You wouldn't hit your best friend, would you?"

Mae shook her head in mock surprise, picked up a handful of sand and threw it lightly at her friend, Savanna. "I would have said no, but seeing as though you two are one and the same ..." Mae tackled Savanna to the ground, pinning her arms down. "You thought you were safe, huh," she asked teasingly.

Savanna used her forearms to strike Mae's arms at the elbow joint, breaking them down. Mae fell in close; her face hovered inches above Savanna's; her warm breath raised the hairs on Savanna's neck. Mae looked deeply into Savanna's eyes as she leaned in even closer. She traced her fingers along Savanna's belly and began to tickle her, releasing a torrent of laughter hamstrung by pleas of, "I give up. You win, you win."

Mae rolled over, smiling and chuckling. Savanna morphed back into Jax.

"Thank you — for everything," Mae said. She extended her fingertips; they found his.

The pair laid on their backs for a moment, staring at the celestial bodies. "Mae, when I first met you, it wasn't by chance. I was sent ..."

"To save me. Yeah, I know."

"But I was too late. I'm always late, I see that, but I'll never stop trying. I'll never stop being in your corner. I promise you that. Even though I never wanted the job, you know."

"Um ... not sure now is the right time to tell me you never really wanted to be there for me," Mae chided.

"Just listen. I was a model ... alright, struggling model, but a model nonetheless. One minute I was minding my business, on my way to eat dinner with my mom, and the next, I was battered from a car accident and then given a choice: Remain mute to the truth of the world, the universe, existence, or be awakened and protect a really hot chick in the process. I'm sure you've figured out which one I chose."

"I would've guessed you'd have taken option number one. I mean, didn't you have a car with the license plate, CHKN-FRID?"

Jax gave Mae's hand a small squeeze. "That's beside the point," he said, smiling. "Look, you should hear a story, and then we can keep talking."

"Shoot, I'll bite."

"*In the beginning,*" Jax began telepathically, "*there was Aletheia. Aletheia was all and all was Aletheia ... and Aletheia still is. This plane of existence, made up of what us humans comprehend to be dark matter and dark energy, houses a number of species, although none are quite like the race known only as the Quintessence. Those non-corporeal beings made up of energy were a powerful, mysterious race as old as time, eventually becoming a property of space itself.*

The Quintessence were once no different from humans, a bipedal race made of flesh, speeding down the evolutionary highway in the fast lane. They had art and beauty. They lived, loved, and died much as humans do today.

Their minds worked in ways we cannot begin to comprehend. Making things came easy to them, which is no surprise as to how they were able to propel themselves through the technological singularity. Creation was their art, and soon their minds and bodies became one with their technology, creating the most beautiful art of all: eternal existence.

Ascendancy did not mark the end of their evolutionary prowess. As the ages went on, the Quintessence continued to evolve, to morph almost into an entirely new species — what they came to be known as: the Quintessence.

Over the course of millions of millennia, the Quintessence no longer needed physical technology in the way other races do. They no longer experienced pain or love; life or death. They simply 'were.'

As the eons went on, the Quintessence continued to spread through the vastness of Aletheia. No longer confined to the physical, and non-dependent on technology, they willed their essence to where they pleased.

As omnificent as the Quintessence had become, they could no longer grasp the concept of life and death, for as long as they could remember, they simply 'were.' It was through ages of watching and monitoring many other beings, that they realized they were missing something.

Not without authority and order, the Quintessence were governed by two very powerful beings — even by their standards — known as Abnar and Nurya.

Abnar wanted to bring back what was lost to his kin so long ago. Through his observation of other races, he knew one inescapable truth. To live is to die, and to have lived and died is to have truly experienced existence. The ride of life would be theirs once again. Anbar would see to that.

After consulting with Nurya, Abnar decided to create a place where his people could experience an entire lifetime of living in the physical as his people once did. But those memories of the flesh were lost to the Quintessence. He needed to know what 'they' knew; he needed to transverse his essence to a focal point in space-time when the Quintessence were of the corporal.

To peer back in time, back to when his people were of the physical sense, Abnar and Nurya knew what needed to be done. Without reservation Nurya relinquished part of her essence to Abnar. The being, who held the entire weight of his kind on his shoulders, then mentally triggered the acceptance process on a sub-quantum level, merging their essence in order to increase his strength.

No other Quintessence ever tried this, nor were they strong enough. The need was never there. But now, fueled by what the closest thing their logical minds could perceive as passion, Abnar and Nurya knew they had to try.

The discontinuity of their essence was a little unsettling. The time dilation field created by the pair placed a heavier toll on the two then either could have anticipated. Both Abnar and Nurya felt different somehow, weakened by the ordeal, as if a part of them had gone missing. It was then, after a thousand passing years — a rather fleeting moment for the Quintessence — that the architectural structure of Aletheia began to unravel. What they saw was unlike anything they had witnessed in all of their travels and time spent 'being.' It was as if the folds of space were churning, breaking and rearranging themselves to produce the first byproduct of such conjoining. And then it happened … another of their kind emerged from the emptied entanglement of the void. 'It' was for lack of a better term, 'perfectly beautiful.'

The thoughts of the 'born' being ripped out from its essence, touching Quintessence across Infinity. It was those very thoughts that set the tone for who and what would be known as the first of her kind. Nurya and Abnar decided to call her Oralee.

Until then, the Quintessence were a finite number of beings. Reproduction for them became a lost art when they transcended into the Quintessence. Oralee's birth was a precarious moment and a very provocative time for the Quintessence!

Abnar and Nurya's joining had been a success! Armed with the forgotten knowledge of his people, Abnar was ready to create, although what he had in mind would take energy, massive amounts of unfathomable energy from Aletheia … and from the Quintessence. After consultation, his kin freely gave small amounts of their essence, and when Abnar obtained enough, he set to work on his creation.

Several thousand millennia passed before Abnar accomplished what he set out to do. Proud of what he created — a pocket universe completely different from Aletheia, although inseparable from Aletheia — Abnar knew his people would be satisfied with their future *experience: The Human Experience. All that is known in the newly formed pocket universe, the planets, stars, galaxies, and life, were all created by design ... his design."*

Mae took a moment before speaking to process everything she just heard. "Wow. That's a ... an ... incredible story. Where did you hear it?"

"I didn't. When I was awakened, my memories came back to me. I'm one of those Quintessence I just told you about, Mae. So is Thourn, he's the most senior of us, besides Abnar and Nurya. Sent here to keep this reality, this experience, going. When he awoke me, he made me his agent, a Watcher, like him. But do you know who else is a Quintessence?"

"No. And by the tone of your voice, I'm not sure I want to know either."

"Mae, you haven't wondered how it is you can do what you did?"

"No," Mae said, lying. She looked around for something to focus on, anything other than Jax's intense mismatched amber and green eyes.

"You, Mae. You're one of us."

"As much as I don't want to believe you, just deny any of this has happened, it's hard. I'm a Coalition Marine. At least I will be when I finish recruit training once I get back. That is who I am!"

"Yes, you're a Coalition Marine, but you are also the Born Princess — Oralee. You might just be the only one who can stop what's coming. What you did to those Voltari, you did without being awakened. You're awakened now, if that is what we can even call you. You're going to have certain abilities — beyond anything I can do — that you must discover on your own."

"How can I stop what's coming! I'm not a real Marine yet. I didn't even finish boot camp. And you speak of my lineage as though I know what that's supposed to mean. I don't," Mae said. "I'm not who you all think I am. You're born, you live, and you die. There are no do-overs. You think I'm going to believe the opposite? If you're one of those all-powerful beings, why aren't you stronger? Shouldn't you be able to make things happen with the snap of your fingers or something." Mae fought to keep her annoyance at bay.

Jax reached over and tugged at one of Mae's stray red curls. "When Abnar's people cross the plane from Aletheia to Mantheia via the Infinity Gate, the Quintessence's essence is transformed into a star while their consciousness is born again, in the physical form of a human baby with no memory of who they were and what they really are.

The sun serves as a homing beacon that focuses and directs us back across the threshold of the Infinity Gate and into Aletheia. This process only happens when the sun receives us back — when our essence returns to it. The only way home is through death, which marks the end of our human experience, our ride of life. When we return home, we regain our memories and our powers, which brings me to my next point. We came to Aletheia without crossing through the Infinity Gate, so if we die here, we don't return home. So, make sure you don't get killed."

Jax stood. "Come on, we should get a move on. The war is going to start without us, and we still need to find a way off this planet."

CHAPTER 36

Arrival

Five hours prior:

Branson's fleet broke through the subspace barrier into light-space, emerging from several distinct focal points. Cosmic particles, riding in on their heels, exploded outward in brilliant cascading radiances.

Branson's white knuckles belied the false calm demeanor he projected. "Helm, execute evasive pattern gamma."

"Aye, sir," Lieutenant Richards said, passing along rapid orders. His hands ran across the controls, eyes flitting back and forth while he scanned multiple lines of data in his mind.

Surprises, Branson thought, not this time. *If you're lying in wait, we'll find you.*

The light cruiser, Conception, and heavy cruiser, Tollbooth, dove down relative to Taranzu's orbital plane. The light cruiser, San Antonio, heavy cruiser, Trinidad, and destroyer, Santiago, broke to the flanks while the battleship, Aurora-1, and destroyer, Victoria, oriented upwards on a hard 90-degree turn pattern. Each warship executed follow-on random banks and turns along predetermined paths.

"Tactical, get me an update on the situation in-system. What's out there, Major?" Branson said.

Major Yutu's eyes held the glossy stare of someone far away, his mind linked with the fleet's AIs. He refocused, flitting his eyes briefly from side to side. "Sir, no hostile action detected. There're thousands of ships in this region. After applying our new detection algorithm we developed after that last engagement with the forsaken Voltari, we're able to accurately tell friend from foe. There is a large contingent of warships 3 AU away from the planet and holding, well outside of engagement range."

Branson studied the situation for a moment, looking at it from his opponent's point of view. "Looks like they're welcoming us with open arms ... pulling their warships back, giving us a clear path to the planet. Solid chess move. But, somehow I don't believe they're completely defenseless." Branson rubbed the light stubble on his chin. "If I was the Supreme Chancellor down there expecting guests traveling in warships, pulling a few warships back would send a non-hostile message, a greeting of sorts, but be of no true tactical hindrance to my plans. No, not if I knew I had an overwhelming strategic advantage. XO, Tactical, put the fleet at yellow alert. I want weapons and ships on standby, ready to go at a moment's notice."

"Sir!" Chief Bassard called out. "We're getting some readings down there that don't seem right."

"Ok, Chief, put it up on the virtual battlespace. Let's see what you've got. Staff, link in."

Branson and the other key members of the bridge, and — through information leakage — the rest of the fleet, viewed the main battlespace individually in their minds. The President floated alone in light-space; in front of him stood a magnificent super Earth rotating in the opposite direction of the large rings encircling it. Mottled purples, greens, oranges, and blues peppered the planet's surface.

The world grew in size from a marble-sized jewel to a

globe that filled his entire vision as he was propelled forward, through massive supercharged cloud layers, before slowing down a thousand miles above a cratered landmass the size of Earth. A dozen virtual windows popped up around Branson. The scene in each window was almost the same. The strange humans that accompanied the Voltari aboard his ship earlier were everywhere on the planet, but what held Branson's attention was the inordinate number of 'regular' humans he also saw. The ship's AIs had a 'human' counter floating above the mass of floating virtual windows. The running tally showed the regular human count in the hundreds of thousands — and climbing.

"My God! Where did all of those people come from?" Branson said. Commander Ode's voice filled Branson's awareness, "Sir, I'm not sure. I'm not overjoyed at the prospect, but we won't get the answers we need up here. Should I prep a team?"

"Bio analysis indicates none of those regular humans evolved on this planet. Correction, that's both the regular-looking ones and the different ones, sir," Bassard chimed in.

"Great, another piece of the puzzle still unanswered," Branson mumbled.

Lieutenant Salisbury cut in, "Sir, gentlemen, we're receiving a message from the surface."

"Is it the Chancellor?" Branson asked.

"No, sir," Salisbury said, excitement in her voice. "It's one of ours, sir; personal ID is registering as Recruit Daniels, Mae, sir. Our records have her missing in training since before we began our voyage."

"What does it say?"

"Huh, sir?"

"The message, Lieutenant, the message. What does it say?"

"Oh yes, it's brief, sir. It says 'Situation dire; Voltari not to be trusted; humans are pets/slaves/food; need immediate extraction — please, to whoever is listening. Respectfully, Recruit Daniels.' The message came with a video file."

"Thanks, Lieutenant. Send me the file. Staff, meet me in my

ready room."

◆ ◆ ◆

The clanging of boots up the Komodo's entry ramp reminded Branson of his time in the Corps. "Marious, are our guests doing alright?"

"Yes, sir. The Voltari delegation have boarded their ships and will be departing from the Aurora in the next five minutes. We'll be right on their heels."

"Good. That's good. Listen, what's about to happen is history in the making. I need to put the right foot forward, but I also need answers. Answers I probably won't get from this Supreme Chancellor. So, I want you to review my speech one final time, and in the process, have General Sherman send some Marines down to investigate that underground city Recruit Daniels told us about in her video. My gut tells me there's something to be learned down there."

"Understood, sir," Marious said while messaging the general through his EMCD. "Orders sent. What do you expect will happen when you meet with the Chancellor?"

"I think ..."

"*Sir!*" General Sherman broke in via his EMCD, speaking into the minds of both Branson and Marious. "*I've sent orders for your pilot to stand fast. You're going to that planet too light. I'm sending a platoon of Marines to escort you.*"

"General, that was the point. I don't want to spook our new 'friends' on our first — no — second diplomatic mission."

"*We don't know their intentions! It would be reckless not to take a large security force.*"

"*This isn't up for debate, General.*"

"*Sir, you are the President, and because of that, I'll follow you to the bowels of hell but here,*" Sherman said, waving to emphasize their location, "*this place, the rules are different. I'm sending at least a squad to accompany you. Nothing less, sir.*"

Marious mouthed, "*The general is hard to control.*"

Branson focused back on his conversation. "*General, if they aren't here in the next three minutes, we leave without them.*"

A squad of Coalition Marines in their black and gold Zeus suits trotted into the Komodo drop ship as Branson's last words flowed from his lips. The Marine leader crossed his pointer and middle finger over the back of his other hand, rendering an armored field salute as he passed the President. Branson returned the gesture with a bit of pride and nostalgia coursing through him.

"Pilot," Marious said, "you're clear to depart. Take us in. We don't want the President to miss his meeting with the Chancellor."

CHAPTER 37

Ruins

"Sir, we're picking up heavy fighting at the LZ," Lieutenant Commander Barnett said, tapping in the command sequence to descend to the planet's surface.

"Captain Marsh, I want all Marines loaded and prepped for immediate infil. Looks like our little get-together is gonna be a full-blown party."

Marsh nodded at Liam; her face took on the signs of intense focus and vague awareness as she relayed the orders.

"Oh, and did you bring the package I asked for?"

"Sure did, sir. Where would you be without me?"

Liam reached out with his mind and caressed Sarah's mental cheek. *Thanks,* he said, before returning his focus to the mission.

"Pilot, set us down on this ridge here," Liam said, sending an image of the new landing zone to Lieutenant Commander Barnett.

"Got it, boss. New LZ locked in," Barnett said, wiping the palm of his moist hand on his trousers.

In the wake of Liam's Komodo drop ship, three dozen more Komodos fell into formation as they shook, their angular, dragon-like fuselages buffeting against the miles of cloud layers each ship fought through to reach the surface.

Major Alexander gripped his harness. "Listen up," he said into the troop-wide communications channel. "We're gonna hit our LZ in moments. Keep your eyes alert and heads on a swivel. This isn't a training exercise. Those training protocols on your Zeus suits were lifted before you jumped. You'll be going into battle with more strength and power than you're used to. I also understand Dr. Grosbeak was kind enough to give us some last-minute in-flight modifications."

"This is the part where I tell you to take it easy. To be careful and limit collateral damage — but I won't. We're landing on an alien world, out of our depth and far from home. If we're gonna make it back alive, I'm gonna need violence. I'm gonna need each of you Marines to do the one thing you were trained for — kick in their shit and kill!"

"Kill with every fiber of your being. Most of you read the Phantom Mamba mission report. You know what a handful of us faced on that Dyson Sphere. Our enemy, these Voltari, will not hesitate to tear any of us apart. Remember that. Everyone comes home. No man or woman left behind! Oorah!"

The resounding chorus of oorahs, yuts, and kills cascading in Liam's ear caused a small smile to creep across his face behind his faceless armor.

They may be inexperienced, but at least they're motivated, he thought. *They're going to need every ounce of it.*

Major Alexander stood on the ledge of a decrepit building in the long-ago abandoned city, Oasis. Thousands of buildings of various sizes and architecture stood old and crumbling. The city might have represented the height of Voltari engineering millions of years ago, but today its ruins, reclaimed by nature, stood as a testament to the end of the Voltari's natural evolution. The local flora slowly eroded away the Voltari's last remaining link to their past. It reminded Liam of one thing. *No matter how magnificent something is, all things come to an end.*

Dozens of drop ships pulled in fast overhead, pausing long enough to allow hundreds of Marines, clad in obsidian and gold TALOS Aegis Zeus suits, to drop to the ground. Explosions blossomed across the battlefield as smaller versions of the Voltari's manta-like ships, known as Skitters, peppered the ground with devastating fires.

Four Marines exited a Komodo before their drop ship took a direct hit to its cockpit.

"Pull up, pull up," cried the co-pilot of the Komodo directly below the one falling out of the sky. Alarms blared as her partner's hands hovered over small threads of ionized energy extending from the flight controls to his fingers. He clenched his fists, flipped them over, and curled his hands towards his chest as fast as he could. Their Komodo's engine groaned as the ship flipped nearly vertical and shot upwards, her belly scraping the cockpit of the downed Komodo as it fell into a nearby building and tumbled to the ground.

Major Alexander linked to his executive officer. "Captain Marsh, get a platoon of Marines on that building to the right. Have them flank that squad of Voltari cornering our fighters. Get another two platoons to flank the perimeter on the port side while the bulk of the forces push forward. For now, we have air superiority three to one. Don't expect that to last. Speed is our weapon. Let's use it."

"What do you mean you blew the factory! Why wouldn't you wait and do a coordinated strike with the human fleet overhead," Mae demanded as she rushed past several people. The almost perfectly preserved underground city was awash with activity. Those decrepit parts of Oasis, sticking up above the earth-domed roof of their underground city's cavern, belied the true beauty of the onyx and crystal city.

"It was a tactical decision," Anise said. "One I had to make. The Voltari are preoccupied with the arrival of the human fleet overhead. That, coupled with the fact that we don't know those humans, which means we can't rely on their cooperation, meant that I had a decision to make. I don't expect you to understand the intricate workings of tactics and strategy — Recruit."

Her mother's verbal jab slapped her in the face. Mae grabbed a pulse rifle and a handful of grenades from a pile on her way to the lift to head topside. Anise and Jax followed in suit.

"Mom, no matter the rationale, you should have waited. Now you brought the fight to us, so I'm going to help my friends. I suggest you help too!"

Jax grabbed Mae's arm. "You'll get killed up there with no armor. Anise's people are putting up a valiant fight, but it's fruitless. Reports have it that Marines have landed. Let them handle things up there. They're armored ... you're not."

Mae pulled her arm away, checked the charge on the pulse rifle, and stepped into the lift. "You're coming or you're not. Either way, don't slow me down."

Mae stepped through the lift into the lobby of a spacious building. She ran across and exited outside. Voltari filled the sky; many were already on the ground. Thousands of people flooded the flora-encrusted streets, buildings, and rooftops from Oasis's subterranean parts.

Mae side-stepped a piece of falling debris and took aim at a woman being plucked from the ground. She raised her pulse rifle's reticle to the Voltari's head and fired. Two of the three rounds Mae loosed struck the Voltari in the leg, gouging out small bits. The last round dropped low, splitting the woman's head in two. Her shots were off. The woman's lifeless body fell from the sky, making a loud thump as it crashed to the ground. Mae cursed herself as she worked to recalibrate the sights of the pulse rifle.

Bringing her rifle to bear on newly acquired targets, Mae took aim and fired. One, two, then three Voltari who were ripping a group of humans apart fell, some staggering as their now-headless bodies hit the ground.

The force of ten men threw Mae into a pylon. She gathered herself up to see what struck her. Jax stood on the back of a Voltari, with one meaty appendage in each hand. Its throat was cut, almost severing the head entirely. Its purple energy wings were fading after having been severed from their owner. Jax winked at Mae before disappearing. Mae smiled inwardly and scanned for more targets.

The sky overhead boomed with the cascading sounds of dropships breaking from a rapid descent to the planet's surface. Mae watched as their plasma cannons opened fire on the Voltari in the sky. The scene reminded her of a swarm of gnats dying in droves after being sprayed with a cloud of aerosol bug spray.

Humans everywhere began to cheer as the killing continued. Explosions clapped in the sky and rocked the ground all around them. Mae dove for cover inside a downed tree. The ground shook, making it difficult to do anything except lay down. When the explosions ceased, Mae peered through a break in the tree and took stock of her surroundings. A number of buildings had been leveled, and a dozen drop ships laid in smoking ruins. Skitters streaked away into the distance with a number of Komodos on their tail. Everywhere Mae looked, Marines were engaging the Voltari.

She exited the fallen tree, taking off at a dead sprint toward a decaying skywalk. Five humans were crouching behind a broken wall fending off a few Voltari. Mae ran harder up the skywalk until she got to the edge overlooking the humans. She jumped; reaching behind her, she pulled a firefly grenade off of her belt, primed it, and …

The talons of a medium-sized Voltari snatched her out of the air. Mae's flesh stretched and bowed but didn't rip as the

Voltari squeezed. She brought the tip of her rifle to its throat and fired. Free of its grasp, Mae fell, her body slamming into the ground between the group of humans and the Voltari on the ground. She let the firefly roll out of her fingers. Two dozen bee-sized plasma rounds shot up and out before being claimed by the grenade's electromagnetic field, bringing them back down to the ground and exploding as they struck the pavement, killing everything within a twenty-meter circumference. Mae sat up and looked around at the carnage before making eye contact with the humans she'd just saved. They ran for their next place of cover with weapons scanning the sky, saying thank you as they passed.

Mae began to chuckle, softly at first, and then more loudly. *God, this is awesome*, she thought.

A shadow overtook her. She looked up to see a human in the obsidian and gold armor of a Coalition Marine, his personal ID hovered in her mind. *No freaking way!* she thought.

"Care if I join you? I hear sitting in the middle of a battlefield fully exposed is great for your health. I've been meaning to do it more, but with Pilates, 'cause, well, you know — I only have room for one dangerous activity in my life at the moment."

"Liam! I mean, sir! What are you doing here? Congrats on the promotion!"

"Thanks. Got your message ... figured we'd come check the place out. You don't disappoint now, do you?"

"It was my mom."

"Um, I'm going to need you to explain."

"Right now, we need to get out of here."

The pair stood. "Right," Liam said. "Let's finish killing some aliens."

"Aliens just doesn't have the same ring as it does in pop culture. Just stick with Voltari, sir."

Liam chuckled. *Same little old Mae, I see*, he thought to himself.

"The Voltari value genetic perfection," Mae said. "I think I might have mentioned that in the data burst I sent you guys earlier. What you don't know is what happened during the time I sent that message and you guys made landfall."

"Yeah, please help me piece this debacle together. We thought we were coming to explore an abandoned city of wonders. Instead, we were inserted into the middle of a war zone."

"Unfortunately, that was my mom. I thought she was dead, but she's alive and kicking — good old mom. And apparently, she's a modern-day Harriet Tubman. She has been smuggling Earth humans away from the Voltari's aerie all over the Home Crater to back here, Oasis, their ancient and long-abandoned city. As the Voltari progressed genetically, they didn't have a need for this place, a bipedal-based city. Instead, they took to the skies, built the insanely high aeries and never looked back. So why not attack the one thing they value above all else? Well, that's what she did. It was their primary Genetic Perfection distribution facility, to be exact, that my mother decided to blow to the ground. She probably has more targets, who knows."

"Why in the hell would she do that!" Liam demanded.

"Apparently, she thought that with the arrival of your fleet, she had the perfect distraction to not only strike at the heart of the Voltari but to do a planned withdrawal using a make-shift rift creator."

"Your mother is in possession of a rift creator? Dr. Grosbeak would love to get his hands on that."

"Yeah, they managed to piece one together. I don't think she planned on the Voltari striking back as fast as they did. She was going to use that device and you guys, us, as a distraction while they get away."

Liam grunted, thinking to himself before tapping into his tactical net. *"Captain Marsh, take a handful of Komodos and Marines and head to the President's coordinates. Something tells me he's going to need some assistance and a hot exfil! Don't hesitate, move now. I want him off planet yesterday!"*

311

Mae continued, "I'm sorry on her behalf because I don't think her pride as these people's impromptu leader and as a Master Gunnery Sergeant will allow her to say as much."

Major Alexander eyed Mae from head to toe. "I see. For now, we're playing to her tune since she set all of this in motion. Let's focus on saving these people and get the hell off this planet. We'll figure out the rest later."

"I agree. That's why I'm out here now. It isn't much, but it's the least I could do to help."

"And you've been out here killing Voltari in that?" Liam said with emphasis on Mae's lack of armor.

"Don't lecture me now, sir. It's either we beat them back or we die. I didn't know killing someone required a specific dress code," Mae said mockingly.

"Listen, I'm a firm believer of 'don't knock it until you try it,' but this ... you have some serious anger issues ... or a death wish. You're gonna need something to complement your battlefield acumen."

Mae began to head into the direction of a Marine engaged in hand-to-hand combat with one of the Voltari. His in-head ID tag registered as PFC Beasley, Mae's second closest friend from boot camp. Liam took up a light trot by her side, his hulking armored frame dwarfing her.

Mae chuckled. "I take it you're offering to give me your Zeus suit."

"Not exactly, although I have something better. Hold right here."

Liam sent a mental signal to his drop ship pilot. Moments later, a Komodo came screeching in low and fast before breaking into a hover over their heads. A large pod dropped from its underside. After releasing its cargo, it took off for the relative safety of the battlefield's rear area command post.

"Voila," Liam said, "put that on and let's do some real damage."

Mae's beaming smile at Liam's thoughtfulness was enough

to melt hearts — Liam's, in particular.

"Check it out, everyone," Private Tall said. "Look who's back!" Mae's old platoon tac-link flooded with a crescendo of 'welcome back' and 'where the hell have you been' questions.

Mae beamed. "Hey, thanks. Glad to be back. So, who has the highest kill count?"

"That'll be Garrett Beasley," Tall said, a hint of jealousy creeping into his voice.

"Ha! Garrett! Wow, way to go, man." Mae felt a pang of pride, knowing her old crew were holding it down.

Mae's stats began flooding the team's tactical network as her Zeus suit uploaded all of the data stored by her EMCD to their shared network.

Garrett's smile turned into a frown and then into the largest smile he could muster. "Guys, hold up. I think that honor goes to Mae now! Check out her freaking kill ratio! Crap girl, what were you out here doing!" Beasley said, chiding his old buddy.

"The same as any of you, I suppose."

"You keep believing that. Glad to have you back, buddy."

Liam ran towards a set of windows. The architecture of the skyscraper reminded him of old Earth. As he ran, he pointed his arm to the right, took momentary aim with its cannon, and fired a plasma round, dropping a Voltari before diving into a spin and flipping his body as he jumped through the window. The sky laid beneath his feet for a few heartbeats until the gray metal of the Komodo replaced it. Through his EMCD, Liam directed the nanoparticles in the feet of his Zeus suit to grip the metallic surface of the Komodo. The drop ship fired at a cyclic rate, loosing round after rapid round as it engaged a handful of

Voltari in the sky. Liam ran along the bottom of the ship until he reached its edge and pushed off.

He sped through the intervening distance between the Komodo drop ship and the Voltari engaged in mid-air hand-to-hand combat with Mae. Liam and the Voltari slammed through the skyscraper, shattering a row of windows in the process.

Deep within the building, the pair skidded to a stop. Liam raised an arm, blocking a razor-sharp claw aimed at this face. Using his free fist, he hammered the Voltari's faceplate in return. Liam's fourth strike fell short, intercepted by the Voltari; his vision spun as he was sent sailing through the air, impacting the far wall.

Mae filled the Voltari vision as she flew in behind the two, morphing her position into a spinning kick and snapping his neck while sending him crashing through the adjacent wall.

"Thanks for having my back," Liam said, picking himself up. The ground beneath him burst apart, birthing something massive from the darkness. A large taloned hand grabbed Liam's leg, yanking him through the hole. His leg disappeared first, followed by the rest of his body. Mae heard Liam screaming in her mind as his body was whipped around the room and beat into multiple surfaces. Liam's suit transmitted his erratic biosigns into Mae's mind, pumping her with adrenaline.

Mae dashed to the hole and dove into the darkness. Her hulking armored frame crashed into the Voltari swinging Liam around like a child's rag doll. It released Liam, his momentum carrying him out of the nearest window. With a powered kick, Mae snapped the Voltari's leg, kicking it in at an odd angle. She followed with another strike to its face. The Voltari caught her second fist, and countering with his other hand, he sent a massive blow to Mae's face and chest, sending her backward.

Liam's lumbering figure burst through the glass window opposite Mae with his Valkyrie wings tucked in tight for added speed, his arm cannon cocked and aimed directly at the Voltari's chest. He fired off two shots while closing the distance.

Using his good leg, the Voltari dodged out of the way of each plasma round. Liam reached the Voltari, gripped his head, and using his forward motion, buried his knee into its chest with the strength of a hundred men. The Voltari flew backward into a punch from Mae, the enhanced strength of her armor aiding in cracking the Voltari's spine, slamming his body to the ground. Mae knelt bedside's her fallen enemy. She studied him for a moment as he screeched, struggling with his arms to find a way to get up.

"How did you say this upgrade worked?" Mae asked.

"Just think about it and the suit's AI will do the rest," Liam replied.

Mae placed her suited hand on the back of the Voltari. Liam watched inquisitively. The armor surrounding Mae's arm burst apart, separating itself into hundreds of pieces and holding position in midair around her. She leaned forward, pushing her disappearing hand into the Voltari.

"What are you doing, Mae?"

"Shush, I'm trying to concentrate ..."

Behind her armored black Zeus suit, Mae's face scrunched in concentration until she found what she was looking for. With little effort, she left her arm in a phased state while rephasing only her hand and wrapped it around the Voltari's beating five-valve heart. She watched her prey jump as she squeezed, only applying a moderate amount of pressure. She loosened her grip for a moment before using inhuman strength to apply enough force to make the Voltari's heart burst between her fingers.

The Voltari dropped to the ground, lifeless, at Liam's feet. He watched as Mae withdrew her arm and noticed her hand rematerialized still clenched, holding the remnants of their enemy's heart.

Liam felt a rush of excitement flood his veins as his manhood rose.

"Recruit, we're going to have to talk about your tactics," he said, trying to hide his excitement at Mae's actions. "Plus, I'm pretty sure that's not how Dr. Grosbeak's upgrade works ... so what was that?"

"No, sir, I don't think we will," Mae said, rising. "Let's go, we have more Voltari to kill."

Liam held his conflicting emotions in check at Mae's actions and seemingly new lack of military bearing. "You mean people to protect?"

"Yea, that," she said dryly as she walked towards the screams and shouts of those in battle.

Destruction bathed the city. All around her debris filled the sky as buildings toppled; Skitters littered the ground as they were blown out of the sky systematically; Voltari and Marines alike were dying.

Mae took stock. Most of her mother's people had withdrawn to the relative safety of the towering flat-topped stepped pyramid, housing the rift generator, bordering the city and a town-sized raging rapids.

Two of the larger Voltari swarmed a trio of Marines, holding them in place with a steady burst of their theta waves. One of the Marines tried to phase-shift out of the psychic net but had trouble focusing enough to do so. A handful of the Voltari's friends flocked to the trio of Marines, using their razor-sharp, graphene-enhanced talons to shred them where they stood — immobilized.

On the edge of her awareness, Mae heard Major Alexander checking on the status of the humans' retreat through the rift they created. She also sensed Jax nearby, taking on a horde of Voltari. He swung his axes in a frenzy of pent-up aggression, guided by his singular desire to protect Mae. A picture formed in her mind of her friend leaping from one Voltari to the next, taking to the sky to confront them on their own turf.

He headed directly into the bulk of the horde, slowing down time around him and hacking away at any Voltari he snared in his time dilation bubble. Mae's feelings of helplessness threatened to overwhelm her again.

A report from one of the scouts sounded in her head loud and clear via her EMCD. *"The last of the civilians are almost clear,"* PFC Sanchez said. *"But we have trouble. More of these things are headed our way. A lot more. I don't think we can handle that many."*

Major Alexander acknowledged the report as he began issuing follow-on instructions to his subordinate officers and the rest of the Marines.

One by one, Marines begin falling back, centering on the flat-topped municipal pyramid off in the distance.

"Get that damned field plasma cannon locked in on my position!" one of the Marines yelled, his hands clutching something long and meaty. Mae's attention drifted towards Garrett Beasley, the Marine yelling. He was running for dear life, his suit propelling him at speeds that would make any Olympic runner envious. The Voltari chasing him was on foot, which was unusual. Its two main wing appendages had been blown off. Mae smirked and shook her head at her friend.

"Got you locked," Gunny Jones said. "On my signal — duck."

"Duck!"

A steady stream of plasma rounds hurtled through the air, across a few blocks, center mass of Beasley's chest. When Jones said duck, Beasley thought he'd do the next best thing. He focused as hard as he could. His body slipped from this dimension into another one for several seconds before reappearing in the present. He'd phase-shifted with enough time that the Voltari wouldn't be able to get out of the way. The rounds struck home, exploding the Voltari and decimating the surrounding area in the process. Beasley stopped running and jumped up and down in a celebratory dance. "Hey Mae, brought you a present," Beasley said.

"What's that?" Mae asked, hoping it wasn't what she thought it was.

"Wing, ar — " Garrett's statement was cut off. He was levitating in the air, arms splayed behind him. Blood seeped from the four holes protruding from his armor. One of the bigger Voltari, the kind capable of producing focused theta waves, held Garrett up on his clawed hand like a skewered piece of steak.

Mae's heart sank at the sight of her friend. Frantic, she closed her eyes, screaming as hard and loud as she could muster. Through her anguish, she felt that door her subconscious worked so hard to close to seal off her abilities beginning to creak open. Mae could feel her grip on reality slipping as she struggled to rectify the loss of her second-closest friend.

The void from before engulfed her. This time Mae wasn't alone. She could sense things normally lost on her mortal form. Spaced throughout the void were lights, thousands of them. With an outstretched hand, Mae grabbed one of the lights and caressed it. The warmth and energy it gave off reminded her of PFC Tall. With a cautious hand, Mae set the small spark back and reached for another one. This one was different. Its energy was significantly higher than the last, and its wavelength didn't feel right. She peered closer. A Voltari fighting a Coalition Marine came into focus. Mae felt the vibration of the spark of light, found more, and then more. She mentally tied them all together, raising her hands towards her intended target. Under heavy strain, Mae commanded each speck of light she'd identified to stop vibrating.

◆ ◆ ◆

Major Alexander stopped speaking as he felt the same thing everyone else did. A widespread earthquake overtook the city. Alexander was attempting to steady himself when he noticed Mae wasn't moving. Amidst all of the shaking, she was as still as a statue. She might have been one if Alexander didn't know any better.

Mae's eyes snapped open. Instead of the beautiful eyes he'd come to adore, Liam found he was staring into the cosmos. Swirling galaxies framed by cosmic nebulas stared back at him. Mae stretched out her arms, and the earthquake shaking intensified.

Nearby, Jax was falling out of the sky as the horde he was fighting crumpled inward on themselves, compressed into a single atom. Mae's attention shifted as she focused her will towards the horde miles away blotting out the sky. Using her last remaining strength, Mae projected enough of her energy at them to cleanse the sky of their presence. She stumbled a step. Liam and one of her squad mates caught her before she fell. "Get to the pyramid now," Liam ordered. "The drop ships are en route for immediate exfil."

CHAPTER 38

All Knowledge Comes at a Price

The Home Crater had amazed Branson upon his arrival at the towering megastructure in the center of it all, the Supreme Chancellor's palace. It's grandiose size, architecture, and beauty left him in awe. The human race had never dared to engineer on the scale of the structure he was standing in. *The palace must cover a landmass probably twice that of Texas. What the Supreme Chancellor needs with that much space is far beyond me,* Branson thought.

Trailing behind his three Voltari emissaries made him feel insignificant. The scale of everything was throwing him off.

Branson, his guards, and the Voltari emissaries came to a halt in a cavernous space he took to be some kind of meeting hall, intended for much, much larger beings than humans. The sort in the 8- to 12-foot category that sported wings of dark energy, talons that could shred metal, and looked like they came out of the closet at night to eat little children.

A voice reverberated in Branson's mind, *"President Branson, you have done us a great honor of joining us this evening."*

"I'd feel much better doing business with someone I can

see."

"*In due time. My two compatriots and I serve as the Chancellor, and it was no accident you were brought here.*"

"Straight to the point. That I can respect," Branson said, surveying the space for the source of the voice. The three Voltari who had accompanied him and his guards had disappeared.

"*As a man of power, someone in a position of leadership — able to speak for species — you understand what it is like to be at the top, to do what must be done for your people and for yourself. Do you not?*"

"Yes. Where is this going? I'd like for you to help me understand why there are so many humans in this world."

"*In due time. In essence, we are a sort of kin. We come from the same stock, you and I,*" the Chancellor said, his voice broadcasting into Branson's head.

"I doubt that, Mr. Chancellor."

"*Ah ... but what would your young mind know of the ways of the universe? Tell me, do you know of the Quintessence?*"

Branson paced back and forth. The cavern was too large to walk across in a short amount of time. "No, I cannot say that I have heard of the Quintessence. Does it have any bearing on the humans on this planet?"

"*You're genetically beautiful, with the exception of your lack of patience, President Branson. Listen, I do not repeat myself. We have a common enemy, you and I ...*"

"I know," Branson interjected, "those pirates of yours."

"*No. The Quintessence. They're a vile bunch who have proven time and again to care for no race except their own. They have stood by and watched countless species wipe themselves off the map across the universe.*"

"Why is that a problem for me? It sounds as though they are a neutral lot."

"*Tell me, if you possess the ability to save a single person from certain doom, would you do it? Would you help them?*"

Branson's thoughts drifted to his wife, Sophia, whom he'd assumed was dead by now; he'd still search for her, no matter the cost. He'd thought about her unfailing love for him and how excited she got when she talked about anything related to science and challenged the conventional way of thinking. The answer was beyond obvious to him, "Yes. Yes, I would."

"*What about a hundred people? A thousand, a billion? An entire species? Would you save them, President?*"

"What you're considering, it's a topic for a philosophical debate for the scholars."

"*I'm asking you, President. What would you do?*"

"I'd save them. Every last one of them."

"*That's what I suspected. It is in your nature, this go-around. Your desire to save those around you burns brightly. I can sense it as easily as breathing.*"

"That's fine and all, but what does this have to do with the humans on your planet or why you wanted to meet with me?"

"*You are a lot stronger than you believe you are, Branson. You humans, you have what we need. You're the best way for us to achieve our goals.*"

"And what goals would that be?" Branson's nerves were beginning to wear thin.

"*Genetic perfection, my friend. Your species is still in its infancy, but together, we can elevate your kind to perfection. My kin are almost there. There is no need to wait, President Branson. Do not let time control you. Consider, President, you extract energy from things like wood, fossil fuels, and atomic bonds. Our very being generates energy. We feel the quantum links between subatomic particles and wield it to our ends. Join us and become us. You will know true power. We will be a perfect union. Once we are genetically perfect, we'll be able to exert our dominance through Infinity, and no species will ever have to fear genocide again. But to achieve this, I need your help. You must deliver your species to me. I give you my word, one leader to another. They will not be harmed when they merge with us.*"

"What do you need us for if you're almost there?"

"*Like any great creation, you need the right parts. When you cook, do you humans not seek the perfect seasoning?*"

"Yes, but ..."

"*Exactly. So, as is for us. When we splice, we seek to use the genetic codes that would allow for the most perfect of unions. You and the human species, President, harbor such codes in great abundance! Man is a slave to biology but a master of will. Imagine what we could accomplish as a singular species, supreme beings of the Infinity. You may even return to your galactic realm if you wish — as Gods.*"

"Wait! You want me to just hand over the entire human race — for what? So, you can play Dr. Moreau and farm us for our genetic code? And then what? Merge and live under your rule, subjugated and slaves to you? Is that the catch?"

"*You're thinking about it the wrong way, President. My terms are the same that have been offered to all other sentient life forms in Infinity. You should consider this a great honor to be considered and offered such a gift. Together, we'd be the ultimate biological being. We'd rival the Quintessence themselves. It is time Infinity had new gatekeepers.*

We were once kin to the Quintessence until they built their Infinity Gate. No being can pass through it unless you're like them, so we created two of our own — one on and one above our planet. The process of passing from our realm to yours left us changed, different, as the beings you see before you. At first, we thought it was a curse, but over time we learned to embrace our ... change. We've even learned to modify our genetic code, but we need new code. Your code."

"I should consider it a great honor to be offered the choice the same way so many millions were offered one as they were stolen from their homes and imprisoned here for your deranged experiments. No. No! I don't think that'll be happening, Chancellor. It won't happen. We're not some cattle you can cull for your own ends." Branson's mind raced with the horrors the humans of this planet must have endured.

"*You selfish fool! Hoarding resources and squandering this chance will be humanity's demise. Your precious toy-land will be my feeding grounds! I had held out hope you were different, but my* assessment was flawed. Even in this form you only think about you and your kind, never anyone else."

What the hell is this guy talking about? Branson shook the thought and tried to link to his security detail — nothing. *Ok, he's jamming me,* he thought. *I've been in one too many scrapes to know that's never a good sign.*

Branson's security detail slid into place around him, forming a protective circle.

"Captain, what is it?" Branson whispered.

In a low even voice, Branson's lead Archie replied, "Nothing yet, sir ... it's more of a gut feeling. Something's not right sir. Comms are down, and Joey said he thought he picked up what looked like cloaked movement."

"Ok, we're going to get ready to go. This meeting isn't proving to be fruitful like I thought it would."

The Chancellor's demanding yell nearly split Branson's mind. *"No! You've heard nothing! You are my permanent guests, so long as it takes us to prep you."* Branson worked to endure the psychic pain, gripping his helmet in an attempt to get to his head.

Branson's Voltari escorts, the Apotheosis and his two associates, reappeared several yards away at a control station that wasn't there moments ago. Their backs were turned as they worked several intricate user interfaces.

"Apotheosis, what's going on here!" Branson demanded.

"President Branson, I'm no more an Apotheosis as you are a President, Abnar. Call me Supreme Chancellor. Forgive the rouse. It was necessary to gain firsthand knowledge of you, to see what you've become. I am not impressed!

All around Branson, the once-stark-white, empty cavernous domed structure transformed into a sprawling hub of activity. An intricate production factory materialized bit by bit, replacing the vast empty space.

Within seconds, Branson and his security were surrounded by two dozen decloaking Voltari.

The Supreme Chancellor strode closer to Branson, stopping

just out of arms' reach. *"This could have been done without the bloodshed. No worries, I will have what we need from you all in due time. There isn't a force in the universe strong enough to stop the full force of the Voltari."*

As if on cue, Branson's Marines sprang into action, each Marine paying particular attention to keep the fighting away from Branson.

Branson pulled his 20-inch obsidian K-blade from his sheath and prayed to God he'd be able to handle the Chancellor. Fighting humans was one thing, but these beings were something else entirely.

Either they go down or I do, Branson thought to himself, *but I'm not backing down from this fight.*

Violent tremors rumbled through the vast space, growing in intensity before anyone could react. The ground buckled and bowed. Cracks appeared in multiple locations, some wide enough to swallow workstations and their occupants. Branson found himself thrown off of his feet. Explosions erupted several floors below their location. Fire, blast overpressure, and massive amounts of debris overwhelmed Branson. His TALOS suit worked overtime to keep him from feeling the raging effects of the explosions. Branson gripped a nearby strut as he rose to his feet, steadying himself. Through the flames and smoky haze, he could see the figures of two very pissed off Voltari — one being the Chancellor dredging through the aftermath, getting closer and closer to him.

The chamber's outer wall erupted in another torrent of flames and destruction. Branson cycled his suit's vision to polarized x-ray, allowing him to see the environment clearly through all of the murk and chaos. He smiled in surprise when he saw the angry-looking Komodo drop ship crashing through the domed wall and ceiling. Another two drop ships stood sentry outside of the new entry hole.

A fresh voice broke through the block, "Mr. President, sorry to crash your soiree, but we need to go — now," Captain Marsh said over the tac-link.

Marsh's cool, collected tone switched to intense concern as she yelled, "Sir, look out! Your six!"

Startled, Branson sent a thought to his suit; a fraction of a second later, he phase-shifted to a dimensional frequency outside of the range of the Supreme Chancellor who flashed past the spot he was just in. He crashed into two large sections of wall that had collided with each other during the explosions. Branson knew he only had half a minute before he re-phased back into this dimension. He eyed his dead security detail then turned his attention to the Chancellor. He checked to ensure the waiting drop ship was still there and then returned his attention to the Chancellor again. With ten seconds left until re-phasing, Branson sprinted.

Captain Marsh helped Branson aboard as the drop ship fired her plasma cannons to widen their exit hole. The rear hatch closed as the ship sped off, leaving a dejected Supreme Chancellor hovering above the destruction, watching them go.

"Care to get me up to speed, Captain? How did you know to come for me?"

"Sir, you have Major Alexander to thank for that. When we hit the ground, heavy fighting had already broken out. He ended up linking up with a recruit, Mae Daniels. Apparently, she was stolen by these fuckers while she was in training."

"Yes, I've been made aware of Recruit Daniels."

"So, as I was saying, sir, she pumped Major Alexander full of all kinds of info, like the fact that these Voltari steal people! That's why there are so many humans on this planet. And when he found out about their need for Genetic Preeminence, by using humans to augment their genetic code, the good major thought it prudent I take some Marines and come get you. It looks like we almost lost you there. The humans Major Alexander is fighting to protect right now are the same damned ones who just set off that bomb in the heart of the palace. Their target was the Chancellor's private Genetic Blessings production plant. They'd already struck the first one right before we made planet fall."

"Well, I don't think they got all of it. I'm pretty sure I was standing inside of that plant or a part of it."

The main pilot broke in over the tac-link, "Hang tight, Mr. President, we have a couple of bogies on our six. I'm setting on a course for the Aurora as per Major Alexander's orders. Komodos two and three are peeling off to handle those Voltari Skitters."

Branson sat back, breathed a sigh, and thought about his next move. He brought up the inter-link function on his EMCD, sent the mental commands to establish a voice-only tight beam connection to the Aurora's command deck, and set to work. The voices of his senior staff came on the line. "General Sherman, contact your troops and get them back on board and debriefed. We're pulling out. Commander Ode, contact the Task Force commanders, prep for immediate withdrawal. Marious, coordinate with the General and Commander. I want everyone planet-side and within the Task Force to conduct an immediate download of their EMCDs for rapid transmission back to Earth. There's no guarantee we'll make it out of this alive. Oh, and get with the Doctor. Tell him to do that thing he did to the Marines' hardware, and see if he can apply it on a larger scale — a much larger scale."

"Aye, sir," came the unanimous response.

"Sir," Commander Ode added, "our sensor tech has been keeping an eye on those warships we saw on the far side of the system when we first arrived here. Shortly before your drop ship began heading for the Aurora, they started moving ... fast."

"Direction?"

"Towards us, sir."

"I feared as much. The Supreme Chancellor, our very own 'Apotheosis,' was fooling us all along. He must have been behind the attacks when we first entered light-space, and now he's coming for blood. He wants to harvest every one of us. It'll be a hot extract. Prep the ships' weapons and ensure the crews are ready!"

CHAPTER 39

Pursuit

Dry-eyed and battle-weary, some Marines hobbled, others meandered, and many stalked out of the dozens of Komodo drop ships landing in the flight bays. Their bulky armored frames created a sea of black flowing from the ships, flooding the flight bays.

As Mae exited her drop ship, she paused at the end of the ramp. Major Alexander walked up beside her. Placing his hand on her shoulder in an effort to comfort her, he said, "I didn't know him, but I saw him out there on that battlefield. He was fearless and fought with a ferocious intensity that'll garner him respect and maybe even legend status as the Marines re-tell his story over and over." A couple of medics floated Jax out of the ship, cocooned in a biopod. After the battle, they had managed to stabilize his biosigns, but not before he slipped into a deep coma. The medics were apprehensive about his recovery.

"Yeah," Mae whispered, "he fought bravely ... and for what? I don't need protecting anymore, yet he still fought for me. This time he took on more than he could handle, and I wasn't there for him, wasn't fast enough, not like he tried to be for me. Now look at him."

The pair stood motionless in the torrent of Marines, crewmen, and equipment, all working toward their own ends.

"Come on, there's nothing more we can do for him here," Liam said, standing beside Mae, who was watching Jax being taken away. "Let's go to the chow hall. We'll eat, shower, and then debrief."

Mae turned numbly and walked away.

"Push it, Lieutenant. Get us to the gate before that fleet catches us. It's our best bet to get home as fast as possible." Branson's nerves were on edge. *After this, I'm going to have to look into finding a capable admiral to take over command of the fleet,* he thought.

Branson felt most comfortable operating in austere environments, the kind of places you didn't want to take a Sunday stroll in, which is why he found himself so adept at politics and working at Capitol Hill — not facing an enemy force that wanted to harvest their DNA.

Major Yutu's voice rang in his ears, "Sir, the enemy is opening fire. The Santiago isn't far enough away. They're going to take a hell of a beating."

"Commander Ode, have the Santiago increase speed. Tell them to break all of the rules ..."

"Sir, it's too late for that. The Santiago's shields are being overwhelmed with the entire Voltari fleet firing on her. Damnit, she's breaking up. We need to increase speed. Her reactors are going to go critical, and we shouldn't be anywhere near here when she does."

"Helm, signal the fleet and push the engines past the red line. Get us to that gate."

One of the comm techs got up and walked over to the command section, "Captain, sir."

Branson eyed the baby-faced tech. He couldn't have been out of high school for long. "Yea, son, what's going on?"

"Sir, you should know, sir, we've just logged a handful of the crew engaging in on-shift, in-head holo excursions. It looks like they're trying to run from what's coming, sir. They're scared."

Branson's eyebrows scrunched in a look of disdain and annoyance. "You're telling me you monitor the in-head activity of the crew?"

The comms tech's eyes began to flicker left to right as he shifted his weight uncomfortably from side to side. "Sir ..." he began.

Commander Ode broke in, "Of course, Mr. President. We need to ensure everyone aboard ship maintains mental focus in the present in order to ensure each ship's departments continue to run at peak efficiency."

Branson didn't know what was worse — the fact that it was so commonplace to spy on the minds of each crewmember or the cold, disconnected way in which the senior leaders became comfortable with their flagrant breach of privacy. "Tech, override their personal security protocols and pull them back. President's, I mean Captain's orders. And when this crisis is over, disable the spying function and report back to me that it's done."

"Aye aye, sir." The tech executed a crisp about-face, returning to his workstation. Another crewmember, slightly more senior than the tech, glared at the kid. Branson figured it must have been his supervisor.

Commander Ode's demeanor darkened. "Sir, you're putting the efficiency of this fleet at risk by doing that."

"XO, by not showing the crew you trust them, you put the efficiency of the ship at risk. No one wants to be a part of an organization they do not feel trusts them. Besides, I'm enacting a protocol that'll shut down the ability to escape in-head, at least until we get out of this mess. For now, this matter is closed."

Half of the Voltari Battle Group overtook the Santiago, disregarding her dead, free-floating dismembered carcass. The leading edge of the Battle Group came within engagement range of Branson's fleet. They opened fire.

Dr. Grosbeak stormed onto the bridge. "Mr. President, I got it. It's done, I've tied in the quantum transistors to the induction feedback point of the ..."

"Doctor!" Branson said with a dismissive wave of his hands, worry lines creasing his forehead. "Just tell me if it's done. Did you do what I asked?"

"Yes, sir."

Branson immediately shifted his attention, "Helm, Navigation, continue on course for the Voltari's gate and phase-shift the fleet. Do it now!"

The Trinidad and Tollbooth's shields wavered under the impact of long-range fires from the Voltari fleet. Each ship in Branson's fleet shimmered before disappearing from the map, narrowly missing the next volley of enemy fire.

The fleet's immediate reemergence into light-space surprised the crew. Warning lights flashed as the alarm klaxon blared. "Doctor, fix it!" Branson said in a stern voice which teetered on yelling. Of course, he didn't have to say it; Grosbeak was already on it.

"Got it, sir. Try it now. My calculations were just a pinch off."

"Your miscalculations just got people killed," Branson said half yelling, hating himself for taking his anger out on Grosbeak, but he could not stand for his people to die. "Helm, reengage the phase-shifting!"

The Santiago drifted deeper into the enemy's fleet. Her reactors crept to critical before going thermo-nuclear.

With the adjustments previously made to their engines by Dr. Grosbeak, exotic particles multiplied the effects of the Santiago's reactor explosions. The fast-moving bubble of explosive matter swallowed everything in its wake. Thirty Voltari warships were caught in the blast. In its wake, heaps of fragmented ship parts remained. The destroyer Victoria and light cruiser San Antonio were the closest ships in Branson's fleet to the Santiago. Their shields strained under the kinetic assault from the expanding debris field.

The surviving ships in his fleet wavered, blinking in and out of this dimension, finally phasing momentarily out of existence.

Emergency crews ran all over the ships, enacting repairs and putting out fires. "Doctor, how long can we hold this position?" Commander Ode asked. "Those remaining ships are gaining speed, fast! We can't hope to outrun them. Our only chance is to continue to hide or fight."

Grosbeak focused, counting on his fingers and mouthing to himself, "Um, at our current rate of travel, if you continue to drain the reactor by pushing the ships as hard as you are, we're looking at a little less than five minutes of dimensional shifting left. After that, we'll need to slow down to recharge the capacitors if we plan to shift again."

General Sherman leaned in. "Sir, we're light on options here."

Branson gripped the arm of his command chair. "What are you proposing, Robert?"

Sherman sent Branson a mental sketch of his plans. Branson sat up a bit straighter. "You're kidding me, right? You want me to knowingly throw away thousands of lives, lives of people who all swore an oath to the Coalition because they believe in it and expect it to afford them certain protections. I am the embodiment of the Coalition, General. I can't execute this plan."

"Damnit, sir, those same men and women you mentioned are Marines and Sailors in the Coalition military. They knew when they signed up that it would come with a certain amount of sacrifice, up to and including their lives. If them giving their lives here and now means we get home and can prep for what's to come, if it means the human race has a chance, I know, without a doubt, they will gladly give their lives, sir."

"Shit!" Branson said as he sent his executive officer, Commander Ode, the ships' captains, General Sherman, and Marious a virtual meeting invite. The mental location was one he'd used many times in the past. Branson found himself standing in the center of a white room adorned with some of the last remaining bits of furniture made of real wood, much of which was a few decades older than he was, long golden drapes and a huge seal in the center of the floor. In the seal, an old American bald eagle stood gripping spears in one talon and 13 olive branches in the other talon.

Aware of the time constraint, Branson eyed each of the ship's captains, explained the suicidal plan, and waited for responses. "We are short on time, Captains. I need to know your answers now." Of course, he'd expected some hesitation. Who wanted to willingly throw their lives away, to volunteer to have their lives cut short in service of another?

The captains of the heavy cruisers Trinidad and Tollbooth glanced at each other before stepping forward. "Sir," Tollbooth's captain began, "it only makes sense that we be the ones to screen so the rest of you can get away. We have stronger shields and more armament. We'll go down but not without punching their shit in first." Everyone in the room chuckled.

Branson strolled forward, taking each man's hand in his own one at a time. "I have met no braver men than the two of you. You and your crews will not be forgotten. You have my word."

"Thank you, sir."

Everyone winked out of his in-head virtual meeting, save for Marious. "You alright, sir?"

"Yeah, son. Come on, let's go."

"Sir, they're opening fire again." the tactical officer, Major Yutu, called out. "All ships have rephased into light-space. The

Trinidad has peeled off to draw their fire away. The tollbooth is now doing the same. Sir, should I hail them?"

"No, they know what they're doing. Keep us on course for the gate," Branson said, his eyes revealing the pain he felt at issuing those orders.

The eight remaining Voltari warships closed the distance to the Trinidad and Tollbooth in just moments following the heavy cruisers reversal in direction. The two ships synced their targeting AIs and opened fire, sending volley after volley of RTD rounds into the bodies of the Voltari's sting-ray-shaped ships. The Voltari executed finely tuned counter maneuvers, gracefully dodging many of the rounds fired at them. Several hit home, their nanite-infused bodies defused as designed, eating away at everything they came in touch with and leaving large gaping holes in their wakes. Three of the Voltari warships lumbered towards the human ships trailing debris.

Branson watched on his screen as the Voltari returned fire. Their rubidium lasers slammed into the Tollbooth first and then the Trinidad, speeding up the mass of sections of their ships to near the speed of light. The combined fire from the eight Voltari ships overwhelmed the Tollbooth and Trinidad's shields, tearing through the ships like a sharp knife through butter. In succession, each one of the heavy cruisers fractured, tearing apart as the strike of the lasers sliced through them.

Branson cursed just low enough for his senior military officers to hear. "Damnit! Those were good men and women we lost."

"You made the call, sir. I just advised you. The decision is yours and yours alone," Sherman said.

"You don't think ..." Branson began to rebuke the general's statement but thought better than to argue with the man who no doubt just wanted to bring him down to his level.

Commander Ode's strained face should have worried Branson, but the man always maintained that look. "Commander, what's the matter?" Branson asked.

"Sir, I'm running the numbers. The Voltari's near c-focused

mass weapons, those rubidium lasers, are too powerful. Collectively, they will rip through the Aurora and the Conception just as easily as they did the Trinidad and Tollbooth."

The Aurora began climbing at an accelerated rate relative to the plane of the solar system. "Lieutenant Richardson, what's going on? Why are we climbing?"

"Evasive maneuvers, sir. We're being targeted by ... Tactical, how many?"

Major Yutu responded immediately, "Almost all of their firing patterns. By our count, twenty laser banks."

Liam and Mae walked onto the bridge. No one noticed the pair as everyone focused on their jobs, trying to do their best to keep from incurring the same fate as the Tollbooth and Trinidad. "Liam, um ... Major — sir, take a look over there. We're climbing," Mae said.

Liam scanned the room until he found who he was looking for. He made his way towards the General, but was being waved off by some civilian whose shirt was soaked through with sweat. Hearing bits of Branson's heated conversation with General Sherman, he caught Mae's eyes. They both stared in wide-eyed amazement as the Conception ignored all hails from the command deck. She pulled away from the Aurora, angling herself between the stream of rubidium lasers and the capital ship. The Conception lurched sideways from the force of impact from the lasers. Within seconds, she began to break apart.

Mae stood there, the world dissolving around here. So much loss and despair. Feelings of helplessness engulfed her once more.

The bridge crew was frantically working to get the ship away from the Voltari. "No ..." Mae said slowly before screaming, "stop!" The bridge crew froze; no one dared to move. A blazing orange glow overtook her body, seeping out through her galaxy-filled eyes. Light-space seeped in through every crevice of the ship, making its way towards Mae in the form of liquid light. The light embraced her, shedding away her earthly possessions.

Mae's feet left the ground. Floor by floor, she sailed through matter, as though it was never there, until she found herself outside of the ship. Mae felt no need to breathe. She felt sustained by the space around her. She sailed to the nearest Voltari ship. Their lasers fired, but it didn't matter. She stared down the barrel of a laser bank. The photons from the laser washed over Mae, tickling her in the process. She didn't smile. There was no need for that now. Reaching out, she placed her hand on the ship. Within seconds, each remaining ship in the Voltari fleet disintegrated. Their existence wiped from Infinity. As the last ship vanished, Mae collapsed, her nude body floating limply in the vast nothingness of light-space.

"Sir, we'll be at the Infinity Gate's focal plane within minutes," Lieutenant Richardson at Helm, reported.

Sherman swore aloud, banging his fist on the console. He turned to Branson. "Sir, we can't jump yet. Major Alexander just leapt out of an airlock in a Valkyrie-enhanced Zeus suit."

"Jesus, what is he doing?"

"Looks like he's going to retrieve Recruit Daniels. Sir, he's a Marine, like you once were. No man or woman left behind. For him, this isn't a question. Daniels comes home."

Branson's cheeks flushed for not having thought to retrieve Mae sooner. "Helm, relay to all ships to hold fast right outside of the gravitational pull of the gate. The moment those two are aboard, jump. Don't wait for my word."

Richardson smiled for the briefest of moments. "Aye aye, sir."

Major Alexander kept Mae in his sights as he course-corrected, aligning his trajectory to match her angle and rate of speed. He eased in close, cutting his main propulsion and switching to thrusters only. His black armored hands reached out and snagged Mae's body. He pulled her in close. Several layers of advanced exoskeletal battle armor separated his flesh from hers, yet her warmth illuminated him from the inside out.

"Aurora, this is Major Alexander. Thanks for not leaving us. I have her. Returning to ship in ten minutes."

"We read you, Major." The voice on the other end said. "Return as fast as possible. We'll have medical standing by to receive Recruit Daniels."

ABOUT THE AUTHOR

Wes Easton, a military scholar with a degree in psychology, spends his days defending his country and his nights writing science fiction. He has spent almost two decades in the Marines with multiple deployments to the Middle East. His keen interest in human nature and science, specifically science's application towards the betterment of the human species, led him to write Origins: Truth Revealed. He currently lives in North Carolina with his family.

www.ingramcontent.com/pod-product-compliance
Lightning Source LLC
Chambersburg PA
CBHW020245200626
46816CB00001BA/138